SLIME SWEETS AND DUNGEON TREATS

Also by Pandora Pierce

Legends and Librarians
Legends and Librarians
Myths and Manuscripts

Divine Duelist
Winning You Over
Playing with Lightning

SLIME SWEETS AND DUNGEON TREATS

SLIME SWEETS BOOK ONE

Pandora Pierce

Podium

Podium

SLIME SWEETS AND DUNGEON TREATS

CHAPTER ONE

Tutorial Zone

The scent of freshly cut grass and campfire smoke teased my senses, pulling me out of what felt like a very deep sleep. Bright light pressed against my eyelids, but I tried my best to ignore it. Sleeping in was one of life's true pleasures, so five more minutes wouldn't hurt.

Except I hated camping . . .

Didn't I?

My memories felt hazy, like a fog had settled in my mind. I obviously wasn't in my bed, but I didn't remember going out either. The last thing I remembered was something about . . . bread? Yeah, I think I was prepping the dough in the middle of the night so it would be ready in the morning. Did I fall asleep while I was working?

A low hissing noise made me bolt upright, eyes wide.

I was in a small clearing beside a mountain that had a door carved into it, covered in glowing symbols. Thick fog blocked my view of anything beyond the clearing, boxing me in as if there was nothing past it. But at the edge was something my mind couldn't really comprehend. I rubbed my eyes, focusing on a group of animal pens that were filled with what I could only describe as monsters from some kind of fantasy movie. Wolves with horns, three-headed snakes, giant bugs, and a bright blue bouncy thing that I couldn't identify.

"What the hell is going on?" I lurched to my feet, but my body felt like Jell-O, all weak and wobbly.

"I'm glad you're awake," a man's voice said, pulling my attention to his unusual appearance. Horns jutted from his head, curling through his fluffy brown hair, and his feet were actually . . . No, that couldn't be right. They were hooves, like what you'd see on a goat! "Welcome to the Dungeon of Eternal Embers."

My pulse raced, pounding in my ears like I was standing at the edge of a cliff. Everything about this place was so very, very wrong, but the worst part was that I couldn't remember what was right. My mind was blank.

"Welcome to the what . . . ?" I needed to grasp onto something, anything that would slow the panic racing through my mind. "What are you?"

"I'm a satyr, half man, half goat, and I'm here to welcome you to the Dungeon of Eternal Embers." He smiled warmly, motioning at the mountain. "Take a deep breath, calm down, and then we can get started."

A crazed laugh threatened to bubble up at the idea of a mythical goat-man welcoming me to a dungeon. This had to be a dream. But my chest hurt too much for it to really feel like a dream. My breathing was uneven and my heart just wouldn't stop pounding, like my body thought it was in fight-or-flight mode.

How did I get here?

I put my hand against my chest, my fingers brushing over the silver buttons of a double-breasted white coat that felt like a uniform, but I couldn't remember what for. My long brown hair hung over my shoulder in a tight braid, and an apron was tied around my waist.

The apron's fabric was soft and well-worn, with specks of flour right where my hands would go if I were to wipe them off. This was *my* apron, something I wore often.

"Good, you look calmer now." The satyr stepped toward me, holding a notebook. "What's your name and age?"

"I'm Hazel and I'm twenty-five years old." The words came out without even thinking about them, as if simple details about myself were easier to remember than how I got here. "I think I'm a . . . baker?"

The word settled into the back of my mind, comforting me. Yes. My name was Hazel and I was a baker.

The satyr jotted that down. "Okay, then, Hazel, please choose a weapon."

"What?"

He motioned toward a table full of swords, daggers, bows, and lots of books. Suddenly the whole dungeon-and-monsters thing was making more sense. I had to be playing a game, one that was far too lifelike for my liking.

I laughed nervously, fiddling with the edge of my braid. "Is this some kind of virtual reality game?"

"No, but many prefer to treat it like one. It helps make sense of their new world. Now please, choose a weapon." He motioned at the table again.

New world? My eyes widened. So this wasn't a dream or a game, but a new world? And I needed a weapon for it? Weapons meant violence and pain, neither of which I enjoyed. Whatever was going on, I wanted no part of it.

"I think you've got the wrong person." I backed up until the damp fog clung to my skin. "I'm a baker, not a warrior."

Wasn't I? The fog chilled my skin, making it hard to concentrate. What was I doing? If he said I needed a weapon, then I should choose one. It didn't mean I had to use it . . .

I stumbled over to the table, searching for a weapon that felt right to me.

Maybe the books? They seemed safe enough, but when I reached out to one, the air around it felt electrically charged, zapping against my skin. Were they magical books? That was kind of cool, but magic sounded like a lot of work and often blew up in people's faces.

Wasn't there anything simple here? Anything that felt like me?

My gaze settled on a sandwich at the edge of the table with a bite taken out of it, as if the person had gotten distracted mid-meal. I couldn't remember much about my life, but every little flash was about food. My entire life apparently revolved around it, so why stop now?

I reached for the grilled cheese, as if drawn to it. "I choose this sandwich."

"What?" The satyr's eyes widened. "No, that's not a weapon. It's my lunch."

"Well, then you shouldn't have put it on the weapons' table." I shrugged, holding the grilled cheese out like a sword. Maybe if I chose the most ridiculous option, he'd send me back home and forget about this whole new world thing. "This grilled cheese sandwich, in all its cheesy glory, is now my weapon."

A light-blue message box appeared in the air in front of me, asking me to confirm my choice of making [Dave's Lunch] my weapon.

"Don't even think about it." The satyr, who was apparently named Dave, shook his head. "You won't win with a sandwich for a weapon."

What kind of name was Dave for a mystical satyr? I pressed my lips together to avoid laughing at the absurdity of all this. "Who said anything about winning? You claimed this wasn't a game, and the grilled cheese was on the weapons' table, so I'm going with my gut and that's leading me to food."

The message box that said [Yes] glowed brighter and then disappeared before another message popped up.

[Dave's Lunch has been assigned to Hazel]

[New Quest: Defeat 1 Monster]

"Defeat one monster?" My gaze fell on the enclosures full of strange creatures. Dave said this was a dungeon, but fighting just didn't feel right. "No way, I'm not hurting any of them. If that's why I'm here, you might as well send me back."

"You can't go back. Not yet, at least. You have to enter the dungeon and level up by killing monsters."

[New Quest: Escape the Dungeon by Defeating the Boss on Floor 100]

This was going from bad to worse if the only way I could go home was to kill things. It didn't matter how strange those monsters looked, they were still animals in my mind, and hurting them just to level up would make *me* the monster.

I clutched my apron, fingers curling into the soft fabric. "There's gotta be another way, right? Something that doesn't involve fighting or hurting anyone? I mean, if you were using the monsters for food, I could understand. Everyone needs to eat. But killing them just so I can go home? It feels wrong."

"You're fighting them to gain experience and new skills." Dave's eyes twinkled like that was supposed to be something thrilling. "The more monsters you defeat, the higher your level will rise until eventually you can fight the boss on the last floor. If you win, you'll not only get out of the dungeon, but you'll also gain the thing you desire most. Just defeat the boss, and it'll all be yours."

"That simple, huh?"

What even was the thing I desired most? I guess I'd have to figure that out on my way to the final boss. But could I really fight through a hundred floors of monsters and beat some epic boss with a *sandwich*?

Guess there was only one way to find out.

CHAPTER TWO

Weaponized Grilled Cheese

My morning was off to a rough start so far. I'd not only woken up in a dungeon and chosen a grilled cheese for my weapon, but I was somehow expected to fight with it too. Against literal monsters.

This new world was so not my cup of tea.

Dave gave me a sad smile. "I understand that you don't *want* to fight, but once you're inside the dungeon, that will change. You need to be prepared, and a sandwich won't help you."

"I know that." I stared at the perfectly golden-brown bread in my hands, wishing it had all the answers for me. "There has to be another way for me to get home. You can't just kidnap me, tell me to fight monsters, and assume I'll be okay with it. That's ridiculous."

The fence keeping the bouncy blue monster locked up suddenly disappeared, as if Dave was trying to force me into action. I'd have backed away, but something deep inside me knew that I shouldn't enter the fog surrounding the clearing.

So that only left one thing: defeat that monster. With a grilled cheese.

I scratched my head, eying the monster bouncing toward me. It reminded me of colorful pudding or blue Jell-O as it hopped closer, body jiggling. It was honestly kind of cute, if I ignored the whole monster thing. Its eyes were a deeper blue than its body, shimmering like sapphires as it blinked curiously at me.

"Hey there." I knelt down slowly, holding my hand out to it. "Are you hungry?"

"What?" Dave shook his head as the cute bouncy thing came closer, his expression pained. "No, you can't feed the monsters."

"Why not?"

Maybe if I treated it like a puppy, I could get through this with some sanity intact. I ripped off the corner of my sandwich, melty cheese pulling away from it in a long string, and tossed it toward the monster. Its mouth opened wide as it gobbled the gooey cheese up, making an adorable *glomp* noise. Then it chittered gleefully and bounced faster.

"You liked that, huh?" I smiled, ripping off another piece for it. "Have some more."

Soon the creature was in my arms, crooning as I fed it by hand. Some monster it turned out to be. I wanted to mock Dave about that, but he looked like his head might explode as he paced the clearing, muttering to himself.

I dared to pet the creature, its squishy body molding against my hand. Its skin was smooth and elastic, reminding me of bread dough. It leaned into my hand as its eyes changed to adorable greater-than and less-than signs, making a *squee* noise like it was the happiest little jelly bean ever.

My heart warmed as the little creature melted some of my worries away. Focusing on things I *could* do, like feed this hungry little monster, eased my mind far more than focusing on all the things I couldn't do. Like remembering my past or going home, apparently. I swallowed hard, determined not to let any feelings of helplessness overtake me.

For right now, I just needed to focus on what I could do. Defeat this monster without hurting it, because that was the only hope I'd have of making it through the dungeon. The phrase *monster tamer* came to mind, so maybe something like that would work. I could feed them, befriend them, and form a bond.

Forming that bond might be easier if the monster had a name.

"What should I call you?" I asked the little blue creature. "Jellybean?"

It wiggled up and down, almost like it was nodding. Apparently, it liked the name.

[Quest Completed: Defeat One Monster]

[It's not the normal kind of defeat, but the slime has definitely been won over. Reward: Starter Gear.]

I blinked at the blue messages in front of me. Was there a system monitoring my actions? That was weird, but at least it seemed to be going with the flow for now. Being able to defeat monsters by feeding them *would* let me go through the dungeon without doing anything I'd regret.

"So, you're a slime, huh?" I asked the little blue Jell-O monster in my arms. It wiggled another nod and gazed up at me with those big, shimmering blue eyes, begging me for another bite. "Don't worry, I'll share my food."

[New Class: Culinary Mage]

Pots, pans, and gold coins rained down from the sky along with bread and cheese, but I ducked before seeing what else was there. Getting hit on the head was the last thing I needed right now. A soft chime replaced the clank of pots and pans, and there was no pain. I dared to look up, gazing at the clear blue sky without any cooking equipment falling from it.

Where did it all go?

"No, she can't get pots and pans." Dave moaned. "She's supposed to get travel gear and potions! What kind of starter gear is that?"

He waved his hands in the air, frantically swiping through menus I couldn't see. When he paused, his face grew pale.

"She's a culinary mage?" He glared at the campfire as if it would have answers. "A *culinary* mage?"

Whatever that was was apparently too much for the poor satyr because he collapsed on the ground beside me, muttering nonsense about how chefs didn't belong in the dungeon and culinary magic didn't even exist.

I felt a little bit bad for him, especially since I'd stolen his lunch, so I handed him what was left of it. "Maybe you should eat something."

He nodded, gulping the sandwich down. Once it was gone, another one appeared in my hand with the same original bite taken out of it.

"What the hell?" I dropped it in shock. The slime gobbled it up heartily before yet another sandwich appeared in my hand.

That was so not normal. I guess I really was in another world . . .

"You'll always have access to your basic weapon, but if you lose other weapons, they won't come back." His voice was a bit calmer after the food, going into what felt like a tutorial. "Rely on your weapon and you'll get through the dungeon eventually." He eyed the grilled cheese. "Probably."

"Very reassuring, thanks." Since the grilled cheese and I were stuck together, I should see what I was working with. I took a small bite but immediately spit it out. "Ugh, that's awful. It tastes like cardboard."

"What's cardboard?" Dave asked.

"It's . . ." I paused, unable to picture it. "How do I know a word but not know what it means?"

Dave's eyes softened. "It happens to every newcomer, but your memories would only be a distraction. I promise that most people end up leaving happier than when they came, so try not to worry."

A bitter laugh escaped my lips. Trying not to worry was easier said than done, but he had mentioned something about gaining the thing I desired most when I beat the boss. Maybe he meant I'd get my memories back? If that was the case, then I just had to keep pushing forward and focusing on what I could do right now. Like level up, bake good food, and get the hell out of here.

The slime leaned into my hand like it was begging for pets, so I smiled and obliged. "Sorry I fed you something so gross. I'll make better food for you soon, I promise."

Its eyes lit up and it made a chittering noise, bouncing up and down in my lap. I couldn't help but smile at its excitement.

More message boxes appeared in the air.

[Title Granted: Slime Friend]

[Level Up: Culinary Mage Level 2]

[Your friendship with a slime has opened new doors, expanding your skill options and giving you a better understanding of slimes in general. You keep getting more and more interesting, Hazel.]

Hazel. Seeing my name, so solid and real on that message box, gave me a warm fuzzy feeling in my chest.

"Slime friend? Slime *friend*?" Dave shook his head, groaning loudly. "That's it. I'm done. You're not normal."

"If being normal means fighting sweet little monsters like Jellybean here, then I'm glad I'm not normal."

Hmmmm, getting a title just for being nice and feeding Jellybean made it seem like this dungeon wouldn't mind if I did things a bit differently. How far could I push that? Far enough to make the final boss my friend with the help of a delicious cookie maybe? Oh, now that opened up some possibilities. If I could cook my way through the dungeon, then I'd be set. I just needed a few more things . . .

My lips curled into a smile. "Where can I get ingredients?"

Dave stared at me for a while, as if waiting for me to say I was kidding, until he begrudgingly gave in. "You can find food as you explore the dungeon, or you can buy ingredients at the town on the fifth floor. It's a safe zone where adventurers stay until they're high-enough level to delve deeper. You've also got a few things in your inventory."

"My inventory?"

As I said the word, a grid appeared in front of me labeled [Inventory]. Tiny loaves of bread and hunks of cheese were inside, along with the pots and pans that had fallen from the sky. But there was more. Images of knives, spoons, spatulas, a portable stove, water, and a few other odds and ends appeared in the grid too. Everything I'd need to start cooking, if I could get them out of this menu.

Maybe if I touched one of the boxes, they'd appear like in a video game. I hovered over the bread, feeling a bit strange. This wasn't how life was supposed to work, but I had a feeling an inventory menu was only the beginning. This world was full of new and strange things. I'd have to get used to them if I wanted to succeed.

I tapped the box, and bread appeared in my hands like magic. The crust was firm, but the interior felt like it would be nice and soft based on a quick squeeze. I touched the bread against the grid again and it disappeared inside.

"Oh, that is so cool." I grinned as I took the cheese in and out next. "I could get used to this inventory thing."

"Great, glad *you're* having fun." Dave's sarcastic tone did nothing to sway my excitement. "Since you're a culinary mage, whatever that is, I should probably show you how to cook."

I shook my head. "I think that's something I already know how to do."

And I wanted to hold on to those few solid memories. Rolling pastry, kneading dough, drizzling chocolate, all of that felt natural to me. Easy, like something I'd done so many times it was ground into my mind.

If I really couldn't go back home without beating this dungeon, then I'd just have to make it work somehow. Baking for the final boss probably wasn't the smartest route to take, but it was the one I was going with. A faint glow pulled my attention to the mountain as the door opened. Inside that dungeon would be all sorts of ingredients I could use. Maybe I'd even remember more of my life if I kept doing familiar things.

I turned back to Dave. "Is there anything else I should know?"

"Yes, but you can learn it as you go like everyone else. You need to be careful though." Worry tightened his voice. "Your class and title aren't normal. The dungeon's been creating things on the fly ever since you stubbornly chose my lunch as your weapon. I'm not sure what'll happen to you now or where that will lead you."

Maybe I'd have been better off sticking with the magic books, but then I wouldn't have this cute new slime friend bouncing next to me. If I had to be here, then cooking my way through the dungeon felt like the right path. I had a feeling I was never one to follow the rules.

So I'd go in there, find whatever ingredients were available, and bake treats worthy of a final boss.

Then I'd finally be free of this nightmare.

"You coming?" I asked the little blue slime as I moved toward the dungeon's entrance. "You can stay here if you want."

Jellybean chittered, bouncing into the dungeon ahead of me without a care in the world. I smiled and followed the brave slime, grateful that I wouldn't be going in alone. Whatever happened next, Jellybean and I would handle it together. Even if the door was slowly creaking closed behind me, sealing us inside . . .

CHAPTER THREE

A Taste Adventure

Hundreds of glowing orange gems lined the stone walls of the dungeon, flickering faintly like embers. Warmth emanated from them, wrapping around me like a soft blanket as the smoky scent of the campfire outside permeated the air. I expected the dungeon to be dark and gloomy, but this was downright cozy.

[New Quest: Defeat 2 Monsters]

Hmmmm . . . I had a feeling the monsters wouldn't all be as sweet as Jellybean, but I still wanted to try feeding them instead of fighting them. I'd need to keep my guard up though and start cooking right away. No monster deserved to eat that awful sandwich Dave called a lunch.

I sat with my back against the wall so nothing could sneak up on me and opened my inventory. Jellybean bounced next to me like he knew food was coming, but a new menu caught my attention before I could take out any ingredients.

[Cookbook]

Knowing recipes from this world would be really helpful, especially if different monsters had different food preferences. I tapped the word *cookbook*, jumping a bit when an actual book appeared hovering in the air in front of me. My eyes widened as I moved my hand around it. There were no wires. It was really floating! Okay, maybe this new world had a few cool things, like cookbooks that flew next to you at the perfect height for reading. That would definitely come in handy.

The cover was a warm brown, like soft leather, embossed in gold with a crossed knife and fork. It opened on its own, flipping through a few pages of question marks that looked like a very confused index before stopping on a recipe for grilled cheese.

I snorted, glad I actually liked grilled cheese since the system seemed to think it was my favorite food. But the "recipe" was basically just an ingredients list, and it didn't include any instructions.

[Grilled Cheese: Bread, Cheese, Butter]

Okay, but what kind of bread? What kind of cheese? It might not matter as much for *this* recipe, but it would for others. I was a baker, not a cook who just threw things together and hoped they turned out. I needed specifics: ingredient measurements, bake time, temperature, and anything else they could give me.

Except, for some reason, it felt like maybe I actually *could* just toss everything on a pan and call it good . . . It wouldn't hurt to try.

I removed a pan and the item labeled *portable stove* from my inventory. There didn't seem to be a fuel source for the stove, and I couldn't find a switch to turn it on either. It was just a square piece of smooth black metal with rounded corners, maybe an inch thick. I ran my fingers over it, feeling some kind of design on the surface maybe? Hmmm . . . this dungeon cooking adventure wasn't going to get very far without a heat source.

I absently set the pan on the stove so I could go through my menus for a hint, but an orange glow pulled my attention back. The stove had activated somehow and the design on its surface was glowing. I pulled the pan off it and the orange glow faded, but when I set the pan down again, the glow immediately came back. Well, that was useful. As long as I didn't accidentally set the wrong thing on it. Just to test, I removed the pan and placed a clump of grass on the stove instead.

Nothing happened. The grass didn't wilt or turn brown from the residual heat.

I held my hand over the stove, but it didn't actually feel warm. Maybe it was like a magical induction cooktop, where the heat went to the pots and pans instead of the stove itself? Now that would be really cool and a good safety measure.

Jellybean nudged my leg, big eyes begging me to actually cook something already.

"Okay, okay," I said with a laugh. "Give me a minute."

The only ingredients I had were bread, cheese, and butter, none of which said what kind they were, so I just pulled one of each out. The bread looked like basic white sandwich bread, and the cheese was orange like cheddar. I cut them into slices, buttering the bread before putting a slice on the pan to cook. Then I layered some hopefully delicious cheese in the middle before adding the top slice of bread. The butter sizzled nicely as the cheese started to melt, but it didn't smell like anything. How strange.

After a few minutes, I flipped the grilled cheese, excited about the golden-brown color the bread had now. The slime slowly made its way onto my lap, getting closer and closer to the stove while the sandwich cooked. I held him back, not wanting the poor thing to get hurt, but felt just as excited to try this grilled cheese. If it actually tasted good, that opened up a lot of options for getting through this dungeon my way.

Anticipation thrummed through me as I took a small bite of the sandwich, and an unmistakable cardboard taste filled my mouth. No! It was just as awful as the last one. Jellybean ate the rest, cooing happily despite its terrible taste. Why didn't that work?

[You cooked your first meal. Congratulations!]

"Are you mocking me?" I felt a little silly talking to thin air, but I needed answers. "I'm sure you know that didn't taste good."

[Does taste matter? The food served its function.]

"Of course taste matters! Food is so much more than a way to survive." I leaned forward as passion surged in my chest. "It's the thing that comforts you when you're sad or the thing you reach for when you want to celebrate. The taste of a good meal is an emotional experience. It's its own kind of magic, so you can't just pretend like it doesn't matter."

[Are you sure? You don't even have any memories.]

"That's . . . true." I slumped against the wall, feeling defeated for some reason. I'd felt so sure about what I was saying a minute ago, so why was I doubting it now? Food was transformative and apparently so meaningful that it left a mark on my soul. One I couldn't forget no matter what tricks this dungeon played on me. "Memories don't matter here. What I said is true. I feel it in my core. There's no point in cooking without flavor."

The message boxes took a while to appear again, but when they did, it felt like the air had shifted.

[You're only a level 2 and you have no skills. Don't give up yet.]

Ohhhh, that was a nice hint. I opened my menu, but the part labeled [Skills] was empty except for the titles [Culinary Mage] and [Slime Friend]. "How do I get skills?"

[You can gain skills related to your class or titles. Normally, I'd say fight strong monsters. But for you? I'd recommend exploring, gathering ingredients, and cooking as often as you can. Food is your weapon, and to wield it, you'll need to enhance every aspect of it. Skills are gained through action.]

Action, huh? Well, since cooking was a total waste until it tasted good, I might as well work on some of the other things it mentioned. I eyed the rest of the dungeon for the first time, taking in the flat grassy area that looked like an extension of the meadow outside. A few trees and bushes dotted the landscape along with a small pond not too far away.

Trees and bushes might have fruit. Water was always a bonus too.

I packed up my things and gave Jellybean a pat on the head. "Ready to explore?"

The slime bounced off my lap, eyes shimmering as he took off. I hurried to follow, not wanting to lose him in the grass. We stopped at the pond first and I knelt down, cupping my hands to drink from it. It was cool and felt refreshing going down. I let out a breath, happy there were normal things here, when my gaze landed on the rocks at the edge of the pond. They had some kind of white powder or crystals on them. I frowned, leaning closer. It looked like salt . . .

Was this *salt water*?

I spat it out. Ugh. It didn't taste salty, but apparently that didn't matter.

How was I supposed to cook if I couldn't trust my own taste buds?

I bit my lip, staring at the light reflecting off the water. The system had said that skills were gained through actions. If I boiled the water down, maybe I'd have salt that I could use to flavor the rest of my food? I wasn't sure that was really how it worked, but salt was the foundation of flavor. It was worth a try. I thought I'd spotted a canteen in my starter gear too.

As I filled the bottle, I searched for other things to gather. A patch of flowers that looked like dandelions lined the far side of the pond while green shoots of something were a bit farther away. Jellybean hopped over and devoured a few flowers. They hovered in his translucent blue slime before dissolving. They didn't seem to affect him, but I had a feeling slimes and humans were pretty different.

I picked a few anyway before moving on to the thin and round green shoots that were about two feet tall. They felt familiar, but I couldn't put my finger on why. I picked one and chewed on it, but I had no idea what it was. Maybe it was just a weed? I almost moved on, but my gaze kept drifting to the brown parts of the plant. I knelt down and started digging it up without really knowing why. It just felt like what I was supposed to do.

Memories whispered at the edge of my mind as my fingers clawed at the dirt, loosening it enough to pull up a white bulb. Was that garlic? The outside easily flaked off under my fingers, revealing small white cloves inside. I grinned, holding it up high. Yup, that was definitely garlic.

Unless this was another trick like the salt water.

I washed my hands in the pool before pulling a clove off and biting into it, hoping the overpowering garlic taste would come through. It was firm and juicier than I'd expected. Everything in me screamed not to eat garlic like this, but the pungent taste sadly didn't overwhelm me. It was bland, like chewing on air.

So much for that. I sighed and added the rest to my inventory for later before continuing my search for flavor.

Jellybean bounced at me, then hopped over to a strange plant with a domed top held up by a simple stalk. He slurped up a few of the plants with a smile, like he was encouraging me to try them too. Well, Jellybean hadn't led me wrong yet . . .

I took a big bite, chewing and chewing and chewing until I couldn't stand it anymore. The spongy texture was just awful, never breaking down and getting a little slimy.

"Ugh, this can't possibly be edible." I spit it out and washed my mouth out with water while Jellybean gobbled up a few more. "I'm never trusting your sense of taste again. Those are gross. No more random things growing on the ground. Let's find some fruit instead."

We wandered around a bit until we came across a tree with purple fruit hanging from it. I let out a breath. That looked a little safer at least, even if I couldn't for the life of me remember what it was. The fruit was oval and three or four inches long. I picked one, rolling it around in my hand. The skin was smooth with small dimples in it, and it felt like there was juice inside.

Almost like a . . . lemon?

The word felt right, but something about it still looked wrong. Was it really a lemon?

Only one way to find out. I cut the fruit open, revealing the pulp inside. I dared to take a bite, and my mouth puckered something fierce. Even though I couldn't *taste* the sourness, my body knew it was there. No matter how weird it looked, or if the dungeon was trying to trick me, my senses knew that was a lemon.

And. It. Was. Sour.

I forced myself to swallow, and Jellybean wiggled in amusement. "Yeah, yeah, laugh it up. Why don't you try some?"

A few had fallen on the ground, and the slime ate them up, no problem. Did slimes even have taste buds? Maybe not, but he seemed happy whenever he ate, so maybe he tasted a different way? I shrugged, picking a few more lemons to add to my inventory. Hopefully them being purple didn't change anything important.

[New Skill: Ingredient Insight]

[Your fearless sampling of mysterious plants has unlocked a new ability. Focus on an ingredient to identify it and determine its rarity.]

My lips pulled into a grin as I held the lemon up in triumph. "I got my first skill!" I leaned down to scoop up Jellybean so we could dance and wiggle our victory out. "That's so cool. Now I won't have to eat weird things without knowing what they are."

I stared at the fruit in my hand until a small pop-up appeared over it.

[Lemon: Common]

"It worked!" I hugged Jellybean close. This felt like the first real step toward making tasty food again. "What's the common part about though? Does that mean there are uncommon ingredients?"

[There's only one way to find out. Rarity might even affect flavor, so keep exploring. You might find what you're looking for sooner than you think.]

Well, that sounded promising. These messages made it feel like Jellybean and I weren't as alone as I'd initially thought. We had someone, or some*thing*, backing us up with information. Daring me to keep learning about this dungeon and striving for the flavors I knew were here. The challenge of it all was kind of exciting.

I'd show this dungeon what real food was *supposed* to taste like and win over that final boss in no time.

CHAPTER FOUR

Dungeon Chickens

Ingredient insight was amazing, letting me quickly identify plants without having to taste test them. Which meant I could finally see what that weird, spongy plant was from earlier. I picked a small one, staring at it until the skill activated.

[Poisonous Mushroom: Uncommon]

Mushrooms! Of course. How could I have forgotten what that awful texture was? I had no use for poisonous plants, but it was the first uncommon ingredient I'd seen so far. I checked a few of the other mushrooms and they were a mix of common mushrooms and uncommon poisonous ones, so the poison seemed to be the uncommon part. Interesting.

"Be careful not to eat any of these, Jellybean."

A soft *cluck-cluck* answered back, and it definitely wasn't Jellybean.

Were there . . . chickens in the dungeon?

I turned around just in time to see my best little slime friend open his mouth wide and gobble a tiny chicken up.

"No!" I shouted as the chicken bawked loudly before it disappeared. Jellybean looked at me innocently with a chicken feather hanging out of his mouth. "Oh, no you don't. Spit it out. Now."

Jellybean tilted his head as if he was confused, but the chicken was clearly inside his translucent body. It was flapping its wings like it was still alive, so I stormed over there and stared the slime down.

"Spit. It. Out," I said forcefully. "We don't eat cute baby chickens here. We just don't." When the slime didn't do anything, I added, "I'll make you something tasty if you spit it out."

Jellybean's mouth dropped open, and the chicken fluttered back to the ground, squawking up a storm and leaving slime-coated feathers everywhere.

I patted the slime's head. "That was nice of you. Thanks."

He chittered, leaning into my hand, and I couldn't help but smile. I knew I should chastise him more, maybe try training him or something, but he was just too adorable. We'd work on slime manners another day. Right now, I had to start cooking, because if there were chickens, then there were probably scarier things out there too. Hopefully these new ingredients would make something tasty. Not the mushrooms though, even though I still had the poisonous one in my hand. I stuffed it in my inventory to study the uncommon aspect later and reached for the garlic instead.

But the ground started vibrating like a stampede was coming our way. I dropped my hand, no longer caring about the garlic as I leaned down to pick up Jellybean. I wanted to be ready if we had to run.

Then came the sounds.

Clucking so loud I was afraid to turn around and look. But I forced myself to peek.

Four monstrous chickens towered over me. They had to be almost six feet tall, and when they opened their mouths, fire shot out, blazing past me like a warning shot.

Fire. Breathing. Chickens.

At their feet stood a ruffled little chicken that looked suspiciously like the one Jellybean had tried to eat. Dammit. Was I about to be a monster chicken's revenge dinner?

"I'm really sorry about what happened, but I don't mean you any harm." I held my hands in the air, trying to avoid meeting their death stares. "It was just a misunderstanding."

A misunderstanding about who was on the menu tonight, but that was beside the point. Jellybean started shaking in my arms and I held him close. We could all walk away from this in one piece, right?

One of the monsters moved closer, clucking in an angry tone as it pecked the air. I winced, picturing how painful that beak would be if it hit me. This was not how my story ended. No way. Not pecked to death by a chicken.

I pulled out my trusty sandwich: [Dave's Lunch].

"Here chicken, chicken, chicken." I ripped pieces off the grilled cheese and tossed them on the ground. "Dinner time."

The monster in front walked right over the sandwich bites, grinding them into the dirt under its talons. I gulped. That was one terrifying chicken. Thankfully the others seemed to enjoy the sandwich as they leaned down to peck at it. I tossed a large chunk of it in the air, waiting for the boss chicken to look up.

The moment its eyes left me, I gripped Jellybean tight and fled as fast as my legs could carry me.

Furious squawking rose up behind us, but there was no way I was looking back. Not a chance. Not when Jellybean was shaking like a leaf, too terrified to make a noise as the chickens closed the distance between us. There was no way I was outrunning them, so we'd have to find somewhere to hide. There weren't any convenient caves or buildings around, unfortunately, so our only choice was going to be climbing a tree and hoping these chickens couldn't fly.

I tossed Jellybean into the tallest tree I could find and raced after him, grabbing branch after branch. A chef's coat wasn't the best for climbing trees though, and I kept slipping. This was insane. I was just a baker, so why was I getting chased by fire-breathing chickens in a *dungeon*? I hauled myself up higher, straddling a branch so I could catch my breath and see what the chickens were up to. They were still spitting fire but thankfully seemed to have terrible aim.

No, that wasn't right. They were avoiding hitting the tree for some reason. The biggest chicken cocked his head at me, glaring up into the tree, taunting me. I was the silly human who'd climbed a very burnable tree after all, what did I expect? They could get me down in no time if they wanted to.

Which meant they wanted to scare me first. Give me time up here to think about all the ways they'd grind me into the dirt like that sandwich earlier.

I leaned back against the tree trunk, hugging my knees to my chest. Dave was right. Choosing a sandwich for a weapon was ridiculous, and I was going to get myself killed because of it. Saying I wasn't going to fight had sounded great in the meadow, but now? I was in over my head with no idea what to do.

Vibrations ran up the tree as the chickens started pecking at it with enough force to knock me out of it.

I clamped my arms around the branch, refusing to give those crispy cluckers the satisfaction. If I couldn't bribe them with Dave's lunch, then maybe I'd have to do something more drastic. I opened my inventory, staring at the poisonous mushroom from earlier. I didn't want to use it, but what other choice did I have? It's not like anything I could make would appease them.

Like the dungeon said, I was only a level two and barely had any skills. I couldn't even make something that tasted good yet, let alone something that would defeat a giant fire-breathing chicken! I was useless, and Jellybean was going to pay the price.

I swallowed hard and grabbed the poisonous mushroom. Holding it now, with the intent to use it, felt so wrong, like its poison was leaking into my skin. Was I really willing to kill those monsters when all they'd done was protect their child? I'd have done the same thing in their place; I could feel it. If only Jellybean hadn't tried to eat that one, maybe we could have avoided this all.

No. Blaming Jellybean wasn't right either. It was my fault for not taking an actual weapon when I had the chance. I pulled out the portable stove, balancing it carefully between my legs on the branch, and started cutting up the mushroom. If I was going to do this, then I'd do it right and make a meal fit for a monster chicken.

My stomach sank as the mushroom slices started piling up. I had to do this. I had to keep us safe.

I glanced up at Jellybean for reassurance, but he was busy gobbling up fruit like we weren't in immediate danger. I frowned. Were those strawberries? Why would they be growing in a tree? The more I focused on them, the more pop-ups started appearing.

[Strawberry: Common]

[Strawberry: Common]

[Strawberry: Common]

Jellybean devoured them faster than my skill could catalogue them all. I sighed. Even if I did make something with those, it probably wouldn't taste good. Better the slime eat them and be happy while he could. I should be focused on the evil mushroom in front of me. I added butter to a pan, letting it sizzle before adding the mushrooms to sauté. Except, I couldn't get myself to drop them in the pan.

This just wasn't me. I wasn't a killer.

I slumped back against the tree. Okay, so if I wasn't a killer, then what was I? An idealistic fool who couldn't protect the only friend she had in this dungeon?

Jellybean had eaten almost every strawberry in the tree by now, his eyes twinkling, and I felt myself smiling despite the danger. "Do they taste good?"

The slime nodded, then hopped from branch to branch until dropping down next to me. I patted his head softly, wishing I'd been more capable of protecting him. He might have been the one who tried eating a baby chicken, but I was the one who'd made him let it go. That spicy lil nugget went straight to Mom and Dad after that, calling in the cavalry.

"I'm so sorry," I whispered to the slime, blinking back tears. "I never meant for any of this to happen. With how well you jump, maybe you could get away on your own. Hop from this tree to another?"

Jellybean tilted his body, then opened his mouth and dropped piles and piles of strawberries in my lap. My eyes widened as the pile grew, some even falling down on the chickens below. I rushed to put them in my inventory before they all fell but couldn't help but stare at the slime.

"Were you collecting all of these . . . for me?" My chest tightened as I watched the little slime nod. "That was kind, but I don't know what I can do with them."

He leaned forward, eating all the mushrooms out of my hand in one big gulp.

"Wait, no! Those are poisonous!"

But they were already dissolving in his body like they'd never been there. Jellybean just wiggled and bounced like he always did, apparently perfectly fine. He had been eating them when we'd first run across them, so maybe poison didn't work on him? Or maybe they were so weak that they wouldn't have done anything anyway.

A weight lifted from my shoulders now that they were gone. This was for the best. Being surrounded by beautiful strawberries was way better than debating violence. Was that why Jellybean had gathered them up for me? To show me there was another way?

I picked up the slime and held him tight. "Oh, Jellybean, I'm going to make you the best-tasting strawberry jam you've ever had!"

And thank him every day for reminding me what really mattered. Food was for healing the soul, not fighting.

I didn't have any sugar, pectin, or anything else I'd need for jam, so I'd have to get creative if this was going to work. Maybe if I spread it on toast, the chickens would be interested enough for us to run away again. Or maybe something else would catch their attention while I cooked. Either way, this was the plan I was going with. This was who I wanted to be.

"Okay, Jellybean, let's make some tasty chicken-taming jam."

CHAPTER FIVE

Monster Treats

Strawberries had an inherent sweetness to them when they were perfectly ripe, so I chose each one with care. Too ripe and they would be mushy, but underripe and they'd be tart with no sugar to combat it. I dried the strawberries off as best I could too, holding them over a warm pan to get as much moisture out as possible. I might not have had all the ingredients for jam, but I'd give it my best shot.

The sweet scent of strawberries filled the air as the beautiful fruit cooked. I'd gotten lucky finding these, their deep red color like precious rubies hidden away in the dungeon. Good food was better than any other treasure that might be here, so I prayed to whatever gods were in this world that the strawberries would finally taste good.

Jellybean bounced next to me, eying the pot with excitement. It was much easier to be confident with a food-lover like him around. No matter what I made, he'd eat it with a genuine smile. The crispy cluckers below us were another story though. They shot fire up at me, probably irritated that this was taking so long.

"Me too, chickens, me too."

I resisted the urge to take the jam off the heat, knowing it was far too mushy still. This just wasn't coming together. I sighed and leaned back, looking up at all the strawberries in the tree that Jellybean hadn't gotten to yet. One in particular caught my attention, high up in the branches.

[Golden Strawberry: Rare]

My eyes widened. "Hey, Jellybean, mind picking that golden strawberry up there for me?"

The slime wiggled a bit, then bounced up through the branches to grab it. When he returned, he opened his mouth and dropped it in my lap just like all the rest. The yellow color was so bright it was practically glowing, and it felt plump but firm. The perfect strawberry. Adding something this rare to the mix would have to help. Better ingredients always made for better food.

I carefully cut the golden berry up and added it to the pot to simmer. Maybe this would work out after all.

"Thank you." I patted Jellybean softly as he pressed against my side. "You'll get some too, don't worry."

His eyes sparkled and he grew a bit taller and skinnier until he was more of a rectangle, trying his best to reach into the pot.

I laughed. "Not yet. It's still cooking!" The poor little slime deflated with the most pathetic sigh I'd ever heard. "I'm sorry. Waiting for food to cook is never fun. But I have a good feeling about this one, just you wait."

This time it would taste like real food, I just knew it. That rare strawberry was going to put this over the top. I squeezed some purple lemon juice into the pot as well, adding just a bit of rind to help thicken it. I'd used every trick in the book to make this work without the right ingredients. This was my only chance. It had to work.

Black smoke rose off the pot and I wrinkled my nose as something acrid filled the air. "No, no, no!"

It hadn't even had time to burn! The pot just went from normal-looking jam to a charcoal blob!

[Your culinary mage level is, uh, too low to use rare ingredients yet.]

"Sure, now you tell me." I glared at the message box hovering in the air. "Any other words of wisdom for me?"

[No. You're actually doing a great job.]

I couldn't tell if the system was mocking me or not until another message appeared.

[Ingredient Insight: Level 2]

[Your insight has grown after inspecting all those strawberries. You'll see a bit more information now and can inspect your finished dishes too.]

Well, that was interesting. I focused on the burnt mess in the pot.

[Crispy Strawberry Jam: Inedible]

I snorted. "Crispy and inedible, huh? You really don't pull any punches."

And I couldn't help but laugh. Crispy jam had to be a first and I'd savor that fail, because it was epic and ridiculous and all mine. My shoulders shook with amusement as I let it all out, laughing despite the horrible situation. Between Jellybean and this system, what should have been a heartbreaking moment was actually pretty fun. This was how cooking should be. Happy and warm, surrounded by people you cared about. Or slimes.

"Okay, Jellybean, time to try this again."

I scraped the charcoaled mess out of the pot and started from scratch, making sure not to use any rare ingredients this time around. I picked the best strawberries again, making sure they were perfectly ripe with my upgraded ingredient insight, before drying them off and adding them to the pot along with lemon juice. Sugar and pectin would be better, but I let it cook low and slow for a long time, thickening it naturally until it finally started looking like jam.

[New Skill: Mana Mix-In]

[You've worked hard to make the best out of a bad situation, using only the few ingredients you have. You can now create one ingredient per recipe out of pure mana.]

"Pure mana? What's that even mean?"

[Mana is the magic that fuels your culinary mage class.]

"Wait, I'm really a mage?" I glanced at my menus, spotting a full blue bar labeled *mana*. "That's awesome. So, how's the new skill work, then? I could really use some sugar, especially if it's magic sugar."

[Speak the skill name to activate it. The more intense you sound, the better your outcome.]

I raised an eyebrow at the message. "Is that a joke or are you serious?"

[Dead serious.]

That still kind of sounded like sarcasm, but I'd do it just in case. I took a deep breath, straightening my back as I focused on the jam.

"Mana Mix-In!" Heat burned my cheeks as I loudly called out the name. At least there was nobody around to hear me say it, but it still felt so awkward. "Use sugar."

The last part was barely audible as embarrassment tightened my throat. Ugh, I really hoped the system was just messing with me, because I didn't want to do that every time. I ran a hand over my eyes and almost missed the glowing white sugar falling into the pot. Each crystal was beautiful, shimmering like diamonds. Okay, being a culinary mage had a few pretty awesome perks.

I stirred the sugar into the jam and let it cook a little longer to macerate the berries before using ingredient insight again.

[Sweet Strawberry Jam: Tasty]

A grin stretched across my face. This was really working! My food was getting better with every skill. I dared to take a sip of the jam and sighed. It still didn't taste like anything. Maybe flavor took a while to unlock. Jellybean didn't seem to mind as he slurped up half the pot, his blue body turning purple from the jam.

"Hey! That's for the chickens, remember?"

At that, we both looked down at the increasingly angry chickens. The smallest one strutted around like it was the general of an army. A very tiny general, but the spicy nugget was still egging the others on into pecking the tree like woodpeckers. Which meant it was time to give them a taste of this jam.

But . . . how was I going to feed the chickens from way up here? I could dump the jam on the ground, but I worked hard on that jam, and it didn't seem right to make the chickens eat it with dirt mixed in. I frowned at the spoon in my hands and then glanced at their sharp beaks, shaking my head. Nope, I definitely wasn't going to spoon-feed them either.

Where did that leave me? Tossing toast from up high? That might work if it didn't land jam-side down, but who was I kidding? Bread always landed jam-side down.

Which meant I'd have to get creative and roll it into balls, so no matter how it landed, the jam would be safe inside.

I buttered a slice of bread and added it to the hot pan. Once it was golden brown and beautifully crispy on both sides, I spread the jam across it and rolled it up like a snowball. Now I just had to hope my aim was good. I leaned over the branch I was sitting on and tossed the first jam ball in front of the smallest chicken.

The little spicy nugget turned its head this way and that before eventually pecking at the jam ball. Excitement rushed through me as it kept pecking, slowly eating it until the whole thing was gone. I tossed a few more jam balls down, so happy that this was actually working! Another small chicken joined the first, devouring the jam balls with gusto.

[Quest Completed: Defeat Two Monsters]

[Reward: Eggs, Fire Peppers, and Gold]

Four eggs, a few peppers, and ten gold coins rained down from the sky, almost hitting me on the head before they disappeared into my inventory with a soft chime. It was like the chickens were giving me gifts for feeding them, and that was so cool!

[New Quest: Defeat 5 Monsters]

Those quests seemed to get harder every time I finished one, but no matter how many jam balls I threw down, the bigger chickens didn't even deign to look at them. They were probably higher level than the little nugget, so maybe bigger monsters needed better quality food? Like how some of the strawberries were common and some were rare?

If that was the case, I'd need to level up fast if I wanted to hold my own in this dungeon. My food needed to be the best thing anyone had ever eaten, and that couldn't happen if the monsters weren't even willing to take a bite.

I still wasn't really sure *how* to level though. Skills were gained through actions, but the level I'd gotten had seemed pretty random after I first befriended Jellybean. No, it was after I'd gained that slime friend title. So maybe I'd level after big events? That felt like it made sense, but I doubted I'd have any big events stuck in this tree.

I sighed and pet Jellybean. "We're probably going to be here a while. Until those crispy cluckers get bored at least."

The slime blinked at me, like that didn't matter to him at all, before slurping up the leftover jam in the pot. A look of utter contentment settled on his face that made this all worth it. If he was happy, then so was I. Cooking for Jellybean was honestly pretty satisfying. I just wished we weren't stuck in a tree while doing it.

"Do you maybe need some help?" a woman's voice shouted up at me.

I jumped, almost falling out of the tree. An older woman with bright red hair, broad shoulders, and toned muscles stood about ten paces behind the chickens, watching the whole thing with a grin on her face like this was the best show she'd seen in ages.

"Uhh, that depends." I glanced over at the very large hammer strapped to her back. "Are you planning on using that hammer to tenderize them? Or would you be open to shooing them away instead?"

"You want me to shoo the monsters away?" Her laugh was raspy but full.

"Only if you won't be in danger." I squinted, wishing I could see her level like I saw ingredient insights. "Are you strong enough for this?"

The woman's face split into a wolfish grin. "Oh, I'm strong enough. You just get ready to jump."

She pulled the hammer off her back, swinging it over her head in an oddly hypnotic motion before striking a fearsome pose. A faint pulse went through the air, and I couldn't take my eyes off her for a moment.

Neither could the crispy cluckers.

They all turned, completely forgetting me high up in this tree. The leader stomped over to the newcomer, pecking the air in front of her like it had done to me earlier, except she laughed about it. She hefted her hammer and slammed it onto the ground in front of them. The monsters jumped back, feathers ruffling as rocks and dirt sprayed a few feet into the air.

"Did you forget the jumping down part?" the woman called out.

I blinked, realizing I hadn't moved at all. "Sorry!"

She'd just been so mesmerizing with skills I'd never seen, but now was not the time to gawk. I shimmied down the tree with Jellybean amid the chaos of chickens bawking as the hammer struck the ground over and over. When my feet finally hit the ground, feathers were flying through the air along with shots of fire. Those crispy cluckers were not backing down!

Something brushed up against my leg, and I jumped so bad Jellybean almost fell out of my arms. It was just the lil nugget from earlier. I let out a breath and bent down to give it the last of the jam balls in my inventory. My cooking might not have been good enough to sway larger monsters, but it seemed like it had won this one over at least. The chicken clucked and devoured the treat as fire shot in front of my face.

The biggest crispy clucker loomed over me, fury in its eyes. I'd made the mistake of interacting with the little one again. I swallowed hard, holding Jellybean close. Should I take my chances and run? Or hope it forgot about me again?

The woman's hammer struck the ground again, but with far more force this time. Dirt exploded everywhere, making it impossible to see. I rubbed my eyes and stood up while everyone was distracted, running as far away from the chickens as my legs could carry me. Jellybean cheered as he bounced in my arms, peeking around my shoulder to watch the aftermath as our savior jogged to catch up with us, leaving the chickens far behind, squawking in the cloud of dirt.

We'd gotten lucky today, but I couldn't count on that forever. If I was going to be a fool, then I needed to be the strongest fool in this dungeon. Which meant I had to level up. Fast.

CHAPTER SIX

A New Friend

My legs burned from trying to keep up with the woman who'd rescued me. She was in far too good of shape, acting like this mad sprint of ours was a jaunt in the woods while I could barely breathe. I motioned for her to stop, hands on my knees as I gulped down air.

Well, that answered one thing about my life: I was not an athlete.

"How are you not tired?" I gasped, still trying to catch my breath.

"Put all my points into strength and endurance." She shrugged, taking a sip of water while I tried to compose myself. "I'm Fiona, by the way."

"Hazel." She passed her canteen to me, and I took it gratefully, gulping down the cool water. She might be on the first floor, but she obviously knew more about this dungeon than I did. "What does putting your points into strength mean?"

She raised an eyebrow. "You never looked at your stats? No wonder you're exhausted." She shook her head with a soft smile. "Everyone starts with two stat points they can put toward agility, charisma, endurance, intelligence, and strength. Every time you level up, you get another point to add to one of those stats, and your health and mana will go up too. For now, try increasing your endurance."

If it meant my side would stop aching and I could breathe again, I was all for it. I opened my stat menu. All the ones she'd mentioned were only at one, but there were also three colored bars at the top: a red health bar that was mostly full, a blue mana bar that was almost empty, and a green level bar that was about halfway to level three. I hadn't noticed I was gaining any XP, but it must have been happening as I cooked? I certainly hadn't fought anything worth leveling up from yet, unless winning over that spicy nugget counted for half a level, which I somehow doubted.

I took Fiona's advice and added one of my points to endurance. A sense of relief washed over me, as if I'd just woken up from a full night's rest. "Whoa, that's amazing!"

Fiona nodded as Jellybean hopped out of my arms and started munching on some plants nearby, reminding me of what had caused all this nonsense in the first place. I could still picture how offended that baby chick had looked, feathers ruffled and out of sorts as it fell out of the slime's mouth. It might have been funny if it hadn't ended up with the monster parents chasing us down.

"You just had to eat that chicken, didn't you?" I asked Jellybean, accusation coloring my tone.

Fiona's lips twitched. "Wait, that's why you were stuck in a tree? Because that slime ate a chicken?"

"I made him spit it out. That should have been good enough, but noooo, they just had to get revenge."

Fiona burst out laughing, practically doubling over. "Revenge of the chickens? That's so ridiculous. I knew when I saw you throwing bread to them like they were pigeons that I had to introduce myself."

My cheeks burned. "Well, what else was I supposed to do?"

"Fight them," she said, as if that was the only logical answer. "They're not as tough as they look. Unless you're planning on feeding every monster?" She laughed, but stopped when I didn't join in. "Wait, that's not really your plan, is it?"

I bit my lip. "Umm, maybe?" No. That sounded way too uncertain. If I was really going to do this, I had to square my shoulders and say it with pride. I lifted my chin, staring her right in the eyes. "I mean yes, that's exactly my plan. I'm a culinary mage, so I'm going to bake my way through this dungeon without fighting anything at all."

Now, that was downright cocky and I kind of liked it. This wasn't going to be an easy path, so I needed to at least *sound* confident. Fake it till you make it and all that.

Fiona blinked. "You're going to *bake* your way through the dungeon?"

"I know it sounds a little silly, but I defeated Jellybean with a grilled cheese." I nodded at the slime playing in the grass. "And I actually did win over two of those chickens. The smallest ones, sure, but a win's still a win! Once I level up and improve my skills, I'm sure I can make this work."

She sat down and started cleaning her hammer, her forehead creasing in thought. "Okay, but *why* would you want to do that? Fighting to level up is tough sometimes, but it's kind of how this whole place works."

"Maybe, but I don't like the idea of fighting the creatures here. Take Jellybean, for example. Does he really seem like a monster you want to fight?"

"No," she paused, staring at the slime, "but he's special. I promise they're not all like that."

I sat down and hugged my knees to my chest. "Honestly, I was kind of worried about that, but it won't sway me from my plan. If Jellybean is nice, then I bet at least some other monsters are nice too, and I'd hate to hurt them just because the system wanted me to. I'd never be happy knowing that I hurt others to get ahead."

"You're pretty strange, but I see your point." Fiona sighed and leaned back on her hands. "Okay, culinary mage, show me what you've got."

"Well, I don't really have many ingredients . . ."

And my food still tasted like cardboard. I bit my lip, wishing I'd managed to get that flavor skill the system had hinted at. She'd understand my plan once she knew what good food tasted like. She had to.

"You can use anything I've got, if that helps." Fiona opened up her inventory and started swiping through menus. "What kind of ingredients do you want? I've got vegetables, eggs, butter, meat, fish, tea, sugar, milk, flour, chocolate, and all sorts of other useless stuff a new shop in town tempted me with. It all tastes the same though."

"That useless stuff sounds amazing to me!" I leaned forward eagerly. "What should I make? Do you have a favorite dessert? Or maybe a favorite meal?"

Her forehead scrunched up. "I'm not sure. I've seen cookies at the market and they always *look* like they'll taste good. But they never do."

The sad tone in her voice was a little heartbreaking. She didn't even know what she liked to eat! That was just wrong on so many levels. Everyone should have a favorite food that made them happy every time they ate it.

Well, if cookies were something she wanted, then cookies were what I'd make. Warm, gooey, chocolate chip ones. The best comfort food around.

"Why don't I make some chocolate chip cookies, then?" I pulled out my portable stove, pots and pans, and everything else I'd need to cook with. "Can I use your flour, eggs, butter, sugar, and chocolate?"

Why she even had all those things if food didn't taste good was beyond me. Between that, the purple lemons, and the strawberries growing in trees,

I had a feeling this dungeon had no idea what to do about food. It was like it knew food existed, but not what it should look or taste like.

I really wanted to change that for everyone here, and the best way to bring some flavor in was to add a little salt into the mix. And thankfully, I had just what we needed: salt water!

The bottle of salt water I'd gathered from the pond earlier barely filled the bottom half of my pot, but it would have to do for now. Fiona's eyes widened and she scooted a little closer as the water started boiling, leaving salt crystals behind. I stirred it slowly, hoping the tiny crystals wouldn't burn as the heat cooked off the water.

The bubbling water grew whiter and whiter until all that was left was [Salt: Uncommon]. I tapped my spoon against it and the salt shattered into large shards that were easily ground up into what looked like table salt.

"That's so cool," I mumbled.

Fiona raised an eyebrow. "Haven't you done this before?"

"I honestly have no idea, but it was fun." I grinned and gathered up all the other ingredients. "These cookies are going to be amazing, I promise."

She nodded and went back to cleaning, humming softly as if she didn't mind sitting here as long as I needed her to. It was nice. I creamed the butter and sugar together, beating them as fast as I could for a few minutes until the mixture became light and fluffy. I shook my arm out. Even with the extra endurance, I was still sore!

Fiona smirked. "One stat point isn't a miracle worker, you know."

"A girl can dream, but I see your point . . ." I increased my endurance stat again, leaving me one point left over in case something came up. Relief washed over me, and I started mixing the rest of the ingredients together until they formed a nice light-brown dough. "So, how long have you been here anyway? You seem to know a lot, but you're only on the first floor like me."

"A few months. I lost a fight and ended up at the beginning again. But . . ." She grinned and leaned closer like she was sharing a secret with me. "At least I got the pleasure of watching your chicken fiasco."

I rolled my eyes, but something she said was nagging at me. "You don't die when you lose a fight?"

"Not really, no, you just reset back to the tutorial zone and lose any progress you made toward your next level." She sighed. "I was so close to level nine too. Now I've got to start all over."

At least death was off the table, then. The knot in my stomach loosened as I broke up a chocolate bar, mixing so many chocolate chunks into the dough that it could barely hold them all. Apparently I had a sweet tooth.

Fiona tilted her head. "Mind if I ask *you* something?"

"Sure, but I don't know how much help I'll be."

"What are you doing with that thing?" Fiona nodded at Jellybean, who was eying up the cookie dough with stars in his eyes. "You do know that slimes are monsters, right? Or are you not strong enough to kill it?"

Jellybean shrank in on himself and moved closer to me, as if the other woman was an enemy now. I pulled him onto my lap just in case she was, but knew there wasn't much I could do if she tried to hurt him. I'd have to get stronger if I wanted to keep Jellybean safe.

"This slime is my friend," I said firmly, patting his head. "What's up with everyone assuming all monsters are evil? The system gave me a title for befriending him, so it must be fine."

"You got a title for it?" Fiona halted her cleaning, entirely focused on me now.

[Slime Friend]

The box appeared as if she'd called it forth, like how I could see the quality of ingredients when I focused on them. Was there a general appraisal skill that worked on people too? That would come in handy . . .

Fiona whistled before going back to her polishing. "That's pretty cool. Most people have slime killer or slime slayer titles, but you're the first slime friend I've seen."

Jellybean trembled in my lap. I wrapped my arms around him, murmuring calming things until Fiona held her hands up.

"I'm not going to hurt your friend, okay?" She leaned closer. "How'd you do it though? Befriend a slime?"

"I fed him."

She laughed. "Okay, maybe I underestimated that baking-your-way-through-the-dungeon plan."

"See? I told you this would work." I started to grin but then remembered I had to use my mana mix-in skill still for the baking powder. I sat up straighter and held my hand over the dough, determined to put as much oomph into this as I could. "Mana Mix-In! Use baking powder!"

Fiona's shoulders shook with silent laughter as she covered her mouth. "Umm, what was that?"

"What do you mean?" The back of my neck warmed. "The system said skills worked better if you shout them."

Laughter burst out of her so intensely that she had to wipe tears from her eyes. "Sorry, I'm not laughing *at* you, I promise. The system is well-known for getting bored and telling adventurers weird things."

"Oh, really?"

My face flushed. The system and I were going to have a long hard talk about that later, but right now I'd focus on shaping the cookie dough into balls until my embarrassment faded. It did feel like a cool magical spell when I was shouting it, something an actual mage would use. So maybe the system had just wanted me to get in the spirit of the dungeon.

Or maybe I was giving it too much credit.

Either way, I had to give these cookies my all and impart as much flavor as possible. Which would be hard to do without a stove, but I'd make a frying pan work for now. After a few minutes, the air filled with the scent of warm, buttery cookies and all other thoughts drifted from my mind. This was the first time food had smelled like anything!

Hope surged in my chest as I took the frying pan off the heat so they'd finish cooking with the residual warmth. I sprinkled a little bit of salt on top and smiled. They might not be the perfect cookie, but they were the first ones I'd get to share with friends in this dungeon.

Jellybean bounced closer, eying them with his mouth wide open. His body jiggled from the effort it was taking to hold himself back.

[New Skill: Flavor Boost]

[No food could taste bland with the care you put into it. As long as you have mana, flavor boost will make everything you cook have flavor. Whether that's good or bad is up to you. It can't stop you from burning things.]

"Yes!" I punched the air, so excited to finally unlock flavor! "Give 'em a try, Jellybean."

The slime gobbled one up, wiggling happily before devouring two more. I'd finally made something worth serving my little friend and it made me so happy. But I still snatched the pan away before he ate them all.

"Fiona, thank you for saving us." I held the cookies out to her. "I hope you like them."

She took a deep breath. "They smell so good."

"Hopefully they taste good too."

Fiona bit into a cookie, her eyes closed as a happy little moan escaped her lips. "These are amazing!" She grabbed a second one before she was even done with the first, reminding me far too much of Jellybean. "You really can bake food that tastes good!"

I grinned with pride and finally picked up a cookie for myself. It was still warm and gooey, falling apart in my hands. I took a bite, sighing as the chocolate melted in my mouth. The buttery taste filled my senses, warming my soul as well as my body.

Chocolate chip cookies really were the perfect comfort food. Nobody could be sad while eating one of these.

All too soon the cookies were gone, devoured between the three of us.

"Wanna make some more?" Fiona asked, already holding out the ingredients with a hopeful look. "I'll keep you safe while you cook."

I laughed. "Sure, I'll make all the cookies you want."

Jellybean bounced happily and Fiona slowly reached out to pet him. He cooed and leaned into her hand as she smiled. Cookies apparently had the power to bond people and slimes together too.

Guess I'd be baking a lot of them, then.

CHAPTER SEVEN

A New Dungeon Floor

[Level Up: Culinary Mage Level 3]

Pretty, colored lights shimmered in the air, and my entire body felt lighter as my health and mana bars increased. That last batch of cookies had really done the trick! I upped my charisma twice, using up all my stat points to hopefully make it easier to charm some monsters with my food.

My body glowed for a moment as the new stats settled in. "Look, Fiona! I leveled up from baking! This plan is really going to work."

She rolled over and gave me a half-hearted thumbs-up. "Nice job." Then she flopped back on the ground and held her stomach. "I think I need to lie here for a bit though. Those cookies are dangerous. They're just too good."

I chuckled. Even Jellybean looked a little too full with cookies hovering in his translucent body, so I packed the leftovers into my inventory and cleaned everything up as best I could. If I wanted to keep leveling, I needed a real kitchen to bake in with proper equipment and tools. Which meant the safe zone was next on my list of places to go. That was still four floors away though . . .

"Why don't we stick together for a while?" I asked Fiona. "I'll keep cooking and you can keep scaring chickens away until we get to the safe zone. Sound like a plan?"

Her forehead creased as she stared up at me. "You're really not going to kill *any* monsters *at all*?"

"Nope. Not unless they don't give me a choice."

"And do you expect *me* not to kill anything either?" She sat up, tilting her head at me. "You know I level up from fighting, right?"

She had a point. I bit my lip, staring at Jellybean as his eyes drifted closed like he was in a happy little food coma. I didn't want anyone as kind and silly as him getting hurt, but I also couldn't tell her to stop leveling up. Not when the reward was getting out of this dungeon and back to our real lives. The dungeon was set up to reward fighters like her, not anomalous bakers like me, so I had to learn to be okay with that. That didn't mean I had to watch it though.

I tapped my fingers on my apron. "What if you agreed not to kill any weak slimes and kept most of your fighting to times when I'm not there?"

She leaned her elbows on her knees, lost in thought. She was silent for so long that I thought she was going to say no, but instead, she stood up and held out her hand. "Okay, deal. I'll keep traveling with you as long as you don't stop me from fighting if we're really in danger. I don't have it in me to watch you get hurt for a monster, I just don't."

"That's fair." I shook her hand with a smile. "Now, let's see what's on the next floor. Wait, how do we actually move between floors?"

"With one of these." Fiona pulled an ancient-looking bronze key out of her inventory. "Hold it out like you're unlocking a door, and one will just sort of appear for you."

"Sounds easy enough. Where'd you get the key from?"

She winced. "They're given out randomly from monster drops, so I don't know how you'll find any without fighting."

This dungeon really was set up for fighting and nothing else. It's like the whole concept revolved around fight, kill, repeat, and it didn't sit right with me.

"You can use mine for now," Fiona said. "This one's a mystery key though, so it could take us one, two, or three floors down. We won't know until we use it."

"So we could end up pretty much at the safe zone if we're lucky?"

Fiona shook her head. "There's a floor boss we'll have to beat before we get there. Even a mystery key won't skip that."

"A floor boss?" She hadn't mentioned that fun little detail before, but how bad could it be? We were still on the starter floors and I had delicious cookies. "I'm sure we can handle it."

She laughed. "Look at you all cocky after leveling up a bit. If we end up at the floor boss, we're screwed though. Level three is not high enough, unless you're okay with me killing it for you, and even that isn't a guarantee. I'm only level eight myself, and this usually requires a party unless you're overpowered."

I reached over to pet Jellybean, who woke up with a jump. "Slow and steady is fine with me for now. I'd rather keep us safe than rush ahead."

"That's the spirit." Fiona stretched her arms high and repositioned her hammer on her back. "You'll want to hold on to that slime tight. Just in case."

"In case of what?"

"You'll see." She held the key out, summoning an old wooden door with intricate carvings on it. "Remember to hold on to the slime."

That warning felt far too ominous, but she opened the door and stepped inside before I could ask again. I picked up Jellybean, holding him close. The other side of the door was so dark I couldn't see anything. Logically there should be stairs since we were going down a floor, right?

Jellybean chirped in my arms, but didn't quiver in fear or anything, so this must be fine. I took a deep breath and stepped through.

The floor was slick and angled down so much that I slipped, almost falling forward. My instinct was to reach out and catch myself, but Jellybean pushed back against me, knocking me safely onto my backside. Then we started sliding, faster and faster down a chute that bent and curved, making my head spin.

The dungeon floors were connected by *slides*?

Before I could think about that too long, I was shooting out the other door into open air. My stomach dropped as we plummeted toward a massive blue slime fighting against a small group of adventurers. I clutched Jellybean tight, preparing for the worst. Even if we survived the fall, how would we win over something like that?

I clamped my eyes shut as we continued to fall. We seemed to be moving slower than before though. Almost like we had a parachute or the air had thickened.

"You'll be fine!" Fiona shouted. "Just relax."

Like that was ever going to happen. I curled into a ball as we gently hit the slime's jiggly body and bounced off it, landing on the ground safe and sound. I opened my eyes in awe as the slime towered over me.

"Thanks." My heartbeat pounded in my ears as the adrenaline from the fall wore off. "You saved us."

The big slime stared down at me, but I wasn't afraid like when those crispy cluckers had chased us. Slimes were different. There was just something comforting about them, even when they were twice my height.

I reached out, running my hand across his side. "You're a good slime."

Jellybean leaned forward to brush against the giant slime too, which seemed to be a deciding factor because he nuzzled us back, rubbing against my hand warmly.

"Awww . . ." A smile spread across my face as I wrapped both arms around the big guy in a hug. "You're adorable."

A man gasped behind me. "What the hell is she doing? Is she trying to get eaten?"

"No," Fiona said in an amused voice. "She's just a slime friend."

My cheek pressed against the big slime as I gave him one last squeeze. It felt like hugging a giant tree when your arms couldn't wrap all the way around it. Then I stood back and glanced at Fiona to make sure she was fine too. "Guess we have bad luck with floor keys, huh?"

She shrugged. "Or good luck. Depending on how much that slime friend title helps you."

The two other adventurers glared at me, one of them stepping forward, hand clenched on his sword. "I don't care who you are, but we were in the middle of a boss battle. Step aside."

The big slime whimpered and the sound tugged at my heart. How could they attack something so sweet?

I stood firm, putting myself between him and the adventurers. "No way. You'll have to go through me."

"That's fine with us," the angry one said. "You'll just respawn far away from here."

"Oh, I'll gladly risk a respawn for a slime." I glanced back, wishing I could see the slime's stats. "Are you okay?"

The slime keened, and a blue box appeared in front of it.

[20/500 HP]

No! It was so close to death.

"Will the slime respawn too?" I asked Fiona.

"I've never asked, but I think so?" Her face scrunched up in thought. "I mean, nothing ever seems to truly die in the dungeon."

She didn't sound very confident about that. Jellybean hopped onto my shoulder and then leapt over to the boss, sitting on top of his head like a little slime hat. My heart melted. They were way too adorable, and I'd protect them with everything I had.

"Listen up." I faced the new adventurers, trying to look more confident than I felt. "I can help you win without fighting the boss at all. So just stand back and leave this to me."

The less angry one frowned. "How would you do that?"

I pulled out my secret weapon: the delicious chocolate chip cookies we'd made earlier. "With these!"

They stared at me, hard, before breaking down laughing. "She's crazy. Let's get this fight over with."

They charged at us. My feet felt like lead, unable to move. I wanted to protect the slimes, but I also didn't want to die even if there was a respawn. Would I still be the same person after that? Would I—

"Knock it off," Fiona shouted before barreling into the men and shoving them out of the way. "The lady said she'd win the slime over. So you're going to let her try."

She clenched her hammer with a gleeful smile, practically daring them to disagree. The adventurers cowered, scooting back just a bit, and I couldn't help but smile.

Fiona had saved me once again.

"How'd I get so lucky meeting you?" I asked.

She gripped her hammer tighter, keeping an eye on the adventurers. "Just feed the slime a cookie, okay?"

"No problem." I turned my back on them and faced the boss slime again. "I can't heal you, but I do have some cookies if you want them."

They weren't exactly the best cookies, made with all common ingredients from Fiona, but they had flavor and that had to count for something. Maybe my new charisma and the slime's low health would affect the outcome too? There was so much I didn't know about my abilities, but I prayed this would work. I didn't want anyone to hurt him again.

I held a handful of cookies out to the boss slime and waited to see what he would do. Jellybean chirped and wiggled on top of him, as if urging the boss slime to take them.

The giant slime opened his mouth wide enough to gobble me up whole but just took the cookies instead, thankfully. The feel of a slimy mouth on my skin tickled, and I couldn't help but laugh. The slime perked up as he munched on the cookies, swaying side to side.

"Do you like them?" I grabbed the rest out of my inventory. "You can have as many as you want. If we run out, I'll bake more."

After eating every cookie I had, message boxes started appearing in the air.

[Slime Boss Defeated]

[Reward: Slime Jelly, Sugar, Gold, and a Boss Slime Bracelet]

Clear gelatinous cubes, sugar, and gold rained down on us, disappearing with soft chimes as they got close to each person. The bracelet only fell for me though, landing in my palm. It glowed a soft blue and felt elastic and smooth, just like the slimes.

[Boss Slime Bracelet is a cosmetic item that adds a passive boost to all slime friend skills. If the boss slime trusts you, so will the others.]

The big slime nudged my arm, staring at me expectantly until I looped the bracelet over my wrist. The cool material settled against my skin, molding to it as if it belonged there.

"Thank you for the bracelet. It looks just like you!" I held it up against the boss slime, admiring the sky-blue color. "It's beautiful."

"What the hell is this reward?" the angry adventurer asked. "Food? We got rewarded with *food*?"

Fiona shrugged. "If you knew how good that food could taste, you wouldn't be complaining."

As they grumbled, the boss slime bounced out of the way, revealing a beautiful metal door behind him.

"Is that the way to the safe zone?" I asked.

Fiona nodded. "Yup, you can only find it once the slime's been defeated. Guess the dungeon uses that term pretty loosely with you though, huh?"

The other adventurers pushed past us, shaking their heads. "Stay out of our way next time, slime lover."

"Yeah, yeah." I rolled my eyes as I leaned against the boss slime and whispered, "I'd save you every time."

He pressed up against me, almost knocking me over. I laughed and gave him a big hug while Jellybean trilled up above us. When the slimes were happy, I was happy.

Fiona cleared her throat. "Sorry to interrupt, but we should get going. The door stays open until the boss respawns, but since the boss never died . . ."

"You have no idea what'll happen, right?"

"Exactly."

I slowly pulled away from the boss. "We've gotta go, I'm sorry. It was nice meeting you."

The slime's body drooped and Jellybean fell off. I caught him in my arms, feeling horrible that I was bringing one of them with me and leaving the other. He was the boss for this floor though. I couldn't just take him with me . . . could I?

Fiona led me toward the door, but when I turned back and saw the boss slime all by himself on this big empty floor, I couldn't help myself.

"Do you want to come with us?" I asked hopefully.

The giant slime bounced in excitement but paused, blinking slowly. Then he shook his body and moved back. Jellybean chirped at him as an ache spread through my chest. He didn't think he should come with us? Was that because he didn't want to or because he wasn't allowed to?

"I'll take care of you," I promised. "I'm not really sure how, but I'll figure it out. You don't deserve to be killed by adventurers day after day, respawning just to fight again. You deserve to relax and eat all the cookies you want."

"Are you sure about this?" Fiona asked. "The town won't like it. They'll probably kick you out."

"Then they'll kick me out. If they're that coldhearted, they don't deserve my food anyway."

The boss slime hopped closer, small hops at first, followed by big hops that ate up the distance between us. The door was far too small for his huge body, but that didn't seem to faze him as he changed his shape into more of a rectangle, just barely squeeeezzinnng through the door.

That silly little squeeze followed by a pop made my heart soar. I saved another adorable slime today, which was the best feeling ever. They were innocents in a violent world that didn't even give them a chance. I'd protect as many of them as I could, and hopefully one day, this dungeon would be a safer place for them.

Everyone deserved to feel safe.

CHAPTER EIGHT

Stealing a Floor Boss

Unlike the fast slide between floors one and four, the door to the safe zone had opened to a stone stairway that seemed to go on forever, and my legs were starting to feel the burn, especially after all that running earlier. I just wanted to sit down, relax, and find somewhere safe to sleep.

"Think it's much farther?" I called out to Fiona. The big boss slime was between us, filling every inch of the stone corridor, so I couldn't actually see her.

The soft *plop plop* of the boss slime hopping down the stairs was the only sound I could hear.

"Fiona?"

I waited, but no answer came. That was not a good sign. I clutched Jellybean to my chest. Fiona wouldn't have just left me, not without saying something. So why wasn't she answering?

The boss slime stopped abruptly, and I face-planted into his jellylike body. I bounced off, stumbling back a few steps.

"Sorry about that. You okay?" I asked Jellybean. He chirped and wiggled, perfectly fine even though he got smushed between us. "Well, that's a relief. Now, what's up, Boss Slime? Can I call you Boss for short?"

The big guy nodded and then moved forward again. The squishing sound of him squeezing through another doorway made me let out a breath. We'd finally found the exit! How had three floors flown by in moments while one floor took ages? This dungeon should come with an instruction manual.

Once Boss lurched through the doorway, I made my escape onto the next dungeon floor: the safe zone I'd been dreaming about ever since I heard the term. I wouldn't have to worry about monster chickens or three-headed snakes or anything else. I could finally relax after far too long of a day.

Except, instead of the picturesque medieval town I'd been imagining, it looked more like we'd stepped into an overgrown jungle. Large vines hung from the ceiling, swaying around me like snakes. The ground was uneven, made of weathered stones covered in moss. Humidity thickened the air, leaving small pools of water everywhere.

"Is this . . . the safe zone?" I asked, turning to where Fiona should be. Except instead of Fiona, Dave was standing there.

Of course that extra-long walk had something to do with him. I wouldn't be surprised if he was the reason I was here in the first place, like some sort of game master.

I turned to go right back up the stairs, but the door swung shut and disappeared. I sighed. "Whatever you're here for, I don't want it."

"You don't even know what I want yet, and you did take my lunch. I think you owe me."

"Calling that a lunch is pushing it." I paused, staring at him for a while. "Is something different about you?"

Were his horns smaller? Or maybe his hooves were trimmed? No, his light-brown fur was fluffier. While I'd been getting treed by crispy cluckers, he'd been getting his hair done!

Dave frowned. "I'm always the same, but that's not the point. You stole a floor boss."

I glanced sideways at the boss in question, who was investigating what looked like a giant Venus flytrap, nudging it curiously. One of its spiny heads opened, snapping at the slimes. Boss was far too large to eat, but Jellybean seemed pretty offended. He bounced at the Venus flytrap as if he was yelling at it.

Wait, was that a monster too? Were there plant monsters on this floor?

[Venus Flytrap: Level 9]

I jumped back, not realizing I'd gained a monster insight skill. Or maybe that was there the whole time, and I just hadn't tried using it? Either way, level nine was crazy for a lowly level three like me. A shiver went down my spine as I stepped away from it, steering clear of the hanging vines too. All I wanted was a place to sleep, so why was I here with Dave and those creepy monster plants?

Dave cleared his throat. "Are you even listening?"

"Yes, of course." I nodded as the monster gobbled up Jellybean. "No!"

I raced over and tried prying its mouth open. This was the chicken and the slime all over again! Except this monster's spiny lips were sealed. Boss backed me up, leaping high and crashing down on most of the flytrap's heads. Even after that, it wouldn't let the little one go, the damned overgrown houseplant.

"Don't you dare hurt Jellybean." I hit the edge of its mouth, hoping to crack it open and get Jellybean back, but the flytrap stayed shut. "No! He's my slime, not yours."

Another one of the flytrap's heads snapped at me, and I was forced to jump out of the way. It thought it could hurt my friend, huh? Well, I'd show it how wrong it was. I opened my item box, searching for something I could feed it that would be tastier than Jellybean, but I was woefully short on food. How long would it take for a plant to digest a slime . . . ?

"Uh, Hazel?" Dave tapped me on the shoulder, annoyance clear in his voice. "Back to the whole you-stole-a-floor-boss thing."

"Seriously?" I snapped at him, my arms tired from wrestling a plant who had zero manners. "Help me deal with this and then we can talk."

He grumbled something about tiresome adventurers but opened his menu anyway, pressed some buttons, and poof, the flytrap was gone. All that was left was the little blue slime I'd grown quite fond of, falling to the ground. He bounced and rolled onto his head, staring up at me with a silly upside-down smile.

I sank onto the ground, pulling him into my arms for a hug. Jellybean quivered against me, nuzzling close like I was his savior. That was actually Dave though. I glanced up at him with grateful tears in my eyes. "Thank you. I really appreciate your help."

"Good. Now maybe we can talk about this stealing-a-dungeon-boss thing." He shook his head at me. "Honestly, you are so strange. The slimes are why you got stuck in the stairway, you know. They're monsters, so they can't enter a safe zone."

He paused, giving me his best *duh* look. I had a feeling he wanted me to say, *Ohhhhh, of course, that makes total sense*, but I didn't have a thing against monsters like he seemed to. So I just sat there, petting Jellybean until he stopped shaking.

Dave scratched the base of his horns. "Don't you get it? Your friend Fiona got into the safe zone just fine, but after her, the door shut again. The dungeon won't allow any monsters into a safe zone. So if you stick with them, you'll never make it out of here. You'll just keep resetting back to the beginning over and over, never making any progress. Is that really what you want?"

"Of course not, but . . ." I glanced around at the jungle floor full of ravenous plant monsters that were far too high-leveled for me. Dave was probably right. If I stayed here, I'd be monster chow in no time. But even so, I couldn't just abandon these slimes. Not after they'd decided to join me. Not after I told them I'd protect them. "I'm staying with them anyway, so I guess I'm just screwed. Any advice?"

Dave sighed. "If you'd chosen an actual weapon instead of my lunch, maybe, but you keep making the foolhardiest decisions. You can't survive here. Please, go to the safe zone. The slimes will be fine on their own."

Would they really? Neither of them was from this floor either, so they'd be at a disadvantage. Plus, adventurers would come to slay them soon enough.

I hugged Jellybean tight and stood up, brushing the dirt off my uniform. "Thanks for the information, but I'm still staying with the slimes."

Dave shook his head, sighing loudly and muttering something about the dungeon always being right. "You're so stubborn, Hazel, but I can offer you one thing that might help. There's a small shack some adventurers built with protections on it. You should be safe enough to sleep there for a few nights, but it's not a permanent solution. Just something to give you time to come to your senses."

He took off in the other direction, away from the snapping flytrap monster that was still taunting Jellybean.

"Aww, Dave, so you really do care, huh?" I grinned and hurried after him, nudging Boss to follow along too. "That shack sounds perfect. Thank you."

We came across quite a few monsters as we walked, but most of them stayed clear of Boss once he started jumping at them. He seemed like he'd be fine on this level at least, but Jellybean and I needed to do some leveling up. If this shack really was protected, then I could bake until I ran out of ingredients at least. But then we'd need to adventure out for more. I really wished Fiona was still here. Maybe she'd find us once she realized we didn't make it to the safe zone.

As we walked, the orange stones in the dungeon's walls and ceiling started changing colors until they were a beautiful sapphire blue. The stones dotted the ceiling like stars, and I couldn't help but stare up at them. They were beautiful!

"Careful." Dave held his arm out before I ran straight into the shack we'd been trying to find. He shook his head with a chuckle. "I bet you only survive here one day, then you'll be tutorial Dave's problem again."

"Tutorial Dave?" I frowned. "Do you always talk about yourself in the third person like that?"

He blinked at me, a faint blush sweeping across his cheeks before he pushed me into the shack. "Just get inside and stop causing problems."

"Yes, sir!" I mock saluted him and went inside. It was small, downright cramped once the slimes joined me, but it was far better than nothing. I patted Boss softly before pulling out my portable stove. "Why don't you come inside, Dave, and let me cook you dinner as a thank you?"

"This isn't a cafe!" He groaned, holding his head in his hands and muttering too softly for me to hear. "Do whatever you want, but I have more pressing things on my agenda than dinner."

I raised my eyebrows. "More pressing than dinner? That's doubtful. Everyone needs to eat." I leaned out of the shack to tug on his sleeve. "I'll even make grilled cheese to make up for the one I stole, so you can't say no."

His ears perked up at that. "A grilled cheese, huh? And does your weird culinary mage class actually make it taste good now?"

"Only one way to find out."

I grinned and went back inside to get the food ready. Dave was kind of a handful, but he'd helped me twice now and I didn't feel right not repaying him. I sliced an entire loaf of bread up and buttered the first four pieces before laying them in the hot pan. Once the butter was sizzling, I added the cheese and put two of the slices on top to make the sandwiches. I checked them a few times, flipping them once the bread was golden-brown and beautifully crispy.

Dave's nose twitched and he leaned closer. "That smells amazing."

"See? Aren't you glad you stayed?" I pressed down on the grilled cheeses, waiting for the cheese to get nice and melty before taking them off the pan. Then I grabbed the final touch: a little garlic rubbed on the outside of the bread. It smelled divine, like cheesy garlic bread. I handed one to Dave. "Here you go, enjoy!"

He took a careful, almost suspicious bite, before his eyes went wide. "It's so good!"

"Flavor boost at its finest." I cut the second grilled cheese in half and gave part to each of the slimes before they drooled all over my stove. They gobbled them up so fast, wiggling with joy. "Don't worry, I'll make more."

As I cooked, Dave pulled out a notebook and pen to take notes. He leaned closer, studying what I was doing carefully, but I had a feeling it wouldn't taste the same if he made it. He wasn't a culinary mage, after all.

"You can come back whenever you want more," I said softly. "If you let me borrow that pen and notebook for a minute."

His forehead creased, but he handed them over. "What madness are you planning now?"

"Just hold on." I laughed and wrote down a silly little menu since he'd joked about this not being a cafe. I ripped the page off the notebook and handed it to him. "We've got grilled cheese, water, and a few cafe rules too!"

"*Be nice or no dessert?*" He stared at me. "Are you serious?"

I leaned over to scribble a few more things. "Yup! No fighting either, and definitely no hurting slimes! Otherwise, your food might have a little extra kick to it."

Jellybean chirped like he approved and Dave just groaned, but before he could say anything, a blue message box appeared in front of me.

[Title Granted: Cafe Owner]

[You've welcomed people into your temporary home, fed them, and even made a menu to keep things organized. You're well on your way to running a cafe, so expect to see new cafe quests and skills.]

"A cafe owner title, huh?" I grinned, staring at the words with pride. "That's so cool!"

"No, that's not cool." Dave scratched his horns, staring up at the shack's roof and around at the walls as they glowed faintly. "No, no, no! She is not a cafe owner because this is not a cafe!"

His panic reminded me of when I'd gotten my culinary mage class, so I had a feeling I'd just broken something again. I smiled awkwardly and waited for him to calm down, but he did the opposite, jumping up and storming outside to stare at the shack's exterior.

"*Cafe Name Here?*" he shouted. "Are you serious?"

Ohhh, that sounded cool. So the building itself was changing because of my new title? I hurried outside to join him and grinned at the little sign above the door just waiting for a cafe name. Now *this* was my lucky break. If I could make a cafe work in the dungeon, then I could level up as much as I wanted without ever leaving this floor. I'd just bake and gain experience and skills until my food was good enough to defeat the final boss! It was foolproof!

I reached over to give Dave a side hug. "Thank you! I'd never have made that menu without your joke about it being a cafe."

"Don't you dare blame this on me." He jerked away from me, far too flustered to deal with my jokes right now, apparently. "This wasn't my fault. This was all on you and your system-breaking class!" He took a deep breath, his shoulders rising high before falling. "I really think you'd be better off going to the safe zone. Your class isn't normal, and I don't know what will happen to you here."

"I'll be okay." I smiled at the slimes peeking out of the shack. "*We'll* be okay. You don't need to worry, everything's going to work out fine. I can feel it."

He shook his head. "If you say so. Thank you for dinner, but I've got a few things to take care of, so I need to get going."

"You're welcome to come back any time!"

Before I could even joke about how he was nice enough to get dessert, he'd already summoned a door and disappeared. He stressed himself out over the little things way too much, so hopefully he was going to get some rest. I covered up a big yawn. It was about time I did the same.

The faint blue glow of the embers in the walls cast the dungeon in a new light, beautiful, but a little eerie too. Hopefully this shack really did have protections on it like Dave said, because I was about ready to pass out. I walked inside, curling up next to Boss, who filled most of the room. Jellybean hopped on my lap, and we all snuggled up together, ready for a well-deserved rest.

"Sleep well, slimes."

They pressed against me softly, as if saying good night back, and I felt myself smiling. My first day in the dungeon had been exhausting and kind of terrifying at times, but it had also been pretty wonderful. Meeting these slimes and cooking tasty food made everything a little less scary.

Hopefully tomorrow would go even better now that I had my very own little cafe shack.

CHAPTER NINE

The Dungeon of Eternal Embers

The Dungeon's mission was clear: Keep everyone leveling up and advancing to the last floor.

It had been fun at first, setting traps for adventurers to fall into, changing the layout of the floors, and hiding treasure chests in the weirdest places. Watching it all play out from the embers in the walls was pretty awesome, but after a few centuries, the Dungeon's mind was practically on autopilot.

Nothing interested it anymore. Not the battles between adventurers and minotaurs, not the monsters swimming in lava pools, and especially not the constant starting over. It just wanted to see something new. Something exciting. New and exciting wasn't the point of this dungeon though. The point was to give adventurers and monsters a place to improve themselves by leveling up.

But the Dungeon was tired of it. Maybe it was time for another dungeon core to take over. Its flames were already burning low, practically an ember itself. If it let things continue as they were, it would disappear entirely. At least it wouldn't be bored anymore.

An energetic satyr bounded into the Core Chamber. He was one of the Daves, but the Dungeon wasn't sure which one.

"My lord," Dave said through wheezes, "something's happened."

Oh? Had the Dungeon's wish for something new and interesting finally come to pass?

Dave took a minute to catch his breath. "The woman you gave the culinary mage class to has been . . . baking."

A culinary mage class? Hmmmm . . . the Dungeon vaguely remembered doing that, but it felt like a while ago. Time blended together after so many years of running the dungeon. To think she'd chosen a sandwich instead of a sword or a bow. How interesting.

But that was probably not why Dave was having a meltdown. Why was baking such a problem? Humans did it all the time, so it was nothing new.

The Dungeon relayed that to Dave through the ember shard in his head, but the satyr just sighed.

"It's not the baking that's the problem, it's what she's doing with it." He stared at the core's flames, at the embers burning brightly inside them, and lowered his voice. "She lured the slime boss on floor four away with cookies. With cookies!"

That last part was followed by a lot of mumbling and moaning as the Dungeon shifted its attention to the fourth floor. Sure enough, it was empty. Nothing was guarding the door to the safe zone. It was just wide open for any adventurer to stroll through.

If the Dungeon could laugh, it would have.

It had never eaten food before, but these things called cookies must be very tasty to have swayed such a dedicated monster. The Dungeon had a sudden urge to try one.

"Why did you even make a culinary mage class, of all things?" Dave moaned, then froze. "Sorry, my lord. I didn't mean to question your vast wisdom."

The Dungeon did not mind, and it relayed that to Dave, who smiled gratefully.

Honestly, that decision *had* been a little impulsive. But that's what happened when somebody got too bored. Plus, all the mortal texts in its memory bank indicated that chefs were the closest thing to using sandwiches as weapons, and mages had the most diversity in skills. Hence culinary mage just made the most sense.

Or at least, that's what the Dungeon had convinced itself of, but maybe it had just wanted to see what would happen.

"So, about the slime boss," Dave continued slowly. "She tried taking it to the safe zone, but the door wouldn't open. They're all stuck in the passageway with no clue what's going on."

Now *that* was a problem. The Dungeon sent a message to the fifth-floor Dave, asking him to retrieve the adventurer and the slimes and hopefully talk some sense into them. Yes, her stealing a floor boss was entertaining, but they really did need somebody protecting that door.

"What do we do now?" Dave asked.

The Dungeon watched as the culinary mage refused to abandon the slimes, no matter how hard the fifth-floor Dave tried to convince her to. Even when monsters attacked them, she still refused to leave the slimes. It was admirable. Maybe the Dungeon should reward her determination.

Its flames grew brighter, dancing in the hearth as it created a small shack with an ember shard in it for protection. The shack would serve as a temporary safe zone until she leveled up enough to move on. It relayed that to the tutorial Dave so he'd stop panicking, but it seemed to distress him even more.

"No, you can't keep encouraging her chaos!" Dave leaned over the Dungeon's flames, full of anxiety. "It'd be better to send her back to the tutorial zone and make her choose one of the original classes instead. I can fix this, you just have to let me try."

That didn't sound like any fun at all and hardly a fitting reward for the entertainment she'd given it so far. But Dave had a point: She had been causing chaos ever since she got here. Every action she took seemed to break the system in new ways. Especially the notification the Dungeon just received about her title potential.

She'd cooked for two monsters and one of the Daves, created a menu, and claimed the shack as her own. The system thought she'd done enough work to earn a title, but should the Dungeon do it? And what should the title be? Its flames danced even higher as it sent a few messages.

[Title Granted: Cafe Owner]

[You've welcomed people into your temporary home, fed them, and even made a menu to keep things organized. You're well on your way to running a cafe, so expect to see new cafe quests and skills.]

"Noooo," Dave moaned. "What kind of title is that? Hasn't she already caused enough trouble with the slime friend title?"

Where the Daves saw trouble, the Dungeon saw potential. This adventurer wasn't like the others. She stood out like a bright flame in the night, drawing everyone in. The Dungeon could either fight against that or encourage it with new rules. All it had to do was keep her leveling and moving out of the dungeon. If she really refused to fight, then the Dungeon had to provide another route for her to take.

Like a cafe that she could upgrade through quests and hard work. The Dungeon could even move some slimes to the cafe's floor to put that slime friend title of hers to use. Not because the core was burning with curiosity over what new skills she'd unlock, but because it would keep her busy and working hard. Maybe it should grow some tea nearby so she had something easy to serve customers starting out. Hmmm . . . the cafe would need a lot of room to expand too in case she gathered a whole slime army.

With the ember shard in it, the building could be like a miniature dungeon, capable of changing shape and size to suit her needs. Yes, that would be interesting for sure. Like a little game between the two of them.

Now, would she prefer a modern design or an old one? Two levels or just one? It should definitely have a big garden out back, maybe overgrown with a bit of a surprise inside . . .

Excitement coursed through the Dungeon's embers for the first time in ages. This was exactly the kind of thing it had been looking for.

"My lord . . ." Dave stepped back as the core's flames shot up. "Do you really think this is a good idea? What if she never leaves and stagnates there like the others?"

This was the Dungeon's fault, so it would make sure she didn't stagnate. It would send so many quests her way that she'd have no choice but to level. Not that it was worried anyway. She was driven and passionate about baking. It had a feeling she'd level with or without it. She was a system breaker, always pushing the limits of what was normal. She'd level just fine.

Dave scratched his horns. "Fine. I've already got a few new sleepers waiting for me, so I'll leave you to it. Just try not to do anything too chaotic."

The Dungeon sighed mentally. The Daves were always so dedicated, but they liked everything done a certain way. Unexpected things made them panic, especially when one thing snowballed into two or three. That kind of situation was like a nightmare for the Daves.

Had the Dungeon programmed them that way on purpose? It couldn't remember.

Dave turned back to ask the Dungeon one last thing. "You're spending a lot of time on one adventurer. Is she really worth it?"

The Dungeon paused for a moment to think about that. Something about this woman called to it, needling its mind like she was an important piece to some puzzle it had been working on. Only time would tell if the Dungeon was right about her or not.

But right now, it had a new cafe system to design.

CHAPTER TEN

Boss Slime

The tiny shack barely fit the big slime's body, but he dared not move. Not when the strangely kind woman was resting against his side. Her deep, sleepy breathing was pleasant to listen to, almost lulling him to sleep himself. He rarely got to sleep for long on the fourth floor, always being interrupted by adventurers demanding passage. It was exhausting and he was very glad to be done with all that.

But what was he supposed to do now?

He used to be the boss of the Dungeon's fourth floor. That title held weight, prestige. Now he was just . . . a slime. A big slime, but nothing special anymore. That was a little unsettling, and he felt his sense of purpose falter until a message from the Dungeon appeared in front of him.

[You can still go back to the fourth floor and be one of my floor bosses again.]

The big slime considered it, but a sound outside the door distracted him. Something tiny was scuttling, no, pecking, at the door. The soft *cluck-cluck* of a chicken made the slime tense up. Where there was one chicken monster, there were usually more.

He glanced down at the kind adventurer sleeping beside him. She'd protected him from others of her kind, fed him delicious food, and taken care of him when nobody else ever had. He would not let that chicken, or any other monster, touch her.

The big slime bounced as softly as he could, the wooden floor creaking under his weight as he moved to block the door. Those monsters would have to go through him if they wanted to get to her, and his jiggly body was surprisingly tough to peck through. The door vibrated as the chicken tried to get in, but it was so faint and its clucks were so soft that the slime had a feeling it was only a baby chicken.

Baby or not, they weren't getting inside this tiny house. Not on his watch.

The woman and the smaller slime shifted in their sleep, and he worried they'd wake up, but she just curled around him tighter. Her warmth spread through him like he was basking in the sun, and it made him so happy that they felt safe with him.

How could he give that up just to protect a silly door?

[I understand. Keep her safe for me, then. Think of it like your new role: Hazel's Protector.]

The slime perked up. He had a new role! Protector of the cookie lady!

New message boxes appeared in front of the woman, but she squeezed her eyes closed and turned away.

[New Skill: Slime Bond]

[Even in your sleep, you managed to form an unbreakable bond with yet another slime. Through this skill, you'll get a better sense of what slimes want and how to connect with them. They might even share some of their abilities with you.]

The slime couldn't usually see other people's messages, but he was very glad the Dungeon had shared these with him. Happiness warmed him to the core. Their bond was about more than tasty food now.

He was her protector, and that was far better than his old floor boss title.

CHAPTER ELEVEN

A Little Chaos in the Morning

B awk, bawk, baaaawwwkkkk."

I squeezed my eyes closed, not at all ready to wake up yet. The slimes felt like soft, squishy pillows perfectly formed to my body, and I just wanted to ignore the day and stay inside with them. Even if it was cramped beyond belief in this tiny shack.

"Bawwwkkkkk."

No . . . please tell me the crispy cluckers hadn't followed me all the way here for revenge! Dave had said this shack was protected, so maybe if I ignored the chicken, it would go away? A soft tapping at the door made my eyes fly open.

Was the chicken *knocking*?

No, it was probably just pecking for food. Or trying to drive me crazy so I'd open the door. I shifted, my legs screaming at me to stretch them out, but there was no room between me and the slimes. This place just wasn't built for three.

The chicken's pecking got more insistent, vibrating through the walls.

"Okay, okay. Don't burn my new cafe down." I fumbled around, realizing that Boss had moved while we slept and was now firmly planted in front of the only exit. "Um, Boss? Could you shift a bit so I can go see what's up with the chicken outside?"

The big slime opened one eye and then closed it firmly before snoozing like he was fast asleep!

I shook my head with a smile. "I know you're awake . . ."

He deflated a bit as he hopped out of my way just enough for me to open the door. Bright daylight seared my eyes as Boss bounced out first, almost smushing the tiny chicken at the door. The spicy nugget squawked and ran out of the way, feathers puffed up like she was ready for a fight. Jellybean joined us, mouth wide open with a bit of drool as he stared at the chicken.

"Don't you dare!" I shouted, diving for the bird before Jellybean could start the chicken wars all over again. He tilted his body, giving me a sad look like I'd just taken his favorite toy away. "Baby chickens are friends, not food."

Jellybean nodded and actually managed to look a little ashamed as Nugget trembled in my hands. Boss looked wary though as he grew a bit taller to intimidate the little thing. What was up with him?

"It's okay, little Nugget. Nobody's going to hurt you." I pet her carefully, enjoying the feel of her soft and fluffy feathers. "Did you come here all by yourself?"

I glanced at the jungle around us, hoping the rest of those monsters hadn't joined her. She leaned into my hand, cheeping softly, and I took that as a yes. I mean, I didn't hear any angry clucking or the pounding of giant chicken feet at least. I opened my inventory, which was far emptier than I'd like. After cooking for everyone last night, I was down to mostly strawberries.

I pulled a few out and laid them on the ground for her, setting her close by. "Are you hungry? I don't have any jam right now, but the strawberries are still good."

Nugget pecked at them slowly, eyes on Jellybean, who was keeping his distance. I walked over and patted him on the head.

"That's a good boy, Jellybean. And you too, Boss." I grabbed a few more strawberries for them both, but my own stomach started grumbling then. "We're going to have to find some more food, guys."

I glanced at the jungle ahead of us, knowing the monsters were all really high-leveled compared to me, but we had to try. I hadn't seen any monsters since we got here, besides the little Nugget of course, so maybe the protections pushed out a little farther than just the shack. Or maybe that was wishful thinking. Either way, we'd have to explore a bit.

"You don't have to come with me," I started, but Boss was already bouncing ahead like he was paving the way for me. I smiled and waited to see what Jellybean would decide. He leapt up into my arms like he was ready to go. I hugged him. "Okay, let's gather some ingredients!" Nugget started following close at my heels, but I shook my head. "Sorry, but I think you should stay here for now. The shack's protected, and we'll be back with good food soon."

The little chicken went back to eating the last of her strawberries without a care. I let out a breath, grateful she was going to stay here where it was safe and where she couldn't suddenly call an army of crispy cluckers on me if things didn't go her way. I turned to follow Boss into the jungle and moved Jellybean to my shoulder so I could grab the notebook Dave had forgotten last night. If we were going to explore, I might as well keep track of what we found and where.

I marked an X on the page for where the shack was and then took off with the slimes, making sure to note anything interesting. As we walked, Boss did an amazing job of intimidating all the smaller plant monsters we came across like he was our group's protector. He even loomed over my shoulder while I got a drink from a nearby river just in case it was full of monster fish.

I didn't want him to feel like he *needed* to fight, but it was awfully reassuring having him with us. I patted his side and stopped to investigate a tall tree with what looked like green fruit on it.

[Unripe Bananas: Common]

Ohhh, bananas were always good, and they'd ripen just fine off the plant. They were kind of high up though. I grabbed the tree, looking for handholds to climb, but this wasn't like the trees on the first floor that were full of easy branches to grab onto. These trees were all big leafy fronds and bunches of bananas.

Jellybean chirped and bounced off my shoulder, leaping high into the tree, where he gobbled up as many bananas as he could. When he plopped back down, he filled my arms with the fruit, smiling wide at his prize.

"Thank you!" I held a hand to my chest, so happy to have found such good friends in this dungeon. "They're not good to eat yet though, so I'll put them away for now and we can try them later."

The slimes nodded, waiting for me to draw a little banana tree on the map before continuing on. My stomach was rumbling something fierce now though, so I hoped we found something tasty soon. Otherwise, those green bananas might have to be it.

After far too much walking, all we found were a few more banana trees. The dungeon seemed to like those way too much. I held my stomach tight, feeling a little lightheaded.

"Maybe we should—"

A giant mushroom blocked my path, moving on tiny little legs that should not exist. It didn't have any eyes or a mouth like other monsters, just legs. Did that make it a plant or an animal? I wasn't sure, but I was definitely hungry enough to wonder. There wouldn't be any harm in eating plants, right?

I shivered. I wasn't me when I was hungry. Guess I should try those bananas after all. After we dealt with the creepy mushroom monster, of course.

Boss booped the walking mushroom, sending it flying a few feet. Its legs wiggled as it tried to stand back up, reminding me of a turtle stuck on its back. I would have smiled if it wasn't a mushroom. But then it stood back up and ambled toward us again. Even though it was my least favorite food, I still didn't want to kill it.

"Let's head back," I told the slimes, nodding at the path back to the shack. "We'll figure something out for food."

Jellybean bobbed a nod as Boss sent the mushroom flying again to give us some time to get away. I marked evil mushrooms on my map while we waited to make sure it could stand up again, then took off toward the cafe. My stomach groaned louder with each step. Maybe it was time to plead with the system for help.

"Hey, system, is there a way to find food nearby? Maybe a skill or something useful?" I waited for a message box to pop up, but nothing appeared. Huh. Maybe it didn't respond to something as open-ended as that? I hadn't actually initiated a conversation with it before. "Mr. System?" I tilted my head, but after a minute or so, I decided to get creative. "Hello? Big Blue? Sweet Potato? My darling dungeon, are you even listening?"

Maybe that was going too far, but a message box did appear.

[Your darling what? And how are my messages like potatoes?]

[Never mind. You have more important things to think about.]

[New Quest: Garden Cleanup. The garden out back is such a mess that it will keep you busy for days, so busy you won't have time for strange nicknames.]

I laughed, coughing quickly to try to cover it up. Those message boxes weren't the normal blue I'd become accustomed to. They had a faint pink hue around the edges, almost like the system was blushing.

Oh, that was far too adorable and made me want to tease it a little more, but I resisted the urge. I didn't want to end up with some impossible quest if I annoyed it. Wait . . .

"There's a *garden* behind the shack?" My eyes widened and I could practically feel my stomach rejoicing. "Thanks for the awesome quest!"

[You are welcome.]

[And . . . you can call me Sweet Potato if you want, but I don't understand why you would.]

That message had the same pretty shade of pink around it as the first one. I really hadn't expected the system to pick a name, especially not the most ridiculous one, but it made me smile. The system was definitely a sweet potato, all warm and comforting. It knew I was hungry and needed that garden, so it had given me a quest to find it. That was kind.

"You're pretty nice, Sweet Potato. I'll clean that garden up in no time and grow the best plants you've ever seen. Just you wait."

[I'm excited to see it.]

Butterflies danced in my stomach as I picked up the pace. A garden meant we could take care of ourselves without wandering off like this again, and that was worth more than gold.

CHAPTER TWELVE

Garden Cleanup

The system wasn't kidding about this garden being a mess! Weeds towered over me, as if daring me to try to pull them out. They'd probably be tricky to get rid of for good, especially since I couldn't really tell what was a weed and what was a plant. Apparently gardening was another thing I hadn't really done before . . .

Thankfully, some of the plants were easy to identify, like the tomatoes bursting through their rusty cages to spill out over the rest of the garden, or the oregano that had swept across the ground like grass, filling the air with an earthy, peppery scent. The other plants were a bit more puzzling since they were all fighting for dominance over the large patch of land.

I smelled mint and basil coming from somewhere but couldn't actually see the herbs through the chaos. The garden took up the entire backyard of the cafe, but it was so overgrown that I'd have to trim it back as I went if I ever wanted to see what was in the middle. Walking through it as is wasn't a good idea unless I wanted to be covered in scratches.

"Hey, Boss?" I turned to the big slime next to me. "Mind keeping watch out front in case any other monsters show up?"

He nodded vigorously before leaping into action. Nugget started clucking up a storm as he drew near, which hopefully meant she was happy to see him? I chuckled and shook my head. No, that lil nugget was too boisterous for that right now. With luck, she'd get used to the slimes soon and they'd all become friends.

A happy little *glomp* noise drew my attention back to the tomatoes, which Jellybean was gobbling up before moving on to some kind of leafy plant. The little slime bounced from plant to plant, devouring all the useful parts of the garden.

"Hey, leave some for me too." I tried to reach him, but he just rolled away like the stealthy little creature he was. "Fine, fine. Eat up. It looks like there's plenty here for all of us."

An old spade stood upright in the dirt, and I struggled to pull it out. The soil was hard and compacted over the years of neglect, so this was going to be a lot more work than I thought. As I followed Jellybean through the garden, I found pruning shears and a shovel too. It was like the tools' owner had dropped them mid-use and never came back. That was a little ominous, but maybe they just leveled up and went to another floor where they wouldn't need any of this anymore.

Either way, this garden was mine now, and the first thing I'd do once it was cleaned up was switch the plants up from savory to sweet. Planting different kinds of fruit would be the most useful. I imagined beautiful red raspberries, sweet figs, delicious apples, and every other fruit this dungeon might have. Mmmm . . . my mouth was watering just thinking about it. Fruit was the perfect thing for baked goods.

I started trimming the plants back, not really sure what I was doing. I couldn't possibly make it worse, right? I harvested some of the rosemary, mint, and basil into my inventory, hoping there would be ginger and pumpkins somewhere too. A nice pumpkin pie sounded really good right now.

Gardening was hard work though, and all too soon I was wiping sweat off my brow, leaving what I assumed was a dirty streak across my forehead. Gardening gloves would be nice, and a new outfit too because this baker's uniform was not ideal anymore. I'd have to make a list of essentials and find that safe zone eventually.

I bent down to trim what I thought was a weed, but weeds didn't shiver . . .

The shiver moved through the plant and into the ground, rumbling through the garden. I dropped the shears, falling on my backside in horror as the plants shifted, moving as if they had a will of their own.

Oh, please tell me this garden wasn't full of monstrous plants, and I'd stolen their harvest. Or worse, pruned the wrong thing and upset them!

"Jellybean," I called out, backing out of the garden. "This place isn't safe, hurry up and get out."

A great mass of plants rose in the middle of the garden, dirt tumbling off the round monster in waves as it shook itself. My eyes widened as it got bigger and bigger, but even more as Jellybean bounced toward the thing instead of away from it!

"No!"

I raced after the little slime and scooped him into my arms, but I froze when the monster stared at me with eyes that looked oddly familiar. Its body was dark brown, blending in with the dirt almost perfectly if not for the translucent shimmer that I'd come to associate with slimes.

That monster was actually a slime!

Moss covered his head with plants peeking out like the slime was a living garden. He moved slowly, as if just waking up from a long nap.

I swallowed hard, holding Jellybean tight. "Hello, sorry we disturbed you."

The great dirt slime groaned, sounding like the earth was opening up beneath us, but he didn't do anything else. Just stared. Well, glared was more accurate.

I took everything I'd harvested out of my inventory and laid it on the ground carefully. "Here, you can have it all back. I promise not to touch your plants again."

Neither of us moved for what felt like ages until something at the edge of my vision caught my eye. Tiny dirt slimes bounced to the food I'd set out, gobbling it up just like Jellybean had. They each had one little plant growing out of their heads, like miniature versions of the giant dirt slime in front of me. One of them had a broken plant, clipped off savagely.

By me.

That was the plant I'd been trimming right before the dirt slime sprouted out of the ground. My chest ached at the sight of the sad little slime.

I knelt down, offering it a tomato. "I'm so sorry. I shouldn't have been trimming anything without knowing what I was doing. I never meant to hurt you."

The little dirt slime bounced back and forth, then hopped closer. I held my hand out in the air between us, letting it decide if it wanted me to pet it or not. After a few moments, the little slime brushed against my hand, nuzzling into my embrace. I pet it carefully, trying to avoid damaging the plant any more.

The big dirt slime groaned again, then sank back into the ground until it was more on eye level with us. The smaller slimes tried to follow suit, but the ground was too hard for them to get into. They kept jumping at it but weren't strong enough to burrow like the big one.

I grabbed the garden spade and broke a little patch of dirt up. The slime hopped in, wiggling around like that was the perfect spot. Awww, these slimes were seriously the most adorable things I'd ever seen! Maybe they wanted water too?

"Hold on a sec." I went over to grab a watering can I'd seen earlier, which was thankfully full.

When I poured a few drops on the little dirt slime, she trilled with excitement, closing her eyes like the feeling was heavenly. I grinned and poured more, letting a steady rain of water cover the dirt slime and the soil around it. Another little slime hopped over, burrowing into the dirt beside us, nudging closer so he could get rained on too.

I laughed and poured water on as many of them as I could find, watching them wiggle and bounce with joy. Sadly, the watering can was empty by the time I got to the big dirt slime, but he just nodded like he approved of my actions. Jellybean bounced beside him, chittering away like they were having a conversation.

This dungeon was full of so many things I didn't understand. I couldn't act rashly, not even when it came to gardening. This was the dirt slimes' home and I had to respect that. I could dig up another patch of land for my own garden or even bring some pots inside for herbs. I'd figure it out.

But the system had told me to clean up this garden. So I had to keep going if I wanted to complete that quest . . .

Jellybean bounced at me until I walked back to the big slime. He blinked at me, then chirped as a carrot popped out of the mossy part of his head, flying into the air and landing in my hands.

My eyes widened. "Is this for me? Are you sure?"

The gentle giant nodded.

"Thank you." I held the carrot close. This was something dear to the slime, so it meant a lot that he'd shared it with me. "Does this mean you want me to keep working in the garden? As long as I break up the dirt and water everything really well for the little ones?"

The big dirt slime hopped out of the ground, nudging me firmly enough that I almost fell over again. I glanced at Jellybean, who hopped excitedly.

"So, if I'm more careful and take care of the garden and the slimes, then you'll let me use some of the food you're growing here?" I offered my hand out to the dirt slime. "Is that a deal?"

He brushed against my palm as all the little ones circled around us, bouncing and hopping as if they'd never had so much fun in their lives.

I grinned, gazing out at the garden full of slimes and possibilities. This dungeon was proving to be a wonderful adventure.

CHAPTER THIRTEEN

Happy Slime, Happy Time

I fell back on the soft, damp soil in the garden, completely and utterly exhausted. I'd removed my chef's coat a while ago to work in my tank top, so the freshly tilled soil was cool and refreshing against my skin. My entire body ached from cleaning up the garden, including muscles I didn't even know I had. I took deep breaths, inhaling the earthy scent of freshly dug up soil.

The little dirt slimes were having a blast, jumping in and out of the ground like this was the best game they'd ever played. I smiled as one hopped onto my stomach while the others jumped over me and into the ground on the other side like I was an obstacle in this new game of theirs.

Their joy made all the effort worth it. I'd spend every day out here digging up this soil and watering them just to catch a moment of their bliss.

One of the slimes hopped onto my chest, staring down at me quizzically. Thankfully they weighed next to nothing.

"I'm okay, just resting for a minute."

The slime nodded, then rolled off me to go play with the others. Their happy little noises as they wiggled in the soil made my heart soar. Not only had I gotten to eat tasty vegetables from the garden, but I'd gotten to make a lot of slimes happy too. That was a win-win.

The quest hadn't been completed yet though, which meant I had more gardening to do!

I sat up, stretching my arms above my head with a happy sigh. That break was exactly what I needed. I was all refreshed and ready to go now.

The dirt slimes and I got back to it, pulling weeds and removing dead leaves. I added it all to my inventory, not sure where else to put it yet that would count as clean. I should really make a compost bin for stuff like this.

Once all the debris was cleared up, the soil tilled, and everything was watered, there was only one thing left: trimming the plants on the big dirt slime. While the small slimes only had one plant growing from their mossy heads, the big guy had about five or six, some of which had overtaken the others. Those were the only plants I hadn't touched yet, so I had a feeling that's why the quest was still incomplete.

"What do you think, Mossy? Mind if I trim those chives?" I put my hands on my hips and stared at him, hoping I'd proven myself after all the other work I'd done. "I promise I'll be careful."

Mossy wiggled deeper into the earth, lowering himself until his eyes were at ground level and I could reach the plants on top of him. I resisted the urge to jump with excitement and walked over slowly instead so I didn't scare him off. So far, he'd just been watching, as if waiting to see how I treated the little ones. This felt like I'd gained his approval, so I didn't want to screw it up now.

I reached up, leaning against his squishy body to trim the chives. They'd spread everywhere, smothering the carrots and radishes. Mossy sighed, closing his eyes as I tended to the plants. I grinned, feeling like a strange hair stylist for the slimes.

"There, all done." I stepped back to admire my work as message boxes appeared one after another.

[Quest Completed: Garden Cleanup]

[Reward: Various Seeds, Bottomless Watering Can, and a New Garden Plot]

[Level Up: Culinary Mage Level 4]

My body glowed and all the exhaustion fell away as my health and mana bars increased. Lights shimmered in the air like fireworks, congratulating me on a job well done as bags of seeds rained from the sky along with a golden watering can. I reached out to grab that before it went into my inventory. What made it bottomless?

I watered Mossy since he hadn't gotten any the first time around, walking around to make sure I got all of him. He sighed in contentment again, wiggling a bit deeper into the ground. Even after I'd watered him and everything around him, the watering can was still full! These rewards were so perfectly themed for exactly what I needed.

"Thank you, Sweet Potato!"

[. . . You're welcome, Hazel.]

Things were looking up. I had a garden full of food and slimes, I'd leveled up, and I'd gotten some great rewards too. I sank to the ground, sorting through the new seeds and plant clippings. There was enough here for me to plant strawberries, apple trees, sweet potatoes of course, vanilla, and lots of tea.

Could I even grow all that? I had little to no gardening experience, so I was kind of counting on the slimes to do most of the work. It would be amazing if they could grow vanilla and tea. A cafe needed drinks to serve people and tea would be the easiest, and vanilla went well with most baked goods.

These were boss-level rewards.

I blinked tears away as a surge of emotions swept over me. I'd worked hard and gotten rewarded for it. That felt really good, especially since it meant I could keep all these slimes fed for a long time. I'd treasure these seeds and make good use of the plants that grew from them.

The system had mentioned a new garden plot too, but I wasn't sure how that part worked. I went through my menus, finding a new one called *Cafe*. My eyes widened. There were rows and rows of options, from adding rooms to expanding the garden to upgrading the kitchen and adding furniture! This place didn't even have a kitchen yet, but I was so excited!

"It's like a house decorating game!" I eagerly browsed through all the menus. "There's so much here!"

The top showed a currency called "cafe points," which said they were accumulated through doing cafe duties. Hmmm . . . since I already had one hundred fifty of them, that probably included cooking and gardening. What could I buy with that?

I glanced at the back of the incredibly small shack and my legs started aching just thinking about sleeping there again. Expanding the size had to be the first thing I worked on. I flipped through the menus, selecting the option for a larger dining area, which only cost fifty cafe points.

[New Quest: Gather 25 Mana Wood to Expand Your Dining Area]

I raised an eyebrow at that. "Mana Wood?"

[It's a type of wood that's infused with magic, so it'll let your cafe change shape and grow.]

"Ohhh, that's cool." It didn't use many cafe points though, so I kept looking through the menus. When I saw the new kitchen option, I pressed it so fast even though it cost every last point I had.

[New Quest: Gather 25 Mana Wood, 10 Clay, and 10 Stone to Build a New Kitchen]

"Ahhh, I can't wait!" I did a little happy dance, my face hurting from grinning so much. "Thank you for the amazing new menu, Sweet Potato. I love this cafe."

[You haven't found all the cool new things yet, so keep looking.]

I scrolled a bit farther, stumbling across a cafe menu option that would let me list different meals I was serving. It only had one food and one drink slot right now, but it looked like there were ways to upgrade it. The best part was, any time I served items off the menu, I gained double cafe points!

My eyes widened. "Did you make all this for *me*? To make my crazy class work better?"

[. . . No?]

That soft pink blush lined the message again, making me smile.

Based on Dave's reaction to my class, I really didn't think the dungeon had anything like this before, so that no was probably a yes. This cafe would give me a chance to succeed without fighting, and I wasn't sure how I'd ever repay that kindness. It looked like it would still be a lot of work, but hard work was something I could handle; fighting wasn't.

"Well, thank you anyway. You're pretty amazing."

[. . .]

[Don't forget to add your extra garden plot.]

I laughed, opening up the garden section of the menu to find one extra plot unlocked already and waiting for placement. I clicked on it and was prompted to choose a location to the east, west, or south of the current garden.

Closer to the cafe would be good since the scent of vanilla and tea might draw in customers. I wasn't sure what kind of environment they preferred though. I felt like vanilla grew on vines, kind of like beans? So I'd need a trellis or trees or something. I could plant the apple trees nearby and make some kind of apple tree, vanilla combo plant.

I laughed. I was definitely a baker, not a gardener. The slimes and I would make it work somehow though, so I chose to the east.

The message box glowed blue before the ground started shaking. The grass and weeds in the area next to the garden disappeared, sinking into the ground as fresh soil took their place like somebody had flipped a garden tile upside down. That was so strange, but I was grateful I wouldn't have to do it all by hand.

I wandered over to where Jellybean was bouncing with the tiny dirt slimes. "Anyone want some tasty seeds? I'm about to start a new garden."

Their eyes widened as three of them bounced faster, gaining more height than usual. I laughed, pulling the seeds out for them to look at. I wasn't really sure how they grew the plants, so I waited to see what they'd do.

The slimes leaned down like they were sniffing the first pack of seeds, then moved on to the next and the next, until they'd investigated all their options. Then the smallest slime gobbled up the strawberry seeds and a tiny plant sprouted from her head. Ohhh, that was cool. I pet the slime carefully as she spun in circles as if trying to see the plant on the top of her head. I couldn't help but laugh, picturing a dog chasing their tail.

The other slimes chose vanilla and the sweet potatoes, but sadly none of them wanted the tea plants or the apple trees, which felt like a good call. Growing an entire tree out of your head when you were a tiny slime seemed like a terrible idea.

The strawberry dirt slime wiggled and smiled at me, brushing against my hand. We both glowed green for a moment before a message box appeared.

[New Skill: Green Thumb]

[The dirt slimes have decided to share one of their passive skills through your slime bond. You'll naturally have a better sense for gardening now, and any plants you tend to will grow a bit faster than usual. Keep gaining their trust by working in the garden and the skill will improve.]

"So plants will grow well even if I screw something up?"

[Especially then. This skill will make you feel like an expert gardener eventually, even if you plant those potatoes in the river.]

"Well, I know enough not to do that," I said with a laugh. "But it sounds amazing."

I turned back to the dirt slimes to find the little strawberry one bouncing happily. A warm fuzzy feeling welled up inside me. These slimes trusted me enough to share their skills. This world showed me something new every day and it was beautiful.

I picked the slime up and cuddled her close. "Thank you. I love the gift."

She cooed and hopped onto my shoulder as we made our way to the new garden plot to test out the skill. I planted two apple trees on the back side of the garden, followed by the vanilla and potatoes. Then I planted the tea in the front, hoping it would grow nice and strong. Beautiful green balls of light swirled around everything I touched, like fireflies in the night, boosting my plants' growth and health with magic. Seeing things like this never got old.

Now that all the gardening was done, there was one last thing on my to-do list for now: cook a delicious meal to thank everyone for their hard work. Except, dirt covered my clothing, streaking across my skin like dried mud, and my shirt was starting to smell bad . . .

Maybe I'd take a bath first.

CHAPTER FOURTEEN

Bottomless Watering Cans
Are the Best

We'd found a river when we were exploring this morning, but it was a little farther away than I wanted to go for a bath. Plus, I was pretty sure I'd seen monster fish swimming around in there, and that was definitely not something I wanted to take a bath with.

I tapped my fingers against my thigh, staring at the bottomless watering can the dungeon had given me as a reward. Maybe I could rig that up into a shower?

After a few tries, I managed to get the watering can set just right on the roof and water started raining down. I reached my hands up and smiled. It was so cool and refreshing, exactly what I needed after a long day in the garden. I took off my clothes and tried washing them the best I could but quickly realized that it was kind of pointless without soap. I really needed to find that safe zone soon and buy some amenities. An extra set of clothes would be really nice too.

This would do for now though. I hung my clothes over a few big rocks to dry out and then stepped under the wonderful watering can shower myself, letting the rain wash away all the dirt and sweat from today. I unbraided my hair and ran my hands through the long strands to soak them properly. Ah, it felt so good to be clean again. The dirt slimes seemed to like this arrangement too as they hopped around in the puddles.

I laughed. "Just be careful not to get mud on my clothes, okay?"

The dirt slimes wobbled back and forth, staring at the clothes drying on the rocks while I took down the watering can and wrung my hair out. I was lucky this jungle floor was warm, but I still didn't like the idea of just standing here waiting for my clothes to dry. I crossed my arms, debating going back into the shack or something, when a few new dirt slimes jumped onto the rocks, rolling all over my clothes.

I sighed. Their happy little smiles made it hard to stay annoyed with them, so maybe I was just doomed to be covered in dirt from now on. The price to pay for our new friendship.

Except, they weren't leaving muddy slime prints like I expected. I walked over and touched my shirt, which was now perfectly dry. The slimes rolled and wobbled across my clothes, absorbing all the water like the ground during a light rain. I grinned from ear to ear, hurrying to get dressed.

"You're all so amazing!" I tried to pet the slimes, but they were too busy jumping with joy at my compliment. The little strawberry one jumped into my arms though and snuggled close. "Thank you for helping me."

She trilled happily while Jellybean rolled over to see what all the fuss was about. He was completely covered in mud from playing with the other slimes, and I couldn't help but laugh. He was practically a different color! I grabbed the watering can and washed him up too. He giggled and rolled around, having way too much fun during bath time.

"Okay, you're all clean." I patted him on the head and smiled. "Why don't we go check on Boss and get something to eat?"

He nodded quickly and followed me out front, along with a little trail of dirt slimes too. It was like the garden was coming with us, and I had a feeling we'd be cooking out back from now on. Keeping these slimes company was my new favorite hobby.

Boss and Nugget were standing guard at the front of the shack—well, Boss was. Nugget, on the other hand, was fast asleep against his side. It seemed like they'd become friends while we were gardening, and it was great to see. The little chicken seemed so at ease now, or maybe that was just because she was asleep. When Boss saw us, he nudged her awake and she jerked up in a flurry of feathers and cheeps.

"It's okay!" I held my hands up to calm her down. "We were just going to cook something for dinner and wanted to see if you were hungry."

Boss's eyes widened. Yup, he was hungry. With everything we'd harvested from the garden, these slimes were about to get a veggie feast. I still had some eggs from defeating Nugget and her friend too, so maybe omelets would be good. I took out the ingredients and studied them.

[Tomatoes: Uncommon]

[Carrots: Uncommon]

[Egg: Rare]

So much for that omelet plan. Memories of the crispy jam fiasco played in my mind. It seemed like most ingredients growing in the dungeon were common, with a few random uncommon ones with special properties like the poisonous mushrooms from earlier, but everything the dirt slimes grew seemed to be uncommon. So maybe growing things yourself improved the ingredient quality?

Homemade food always tasted better, so I bet if I used homegrown ingredients and made everything from scratch, I'd make even better-quality food.

"Hey, Sweet Potato? What level do I need to be to start using rare ingredients?"

[Level 5.]

Just one more level, then. That was a relief. "And what about after that? Is there something better than rare?"

[Epic and legendary, but you won't be finding those kinds of ingredients for a long time, and it'll be even longer before you can use them.]

"Legendary food for a legendary boss, then, huh?" I grinned as I started cutting up the veggies for a nice stir-fry. "Thanks, Sweet Potato. That makes me think I can actually make this work."

[There's no challenge in this dungeon that can't be won with enough hard work. Keep cooking and improving your skills. I have no doubt you'll succeed.]

My face felt a little hot, but that was probably just the humid jungle air. Sweet Potato did seem to have a lot of faith in me though. Before I could think on that too much, excited clucking pulled my attention to the chicken riding on top of a dirt slime. The pair raced around the yard, bouncing and clucking like they were having the time of their lives. I'd been worried about Nugget fitting in here, but apparently the slimes liked her just fine.

This little cafe shack was turning out to be a place where everyone could get along, eat a good meal, and have fun. It warmed my heart seeing it come to life like this.

But if I was really going to turn this shack into a cafe, I'd need dishes and flatware.

Up until now, all I'd been making were sandwiches and jam balls, but these sautéed veggies weren't nearly as portable. I could use my fingers for now, but what about the slimes? I scooped some veggies up with a spoon and offered them to Boss.

"Sorry I don't have plates or anything . . ."

The big slime opened his mouth wide and gobbled everything up, spoon included.

"Hey, the spoon's not part of the meal!" I said, laughing so hard I doubled over when he spit the spoon back out. "Everyone come on over and get some food."

As I passed out spoonfuls of food, the slimes ate and played and laughed. It's what I thought a family meal should feel like, everyone all gathered together and having a good time. This cafe idea felt more and more right. Which meant I should start focusing on those upgrades now that I was clean and had a full belly.

I brought up my menu, glancing at the current quest list.

[Escape the Dungeon by Defeating the Boss on Floor 100]

[Defeat 5 Monsters: 1/5]

[Gather 25 Mana Wood to Expand Your Dining Area]

[Gather 25 Mana Wood, 10 Clay, and 10 Stone to Build a New Kitchen]

I'd seen a bunch of stones in the garden, so those should be pretty easy, and maybe I could find clay in the river? I frowned and took out the little map I'd drawn earlier. It was worth taking a look, except the embers in the walls were already turning blue. Maybe I should rest and take on the world tomorrow.

I gathered up the last of the food and took it out back for Mossy and the rest of the dirt slimes who hadn't followed us. Then I rinsed off the pots and pans with the bottomless watering can and filled up my water bottle too. I took a deep drink, so happy to have fresh water.

This watering can was my new favorite item.

CHAPTER FIFTEEN

Accidentally Overpowered

Yup, this river was definitely full of monster fish, but if there was any clay there, I had to get it.

"What do you think?" I asked Boss and Jellybean. "Should we look for another spot or just jump in and hope they swim away?"

The two of them chittered at each other like they were weighing the pros and cons, before Jellybean hopped right in with a splash.

"Be careful!"

The little slime swirled with the current, squealing excitedly as he drifted away. The fish darted after him and so did I. That reckless curiosity of his kept getting him in trouble! Boss jumped high in the air, crashing into the water with such force that it created a giant wave, pushing Jellybean out of the river. The little slime rolled toward me, a happy smile on his face as water droplets glistened off his blue slime body.

I let out a breath, but before I could stop him, he went right back in for a second ride!

At least all the jumping around had scared the fish away. I shook my head and leaned down, searching the edges of the water for any pockets of clay. After a while, my fingers slid over an extra smooth patch of mud that was reddish-brown and held together really well when I picked it up.

I added some to my inventory and checked the quest status.

[Build a New Kitchen: 0/25 Mana Wood, 1/10 Clay, 10/10 Stone]

Heck yeah! Between that clay and the stones from the garden, I was well on my way to a new kitchen. I scooped up nine more clumps of clay and then washed my hands off before marking the location on the map in case I needed more later. This river was pretty handy.

[New Skill: Ingredient Tracker]

[You've worked hard exploring the area and tracking down everything from food to clay. Your map improves with each new item and will now help you track down things you've never even seen before. Just ask and let the map guide you.]

The notebook in my hands shimmered, glowing brightly as my terrible drawings turned into more accurate versions with an X on the map for where we currently stood. Now that would come in handy for sure. I glanced at the quest, noting all the mana wood I still needed.

"Uh, map? Can you find me some mana wood?"

The page flipped as the ink shimmered, drawing a grove of trees that looked like it was at least an hour's walk away. So much for my plan of not going too far away from the safety of the shack. I took a deep breath and turned to orient myself with the map.

"Okay, slimes, it's time for an adventure."

The two of them perked up and hopped out of the river, shaking water all over me like dogs after a bath. I winced and turned away, laughing. "Thanks for that."

Jellybean rolled over with a silly smile before hopping on top of Boss so the three of us could get going. I patted his head, grateful they were coming with me, before taking off to find that mana wood!

We walked for a while, dodging some monsters and tempting others with tasty food, until we finally located the patch of trees the map had indicated. Something about them felt off though as I stared at the knots in their bark. Whenever three circular shapes were close enough together, it always reminded me of a face. Like when my bread dough suddenly seemed like it wanted to talk to me. That's what these trees reminded me of right now.

They were downright unsettling with their gnarled branches stretched out like hands and the way I swore they changed positions whenever I looked away. The dense canopy overhead blocked out a lot of the light from the embers, casting shadows that played with my mind. Leaves rustled without a breeze, and it was too quiet, as if there were no animals living in this part of the jungle.

Jellybean bounced softly on my shoulder, apparently unaffected by the strange vibes surrounding us, which was kind of reassuring.

I didn't have anything to cut with, so I searched the underbrush for fallen branches instead. Most of the wood there was rotten and not something I wanted to use to expand the cafe, so I kept moving deeper into the jungle. Excitement filled me as I started finding usable branches finally, fulfilling half my quest in record time! Boss delved into the jungle with me, but his bounces were getting slower as we went. He kept staring at the trees, sometimes bouncing at them with enough force to make a thunking sound.

"Calm down," I told the big slime. "We'll be out of here soon."

We stepped into a clearing that looked like the heart of the jungle according to my map. In the center was an ancient tree, twisted and gnarled with a lot of its bark missing. Large branches littered the ground, perfect for the cafe. I rushed forward, but Jellybean bounced hard, hitting me in the cheek before I could collect any of it.

"Hey! What was that for?" I rubbed my cheek while the groan of bark rubbing against bark filled the air.

The trees started shifting, moving with a life of their own. All those circles that had looked like eyes before turned toward me, staring at the intruder in their jungle.

[Living Trees: Level 9]

I swallowed hard, backing up until I ran into Boss. His doughy body stood firm next to me, as if willing to fight whatever came at us.

The trees were alive. Holy hell, the trees were alive.

"Hello, my name's Hazel." I cleared my throat, trying to stop my voice from shaking. "I'm a baker with a cafe on this floor. Any chance you like tasty treats?"

I took the leftover veggies out of my inventory and offered them to the trees, laying them on their roots as my pulse raced in my ears. The food sank into the ground with an earthy crunch.

"Moooooooorrrrrrreeeee." The tree's voice was so slow I could barely understand the word, and its missing bark made it seem sick or dying. If it wanted more food, then the least I could do was make a bit more. Except, I was out of leftovers, and I didn't have any carrots left to make another batch.

I forced a smile on my face. "Okay, just give me a few minutes to make something."

What did trees even eat? Fertilizer? I frowned, swiping through my inventory. I did have all the debris from the garden cleanup in there, plus some food scraps and other odds and ends that I hadn't known what to do with.

I bet I could actually make a decent fertilizer and it might even help the tree recover too. Okay, I'd make that work somehow.

I took out some plant clippings, grass, and banana peels, grinding them all up in a pot. I'd never actually made fertilizer before, but it felt like it needed something else. "Mana Mix-In! Add eggshells!"

Beautiful white eggshells appeared in the pot, shimmering with mana as I crumbled them up into the mix.

But now what? I didn't have time to let this compost properly. Trees drank water from the ground, so maybe a fertilizing *tea* would be good here?

I poured water in the pot, heating up all the ingredients together until it made a grassy, kind of ugly, brown soup. Mixing this up in the middle of all these trees made me feel like a witch in the woods, but I resisted the urge to cackle because now was not the time to break down and start laughing. The tree monsters were watching me.

The fertilizer smelled earthy and dank, not the most appealing thing I'd ever made, but I took it off the heat before it started bubbling too much. I turned back to the older tree in the middle of this clearing, sensing that it was important to the others since it had all this room around it. Once the mixture cooled, I carefully poured it around the tree's roots.

The soil around the tree glowed with a warm light as the tree slowly absorbed the fertilizer. The glow moved through the tree as new growth sprouted from every branch, straightening the broken pieces and regrowing the missing bark. The tree shook its branches, opening its eyes for the first time since I'd gotten here.

Then it stood up straight, towering over all the other trees by far. Its strong, root-bound legs broke free of the earth, standing tall and proud among the other trees.

My mouth dropped open. "How did simple fertilizer do all that?"

Boss swayed side to side like he had no idea either as a message box appeared.

[Your new passive gardening skill apparently works on plant-based monsters too. That tree's enjoying the benefits of Green Thumb.]

"Didn't you say that would make plants grow *a bit* faster?" My mouth dropped open as I stared up at the tall trees. "That's more than a bit."

[It was meant for plants, not monsters . . .]

"Well, if it worked that quickly for one, then maybe I should make some more. They all look hungry to me."

[Wait, no, that's not how the skills are meant to be used! Please remember these trees are monsters.]

I shrugged, cackling as I mixed up another batch, adding ingredient after ingredient to really make these trees be the best trees they could be. When it was cool, I ladled the fertilizer on as many trees as I could, grinning as the golden light whooshed through their trunks and into all their branches.

Wood creaked and groaned as the trees grew taller, their branches thicker, and their leaves shinier. It was like I was giving them new life, filling this jungle with the best trees it could possibly have. They crowded closer, handing me more grass clippings, fruit, nuts, and anything they could get their twiggy little hands on for me to cook with.

I made batch after batch, relishing the feeling of being useful. They were just so happy, bounding around with renewed vigor. Jellybean and Boss were even playing catch with a group of saplings, tossing an apple back and forth. It was all so silly and amazing. If this fertilizer could work this kind of magic on jungle monsters, imagine what it could do for my garden.

[Living Tree Defeated]

[Living Tree Defeated]

[Living Tree Defeated]

[Living Tree Defeated]

[Quest Completed: Defeat 5 Monsters]

[Reward: Wood, Sap, Seeds, and Gold]

I glanced up as all the wood I could ever need rained down from the sky. I ducked even though it all disappeared right before hitting me, filling my inventory with more than enough to finish my cafe upgrade quest. I grinned, patting the closest tree as I poured even more fertilizer around it as a thank-you.

[New Quest: Defeat 10 Monsters]

[New Skill: Buff Baking]

[I guess even nonsense like that will unlock a skill if you put enough heart and repetition into it. By trying to replenish these trees with your food, your baking can now temporarily boost stats when you use this skill.]

"Really? Oh, I've gotta try that." I whipped up one last batch of fertilizer, the biggest one yet, and held my hands over it. "Buff Baking!"

The grassy soup glowed green, making it look even less appetizing, but when I focused on it, a wonderful message appeared.

[Strengthening Fertilizer: Uncommon]

[You really probably shouldn't give them that . . . These are monsters, Hazel. They might attack you.]

I paused. It had a point, but the trees were reaching out to me so eagerly that I couldn't help but let them try it. They were nice trees, and one little pot of fertilizer couldn't hurt, right?

The trees creaked and groaned as they bulked up with bark that was twice as thick as before. They looked healthy now, a far cry from the droopy and half-broken jungle I'd walked into.

[Sorry, Hazel, but I have to do this . . .]

[Alert to all adventurers in the area: Living Tree rampage commencing. The trees are overtaking floor 6 and are now boss-level monsters. Good luck.]

"Wait, what?"

I dropped the ladle into the pot, splashing fertilizer all over. I stared at the massive trees surrounding me. They had to be at least two times larger than they were before, maybe three. Some of them were even level fifteen now. I covered my mouth as a laugh bubbled up. My cooking caused a monster rampage!

"Maybe it's time to go," I whispered to Jellybean and Boss. "Before the other adventurers get here and blame us." I turned to the trees, biting my lip. What about them though? "Um, maybe you should hide for a while until things calm down."

The trees shook their branches, leaves rustling as if they were laughing. I had a feeling they were too hopped up on my fertilizer to think anyone could hurt them. Maybe they were right. Maybe my true skill was making crazy-awesome monster food. This was probably going to go horribly, horribly wrong.

"Please don't hurt anyone." I pressed my palm against the old tree I'd helped first, feeling the magic seeping through it like sap. "I won't come back with more fertilizer if you do."

The old tree bent forward slightly in what I hoped was a nod before holding out gnarled hands filled with fallen branches. The other trees followed suit, holding out enough wood to expand my cafe three times over. Warmth blossomed in my chest as their kindness washed over me.

"Thank you." I filled my inventory to the brim with wood. "I'll visit you again soon, just please, keep yourselves safe and don't hurt anyone."

I waved to the trees and we started making our way out of the jungle, but the sounds of adventurers yelling and metal clashing filled the area. I glanced to the side just in time to see a man flying through the air, tossed by one of the trees. I winced as another followed, screaming as he soared in a perfect arc before landing in a swamp with a great splash.

He sat up, cursing and rubbing his backside. "This is why I should have become a mage instead. I hate all this frontline fighting!"

"Yeah, yeah, Bruce," another adventurer said as she offered her hand out to him. "Time to get back to it if you want those rewards."

Dammit. I definitely screwed up here. I meant to help the trees, not start a war. They were way stronger than anything else on this floor, but at least they weren't killing anyone, and the extra buffs would wear off soon enough. Still, it didn't feel right just leaving them like this. I glanced between the adventurers and the trees, neither of which really seemed to be doing much harm to the other in the long run. Should I just wait it out, then? Or talk to the adventurers?

"Of course this mess has to do with you," a woman's voice called out. I whipped around to find Fiona shaking her head at me. "Any time something weird and dungeon breaky happens, I'm just going to assume it's you."

I let out a breath. "Thank goodness you're here. I could really use some help." I moved closer, lowering my voice. "I sort of, maybe, buffed the trees with some tasty magical fertilizer, and then all these people showed up, and I have no idea what to do." I winced. "The strength buffs won't last long, and I swear the trees are nice when you get to know them."

She pinched the bridge of her nose. "You did what? How can I even help with that?" She stared at the trees, who looked like they were having way too much fun playing with the adventurers. "You probably don't want me to fight them, so do you expect me to protect them and fight the adventurers?"

"No, of course not!"

"Then what *do* you want?" Fiona's voice was soft, but her question ate at me.

I thought just asking her to fight while I wasn't around would be good enough, but now the tree monsters were right in front of me mixed up in a mess I caused. Why couldn't this dungeon just let us all get along?

The longer I debated, the more damage the adventurers took. The trees were obviously holding back, but the people seemed to think that meant they had a shot even though anyone with eyes could tell they didn't. The sound of people crying out in pain made me flinch.

"Just stop!" I shouted, moving between the two groups with Boss and Jellybean backing me up. "Just stop already. This is all my fault, okay? I don't want any of you getting hurt because I didn't know how my skills worked."

"Let's listen to her." The man who'd gotten thrown into a swamp was breathing heavily, hands on his knees. "I could really use a break."

"No way, we're not done yet." The woman who'd helped him before clung to her staff, legs shaking. "If we hold out, I'm sure other adventurers will join us."

She glanced over at Fiona, who just shook her head. "Sorry, I'm neutral today."

I turned back to the trees. "Remember our deal? I'll bring you tasty fertilizer if you don't hurt anyone. That'll go easier if you make yourself scarce until this quest is over."

The trees slumped like they were sighing, and the adventurers did the same. They all sank onto the ground like they were completely exhausted. This was probably a terrible idea, but I grabbed the last bits of fertilizer and brought it over to the adventurers.

"This probably won't taste good, but it'll help you recover." I held a spoon out for the woman.

Her nose wrinkled. "That smells awful. We're good."

"Super good." The man flopped onto his back and held his thumb up in the air. "But what skills did you use that made this your fault?"

I bit my lip. Admitting that I could buff monsters probably wasn't the best idea. I trusted Fiona, sure, but these other two were strangers, and I had no idea what they'd do when they found out about my weird class and monster-loving ways. Thankfully the trees slowly started shuffling off, so that was one less thing to worry about. Now we just had to deal with these two . . .

Fiona clapped a hand on my shoulder. "I think it's time to call it a day. It took me forever to find you and we need to catch up, right?"

"Right." I nodded, smiling awkwardly. "So, we'll be going, then. Stay safe."

We made our escape before they could respond, bouncing away with the slimes like we were never there. Avoidance at its finest, but at least everyone was safe. We'd find a better solution soon; I just knew it.

CHAPTER SIXTEEN

Upgrading the Cafe

The slimes were amazing, but having somebody to talk to who could actually talk back was refreshing. Fiona was doing more laughing than talking though as I regaled her with stories of my adventurers since we got separated.

"So, you turned a shack into a cafe?" She doubled over laughing. "And Dave was just okay with that?"

"Well, no, he actually seemed kind of annoyed. But he did like my food."

She wiped happy tears from her eyes. "Who wouldn't? My stomach's grumbling just thinking about those cookies."

"We'll be there soon, and I'll make us something nice." A warm feeling settled in my chest. My food mattered to people, and that was the best feeling in the world. "Just try not to be too disappointed when you see it. It is still a shack, after all."

Furious clucking filled the air as Nugget spotted us. The little chicken raced toward me and started pecking at my ankles.

"Hey! What's wrong?" I hopped in place trying to avoid her sharp beak.

She puffed out her feathers, glaring at me. I glanced around the cafe, but nothing seemed to be out of the ordinary. Maybe she didn't like being left home alone?

"Sorry we were gone so long." I leaned down to run my hand over her fluffy feathers. "Thanks for protecting the cafe for me."

Nugget tried to keep glaring at me, but her eyes closed tight as I apparently scratched just the right spot.

"Is that one of the chickens who treed you?" Fiona's smile was wide and bright as she shook her head, turning to take in the cafe. "And what's with that sign? *Cafe Name Here*? You didn't even name it yet?"

"Huh, I kind of forgot about that sign." I'd been so busy working on quests that it completely slipped my mind. "Any ideas?"

"Ohh, what about Dungeon Delights?" Fiona's eyes lit up as she tapped her cheek. "Or Slime and Dine? Maybe Hazel's Hideaway?" She held up a finger. "I've got it: Monsters and Mochas! You know, since you're apparently gathering a monster horde."

She nodded at the chicken and the slimes, and I couldn't help but laugh.

"Honestly, between them and the trees I just befriended, I probably could make a monster horde if I wanted to." I held up my hands. "Not that I'd do it, of course, but it's nice to have options."

Fiona chuckled. "You keep getting stranger. But back to the names though, Hazel's Hideaway is pretty good, right?"

Hmm . . . naming it after myself when I'd be leaving eventually felt kind of strange, and I didn't want to get too attached. This was a means to an end after all. Just a way to level up and get out of here.

I tilted my head. "What about the Level-Up Cafe? Or the Get-Me-Outta-Here Cafe?"

"Seriously?" Fiona shook her head with a sigh. "You're terrible at naming things."

"Let's just get this place upgraded first." I opened my inventory to remove all the stone, clay, and wood the quests required.

[Quest Completed: Expand Your Dining Area]

[Quest Completed: Build a New Kitchen]

[Would you like to upgrade now?]

"Yes," I said softly, surprisingly anxious about this moment. "Upgrade the cafe."

[As you wish.]

Fiona and I stepped back as the shack fell apart, the wooden pieces floating and spinning in the air like a puzzle that was deconstructing itself. Then the new materials joined in, spinning and reshaping themselves into solid planks of wood that would be great for flooring or walls. The stones and planks started setting themselves back up, forming a building that was four times larger than the shack, with beautiful windows that would bring in so much light.

As the door settled back into place, a smile stretched across my face. These were just the first upgrades, but there had been dozens of other options. I could make this cafe something really special if I kept working hard.

I could bake every day, meet new adventurers, and befriend all the adorable monsters as we shared this cozy little cafe. It could be like a safe haven from the rest of the dungeon where monsters and adventurers commingled and enjoyed delicious food together. What kind of name would be good for that? Something with *sanctuary* or *haven* maybe?

"So, are we going in?" Fiona asked, grinning. "You look like you want to. Even if it's just a level-up cafe."

I rolled my eyes. "Yeah, let's go inside."

Soft light glowed against the new wood flooring, table, and chairs in the first room. Wooden beams crisscrossed the ceiling, with small hooks that I could hang herbs from so they could dry. There was a back room too, which I hoped was a kitchen, but a blue message box appeared before I could explore more.

[Welcome to your new cafe, Hazel.]

My new cafe. I put my hands over my face to cover my giggly grin. "Thank you, Sweet Potato."

Fiona's mouth dropped open. "Did you just call the system *Sweet Potato*?"

"Yes?" I shrugged, tugging her into the back room to see what else was upgraded. "I've got a kitchen!"

It was pretty small and didn't have any counters, but none of that really mattered, because it had a stove!

I clapped my hands, practically jumping with joy as I rushed over to it. It was an old-style stove made of clay, with two openings to build a fire underneath each pot. I'd never worked with something like that before, but it still brought a smile to my face. I had an actual stove again! Excitement danced through my fingers as I ran them over the solid clay, remembering how soft it had been when I collected it from the river earlier.

Jellybean bounced in to examine the stove with me, hopping softly like he didn't really understand what I was so excited about.

"What should we make first?" I patted him on the head. "We could check on the dirt slimes and see how the tea's growing or make something with the last veggies I've got."

Fiona made a choking noise covered up by a cough. "Sorry, did you just say slimes were growing tea for you?" She shook her head, holding her hand up. "Never mind. I'm sure I'll see it all later. Just use my tea leaves for now."

Apparently even she couldn't handle all this strangeness without a reaction. I took the container of tea leaves from her with a smile and went to the sink. It sadly didn't have running water though. I pulled up the cafe menu and saw an upgrade for that, but I didn't have enough cafe points to unlock the quest just yet.

"Hold on a sec." I hurried into the backyard and grabbed the bottomless watering can, saying a quick hello to the dirt slimes before going back inside with my prize. "Here we go. All the water we could ever need!"

She frowned. "You know what, I'm not even gonna ask."

I laughed and filled a pot up with water before placing it carefully inside one of the openings on top of the stove.

And then I stared at it.

There was wood underneath, but I hadn't seen a lighter and I had no idea how to start a fire without one. I rummaged around, thankfully spotting a box of matches that I somehow hadn't noticed earlier. I struck one against the stove. The flame glowed softly as I bent down to light the wood.

Warmth emanated from the stove and the water slowly started to heat up, which made me realize I was missing something else too.

"Hey, Fiona? Do you have any mugs?" I winced, hating that I kept needing to ask her for everything. "And do you think you could take me to the safe zone soon? I need to buy some essentials."

She nodded and handed me two mugs. "Sure, let's go tomorrow. I need to stop by the blacksmith anyway."

"Oh, good, because my list is growing longer and longer all the time. The system gave me a really cool cafe upgrade menu, but it doesn't seem to have things like dishes on it anywhere."

Fiona frowned. "A cafe menu?"

"Yeah, think of it like skill upgrades, but for the building. That's how the shack grew." I spooned leaves into our mugs as the slimes watched with eager eyes. Guilt gnawed at me, knowing they'd want to try some too. "Mind if I make tea for the slimes? I can refill your container soon once the tea grows in the garden."

"Sounds good. Your tea will probably be better than mine anyway."

[New Quest: Serve 5 Cups of Tea]

Well, wasn't that a timely quest. I still wasn't really sure how they were given out. Some quests seemed to be exactly what I needed at the time, like they were triggered by what I was doing, while others seemed to be more standard, like the ones about defeating monsters.

But the water was already boiling, which was too hot for green tea. I took it off the stove and let it cool for a bit before ladling it into our mugs. Boss was too big for a mug, so I used pots for the slimes instead. Steam curled around me, teasing my nose with the fresh green scent of tea as I carefully set a pot in front of each slime. I felt bad that they had leaves in them, but I didn't have a strainer, so it would have to do for now.

I took a sip, nearly choking as Jellybean jumped *into* the pot of tea!

"Hey, that's hot!" I handed my mug to Fiona so I could check on Jellybean. He barely fit inside the pot, but he was spinning and trilling with excitement as he gulped the liquid down. I shook my head at him. "You are too cute for your own good, you know. I hope you like it."

All too soon, the pot was empty and Jellybean was staring at me with big puppy-dog eyes again. He was getting too good at that look.

"I think the slime wants more," Fiona said with a laugh, sipping on her own tea as she watched the show play out.

Jellybean jumped out of the pot, landing in my lap without a single drop of tea flying anywhere. He'd drained the pot dry, which had to mean he really liked it. I'd have to start keeping track of which food and drinks the slimes liked best and which they were kind of meh about.

I put the pot back on the stove and refilled it with water as Boss nudged his own pot of tea closer to Jellybean.

The little slime's eyes widened as he hopped inside, basking in the warmth of the tea like he was at a hot spring. His blue body started turning green from drinking so much, making him a beautiful turquoise.

I patted Boss's side. "That was nice of you."

He nodded, rubbing against my hand like he wanted more pets. I laughed and hugged the slime close. Meeting these two slimes really was the best thing that had happened to me in this dungeon. Taking care of them was so satisfying, warming my heart even more than the tea warmed my body.

Once the water was almost boiling, I split it between the two pots, making sure Boss would actually get some this time.

"Do you need a refill?" I asked Fiona, but she just shook her head, watching as Jellybean jumped into the pot of hot tea again.

I sighed, glad he wasn't hurt, but I wished he'd wait for it to cool down a bit. He sank into the hot liquid with a little sigh of contentment. He didn't even drink the tea this time, just seemed to enjoy sitting in it. His body turned even greener until he matched the tea so perfectly it would have been hard to tell where one started and the other began, if not for the slime's jellylike body.

[Quest Completed: Serve 5 Cups of Tea]

[Your cooking brings so much joy. You're on your way to becoming a wonderful cafe owner.]

I smiled against my mug, far too happy at the system's compliment. The tea hadn't been anything special, but it was the first thing I'd made in my new kitchen, and Jellybean loved it.

[Reward: Teapot, Teacups, and a Tea Strainer]

My eyes widened as a beautiful green teapot, four teacups, and a strainer appeared before me. I brushed my fingers over the cast iron, grateful the system had given me exactly what I needed right now. Green tea leaves decorated the teapot, swirling around it like leaves on the wind. I couldn't wait to use it.

"Now that's a nice reward." Fiona leaned closer, examining the teapot. "At this point, I think the system's playing favorites though."

Honestly, so did I, but that just made me feel even warmer inside. Somebody was looking after me.

[New Quest: Serve 10 Cups of Tea]

Jellybean hopped out of the pot to look at the rewards with us, but something was different about the little slime. Even after he left the tea, his body was still green and full of tea leaves. Something was sprouting from the top of his head too, almost like the dirt slimes after I'd given them new seeds. My mouth dropped open as a tiny sprig of tea grew out of Jellybean's head.

"What's going on? Are you okay?" I rushed to check on him, but a message box appeared in front of me.

[Blue Slime has evolved into a Tea Slime]

"Slimes can *evolve*?"

[Slimes usually evolve based on what they eat. If they end up loving a food and eating enough of it, an evolution is triggered.]

Fiona's eyebrows raised. "I didn't know the part about them having to love the food. I just thought they evolved if they ate a lot of the same thing. Interesting."

"That's amazing! I'll make you all the tea you want," I told Jellybean, hugging him close as Boss started bouncing. "You too, Boss. I'll make you all kinds of treats in case you want to evolve like Jellybean." I frowned, holding the little slime out to study his new tea shape. "Hmm . . . do you still like the name Jellybean? Or do you want something more tea themed now that you've evolved?"

Jellybean's eyes got all starry when I mentioned a new name.

"Ohh, what about Steepie?" Fiona asked, eyes lighting up again. "Or Brewster?"

The little slime swayed back and forth like he was undecided.

"Okay." I patted the side of his body instead of his head to avoid the tea leaves. "What about Boba? Or Chai? Maybe Matcha?" He started bouncing so fast in my arms at that last name that I almost dropped him. I laughed. "Okay, Matcha it is! Congratulations on evolving into a tea slime, little Matcha."

Fiona gave me back my tea mug, clinking hers against mine. "And congratulations on your Get-Me-Outta-Here Cafe."

"Okay, maybe it deserves a better name than that after all." I laughed, setting Matcha down to play with Boss.

My tea was going a bit cold at this point, but I finished the last few sips, enjoying the earthy taste. Drinking tea with friends was such a cozy experience, warm and homey.

A name for the cafe tugged at my mind, inspired by Matcha's new love of tea. I hovered over the menu as the weight of this decision loomed over me. If I picked a bad name, people might easily forget it, but if I picked something good, they'd be more likely to talk about my cafe.

No matter what I chose, I wanted slimes to be part of it so everyone knew how important they were to me. I not only wanted to protect these slimes, but make a safe space for them to feel comfortable without worrying what the adventurers might do to them.

This was a place for me and the slimes to feel at home. To feel safe and secure. The name should be something warm like tea . . .

A smile tugged at my lips as I entered the name. The menu asked for a confirmation and I pressed [Yes] then hurried outside to see if the sign had updated.

The name *Slime Serenitea* swept across the sign with shimmering green letters that looked like they were mimicking the slime's texture. The sign even had a little version of Matcha on it, relaxing in a big cup of tea.

I pressed my hand to my chest, overcome with emotions at the sight of it. This felt like everything I'd wanted for so long and more.

This was the Slime Serenitea Cafe.

CHAPTER SEVENTEEN

The Dungeon Wants a Cookie

Dave scratched his horns. "We need to make a plan for those living trees on floor six. The adventurers who are strong enough to defeat them already went past that floor while the lower-level adventurers are complaining that we've stuck them in an unwinnable situation." The satyr clutched his clipboard to his chest. "My lord, you have to do something about that culinary mage!"

The Dungeon had been hearing many such reports from Dave ever since it had allowed Hazel to become a culinary mage. It was all *she's-breaking-the-system this* or *she's-ruining-the-dungeon that.* How could Dave not see the sheer joy she was creating too? Sure, there was a bit of chaos, but she hadn't done any of it intentionally.

Everyone had to learn their class somehow. She was just working out the kinks. And while she did that, the Dungeon got to enjoy the most amusing sights it had ever seen. Never had such an innocent adventurer caused such a monster surge! Not only had the living trees grown and become stronger, but they seemed to be sticking to her request to not hurt adventurers too. They just toyed with them a bit.

The baker was like a monster whisperer at this point. She gave them food, and in return, they obeyed her requests. It was marvelous and highly irregular.

The Dungeon had read about food before and knew that humans required it to survive, but it hadn't realized that the taste changed the experience so much. It was still the same ingredients, but Hazel's food had an entirely different effect on people. At this very moment, she was baking cookies that had all the slimes crowding around her like they were nectar from the gods, and she'd earned yet another level from all her hard work.

[Level Up: Culinary Mage Level 5]

[Your love for food is hard to ignore. You can now cook with rare ingredients and access new items in the cafe menu. Keep working hard and making even more delicious food.]

A warm smile appeared on her face as she finished the last cookie she'd made and hugged the nearest slime. The lights from the level-up shone around them, casting her in beautiful colors to celebrate her achievement.

The Dungeon had never eaten food before, but to fully understand this new culinary mage class, maybe it would need to change that. One could only balance a power if it knew how it worked, after all. The Dungeon would need a human body for that though.

Maybe it could construct a living spark like how the Dungeon had created all the Daves. With a shard of the dungeon core's embers, new life could take shape, slowly growing and evolving until it surpassed its original creation and became real.

Yes, that was exactly what the Dungeon would do. It couldn't wait to meet Hazel face-to-face and to try the cookies she thought could defeat the boss on floor one hundred . . .

"My lord!" Dave shouted as he fell on his backside, frantically patting out embers that had drifted into his hair. "Every time you think about that woman, you almost burn my eyebrows off!"

Oops.

The Dungeon relayed its apologies to Dave. It never wanted to cause the poor satyr harm, but it just got so excited whenever it thought about Hazel that its flames couldn't help but blaze up. The Dungeon had gone from a smoldering pile of embers, about to be snuffed out, to a raging flame that would fuel the entire dungeon for years to come.

How did one woman have such power? It was exhilarating, and the Dungeon wanted to know everything about her. To balance the system, of course, not because it wanted to try her cookies that badly.

As Dave went back to his report about the living tree incident, the Dungeon drifted off, creating its new body. It had many choices to choose from: short or tall, round or skinny, long hair or short? The possibilities were endless.

What kind of body would Hazel prefer? Based on the situations it had seen so far, she seemed to prefer small, adorable creatures, so maybe short and plump would be best? Possibly something shaped like that sweet potato she always spoke so fondly of.

No, it didn't want to be confused with the slimes. The Dungeon wanted to make her feel safe, like she could trust it to protect her on tougher floors if needed. To help her adventure, of course, not to impress her.

So a tall body, then, one with an athletic build and lean muscles, but what about the custom characteristics like hair and eye color? And what class should the body have? Fighter? Archer? Mage?

Or maybe the Dungeon should take a page out of Hazel's book and create a whole new class . . .

"Sir, are you even listening?" Dave sighed with exasperation as he walked closer to inspect the embers in the walls. "Wait, are you creating a new spark to help me with all this? Oh, thank the gods, I really appreciate it!"

The Dungeon had no idea how to answer that without upsetting Dave, so maybe it would need to make *two* living sparks. One for its own secret use and another to help Dave and keep him busy. Too busy to notice if the system went on autopilot once in a while . . .

"This is a great idea!" Dave sat next to the dungeon core, marveling at all the different character creation options. "Oh, the long black hair looks great. Very dark and mysterious. I bet the adventurers would listen to somebody like that better than me."

The Dungeon thought Dave was doing a wonderful job, no matter what the adventurers said about him. The satyr was a dutiful worker with an attention for detail that none of the other sparks had ever fully developed. Dave was the only reason the Dungeon would even consider getting away with a secret like this, because it knew the system was in good hands with the Daves around.

If anything truly serious happened, they'd be able to find the new body. The Dungeon would leave a trail of breadcrumbs for them to make sure of that. Its flames danced in amusement at the thought. Soon it would be trying real breadcrumbs that had fallen off actual bread!

Together, the Dungeon and Dave spent the afternoon messing with all the possible options for the new sparks. It settled on a fighter class for its own body with dark armor and a sword that had red gems in it that would glow with a bit of its flames. For Dave's new assistant, they chose a kindly older woman with a hidden strength, who nobody would feel comfortable saying no to.

Not twice, at least.

The decision made Dave cackle with glee, which in turn made the Dungeon happy too. This was a nice way to pass the time.

"Wait, what's the second spark for?" Dave tilted his head.

The Dungeon tried to shove it aside in a place far away from Dave's reach, but the satyr was like a dog with a bone sometimes. He leapt up, staring into the Dungeon's flames.

"You're trying to run away from all this paperwork!" His eyes widened, glancing at his piles of reports from earlier that all mentioned the new baker. "And I bet I know where you're going . . ."

Alas, the Dungeon had been caught red-handed. Actually, once it had hands, it wished to get them caught in a cookie jar.

Before Dave could get too anxious, the Dungeon reassured him that this spark was only for emergencies. It was the Dungeon's plan for dealing with the living trees and any other issues that might come up. Not that it would interfere directly, but with a body, the Dungeon could pull a few more strings.

Dave's eyes narrowed. "Just for emergencies, huh?"

The Dungeon's flames shone brighter. It wouldn't lie to the satyr, but it didn't have to tell him everything either. It was the ruler of this dungeon after all, so if it wanted to deal with a cookie emergency, it would damn well deal with it.

With that, the Dungeon continued to design both new sparks, eagerly awaiting the day when they would be ready for use. Hopefully Hazel would be just as excited as the Dungeon was.

CHAPTER EIGHTEEN

Safe Zone Shopping

It was finally time to leave for the safe zone, but it felt so weird going without Jellybean, I mean, Matcha. He'd been with me the entire time I was here, and he was giving me a sad look like he knew what I was up to. I knelt down, hugging him tight while I leaned against Boss and tried to cuddle the little dirt slimes too.

"I won't be gone long," I promised them, patting their little slime heads. "I hate that I can't take you with me, but monsters aren't allowed in safe zones. You'll be fine here though. Boss and Mossy will take care of you."

I glanced at the two biggest slimes, the only ones high-enough level to actually protect anyone here. They stared back at me, nodding slowly in agreement. There were more dirt slimes than before, like they'd been multiplying, and it was so adorable watching them leap in and out of the garden.

"You're sure they'll be okay, right?" I whispered to Fiona.

She sighed and tried to hit me on the head, but her hand just bounced off.

[No-fighting rule activated.]

[Remember to be nice or you won't get dessert.]

I pressed my lips together, trying not to laugh at the silly rule I'd written as a joke on that menu for Dave. The system had taken it to heart and made this a no-fighting zone that covered the inside of the cafe as well as the grounds around it. It meant a lot, and my shoulders relaxed. The slimes would be fine while we were gone.

Matcha pressed against my cheek, his new tea body warm and comforting like a hot-water bottle.

I ran my fingers over his side, petting him. "You'll be okay. Just stay close to the cafe."

Fiona knelt to join us, playing with the slimes as she studied me. "I think *you're* the only one not okay with this. They'll be fine, and you said you have a whole list of things you need. Like more ingredients. You can't run a cafe without food."

"I know, you're right." I sighed and stood up as Matcha hopped off my shoulder, bouncing into the back of my legs until I got moving. "Okay, okay. I get it. We're going."

Fiona grinned at the slime. "Thanks for the assist. We'll bring you back a treat."

Matcha started bouncing excitedly and Boss's eyes widened. Trills sounded from the garden as the little dirt slimes cheered when they jumped out of the dirt, but were muffled once they hopped back in. It was all so warm and happy, lifting a weight off my shoulders.

"Thank you," I told Fiona. "Treats are a great idea. Let's head out and find something good."

She pulled a key from her inventory and held it in the air until a door appeared around it, revealing stairs that led up. I turned back one more time to wave goodbye to the slimes, only stopping when Fiona dragged me inside.

"You'll like the safe zone, and you want new clothes, right? Not to mention tables and chairs for customers." She frowned. "How much gold do you even have?"

"Uhhhh . . ." I flipped through my menus, not really sure since I hadn't needed to use it yet. "Three hundred seventy?"

"That's way more than I thought you'd have. You must not have used your starter gold at all yet, so let's hurry and get shopping!" Fiona raced up the stairs with me until we reached the other door. It flung wide open, and bright light filtered into the stairway. "Welcome to floor five's safe zone!"

I blinked, adjusting to the bright light. The cacophony of lots of people talking at once pressed against me as people milled about a wide-open street full of stalls forming a marketplace. Larger buildings that looked like permanent shops stood behind them with people coming and going frequently. I kept close to Fiona as she confidently strode into the throng of people.

There were so many people! Adventurers decked out in full plate armor clinked and clanked their way down the road while ones wearing simple leathers or cloth were more silent. Almost everyone had weapons of some kind, ranging from bows to swords to maces even. The only people without something deadly looking were the ones with magic books strapped to the smalls of their backs.

It was all just so jarring compared to my quiet, secluded, slime-filled life up until now.

"You doing okay?" Fiona turned back with a smile. "It's a little overwhelming at first, but you'll get used to it."

I nodded, trailing after her as I tried to avoid bumping into anyone. There were so many stalls! Where should we start first? Avoiding all the weapons sellers and armorers was an easy answer, but that ruled out over half the market. Nothing screamed *come here for baking pans* either.

"Any ideas?" I asked Fiona as she stopped in front of a shop full of vibrant clothing. A smile stretched across my face as the colors drew me in. "Okay, we can start with the clothes, sure."

She laughed. "Figured it would be an easy win. We might need to get creative with the rest of your list."

A bell rang as we opened the door, stepping into a world of cloth and leather. Fully made outfits were displayed in the window while bolts of cloth scattered all over made it seem like they made custom designs too. As we carefully made our way through the maze of fabrics, a woman called out from the back.

"Welcome to Stitch and Spell!" Her voice was cheerful, but the closer she got, the stranger she appeared. Her body was made of fabric, smooth silks and intricate brocades. Her thread smile beamed. "How may I help you?"

Fiona smiled back as if talking to a living doll was totally normal. "We're looking for a few new outfits that are more cozy than armored. Something my friend could use as a cafe uniform, with an apron too."

"You've come to the right place." The living doll spread her arms, shimmering blue sleeves swaying in the air. "Here at Stitch and Spell, we imbue all our fabrics with the best enchantment spells. I can have a fireproof apron made for you in a jiffy. What else can I make for you?"

"What is she?" I asked Fiona softly.

Fiona shrugged. "Nobody's really sure, but all the shopkeepers are like that. Some have more personality than others, but none of them are human. They seem willing to help us though, and people trust them."

The tailor kept staring at us, patiently waiting with eerie button eyes. Fiona hadn't led me astray so far, so I should at least try talking to the doll. Especially if it meant getting out of this suffocating chef's coat. It really wasn't ideal for a jungle floor.

I stepped forward with a smile. "Hello, I'm looking for a half apron that goes from the waist down. Maybe in a warm brown or green with clothes that look good with it too. Something flowy so it's not as hot on the dungeon floor I'm on."

"I can accommodate that." The doll held up a tape measure as her buttons sparkled. "Time to get your measurements and make you the outfit of your dreams."

In a tornado of measuring tape, thread, and lots of fabric, the doll spun me this way and that until she stood back with a pleased smile on her face. A white shirt with long billowy sleeves hung on a nearby dress form along with a beautiful green skirt that had a golden floral pattern on it. A frilled brown apron tied it all together.

My eyes widened. "How'd you make that so fast?"

"It's my job, dear," the doll said. "What else can I make for you?"

I was still hung up on the first thing she'd made. The fabric was softer than anything I'd felt before, smooth and airy. The golden flowers on the skirt were intricate, like a garden blooming from the bottom of the fabric. This was exactly what I'd been hoping for in a new uniform, but I had a feeling it would be pricey.

"Umm, how much is this going to cost, first?" I asked.

The doll tapped her chin. "Ten gold should suffice. If you plan to order more, I could bundle them together at a discount."

"That's it? I'd love a few outfits, then! I kind of get covered in dirt a lot . . ." I rubbed the back of my neck with an awkward laugh. "Do you have anything good for gardening?"

Fiona laughed. "And a futon or something she could sleep on too, if you've got one. She's been sleeping in a pile of slimes."

"Hey, they're cozier than they look!"

The doll blinked. "You sleep with monsters? Are you quite all right, dear?"

"I'm fine." The back of my neck warmed as Fiona snorted. "And they're more like friends than monsters."

"And friends deserve nice beds to sleep on, right?" Fiona nudged my arm with a grin.

The doll paused before nodding. "I can accommodate your requests. Please give me a few minutes."

The doll rushed to create the gardening outfit along with the futon, fabric and needles zipping through the air like magic. The cafe didn't have any bedrooms, so Fiona had slept outside in a tent while I'd been sleeping in the middle of the dining room, which really wasn't the most comfortable even after the size upgrade.

After a few minutes, the doll's needles stopped moving, and she turned to us with a smile. "All done. That will be thirty-five coins in total, dear."

I handed her the coins with a grateful smile. "Thank you. These look wonderful."

"Thank you for your business." The doll smiled as she bagged up our items. "Please come again."

"Um, actually . . ." I held up the new outfit she'd made for my cafe work, not wanting to put it away so fast. "Do you mind if I change into this here?"

"Of course, right this way." The doll led me to the back of her store where there was a fitting room.

I removed my heavy chef's coat. This had served me well up until now, the only real link to my past, but it just wasn't suited for my new job. I couldn't bring myself to get rid of it though, so I put it carefully into my inventory before trying the new outfit on.

The fabric was as soft as butter, wrapping me up like a cozy blanket. It was really breathable too and looked beautiful when the light hit it. I stepped back outside, twisting and turning to see the skirt sway around me and the sleeves fall against my arms.

"What do you think?" the doll asked. "Do you like it?"

"I absolutely love it!" I pulled the tailor into a hug. "Thank you. I really appreciate this."

When I moved back, the doll just stood there, frozen for a moment before she reached over for a green ribbon that matched my skirt.

"Here, this is on the house." She tied it around the bottom of my braid, letting the ribbon hang loose. "There we go. You're all set now. Do come back again soon."

"We will!"

Fiona and I waved as we left the Stitch and Spell shop. I glanced back to see the living doll in a flurry of fabric and thread again, stitching up a storm. She might not be human, but she was definitely passionate about her craft. I hoped I'd see her again soon.

CHAPTER NINETEEN

Potatoes Make Everything Better

Fiona and I browsed various food stalls full of fresh fruit and vegetables, meat and cheese, and even what looked like protein bars, but there was nothing remotely like the ingredients I'd need for baking. Everything here was finished, ready to eat, and painfully [Common].

"Where'd you get the flour from when we first met?" I asked Fiona. "I think you said there was a new shop that tempted you or something?"

She chuckled. "Yeah, it opened the day I met you, but nobody cared about anything they were selling since it needed to be cooked. I grabbed a few of everything just to see what it would taste like." She frowned, moving around the market slowly. "I don't remember where the shop was though."

As we browsed, we came across a stall that only sold one thing: potatoes. There were hundreds of them, piled high enough to form little potato forts. It was so ridiculous that I had to stop and get some. Warm potatoes with melted butter and cheese were delicious. Maybe I'd cut some up and make chips for the slimes too.

"Hello, can I get a dozen potatoes, please?" I asked the young shopkeeper.

She nodded and bagged them up for me. "No problem. That'll be one gold."

One gold seemed ridiculously cheap, but I handed it over and took my potatoes while the shopkeeper helped the next customer.

The man wrung his hands. "I don't have any money."

"That's okay, have a potato on the house." The woman smiled and handed him a single large potato. "Come again soon, but do try to go out adventuring to make more money first. This is your three hundred thirty-second free potato."

"Well, that was rude," I mumbled to Fiona as we started walking away.

"Potatoes are the cheapest food you can buy, so adventurers tend to stock up. And if you run out of money, the shopkeepers will give you one a day to keep you from starving." She nodded at the anxious man walking away with his sad potato. "People like him have given up on getting out of here. They just wallow and eat potatoes. It's sad, but there's nothing we can do about it."

The man wandered over to a group of tables outside and sat down, biting into his potato like it was an apple. He wasn't even cooking it! No. I couldn't let him think that's how potatoes were supposed to be eaten, not when they should be warm and comforting. He looked like he needed that more than anybody right now.

"Could you go buy all the cheese from that stall we passed?" I pulled out some coins and handed them to Fiona. "I'm going to keep looking for that baking stall to hopefully find some butter. Meet back at those tables?"

"Okay, but why are we splitting up?" Fiona frowned, following my gaze to the man from earlier. "You're going to cook him something, aren't you?"

"Of course I am. He can't keep eating potatoes like they're apples!" I laughed and hurried off to find that elusive shop Fiona had mentioned.

It took longer than I wanted, but I eventually found it at the very edge of town. The stall was about half the size as the others but was filled to the brim with ingredients. Large bricks of butter were stacked up like a wall along one table while cinnamon sticks the size of actual tree limbs stood proud in a barrel. Bags of flour and sugar covered another table with a few bars of chocolate and cannisters of tea.

Basically everything Fiona had given me that first day, but I was hoping for a few more things. Like milk.

"Hello, can I buy a bit of everything, please?" I smiled at the shopkeeper, who looked oddly familiar. "Are you related to the woman working at the potato stall?"

She shook her head. "No, I'm my own person."

What a weird way to phrase that, but I decided not to ask more as we went through everything I wanted to buy, which was admittedly most of the store. I should have been saving some for temporary furniture and dishes, but buying ingredients was just too exciting! Think of all the bread I could make with this flour! And the pies. Ohhh, the pies would be tasty with fruit from the garden.

"That'll be two hundred twenty gold." The shopkeeper held out her hand.

Yikes. That was a lot of money. I bit my lip, staring at the piles of ingredients. Maybe I could grow my own wheat to save costs? It would probably be better quality too. I'd have to get the right seeds for that though and learn how to mill it . . . neither of which would be happening soon. I sighed and handed over the gold.

The woman smiled. "Thank you. Come again soon."

"Probably not for a while." I chuckled and shook my head as I gathered all the ingredients into my inventory. "Thanks!"

Hopefully Fiona had gotten the cheese by now and was keeping that adventurer busy so he didn't leave before I got there. I probably should have told him what the plan was instead of running off like that, but when I made it back to the dining area, he was still sitting at his table just staring off into space. It bothered me more than it should.

Why were we all dragged here if some of us just ended up like that? What was the point of all this?

Fiona waved me over before I could dwell on it. She had five huge blocks of cheese and what looked like seasoned chicken skewers.

I raised an eyebrow at the meat. "You know that's already cooked, right? I can't make it taste better."

She opened her mouth but snapped it closed and slumped over the table. "I hadn't thought about that. It just looked so good!"

"Don't tell Nugget that." I laughed and sat down next to her. "Thanks for getting all this. I really appreciate it. The potatoes will taste amazing now."

"So you found the baking shop?" She raised her head, eyes sparkling. "I can't wait to try these potatoes."

I glanced over at the man from earlier, raising my voice enough for him to overhear. "Same. Baked potatoes with butter and melty cheese taste amazing. I've got enough to share too."

His gaze darted over to me, but he didn't take the bait. A few other adventurers looked over with curiosity though as I poked holes in the potatoes and covered them in butter and salt. I arranged them on the bottom of a pot and covered it to keep the steam inside, wishing yet again for an actual oven instead of my tiny portable stove.

Maybe there was a quest for that. The potatoes would take a while to bake, so I might as well look through my menus a bit more.

Cooking dinner and breakfast for Fiona and the slimes had gotten me enough cafe points to grab a few more quests. I probably had enough wood to easily complete the table and chairs upgrade, so I grabbed that one first. Eating on the ground was getting kind of old.

[New Quest: Gather 10 Wood to Build a Table and Chairs]

I'd wait to complete it until we got back, but kept scrolling to see if there was an oven quest in here somewhere, immediately grabbing it when I found it.

[New Quest: Serve 25 Customers and Gather 25 Clay and 25 Stone to Build a New Oven]

That was so exciting! I couldn't wait to have an actual oven to bake bread or pies in. Cookies would be so much better that way too, instead of being cooked in a frying pan.

I kept browsing through the menus and found a few other upgrades that looked really nice: a second floor for the cafe, a cold cellar, and an irrigation system for the garden. But they all had lock symbols next to them. I clicked on one and a message appeared.

[Available at level 10.]

I clicked the irrigation system upgrade and got a different message.

[Available after completing the running water upgrade.]

Interesting. So some upgrades were locked behind levels while others built off one another. I should probably get started on that running water quest in case other upgrades needed it too. It would take all my remaining cafe points, but it would be worth it.

[New Quest: Gather 5 Metal and Redirect the River to Flow Beside Your Cafe]

"Redirect the river?" I said a little too loudly.

Fiona laughed. "Well, that sounds complicated. What do you get from it?"

"Running water, which would be nice." I thrummed my fingertips against the table. "Maybe the dirt slimes could help me dig a new route, but we'd have to do something to keep the monster fish on the other side. A net or filter maybe . . ."

While I thought, the potatoes finished cooking. I took them out of the pot and cut them, adding pads of butter and lots of cheese. It all melted together beautifully as the scent wafted across the area and had more than one head turning our way. I got a few more potatoes ready, adding them to the pot in case anyone wanted some. I really hoped the man from earlier would accept our offer, but at the very least, I could tell people about my cafe and spread the word about good-tasting food.

I nudged a potato toward the nervous adventurer. "They're a lot better than that last one you ate, I promise."

His nose twitched. "Food doesn't usually smell that good. What's going on?"

"My friend here's a culinary mage." Fiona beamed with pride, like my class was somehow her doing. "And believe me, you'll never want to eat anywhere else except her cafe after you try her food."

Murmurs rose up as a few people wandered over, but I was most excited about the adventurer who moved one table closer to us. The bait was set, and our target was on his way. Mission warm-and-comforting-potato was a go.

"What's a culinary mage?" he asked softly, pretending like his gaze wasn't locked on those potatoes.

Fiona grinned. "So, basically, when this goofball was supposed to pick a weapon in the tutorial zone, she chose a grilled cheese instead. Now she's a culinary mage and any food she makes tastes amazing."

A nearby woman's eyes widened. "That sounds ridiculous, but, um, can I try one?"

"Sure, the first sample's free." I slid a potato her way. "I hope you enjoy."

She bit into the potato cautiously, but then almost dropped it in shock. "It tastes . . . delicious! I don't even know how to describe it." She proceeded to devour the rest, a soft moan escaping her lips. "Are you selling these? Your friend mentioned something about a cafe, right? Where is it?"

"On floor six." I cut the next potatoes in quarters to split with the crowd coming our way. "It's safe though, so you don't have to worry about monsters while you eat."

The anxious man moved another table closer, raising his gaze to mine. "Can I try one?"

"Absolutely." I grinned as I took out a freshly baked potato, adding extra butter and cheese just for him. This entire potato party was to make his day a little better, so it felt like victory when he took his first small bite. "What do you think?"

His eyes lit up. "It's amazing!"

Happiness surged through me. This was the best part about my class: sharing tasty food with nice people. I glanced at Fiona, and she clapped a hand on my shoulder with a smile. Yup. This moment was everything. I wanted everyone in the dungeon to try my food and find a little happiness in their day.

The man devoured the rest of the potato and licked his fingers with a sigh of contentment. "This was nice, thank you. My name's Marvin, by the way. I wish your cafe was in the safe zone though. Have you asked Dave about it? I'm sure he'd rent you a space."

"Ohhh, I really doubt he'd go for that." I chuckled, picturing his head exploding at the idea. "He's the one who kicked me out of the safe zone in the first place. No slimes allowed, he said."

The happy chatter of the group quieted down as Marvin flinched. *"Slimes?"*

"Yeah, my cafe's called Slime Serenitea," I said confidently as Fiona tensed up. "The slimes are my friends, and they help out at the cafe. See?" I held up my wrist to show off the blue slime bracelet that Boss had given me. "We're bonded."

"Bonded? With a slime?" He shuddered.

"Is something wrong?" I frowned. "I thought you liked the food, so what do the slimes have to do with it?"

The woman who'd first tried our potatoes patted him on the shoulder. "Marvin's just a bit traumatized after a slime, well, ate him. Twice."

"Oh . . ." I bit my lip, trying not to picture him as a baby chicken being gobbled up by Matcha. "That would never happen at the cafe, I promise. I feed the slimes every day." He flinched and scooted farther away on the bench. I held up my hand. "I meant with actual food, not people! I feed them baked goods, like a civilized cafe."

Fiona was obviously trying not to laugh but lost the battle entirely as her shoulders started shaking with mirth. "Sorry, I've just seen that happen before, and it's always so strange. But the slimes at the cafe really aren't like that, they're nice. Plus, it's like a mini safe zone, so there's no fighting allowed."

The adventurers around us didn't look quite convinced by that as they smiled and waved, making awkward excuses to walk away. A few promised to stop by during their adventures though, so that was good. I couldn't expect to win everyone over in a day, but if we got just a few people to give the slimes a chance, that was worth it to me. I just wished we could help Marvin somehow.

"They really are nice, you know." I handed him the last potato and started heating a pot of water to make tea to calm his nerves. "I'm sorry about what happened to you though. It sounds awful. This dungeon really pits people against one another, and I wish there was another way. The slimes I've met don't actually want to fight; they just do it because they have to. Just like everyone else here."

Fiona nodded. "Yeah, it sucks sometimes, but we've gotta get through it. I can teach you to protect yourself if you want." She held her hands in the air. "Without hurting the slimes, of course."

"Of course." A smile stretched across my face. Fiona was the kind of adventurer I liked. The kind who leveled up, but not mindlessly. Maybe Marvin was the same way. I turned to him, pulling one of the teacups out of my inventory. "Do you like tea?"

"Probably?" He shrugged as he scooted a bit closer again. "I'd love to try it, I mean. If you're offering."

"Sounds good, it'll just take a few minutes." I scooped tea leaves into his cup and let them steep for a bit. "The first slime I met in the dungeon was a little blue slime, but he loved tea so much that he evolved into a tea slime. Hopped right into the pot and just drank it all in. Now he's got tea leaves growing out of his head!"

Marvin's eyes widened. "Slimes can evolve like that?"

"Slimes can do all sorts of things," Fiona said, leaning closer. "There's even some slimes that grow food. Honestly, carrots pop right out of their heads and fly through the air!"

Marvin rolled his eyes as a blush crept across his cheeks. "You don't need to make up stories. Tell me what they're really like."

"That is what they're really like." I pulled out a few carrots I hadn't used for anything yet. "Mossy, a giant dirt slime, gave me these. The dirt slimes live in the garden behind my cafe, and they love growing food. They appreciate freshly tilled soil and a lot of fresh water in return."

Marvin blinked. "You're serious?"

"Dead serious," I said, smiling as I remembered the system telling me that one time. "You can meet them if you want."

He shook his head fast, shoving himself away. "Oh no, I'm much safer here. I'll just listen to your stories, that's all."

Fiona frowned, glancing at me like I should do something, but what was I supposed to say?

The tea was done steeping though, so I strained it and passed it to Marvin. "I'll tell you all the stories you want."

As I told him all about the time Matcha and I were treed by monster chickens, leaving out the part about how the slime had started the whole thing, Marvin's shoulders visibly relaxed. He drank the tea deeply, smiling and even laughing here and there as I told him about the first time I met Mossy in the garden and how much fun all the little dirt slimes were.

Fiona even added the silly part about how Nugget liked to ride on the slimes and how I slept curled up with them like a little cat.

"Seriously?" Marvin laughed. "You're braver than I am, that's for sure."

"It's not bravery, it's just that I trust them." I refilled his empty cup with a smile. "The slimes are my friends. I even have a title for it."

At that, the words [Slime Friend] appeared in front of me.

"Incredible. If you and Miss Fiona are with me, then *maybe* I'd like to visit that cafe." He stared into his tea for a while before lifting his head again. "I'm tired of being stuck here, and if something doesn't change, I might never leave. I've already been here for a year."

His quiet admission made my heart ache. If I hadn't chosen a grilled cheese for a weapon, would I be stuck here too? I refused to fight just like he did, even if it was for a different reason. Getting stuck here because of my ideals would be awful, and I was beyond lucky that I'd gotten a culinary mage class.

But . . . what gave me the right to have a class like that when nobody else seemed to be able to?

"I'm so sorry, Marvin," I whispered, hating that I couldn't do anything more for him.

Fiona put a hand on his shoulder. "I'll keep you safe if you ever decide to visit. I promise it'll be worth it. Hazel makes wonderful food, and the slimes are always a lot of fun."

"You know what? Maybe I will visit." Marvin gulped down the rest of his tea and slammed the cup on the table. "I want to get over my fears. Introduce me to the slimes!"

I let out a breath. "That's great! We've just got a few errands left to run, but we can go right after that."

"Now?" His voice rose so high it was almost a squeak. "You want to go that soon?"

"Unless you don't want to?" I asked as he put literal distance between us again, scooting almost all the way off the bench. "It's fine."

He slumped over on the table, head buried in his arms. "You think I'm a coward now just like all the rest, don't you?"

"Not at all." I debated patting his shoulder but wasn't sure if that would be too personal. "Why don't you think on it for a while? I'll need to come back for ingredients often, so you'll have plenty of opportunities to join us."

"Really? That sounds great." He lifted his head, taking a deep breath. "You don't happen to have any more of that tea, do you? It was so calming, the best I've ever had. Without it, I'd have ended up on the ground quivering."

He laughed, rubbing the back of his head as his face burned bright red. If a simple thing like tea could help him, then I'd give him as much as he wanted, but I didn't have anything to store it in . . . I mentally added storage containers to my shopping list, cursing myself for spending so much money on ingredients.

"Do you have any water bottles I could use?" When he nodded, I brewed up another batch, pouring it into a bottle he handed me.

Marvin smiled widely. "Thank you. Honestly, thank you so much. You're both so nice and just wonderful."

He clutched the tea tight to his chest and backed away, thanking us over and over as he went. He seemed nice, so I hoped he really did visit the cafe one day. For now, I'd focus on making it a wonderful place to visit so that every adventurer could have a moment of peace and happiness like he just did.

CHAPTER TWENTY

Clubs Make Good Rolling Pins, Right?

We'd gone to every single shop and stall in the safe zone, but nobody, absolutely nobody, sold baking equipment. We'd managed to find the basics, like dishes and flatware, and even some mismatched lanterns to hang from the ceiling, but nothing like baking pans or display racks. Nobody even sold tables or chairs, which felt really odd. The cafe upgrade menu could help, but only once I had enough points to spend on quests. I needed temporary things to fill in the gaps for now, because one table wouldn't be enough if we had multiple guests.

"Okay, so hear me out." Fiona held up a battle-worn wooden club. "Imagine this as a rolling pin."

"But that's a club . . ."

"A very rolly club," she said with a grin. "Seriously, once we whittle it down and sand it, it would make a great rolling pin. It's a good length and weight."

I frowned at the weapon, wishing I had a better option, but honestly? The club was the best thing we'd found.

"Okay." I tapped my chin, looking around at the rest of the weapons store. "What about serving trays, then?"

Fiona's eyes lit up. "Oh! We could use shields!"

She rushed to grab the nearest one, handing it to me. The large metal shield was so heavy that it felt like my arm might rip off as it crashed toward the floor, but thankfully Fiona caught it in the nick of time. I didn't want any you-break-it-you-buy-it moments here.

"Okay, maybe not *that* shield," she said sheepishly, "but we can find lighter ones."

With that, Fiona and I set off on a scavenger hunt of strange things we could repurpose for the cafe. I drew the line at her trying to convince me to use an old helmet as a mixing bowl, but various other pieces of armor would work fine as cooling racks and things like that if we could flatten them out. We even found whole crates full of empty potion bottles that would be great for drinks or single serving desserts, especially the ones with wider openings.

"Why not take the crates too?" Fiona asked. "If we put some of them together, we could make extra counter space for you. Or tables and chairs maybe?"

"I guess that could work?" My sense of what was a good idea versus a bad one was starting to get skewed here. "Hmmm, maybe this old treasure chest could store my pots and pans?"

Fiona grinned. "Definitely. If we find some others, we can make the cafe feel really homey. Like treasure's around any corner."

"Is that what homey feels like?" I laughed, shaking my head at her. "What about those wine barrels we saw at the market? Those would make great stools."

"You're right! We should go back to all the other shops with this new-found sense of adventurous shopping!"

Fiona's excitement was infectious, so we took off with a new outlook on what would work for the cafe. We rented a cart for the things that didn't fit in our inventory and went to town, buying up so many strange things I'd probably regret later. Thankfully, they were all dirt cheap since nobody else wanted them.

But after a while, we finally had to accept that some things just couldn't be found.

"I think it's time to call it quits." I sighed. "Maybe the dungeon will reward me with muffin pans and baking sheets from quests. I can get by without pastry cutters and things like that. It's fine."

"No way, that is not fine." Fiona linked her arm through mine, confidently tugging me in a direction we hadn't gone yet. "We're going to talk to the blacksmith."

"There's a *blacksmith*? Why didn't we stop there to begin with?" I pushed the cart a bit faster.

"Well . . ." Fiona tilted her head, frowning. "He's not exactly the most imaginative guy. I've asked for customizations a few times, but they go right over his head. So baking pans will probably be a hard pass, but we might as well give it a try, right?"

"Right."

The sounds of metal clanging against metal drew us to a large forge at the edge of the safe zone, all the way past the housing district and other shops. I felt kind of bad for the smith actually, like nobody wanted the sound of his shop anywhere near them. But the closer we got, the more excitedly Fiona talked about it.

"He let me watch when he forged my hammer, and it was one of the coolest things I've ever seen." She patted the hammer on her back. "The way he changed it from a hunk of metal to a weapon this fine was a sight to behold."

Her eyes were bright and sparkly like she was talking about her first love, not her favorite weapon. But hopefully that meant she and the smith were close and he'd be willing to make the baking pans I needed.

The air grew hotter as we walked into the shop, so hot it was almost hard to breathe. The smoky scent of coal burning filled the air, and the fires created a beautiful ambiance.

"Welcome to the Obsidian Forge," a gruff voice called out. "I'm in the back."

"Hey, Brennic." Fiona waltzed over to the anvil he was working at, already peering at the metal. "What are you making?"

"A dagger. Are you buying something or just here to watch again?"

The blacksmith was broad-shouldered and muscular, and his skin was black with bright molten cracks in it like he was made of lava rock. The orange-and-red glow beneath his skin pulsed like a heartbeat, spreading out from his chest. With each stroke of his hammer, the fire inside him blazed.

"We're buying." I moved closer to the intense heat of his forge. "I'm looking for muffin tins and cookie sheets. Maybe some pie pans too and dough cutters."

The big lava man finally stopped hammering. "Does this look like a bakery to you? I make weapons, not whatever those are."

Yeesh. I turned to Fiona, silently pleading with her to help. She was the one who thought this was a good idea.

She motioned with her hands for me to calm down before turning back to Brennic. "I know you usually only make weapons, but wouldn't it be fun to branch out? Imagine the interesting things you could make. Plus, she's a culinary mage, so baking pans are basically her weapons."

Brennic raised an ashen eyebrow at me. "Will you be hitting anything with said muffin pans?"

"Um, no?" I winced. "They're just for cooking. But my food does increase people's buffs and all sorts of other things. So it is how I fight."

"Interesting." He went back to hammering, but he kept glancing at us. "Look, even if I wanted to help, I wouldn't know how. I make weapons."

"Just give it a try. What's the worst that could happen?" Fiona smirked, leaning closer. "Unless you're worried you'll be bad at it?"

"Everyone's bad when they first try new things." He shook his head. "What I meant is that I only know how to make weapons. That's all I do."

I blinked. "But if you wanted to try something else, couldn't you just—"

"No." He shot me down hard as he put the piece of metal he was working on back in the forge to heat up again. "I was only told to make weapons. That's my job."

Fiona and I shared a look. This must have been what she meant about customizations going over his head. It was almost like he'd been given a set of skills and literally didn't know how to do anything else. Like he was . . . programmed or something.

"Hey, Sweet Potato? Got any ideas here?" I asked softly.

If the blacksmith was part of the system, then maybe the system could allow him to experiment with new things. But after a few awkward minutes of us all staring at one another without a single blue message box to be seen, I gave up.

"Fine, let's just go. Thank you for your time."

Brennic nodded. "Sorry I couldn't be more helpful. If you need a sword or an axe though, I'm your guy."

Fiona crossed her arms, staring at the forge with a strange look on her face. "What if . . . you let me try to make them?"

"What?" He stopped his hammer midair with a confused look. "You're not even a blacksmith."

"It's fine, Fiona, don't worry about it." I tried to tug her away, but she went and grabbed a spare leather apron instead.

It was far too big for her, but she didn't seem to care as she used a set of giant metal tongs to pick up a metal bar and add it to the forge. "I'm doing this. I'll pay for the materials, but I'm doing this."

Brennic sighed. "Fine, just don't burn yourself. Or set anything on fire. Or—"

"I get it," she said with a laugh. "I'll be careful."

"You don't have to do all this for me," I said. "I'm really fine."

Fiona stared into the flames, as if in a trance. "There's something about this place that calls to me. Something . . . familiar. I need to do this for me. Plus, if I end up making a lumpy ball of metal, then that's that. I'll finally have my answer." The light from the forge flickered against her skin. "But if I make the best muffin tins you've ever seen, then that would be something else entirely."

The way she was talking made it sound like this was much bigger than me, like she'd thought about forging something for a while but hadn't had the nerve to actually do it. If my baking pans could give her that push, then more power to her.

"Want me to stay?" I asked.

She shook her head. "This might take a while. I'll stop by the cafe once I've made everything on your list."

"Or she flames out." Brennic chuckled. "Honestly, a fighter coming in here thinking they can shape metal. It's not that easy, you know."

But when Fiona took the metal out of the fire and set it on an anvil, she looked like a complete natural. She picked up one of Brennic's hammers and went to work, hitting and shaping that hunk of steel like she did it every day. Baking was the only thing I could really remember of my past, like the motions were ingrained in my mind, but for her? Maybe it was smithing.

This could be a good thing for her, so I left the two of them in the forge bickering about the finer points of blacksmithing while I got ready to head back to the cafe.

It had been a long day, and I wanted nothing more than to cuddle up with the slimes.

CHAPTER TWENTY-ONE

Fiona's Blacksmithing Adventure

Fiona loved every minute she spent watching Brennic smith weapons, but for the first time, she'd actually picked up some metal and started making something herself. The warmth of the forge on her skin felt so right, and every swing of her hammer was exhilarating. The *ting ting clang* of metal created beautiful background music for her first project: a pie pan for Hazel.

Except, this wasn't just for Hazel. This was for Fiona too. Because something about being in this shop just felt right, like it was where she was supposed to be.

The warm metal moved under her hammer like it knew exactly what she wanted it to be. The orange glow was mesmerizing, but it kept cooling down faster than she'd like. She put it back in the forge and waited for it to heat up again.

She could feel Brennic's gaze on her. He hadn't said a word since she started, but he'd been keeping a watchful eye while he worked on his own project. Was it out of curiosity or was he waiting for her to fail?

"Got something to say?" Fiona asked.

He just grunted and kept shaping the dagger he was working on. The design was simple, but the curve of the blade was gorgeous. That was why she loved watching him. He was a master at his craft, even though he was on such an early floor. He should really move farther into the dungeon where his weapons could really shine. But then she might never have met him, and that would be a shame. She kind of liked the grumpy blacksmith.

She took the metal out of the forge and started shaping it again, adding curves of her own to shape the sides of the pie pan. Hazel had drawn pictures of various baking pans, and this one felt like a good starting place. She probably should have gone with cookie sheets first, but there was a fire in her that begged for a challenge.

A smile tugged at her lips as the metal did exactly what she wanted. This was so much more satisfying than fighting monsters. How could she have never tried it before?

Right as the pan started actually looking like Hazel's drawing, the metal collapsed, curling in on itself in unnatural ways that didn't make sense.

"What the hell?" Fiona's mouth dropped open as she stared at the lump of metal, which had gone back to its original form. "Did I do something wrong?"

Brennic moved closer to study it, running a hand over his strong jaw. "No, that's not normal. You seemed like a natural, swinging that hammer like you'd been doing it your whole life. Up until it all failed, of course."

"Gee, thanks." She rolled her eyes. "Should I try something different? Maybe another kind of metal, or was I heating it wrong?"

"I don't think so . . ."

The heat from Brennic's body warmed Fiona's skin as he moved even closer, focusing on the metal with such an intensity that she wasn't sure he even knew she was here anymore. The light pulsing through his body was hypnotizing, reminding her so much of how the metal had looked when she was shaping it. Brennic wasn't just a smith, he was heat and fire incarnate. She'd even seen him heat metal with just his hands.

Eventually he turned those amber eyes of his back to her. "Try again, but with some of the steel over there."

Fiona nodded and added an ingot to the forge to heat up, keeping an extra watchful eye on it this time. She moved through the motions of shaping it again, with tips and tricks from Brennic along the way, and it started coming together even better than before. Hope surged in her chest as she got ready to finish it, warming the pan up and slowly cooling it down to let the metal settle into its new shape.

Except, what should have made it less brittle ended up shattering it. Cracks spider-webbed across the surface of the pan, mocking her.

"I just don't understand what I'm doing wrong!" She threw the pathetic excuse for a pan into the waste bin and dropped her tongs. "It feels right, but it keeps ending up so misshapen."

Brennic moved over to a barrel of oil, quenching his perfect dagger to harden it and give it strength. It came out beautiful, not a single crack or warp in the blade. His projects never failed, especially not as spectacularly as hers. Once he was done, he ran his hands over the pans she'd been trying to make. His silent assessment had her on edge, her shoulders tense as if she was waiting for a monster to jump out at any moment.

"The metal's fighting you." His deep voice rumbled through her as he passed by to grab another ingot to add to the forge. "You should probably give up. You're a fighter class, not a blacksmith."

He was right, but she refused to give up just yet. She knew she could forge something wonderful if the metal would let her. She took a deep breath, inhaling the scent of hot metal and coal. This was where she wanted to be right now, working on a project that meant everything to Hazel and her.

"I hope that metal you're heating up is for me, because I'm not going anywhere until this is done." Fiona grabbed the tongs again, determination in every movement she made. "It's only my first day. I shouldn't have expected to be perfect."

Brennic frowned. "So you're just . . . going to stay here? Where will you sleep?"

"Right here in the forge, if I must." Fiona shrugged and put metal on the anvil again. "The only thing I know is that I'm not giving up."

The burly blacksmith stared at her, light pulsing through the cracks in his skin. Then he smiled softly and went back to work at the anvil next to her. "You can use my cot in the back."

Fiona glanced up at him. He was already lost in the rhythm of his smithing, but his demeanor had changed. He almost looked happy that she had decided to stay. She swung her hammer with a newfound energy. If he thought she was doing the right thing, then she'd give this project her all. She'd make at least one pan by the time this was done and prove that it was possible.

CHAPTER TWENTY-TWO

When the Baker's Away, the Slimes Will Play

Pushing the cart had been no problem on the well-kept roads of the safe zone, but in a jungle? I was struggling, putting all my weight behind it to move the wheels over a rocky patch and hoping no monsters showed up. I thankfully didn't have far to go though as I spotted the cafe in the distance. Bright and colorful slimes bounced in the front yard, beckoning me home. I pushed the cart with renewed vigor, excited to see them again.

Except, at least four or five of the slimes were bright orange and red with what looked like campfire flames dancing around them. I rubbed my eyes, staring at them. Yup, they were definitely fire slimes, and Matcha was rolling around with them like they'd been here the whole time. He was even nuzzling up against one like they were suddenly best friends.

Boss slept against the side of the cafe while the little dirt slimes set rocks around him in precarious piles like they were hoping he'd knock them over when he woke up. Their little noises sounded so much like giggling children that I couldn't help but smile.

The slimes had thrown a party while I was gone! I leaned against the cart, watching them leap and play. Even Nugget had joined in, riding on one like some great commander. Ah, it felt good to be home.

"Hazel?" a male voice called out.

I flinched as a man dressed all in black appeared beside the cafe, as if he'd been hiding in the shadows.

A sword hilt peeked over his shoulder, and before I knew it, he was running straight at me. "You're finally back!"

"Who are you?" I tried to keep the cart between us, but he was far too agile and moved around it with ease, a huge grin on his face. "What do you want?"

"You. Isn't that obvious?"

My pulse raced. He wanted me? What did that even mean?

"Boss, wake up! We've got a weirdo at the cafe."

The big slime jerked awake, knocking all the piles of rocks over. The dirt slimes chirped, rolling around like they were laughing, but Boss immediately focused on the man about to grab me. He bounced over in two big leaps, putting himself between me and the stranger.

"Wait, I think I said that wrong," the man called out, but I couldn't see him behind Boss. "You're usually always here, so it was weird when you weren't. I decided to wait for you."

"How do you know I'm usually here?" My chest tightened as all the alarm bells rang in my head. "Are you a stalker or something?"

"What? No." I heard the man sigh loudly. "I'm messing this all up. Dave's going to be so mad."

"You're friends with Dave?"

"Yeah." The man's voice was sounding kind of shaky, so I peeked around Boss just in time to see him fall against the cart, gripping it for support. "But don't tell that nosy satyr I'm here, okay?"

"Maybe tell me who you are first and I'll consider it."

Not that I knew how to contact Dave anyway, but the threat seemed to work, because the man straightened up and gave me a pleading look with amber eyes that felt familiar. His gaze was warm, like I'd met him somewhere before. Which was ridiculous since I'd only met a few other adventurers, and I'd have remembered somebody who looked like him.

His long black hair drifted in front of his eyes as he swayed on his feet, gripping the cart tighter.

"Are you okay?" I moved closer to him despite my better judgement.

Ugh. Why was I worried about some random stalker outside my cafe? I should go inside and wait for him to leave, not check on his well-being.

The man smiled faintly, his forehead glistening with sweat. "I'll be all right. I just need—"

His eyes filled with confusion as he swayed, grabbing onto my shoulder for support.

"Hey, now—" His body went limp before I could finish, falling against me. "No, no, no. This is not happening!"

My stomach lurched as we careened backward. A slime darted under my head right before it cracked against the ground, but the adventurer's dead weight pressed against my chest like a rock, making it hard to breathe. Did he pass out because he was sick or something?

His head rested on my shoulder, deep even breaths warm against my skin like he was fast asleep. Well, at least *he* was cozy.

"Hey, Boss?" I craned my head back to see him. "Think you can help?"

The big slime just stared down at me, shaking back and forth. Okay, that left it up to me, then. I struggled to push the adventurer off me, but it was no use. The big lug was way too heavy! I let out an exhausted breath, wishing I'd stayed in the safe zone with Fiona. I could really use more friends with hands.

"Hey, mister?" I tapped the adventurer's back. "Time to get up. I promise I won't tell Dave about . . . whatever this is, but please, get off me."

The man shifted with a groan, but instead of standing up, he nuzzled closer. Great. Just great. Nothing like being pinned beneath a total stranger in the middle of a dungeon. The faint scent of campfire smoke wafted off him, which was oddly comforting. My pulse slowed as the adrenaline from our fall finally wore off. If I couldn't move him, then I was going to need some help.

"Matcha, think you and the other slimes can work together to lift this guy off me?"

The green tea slime wiggled underneath one of his arms while the fire slimes moved under his legs. One of the dirt slimes even managed to wiggle between my stomach and his, and together, they rolled the adventurer off me.

I took a few deep breaths, grateful to be free of that extra weight, before sitting up. The fire slimes had crowded around him, pressing against his body in concern. They kept looking over at me with worried eyes too, like they expected me to do something about him. Matcha hopped onto my lap, pressing up against me like he was worried too.

"I'm okay, thanks for the help." I patted his head before turning around to the dirt slime who'd broken my fall to pet him too. "Thank you both. But what are we going to do about this weirdo?"

The adventurer turned over, a faint smile on his face like he was dreaming about something wonderful. Seriously, who the hell was this guy that he could just take a nap in the middle of all this?

He said he'd been waiting for me, which meant he'd had plenty of time to lure the slimes away from the cafe and kill them if he wanted to, but he didn't. That was one point in his favor at least. Plus, he'd seemed excited to see me, not angry or creepy. I mean, kind of creepy, but I didn't actually get a dangerous vibe off him. Every slime here was circled around him like he was some sort of fallen king. Even Matcha was giving me that puppy-dog look of his.

I sighed. "Okay, okay, let's get him inside. I'll try using buff baking to make healing soup for when he wakes up, but then he's outta here. This is all just too weird."

The slimes chirped, positioning themselves under his body so they could move him as a group. It reminded me of ants carrying big pieces of food as they shuffled forward, moving the sleeping adventurer as carefully as they could.

I grabbed the futon and blankets from the cart, laying them on the floor of the cafe as a bed. The slimes deposited the adventurer on top and snuggled inside the blankets with him. The warm glow of their fires looked so cozy and somehow didn't catch anything on fire.

"So who are all of you, hmmm?" I asked the new fire slimes. "Did you come with this guy?"

They nodded, chirping and wiggling like they were telling me some big story I wished I could understand. Matcha nodded along with them, mouth wide open in an O sometimes. Man, a slime communication skill would be really helpful right about now.

"Okay, well, feel free to stay, as long as you play nice with the other slimes. I'm going to make that soup so I can get this guy out of here as soon as possible."

But first, I took enough wood out of my inventory to complete my table and chairs quest. There was no way I was serving a stranger without somewhere for him to sit properly. It would ruin the whole cafe vibe.

[Quest Completed: Build a Table and Chairs]

The pieces of wood rose in the air, spinning and flattening into long planks that pressed together to form a table and two chairs. The design was simple, but they'd be way more comfortable than the wine barrels I'd bought at the market.

These cafe upgrades were really handy, and I couldn't wait to get more points to try other options. The only way to do that was to keep making food and working in the garden though, so I headed into the kitchen to work on that soup for the adventurer.

I pulled a large pot out of my inventory, filled it with water, and put it on the stove. Before I could light the fire, one of the slimes wiggled into the opening underneath the stove. His flames grew warmer, verging on hot as the water started simmering.

"Well, aren't you useful." I grinned at the fire slime. "Thanks for the help."

He trilled, wiggling deeper into the stove like it was his new home. That would make cooking so much easier, especially if he could regulate his heat output well. These slimes were constantly surprising me.

I went into the backyard to gather some vegetables for the soup, catching carrots and garlic as they popped out of the heads of dirt slimes. Food started flying every time I walked into the garden, and it had become a fun little game of catch with the slimes as I harvested ingredients. Once I had enough for the soup, I went back into the cafe.

Five fire slimes had crowded beneath the stove and the water was boiling over, sizzling as it hit the slimes. I rushed forward, dropping the ingredients.

"Are you okay?" I snatched the water off the stove. The slimes pushed against one another, barely fitting in the open space. "You can't all be there. Only one or two will fit."

They started shoving one another, battling to see who would get to stay and who would get shoved out of the stove. I sighed, wanting to grab them, but they were still too hot. Matcha made a noise outside the kitchen, leaning toward the sleeping adventurer. Was he why they were being so insistent on making this soup?

"Calm down!" My shout drew their attention. "If you're doing this to help that adventurer, then you should take turns. He needs some of you to keep him warm too, right?"

The fire slimes tilted their heads, chirping before three of them squeezed out of the stove and bounced back into the main cafe, presumably to comfort their fallen friend. He must be some kind of wonderful to have their support like this. Hopefully he'd wake up soon so I could ask him about it.

I smiled at the little fire slimes still here and put the pot back on the stove. Their flames danced as the water started to boil again. I chopped up the carrots, potatoes, garlic, and herbs, then added them to the water. Finally, I used my mana mix-in skill to add some tasty chicken bouillon to the mix, and things really started to smell good. I stirred the soup, breathing in the comforting scent as I pictured the adventurer drinking it and having all his health and vitality restored.

This soup wouldn't just taste good but would make him feel better too. No more sweat on his forehead or sway in his steps. Any sickness he might have had would be gone. The slimes needed him to feel better.

I took a deep breath and held my hand out over the soup. "Buff Baking!"

The surface glowed for a moment before going back to normal. I focused on it, hoping I got the right buff from that skill.

[Healing Soup: Uncommon]

"See that, little slimes?" I leaned down to peer inside the stove with a grin. "This soup is going to heal your friend right up."

They wiggled and danced, almost boiling the soup over again in their excitement. I laughed and took it off the stove before it got everywhere. Anyone who could make the slimes this happy was worth getting to know.

"Hazel?" the man's voice called out. "Am I in the cafe? And what's that smell?"

I sucked in a breath, gaze darting to the kitchen door. He was awake. Time to meet this friend of the fire slimes properly.

CHAPTER TWENTY-THREE

What's My Name?

Warmth surrounded the Dungeon, but something was different. It felt the softness of a blanket against its skin and the weight of slimes sitting on top of it. It opened its eyes, blinking in the soft light of the cafe. Everything was so bright and colorful with these new eyes.

His new eyes. He was a human now, or as close to one as he'd ever get, so he should use their words.

A fire slime cuddled closer and the Dungeon frowned. These slimes had almost given his identity away. Fire chasing fire. He shook his head at them, all squishy and smiley. What exactly did Hazel see in them anyway? They were cute, he supposed, but they weren't anything amazing. Not like a dragon or a hydra. They were just slimes.

And yet, they'd captured her attention just as much as she'd captured his.

He held a hand out to the fire slime, marveling at the way his new limbs moved so smoothly. He pet the creature, letting the slime's warmth seep into his skin. The slime cooed, rubbing against his palm as his flames blazed just a bit brighter. Getting warmth from another felt better than he expected, and it made him want to curl back in the blankets and sleep some more. But a curious scent was filling the air, and his body was making a loud grumbling noise.

He clutched his stomach. What was that? Was he sick? Or . . . was this hunger?

The Dungeon had never been hungry before. He leapt out of the blankets, causing a few slimes to tumble across the cafe's floor. He rushed to put them back on the blanket, giving them an apologetic pat, then followed the scent.

Hazel stood in the kitchen leaning over a stove filled with fire slimes, mixing what looked like a pot of soup. Her long brown hair was in a braid over her shoulder, and her eyes were closed as she inhaled the scent of the soup, a smile on her lips. Her clothing was different than before, with a flowing green skirt and a loose white shirt.

As she moved, the shirt tugged down on her shoulder a bit, revealing more of her fair skin than she'd ever shown before.

Something fluttered in the Dungeon's chest.

He pressed a hand against it, feeling his heartbeat thundering under his palm. He backed away, not wanting Hazel to see him in such a state. What was going on? First he fainted and now he was feeling lightheaded? He'd rushed to make this body, too excited to even test it out before coming here. Maybe he'd made a mistake somewhere in its creation.

Thankfully the feeling subsided in a few moments. He took a deep breath. Everything was fine.

That delicious scent was getting stronger though, filling the air with smells he couldn't identify. He'd never needed to know what things smelled like before, just like he didn't need to know what they tasted like. But now, now he could experience both.

A smile tugged at his lips. He was going to get to taste Hazel's cooking!

"Hazel?" he called out, pretending like he had just woken up. "Am I in the cafe? And what's that smell?"

He dared to walk back to the kitchen, pretending to be just a regular adventurer. He wasn't in control of any systems or tasked with looking out for an entire dungeon's worth of inhabitants. No. Today, he was just a man standing in front of a woman cooking soup.

Her eyes widened when she saw him. "Oh, good, you're up."

"Sorry about that, I just—" He paused, not really sure what to say. Sorry he created a human avatar and didn't wait long enough to figure out how it worked? No, that was definitely not something a "normal adventurer" would say. "I, uh, just was really tired! Yeah, tired, that's it."

"Okay." She frowned but nodded. "I thought you might be sick, so I made soup with a healing buff."

Sick. That made way more sense. Come on, Dungeon, get it together.

"Wait, that soup is for me?" he asked, suddenly very interested in the vegetables swimming in the golden broth. "Can I try some?"

"Let's start with your name first." She crossed her arms, letting the soup bubble away without her attention. "You passed out before you could tell me."

Ummmm . . . what *was* his name?

How could he be so shortsighted to not even think of a name for himself? Every human had one, so if he was going to be a good human, he needed one too. The closest he'd come was the name she'd given him, but he couldn't exactly call himself Sweet Potato right to her face. That would definitely blow his cover, and he could already feel his face warming at the idea.

No, he needed a human name. An adventurer's name. Something worthy of his flames.

Hazel tilted her head, frowning at him again. "That was supposed to be an easy question, you know. What are you trying to hide?"

"Nothing." He shook his head, getting his long black hair in his eyes. Black was a color he knew well, giving him an idea. "My name's Cole."

He waited to see how she'd react, hoping the name met her approval, but she just kept staring at him. He started to squirm. She'd given him so many options when she named him, but this one was his own creation. Did she dislike it?

"Nice to meet you, Cole, and welcome to the Slime Serenitea Cafe." She grabbed a bowl and started spooning soup into it. "Now eat this, get better, and tell me what the hell you're doing here. Because if we're going to get along, you need to convince me that you're not a stalker first."

There was that word again: stalker. His nose crinkled, but he couldn't really refute it. He had spent day after day watching her, but it was his job! He watched everyone, not just Hazel. He had a feeling that wouldn't work in his favor though.

He needed to seem trustworthy, and the most trustworthy person he knew was Dave. He was a guide, so bringing him up should ease her worries a bit and give Cole a plausible reason for his so-called stalking.

"Dave sent me."

Hazel's frown deepened. "Really? Do you work with him?"

"Something like that. He can't leave the training meadow very often, so I check up on things for him." He winced as the lies kept tumbling out of his mouth. "Like this cafe. He was wondering if you were actually going to serve guests or not. He thought it was a kind of crazy idea, but you seem well suited to it."

There. A true answer. That would hopefully bring this back around to trust. He wished he could just tell her who he was, but that would cause all sorts of issues for her. He wanted to keep her life as simple and happy as possible, not complicate it.

"He would think I was crazy, wouldn't he?" She shrugged, handing Cole a bowl of soup. "Well, I haven't officially opened yet, but I made food for you. Does that count as serving guests?" She smiled, pouring a bowl of soup for herself as well. "Let's eat before it gets cold."

That smile tugging at her lips changed everything. Her eyes no longer frowned at him suspiciously and her body was more relaxed. Bringing up Dave really worked!

Cole wanted to leap with joy at her acceptance but didn't dare spill a single drop of soup. This soup was made by her beautiful hands to heal him when he was sick. He'd made so many things over the years, from traps to treasure chambers, but he'd never had anyone make something for him.

Something wet made his eyelashes heavy. He blinked. His eyes were tearing up. This human body was so strange, doing things of its own accord with no care for what the person wanted.

"Why don't we go sit down?" Hazel led him back into the front room of the cafe where there was a single table set up for dining. She eased herself into a creaky chair and motioned for him to do the same. "So, how's Dave doing anyway?"

"He's stressed out, like usual, but doing well." Or at least, he would be until he realized Cole had left his post. He winced, hoping the satyr wouldn't be too upset. "I'll make sure he comes to visit soon."

"Thanks."

Hazel dipped her spoon into the bowl, blowing on the soup. Cole mimicked her movements. Steam curled around his face as he finally swallowed his first spoonful. Warmth traveled from his spoon, down his throat, and spread through his entire body like he was being enveloped by something cozy and comforting. The broth was rich, full of flavors he didn't recognize, but it paired perfectly with the chunks of vegetables.

He couldn't describe it, but he wanted more. He ate spoonful after spoonful, eventually giving up and drinking straight from the bowl. This soup was absolutely delicious! How had he been missing something so wonderful this whole time? It was like the door to flavor had been opened and now no amount of coal or wood would satisfy his flames. He wanted food, real food, and as much of it as he could get.

His body seemed to relax, as if the soup was unraveling tension he didn't even know he had. If this was the power of a good meal, then he had done the adventurers a horrible disservice by making food tasteless. If only somebody had told him . . .

A soft laugh pulled him from his thoughts as Hazel smiled at him. "There's more, if you want."

"Absolutely." He rushed to pour more of the golden soup into his bowl. "Thank you for making such a fine meal. I will cherish it forever."

"Well, you look better at least," she mumbled, hiding behind her bowl. "That's good."

Her cheeks had a pretty pink hue to them. Was that . . . a blush?

That fluttering in his chest was back again. It always happened at the worst times! He busied himself with eating until his stomach felt nice and full. It was a satisfying feeling, one he hoped to feel again soon.

He sighed and set his empty bowl down. "That was wonderful." A fire slime started nudging his leg and he tried to shoo it away, but that only drew another slime his way. "What do you want?"

"They probably just want attention." Hazel stood up, moving toward the slimes. Her fingers hovered over one of their flames. "How can they be hot enough to cook soup one minute and then cool enough to touch the next?"

She set her hand on the slime's head, petting it cautiously, eyes full of wonder. Her entire face lit up when she was curious about something, and it was so much nicer seeing it in person like this.

Cole leaned forward, petting a slime as well. "You really love these slimes, don't you? What drew you to them?"

She sat cross-legged on the floor, drawing a slime into her lap as she pet him. "Well, the easy answer is that they're adorable, but I think there's more to it." Her voice was soft, like she was sharing a secret. "They're small and seem insignificant to most people here, but they're full of potential if you take the time to really see them. I think that's beautiful."

He frowned, studying the little wiggly balls of fire. He'd obviously overlooked how important good-tasting food was to humans, but had he also overlooked the monsters? He'd assigned them to specific floors to keep everyone fighting hard, but maybe there was more to them than just being sparring partners. Maybe there was more to everything than what he'd thought.

That made his head hurt, and he didn't like that feeling. He'd have to talk to Dave about it later, but for right now, he just wanted to enjoy the time he had with Hazel. He wasn't sure how often he'd be able to come visit like this. The dungeon couldn't run on autopilot for too long, not without chaos breaking out. Or worse, Dave catching him.

Hazel stood up, stretching her arms high to the ceiling as she let out a breath. "Okay, time to get back to work. I have a whole cart of goods outside. Mind helping me carry them in?"

"Do I mind?" He leapt out of his chair. "Not at all! Show me the way."

She shook her head, smiling. "You're an odd one, but I kind of like it."

A grin swept across his face so wide it hurt. She liked his oddness.

CHAPTER TWENTY-FOUR

Decorating the Cafe

We hauled the last of my purchases inside, filling the cafe with a strange array of treasure chests, crates, shields, empty potion bottles, and even a few clubs that would hopefully work as rolling pins. It all looked pretty ridiculous now that it was inside the cafe.

"What was I thinking when I bought all this?" I slumped onto a crate, nudging a shield on the floor. "Cafes are supposed to be warm and cozy, maybe even cute. Not full of weapons."

Cole hung a few mismatched lanterns from the ceiling, rearranging them to make a semblance of a pattern. "It's unique, that's all."

"Unique. That's a kind way to put it." I laughed, shaking my head as Matcha hopped inside a treasure chest full of fabric, wiggling like he was finding just the right spot to settle down. A small smile tugged at my lips. "I'm sure it'll work out. We're in a dungeon, after all. People can't expect it to be nice, not like a real cafe."

"What's that supposed to mean?" Cole frowned. "You don't think the dungeon's nice?"

"Of course not. It's a dungeon." I stacked a few crates into makeshift shelves, smiling as a fire slime got close enough to one of the lanterns to light it. The flame danced inside the glass. "I think he wants to help."

I nodded at the fire slime, but Cole seemed lost in thought, clutching a lantern to him without moving.

"You okay?" I asked.

"You really don't like the dungeon? But it's full of adventure and new experiences. You get to level up and feel accomplished. Isn't that what everyone wants?"

He tilted his head, his brow furrowed. It was the first time I'd seen such a serious look on his face, and I honestly wasn't sure how to respond. I picked up the fire slime, lifting the lil guy up to the lanterns Cole had already hung so he could light those too. The slime's flames brightened as he made a happy noise, slowly filling the room with the warm glow of dozens of lanterns.

"Well, the slimes are pretty wonderful," I admitted, "so I'm sure there's more to like in the dungeon. I just meant that it's not really, well, cafe-friendly, you know? You can't even buy a mixing bowl or a whisk." I motioned at the crates we'd stacked into makeshift tables. "Or furniture . . ."

The fire slime was warm and toasty in my arms but somehow didn't burn me. It was a pleasant feeling, like a hot water bottle or a heated blanket. My fingers slid through his flames without any harm. These slimes really were amazing.

Cole finally hung the lantern in his hands. "That's fair. So furniture would make you like the dungeon better?"

I laughed. "What's with this weird conversation? Sure, comfortable furniture would make it better. So would a decent rolling pin. It's like the dungeon is only focused on fighting and slaying monsters, so there's nothing left for a baker like me. I am grateful I got this cool class though. I just—"

The lid to Matcha's treasure chest slammed shut, making me jump. The slime squealed inside. I rushed to open it. Matcha's green eyes were wide in shock, and the fire slime in my arms hopped inside, nuzzling up to him.

"Are you okay?" I asked. "Maybe a treasure chest isn't a good place to get cozy."

Matcha leaned into the fire slime for a moment, then chirped and hopped out of the treasure chest. I pulled the fabric out and let it pool on the floor for him to curl inside safely, and he happily wiggled into his new makeshift bed.

Then I turned to the fire slime. "You're a really nice slime. I wonder what kind of food you like?" The slime shifted this way and that but obviously couldn't answer. I glanced back at Cole, since they seemed to like him so much. "Any ideas?"

"Something charred?" He shrugged. "I don't know. I don't feed the slimes."

I stood up with a sigh. "Nobody does and it's a real shame. They're so adorable." I crossed my arms, staring at the fire slime. He reminded me of something. I kept staring into those flames until the idea finally came. "Marshmallows!"

Images of golden marshmallows toasting over a fire came to mind. The sweet, sticky treat was exactly what I wanted, but how could I get marshmallows in a dungeon? I'd need sugar, vanilla, gelatin, and corn syrup. Better yet, if I had graham crackers, I could make s'mores with the chocolate I had. Now that sounded tasty.

I tapped my finger against my thigh, wishing I had all those ingredients. This was really going to become a problem as time went on. Sure, I'd managed to find enough ingredients to cook for me and the slimes, but running a cafe was a whole different story. I'd need all sorts of things, especially if I wanted to create any semblance of a consistent menu.

Wait. I forgot about the menu feature. I opened my cafe menu to find two empty slots for food and drinks that would give me bonus XP if I served them. I selected tea as the drink and hovered over the other spot. I had enough flour to bake bread now, so I could probably add grilled cheese to the menu, but I didn't have a good source of cheese without going to the safe zone all the time. It wasn't like I could grow cheese in the garden. If only I had cows or something . . .

"What's on your mind?" Cole asked as he finished hanging the last lantern. Warmth glowed around him, shining against his dark hair and clothes. "Maybe I can help."

"Just thinking about how to make a menu for the cafe when I don't have a good supply of ingredients. The market had some things, but not nearly as much as I'd like. Milk would be good, for example. Maybe I could make my own cheese and have the quality of it shoot up from being homemade. Rare grilled cheese would be pretty tasty, I bet!"

Cole grinned. "I bet it would, so let me help. There's a herd of goats on floor thirty-eight that have the best milk."

I whistled. "You've been to floor thirty-eight? You must be pretty high level, then, huh?" A bar appeared above his head full of question marks instead of an actual level. "Or maybe not?"

"Uh, yeah, I am." He smiled awkwardly, rubbing the back of his neck. "You just can't see a level if it's too much higher than yours."

"That makes sense, I guess, but I'm still not sure about the whole floor-thirty-eight thing . . ."

"Just think about it. You could bring a goat home with you!" His grin widened. "You've already befriended so many monsters. Why not a goat too? I'm friends with them already, so it'll be fine. They're practically pets."

Something about his excitement had me more concerned than reassured, but I did want milk. I could make so many things with it. Like pudding or maybe even ice cream if I could find a way to keep it cold!

I bit my lip, staring at him. "But how would I even get to floor thirty-eight? I'm only a level five, you know."

His face fell. "Oh, well, um, I can take you? We'll go from here to there, no need to risk the other floors." He leaned forward, lowering his voice. "Just don't tell anyone I did it. This will be our little secret."

Should I really trust a man I'd just met who apparently could skip almost thirty floors? Not only was his level a big question mark, but so were his motives.

"Why would you do that for me?"

"Because your food tastes amazing." He closed his eyes with a sigh. "That soup was wonderful. I want to try everything you make, but I can't do that if you don't have ingredients. Plus, you're always doing something interesting. It's kind of fun."

The look on his face was so pure and innocent, like he really did just want to eat my food and have a good time. I felt myself nodding even though it was a terrible idea. But if the goats were like pets, it couldn't be that bad, right?

"You're sure this is safe?" I asked.

"I'm sure. I won't let a single monster touch you, but take this key just in case. It'll get you back to the cafe in no time." He smiled as he handed me a black key that felt warm to the touch, like it had been sitting next to a fire.

I held the key close, oddly soothed by its warmth. "Okay, let's go befriend a goat, then."

Cole pulled a different key from his inventory, holding it in the air to summon a door. Matcha bounced against my leg, but I shook my head. If the goats were dangerous, then I didn't want the slimes anywhere near them.

"Sorry, not this time. Keep the cafe safe for me, okay?"

Matcha deflated with a big sigh. I bent to pet him.

"When I get back, we can harvest the tea and experiment with different kinds. How does that sound?"

He bounced faster, eyes bright.

"It's a deal, then. I'll be back as soon as I can."

Cole offered me his hand as a door opened to a new floor. "Ready?"

"As I'll ever be."

I paused just outside the door to glance back at the cozy cafe I was about to leave. These goats better be worth it.

CHAPTER TWENTY-FIVE

Adorable, but Terrifying

The slide between floors was extra twisty this time, going on so long that I lost the adrenaline rush of falling and was now just zooming along behind Cole, who couldn't stop giggling like he was having the time of his life. I shook my head. He really was an odd duck, but I might be even odder for following him.

While it would be great to have a reliable source of milk for the cafe, going to floor thirty-eight on what felt like a whim might be pushing it a bit too far. I didn't even have a plan, let alone any idea what to expect besides goats. Cole had just sounded so confident, but the longer this slide went on, the more worried I got, until a door opened and we shot out into the foggy air of a new dungeon floor.

My heart pounded as a rocky cliff side got closer and closer. I clamped down on the scream trying to escape. Last time this happened, a giant slime had broken my fall, but there was nothing but golden grass below us now.

Golden grass and goats.

Massive goats that got bigger and bigger as we fell. My chest tightened and I squeezed my eyes closed. I should have cooked a feast for goats this size instead of just the odds and ends I had in my inventory. What did goats even like to eat? Grass? Hay? If Cole hadn't actually tamed these goats like he'd implied, then this was all going to go horribly wrong . . .

"It's fine!" Cole called out as he took my hand, obviously misunderstanding my worry. "The Dungeon would never let you fall."

His skin was smooth against mine as he pulled me to him. Time seemed to slow down as I opened my eyes, seeing nothing but his innocent little grin. He was so full of life and excitement, like everything was a fun new experience. Time might not have been slowing for real, but our descent sure was as we gracefully landed in golden grass that came up to my waist.

"See? Nothing to worry about." He squeezed my hand before letting it go and turning to the biggest goat in the area, who towered over us by a good ten feet at least. "Hello, friend."

The goat's shaggy fur was a mix of dark brown and cream, with a shimmer of gold when it caught the light just right. His massive horns curled behind his head, etched with cracks of golden light that pulsed faintly, like a majestic power that was too much for the goat to fully contain. When he moved, the light seemed to ripple, casting faint patterns on the jagged cliff sides that stretched high to the sky around us.

The goat's eyes had that same golden glow, piercing and regal, as if daring us to challenge him. He stood motionless, an unyielding force of nature that was just waiting for us to make the first move.

I gulped, resisting the urge to step back. Or bow. This goat gave off the aura of a primal nature god, so falling to the ground and begging forgiveness for intruding on his domain felt like the appropriate answer here.

Too bad Cole was already rushing toward him with a big goofy smile on his face. "How have you been? It's been ages since we had a good chat."

The goat lowered his head, eyes narrowing as his hooves scraped big ruts in the ground.

This time I did back up. No milk was worth facing off against that beast at my low level of five. "Maybe we should go . . ."

"No way, we haven't even gotten the milk yet." Cole scoffed. "Heliandor and I go way back, it's fine."

Cole seemed nice enough, but I'd just met him. And this whole plan, if you could even call it that, seemed pretty foolhardy. I glanced at his level, once again seeing the *???* that gave me no information at all. The goat's level shone bright.

[Solhorn Goat: Level 40]

Something bumped against my leg, and I jerked away, yelping. A tiny goat gnawed on my apron, digging around in the pockets like they were full of treats. The goat pulled out a sprig of thyme, chewing it before bleating softly.

This had to be fate: We'd come here for a goat, and within moments, one had literally bumped right into me. Her fur was light yellow, as if it hadn't grown into the warm golden-brown hues of the other goats yet. I carefully patted her on the head, avoiding the adorably tiny horns poking out of her fur.

"Hello there," I whispered, "aren't you a sweet little goat?" She bumped against my leg again, chewing on my apron like it would be just as tasty as the thyme. I stuffed my hands in my pockets, but they were empty. "Sorry, that's all I had."

As the little goat hunted for more treats, the eerie bleating of dozens of other goats carried on the wind like a song coming from all directions. The cliffs loomed over me with glints of golden eyes sparking in their shadows. This one little goat was fine, but dozens of others?

Cole was still chatting with the one he'd called Heliandor. "So, after hearing all that, you see why I need to borrow a goat, right? Her food is just amazing! And I promise we'll take good care of any goat you give us."

Could Heliandor actually understand Cole? If it was as easy as asking for a milking goat, then there was no reason to worry. Except, the giant Solhorn was lowering his head and rushing forward. If he did understand, his answer was obviously no.

"Get out of there!" I shouted, but it was too late.

Heliandor headbutted Cole with those terrifying horns of his. I gasped as Cole flew through the air, collapsing in the tall grass.

I wanted to rush to check on him, but my legs were shaking as the Solhorn turned his golden gaze on me. Power rolled off the goat in waves, making me shiver as the others climbed down the rocks to join their master.

"I'm fine!" Cole shouted as he sat up, brushing grass off his clothes like getting headbutted by a goat god monster meant nothing to him. "Huh, maybe he doesn't recognize me. I mean, I guess I do look a bit different, but still. How could he do that?"

"Is that really important right now?" I let out a breath, almost collapsing on the ground myself. "You idiot, let's go back to the cafe and forget this whole plan. That goat obviously doesn't think you're friends."

Cole tilted his head, studying the monstrous Solhorn. "Maybe that's just how goats say hello?"

The beast pawed the ground again, looking like he was getting ready to headbutt Cole a second time since the first obviously hadn't left enough of an impression. Cole's curiosity was going to get him killed. I forced my legs to move, hurrying over to the fool.

"That is not how goats say hello. It's how they say goodbye." I grabbed his arm, hauling him up. "Take the hint and let's get out of here."

Cole's eyes widened. "You speak goat?"

I sighed, pushing him to get moving. "Yup, and I'll tell you all about it once we're back in the cafe."

"But your milk . . ."

"Screw the milk. We'll come back later."

To run a cafe properly, I needed a steady source of ingredients. Yes, I wanted milk to make cheese and pudding and all sorts of other things, but that wasn't worth anyone's life. I took a deep breath, resigning myself to whatever ingredients I could get from the safe zone.

"If you're sure." Cole glanced back at the Solhorn with sad eyes. "Until next time, old friend."

The Solhorn made a noise that sounded an awful lot like a snort, then went back to grazing on the tall, golden grass as if we'd never been there. I didn't like giving up on something so important, but coming back later was a valid plan. I'd figure out what food goats loved the most and make some glorious treats that would be sure to impress the Solhorns. It was the only option we had right now . . . right?

Except, the little goat from earlier was following me, practically begging for me to take her with us. It would be so easy to just open a door and flee before that monster even knew what we were doing.

Memories of the crispy cluckers chasing me down after their chick was gobbled up by Matcha came to mind. Messing with baby monsters was probably a terrible idea.

"I'm sorry, but you can't come with us," I said softly. "I don't want to be part of a kidnapping. Not with that big guy looking all terrifying."

The little goat bleated at me, sniffing my hands like the scent of herbs was still on them. She hopped, bouncing in such a similar way to the slimes that my good judgement started fading. The goat was only level ten, which was perfectly acceptable for my floor . . .

"Okay, fine, but we have to be quick about it." I glanced at Cole. "Think you can distract him for a bit?"

Cole nodded. "Definitely. Somebody's gotta remind Heliandor who's the boss around here."

I bit my lip. No way was Cole the boss of that goat or any other monster. Even the slimes didn't listen to him. I pulled the key he'd given me from my inventory. It was still warm somehow. I smiled, grasping it tight. Time to go home. The little goat bumped the back of my legs, urging me to go through with this crazy new plan.

I pet her fur softly, but froze when a high-pitched bleat shook the air, rumbling the ground so much I almost fell over. Heliandor charged, racing toward us faster than I could summon a door. Did he know I was about to take a goat home with me? I dropped my hand, backing away.

"I'm not kidnapping her, I swear! She's all yours!" I dropped the key in shock, losing it in the tall grass. The little goat just kept hopping next to me, bleating back at Heliandor as if egging him on. "Hey! I gave you herbs!"

"Time to prove my friendship." Cole pulled me behind him, cracking his knuckles as he stood firm in front of the charging monster. "Heliandor! Sit!"

I gaped at him. "Sit? Seriously?"

Every goat in the area besides Heliandor plopped down on their backside with a soft thud. I blinked, staring at the ridiculous sight of so many goats sitting in the grass. The little one beside me was too short to even see over the swaying golden fronds.

Huh, so Cole really was a friend of the goats. I had not seen that coming.

Heliandor bellowed, his voice shaking the very air as the golden glow spilled out of his horns like sunlight. The light got brighter and brighter, until I had no choice but to squeeze my eyes shut.

"Okay, maybe we're not friends," Cole muttered darkly. "Hazel, go back to the cafe without me. I'll be there as soon as I can."

"I can't just—"

"Go!"

I fumbled for the key in the grass, accidentally grabbing the little goat's hooves. "Sorry."

When I finally found the key, I stumbled up to summon a door, but the light was searing my eyelids and tears were welling up. I brushed them away, stumbling as I moved, trying to escape the light just for a moment. It felt like I was moving in circles though, getting farther and farther away from Cole.

"Be careful!" he shouted right before my foot met open air and the tall grass disappeared. Air whooshed around me as I fell off the very cliffs the goats had been climbing on earlier.

Damn goats. Adorable, but terrifying.

This probably would have gone better if I'd brought cookies.

CHAPTER TWENTY-SIX

Back to the Beginning

Breathing was easier than I'd expected after dying. I even felt good too, like my body was being pillowed by soft grass. A familiar smoky campfire scent filled the air. My eyes snapped open. I was in a small clearing surrounded by fog on three sides and a mountain on the other. A table full of very familiar-looking weapons stood nearby, along with monster pens.

This was the starting area!

I jerked up. How did I get here? The last thing I remembered was that goat searching my pockets for treats. Wait, no, something came after that. I think I fell . . . off a cliff?

"Seriously, Hazel? Floor *thirty-eight*?" Dave's irritation was obvious even from across the clearing. I flopped back onto the grass, closing my eyes as he walked closer. "You're only level five. How'd you even get to that floor?"

"Some weird guy took me." I winced and put a hand over my eyes, the feeling of falling off that cliff still fresh in my mind. "Did I die?"

"Almost, but you were transported back here the moment *before* you would have hit the ground." The fabric of Dave's clothes rustled as he knelt by my side. "Do you think that maybe it's time to take this dungeon seriously? I'll admit, I've been impressed by how far you've gotten with cookies and kindness, but you can't win over every monster like that. You'll need to fight if you really want to get out of the dungeon."

I was pretty confident in the baking-my-way-through-the-dungeon plan a few hours ago, but Heliandor's power had been overwhelming. How could I ever win over a monster like that with food?

Dave patted my shoulder. "Let's start with your stats and use the time we've got to make a plan."

"Wait, I can't just go back to the cafe?" I opened my eyes, sitting up so quickly that I almost bumped into him. "How long am I stuck here?"

"You're not *stuck* here," Dave snapped, standing up to pace. "Why do adventurers always say that when I'm offering to help them? They die, I try to help them not die again, and they complain. Every. Single. Time. Why do I even bother?"

Oof. Looked like I hit a nerve there. Going through my stats wasn't a terrible idea, especially if he could give me some pointers.

"Sorry, Dave. I'd love any help you can give me." I sat cross-legged and opened my menu. "Where do you want to start?"

He scratched his horns, studying me. After I sat patiently for a while, he sighed. "Fine, show me your stat screen."

"And how do I do that? I thought only I could see my menu."

"Just think about showing it to me and I'll see it." Dave sat down next to me as I did just that, and his eyes skimmed my stats.

[Culinary Mage: Level 5]

[Agility: 1]

[Charisma: 3]

[Endurance: 3]

[Intelligence: 1]

[Strength: 1]

[Available Stat Points: 2]

"Well, you're okay on endurance, but what's with the single points in strength and agility?" Dave laughed, eying me sideways. "No wonder you lost to a baby goat."

I crossed my arms. "I did not lose to a goat. I lost to a cliff."

"Riiiight. You know what would help with that?" Dave raised an eyebrow. "Agility."

"I do have some extra stat points, but it feels like a waste. Agility won't really help my baking."

Dave tapped his thigh, looking lost in thought. "Haven't you ever dropped a tray of cookies before? Or bumped against a hot stove and burned yourself?"

"Wait, agility can fix my clumsiness? Sold." I added one of my points to agility without a second thought.

He laughed. "And what about strength? I bet those big bags of flour get annoying to carry sometimes."

"True, but shouldn't I put more into endurance or charisma?"

"Charisma's nice," he said slowly, "but do you even know how to use it?"

"Haven't I been charming you this whole time?"

Dave snorted. "Hardly. You've actually been giving me a headache since you got here."

"Fine, then I'll use some charisma now." I cleared my throat and sat up straighter. "Oh, wise and wonderful Dave, please give me more stat points so I can level everything you tell me to all at once."

"Yeah, I'm not feeling it." He might have said that, but he was smiling just a bit. "Charisma isn't something you can force. Sure, the stat helps, but it's more like it boosts your sincerity. Those moments where people would be more likely to side with you in the first place become stronger. It's almost like people can feel your intentions, your heart."

"Is that how I managed to win over tough monsters even with lower-level food? Like the slime boss?"

He nodded. "The monster could probably sense your desire to protect it."

"Well, that's awesome. I should put even more into charisma, then."

"Wait!" He grabbed my arm before I could touch anything. "Honestly, you really should have at least a little bit of strength. As is, you'd be a goner if a monster sneezed on you."

I laughed. "Well, thankfully that hasn't happened yet, but I see your point. I'll up my strength for now and work on my charisma later. You know, you're actually a pretty good teacher. I'm sorry so many people treat you like a hassle or a tutorial they want to skip over. You deserve better than that."

He dropped his hands, eyes wide. "Thank you. That's so kind—wait, no, you're trying to use charisma right now, aren't you?"

"Guilty." I held my hands up, grinning. "This training thing is kind of fun. I appreciate your help."

Dave shook his head, sighing. "At least you're a fast learner. I don't agree with your nonviolent approach, but if you're determined to keep doing it, try to balance your stats a bit better. That way you won't be completely useless if you need to run away or defend yourself."

"Yes, sir." I mock saluted. "I'll be more careful, honestly. Anything else we should go over?"

"Not right now, no. Just keep working hard and leveling up." He paused. "Actually, let's go back to the whole goat fiasco. You said a strange adventurer brought you to floor thirty-eight? Skipping that many floors shouldn't be possible."

I shrugged. "He just opened a door and poof, we were there. I think you know him, actually. He said he works with you. His name's Cole."

Dave's eyebrows shot up. "I've never heard of him before."

"Long black hair, dark clothes, crazy high level." I tilted my head. "I actually couldn't see his level, now that I think about it. It was just question marks."

"Was he, by any chance, super excited to try your cooking?" Dave asked, and sighed when I nodded, muttering something about a "damn core." "I think I know who you're talking about, but I didn't think he'd ever be quite that irresponsible. I'm really sorry he put you in harm's way."

"I don't think he meant to. He seemed to think the Solhorns would be friendly toward him, but then Heliandor headbutted him into a bush and that all kind of fell apart."

Dave barked out a laugh, then slapped a hand over his mouth. "Sorry, that image is just too hilarious. A goat headbutted him?"

"Yup, he flew right through the air too, but got back up like it was nothing."

"I guess he's already been punished, then," Dave said, still laughing. "But why don't we head back to your cafe so I can have a little chat with him anyway?"

I bit my lip, suddenly remembering that Cole hadn't wanted me to tell Dave about him stopping by. "Uh, sure, but aren't you pretty busy?"

"You're the one who said I should visit again sometime . . ." His gaze dropped to the ground. "Unless you were just being polite when you offered that. Or maybe trying to use me?"

"Of course not!" Man, what kind of life did this satyr live? If that's how people usually treated him, then I'd have to show him what actual kindness looked like. Cole would understand. "Okay, let's go. I'll make you the best sandwich ever. One worthy of such a good teacher."

"Thank you." His voice was soft and heartfelt, as if nobody had ever offered him something like that before. It made my heart hurt.

"Why do you keep working here if nobody seems to appreciate you?"

His hands clenched. I'd asked the question without really thinking about it, but it was probably something I had no business asking. I'd caused nothing but trouble for him, so what gave me the right to dig into his personal life?

"Never mind. I'm sure everyone's worried about me, so we should get back." I pulled out the key Cole had given me and summoned a door, looping my arm through Dave's. "You're welcome to stay as long as you want."

His eyes widened as I tugged him through the door. If my cafe could give him even a little bit of joy, then I'd gladly bake all the food he wanted. He'd given me good advice, and I needed to take it seriously. I couldn't keep hoping I'd get out of here on sheer optimism. I had to focus and level up. Make that cafe of mine a true training ground to improve my skills so that one day I'd be strong enough to befriend that Solhorn goat and get out of here.

Plus, the slimes would love all the treats I'd have to bake in the name of training. Things were about to get a whole lot tastier.

CHAPTER TWENTY-SEVEN

Good Company

I stepped out of the dungeon corridor and walked straight into my cafe, as if the key had opened up the front door. The key didn't disappear either, like all the others I'd seen had. That was weird but also really handy. I glanced around the cafe, expecting to be welcomed by happy slimes, all jumping around to show how much they missed me.

Except, all I saw was the new furniture we'd set up. The mismatched lanterns shone brightly from the ceiling, and the new stools made out of crates were pulled out as if somebody was about to sit in them, but nobody was here. Not a single slime. Anywhere.

How strange . . .

Dave joined me, closing the door behind him. "Wow, this is a far cry from that little shack you had last time."

It wasn't really that impressive yet, but it was a huge improvement from that cramped shack I'd cooked dinner for him in so long ago. My heart warmed as I looked around at all the improvements. The cafe not only had tables and chairs now, but a real dining room and a kitchen too. It wasn't perfect, but it was coming together, and it would just keep getting better as time went on.

I turned to Dave with a smile. "Welcome to the Slime Serenitea Cafe."

Minus the slimes, apparently. I glanced out the window. In the corner of the property, a man was slumped against the wall, slimes plopped all over him like a squishy blanket. His long black hair was easily recognizable: Cole. What was he doing out there?

"Give me a minute, Dave, I'll be right back."

The satyr nodded, glancing out the window as I walked outside. Fire slimes were piled in Cole's lap, flames glowing brightly, nudging him. Matcha sat nearby with a cup of tea on his head, spilling drops of it every time his little slime body wiggled. He slurped them up before offering Cole the cup again. Even a few dirt slimes had joined the party, offering him their best potatoes.

With all those slimes, Cole should have been grinning and having the time of his life, but his face was empty. Dejected.

"Everything okay?" I asked. "Looks like the slimes are on cheer-up duty."

His eyes widened. "You're back!"

"Of course I'm back." I laughed softly. "This is my cafe. Did you think a little cliff was going to stop me from coming back to it?"

Those dark eyes of his stared at me, roving over my entire body. I squirmed awkwardly, leaning down to take the cup of tea from Matcha. It was empty by this point, so I would need to make some more. The little slime chirped, bumping into my hand.

I picked Matcha up and held him close. "Sorry I was gone so long, but I'm home now. Do you want some tea?"

Matcha wiggled in my arms, making a bubbly noise only a slime could make. I smiled. This was where I wanted to be right now. Leveling up with the best companions I knew: the slimes. I turned to go heat up some water, but Cole grabbed my hand. He stood up, pulling me into a fierce hug that I was entirely unprepared for. Fire slimes tumbled all over from his abrupt movement, and Matcha squeaked, squishing between us.

"Hey!" I called out, but I could feel Cole trembling for some reason. I patted his back, not really sure what to do here. "Honestly, are you okay?"

"I should be asking you that." His voice was low next to my ear, raw and full of emotion. "I never should have taken you to that floor without knowing I could keep you safe. I thought I was stronger than that. I thought I could—"

"Stop." I pulled away, looking him in the eyes. "This wasn't your fault. I'm the one who agreed to go, and I'm the one who tried to kidnap a baby goat. I'm also the one clumsy enough to fall off a cliff, but hey, all's well that ends well, right?"

"I guess . . . I just never want to put you in danger again."

"Well, next time I need ingredients, we'll go to a lower-level floor, then." I grinned. "Or I'll level up really fast and take on that monster goat again!

Yeah, we're definitely doing that one day. That baby goat wanted to come back here, and I can't let her down, can I?"

"Next time?" Cole's voice was full of hope and his eyes were brighter. "Yeah, next time we'll do better."

"Exactly. That's what this dungeon is all about, right? Trying, failing, leveling up, and doing better next time."

Or at least, that's what it seemed like. What else was the point of all the floors getting stronger as you went and us not actually dying? It had to be so we could get stronger. But why? I stroked Matcha, enjoying the warmth his new tea evolution possessed. He was like a hot-water bottle, cozy and comforting. We'd figure this out, but right now I had some tea to make.

"Come inside, I'll make tea."

Cole nodded, following me into the cafe with a trail of fire slimes bouncing behind him like little ducks. They really were attached to him, and if the slimes trusted him, then he had to be a decent guy. Plus, he waited for me here after I fell. Knowing there was somebody worried about me, somebody who would keep the slimes company until I got back, felt really good. Like I had people I could rely on. First Fiona, and now him. I hadn't known them long, but it felt like we'd formed bonds already.

Bonds of friendship.

I blinked as my eyes got a bit misty. This cafe made all that possible, and I was so grateful that the dungeon had set up a system for it. I nodded at Dave as I passed him on my way to the kitchen, where I filled the kettle up with water so we could have tea. A fire slime followed me into the kitchen and hopped into the stove with excitement, like he couldn't wait to help me cook again. These slimes were so sweet. I had no idea how people thought they were monsters.

"Dave?" Cole's voice sounded strangled. "What are you doing here?"

"Oh, just getting a sandwich." His voice was teasing, with a hint of something . . . else. "The real question is what are *you* doing here?"

I leaned out of the kitchen to find them both staring at each other—actually, *glaring* described it better—with Dave tapping a hoof on the floor. Cole sighed, glancing away like he'd lost some kind of silent battle.

"What's going on out here?" I asked. "You two are *friends*, right?"

Cole nodded. "Good friends, yes."

"Best friends," Dave said. "Right, Cole? The kind of friends who would never leave important work undone while they rushed off on their own to eat tasty food?"

So *that's* why he had wanted me to keep his visit a secret. I shook my head at him. "Really? You skipped out on work to come here? I thought Dave sent you here to check on me."

"Did I do that?" Dave frowned. "Sounds like me, but I don't recall . . ."

"Fine, I was too excited to wait." Cole gave him an *are-you-happy-now?* look. "Her food just sounded so good! Cookies! And grilled cheese! Oh, man, Dave, you should have tried the soup she made. It was glorious. The way it warmed me up was magical."

My face warmed at that, but thankfully I heard the water bubbling. Time to make that tea. I didn't have many leaves left, so hopefully the tea I'd planted earlier had grown and matured by now. I'd never harvested it before, but maybe the dirt slimes could help. Matcha was a bottomless pit for tea, so I couldn't really go without it.

After a few minutes, the water was a nice golden-tan color. I poured two cups and added the rest to the pot I'd dubbed Matcha's cup, carrying them all on a flattened-out shield. I placed each cup carefully on the table and set Matcha's pot on the floor. The little tea slime hopped in, barely making a splash, while the other two sat down. It was nice having people here at the table ready to eat.

[Quest Completed: Serve 10 Cups of Tea]

[Reward: Tea-Drying Screens and Racks]

Now that sounded useful. Exactly what I needed if I was going to start harvesting that tea outside.

[New Quest: Serve 25 Cups of Tea]

"Maybe we should think of this like a dry run for opening the cafe," I said. "You can be the customers and I'll be your hostess. What would you like to order today?"

I pressed the menu option under the cafe tab, grinning as two physical menus floated out of my system screens just like the cookbook had. There were only two items on the menus, but it was still really cool to see.

Dave read them and laughed. "I guess I'll have the grilled cheese, then."

"Me too." Cole turned the menu this way and that, inspecting it from every angle. "This is pretty cool. Your cafe has a lot of nice features."

Dave rolled his eyes. "Yeah, the dungeon must just love her, huh?"

Cole choked on his tea while Dave sat there looking smug for some reason. There was obviously more going on there, but I wasn't about to pry. A cafe should be a warm and welcoming place, not an interrogation. I went back to the kitchen and put a pan on the stove.

I leaned down to see if the fire slime was still inside the stove. "Well, hello there. Mind helping me cook again?"

The fire slime chirped his agreement and started wiggling as his flames rose, dancing in the stove. They blazed brighter and brighter until I had to look away.

"Maybe a little less flame? I don't want to melt the pan."

The slime made a noise that sounded like laughter and lowered his flames to a perfect temperature. This really was the best cafe ever. I sliced up a loaf of bread, spreading beautiful golden butter evenly across it. A grilled cheese was simple, but it still deserved all the love and attention that a more complex meal required. The butter should reach the edges of the bread, leaving no part unbuttered. Then the cheese. Using multiple kinds was best, but all I had was cheddar, so that would have to do. I cut it thinly, adding layers mixed in with herbs and thin slices of tomato to spice things up a bit.

I set two slices of bread in the pan, enjoying the sizzle of the butter hitting the heat. Then I layered everything else on top so the cheese could start melting. After a few minutes, the nutty smell of cooked butter filled the room. I flipped both sandwiches over and waited, pressing down slightly for even cooking. The cheese started oozing out, perfectly melty.

When I took the grilled cheeses out of the pan, the fire slime opened his mouth wide, about to gobble them up.

"Wait! These are for our guests, but I promise I'll make you all the tasty food you want after we serve them. Does that sound good?"

The slime tilted his body back and forth, but then nodded. Excellent. I'd really need to start keeping slime treats on hand if the fire slimes were going to be helping me cook every day. It was too cruel for them not to get tasty food along with the guests. I brought the sandwiches out to the table, and Cole's eyes lit up as he dug into his immediately, probably burning his mouth on that cheese.

He just kept eating though, smiling and mumbling around the food. "It's so good!"

Dave was more cautious. "It does *smell* good, but does it really taste that much better than my normal grilled cheese?"

"You've already had my food, so you know it'll be awesome." I nudged the plate closer to him. "Or did you forget?"

"Of course not . . ." He took a tiny bite, chewing it thoroughly. Then he stared at me.

"Well, do you like it?" I asked slowly. I wasn't looking for praise, but I did want him to enjoy it. Maybe the tomatoes were too much. I should have kept it simple. "Sorry, I can make another if you want."

"No, no need for that."

He took another bite and another, his floppy goat ears twitching. It reminded me so much of the goats from earlier that I couldn't help but smile. I moved back into the kitchen, loving all the happy little noises they were making as they enjoyed their grilled cheeses. This was what I wanted to do for as long as I could. Cook food that made people happy, because knowing they were happy made me happy too.

Now for the slimes. I made another grilled cheese and divided it between the slimes, giving the biggest portion to the fire slime who'd helped me cook. Sparks danced around him like fireworks as he wiggled with happiness.

"I like your spark. What do you think about that for a name?"

The slime wiggled even more, lighting up the stove with the warmth only a fire slime could bring.

"Okay, Spark it is, then." I grinned and started making another sandwich for him. He deserved it. "Thanks for helping me cook."

But if I was going to be cooking multiple meals at once, I really needed a bigger oven. I opened my quest menu to check on the progress of that. I'd made food for a bunch of adventurers in the safe zone along with Dave and Cole, so hopefully I'd be pretty close to done with that serve-twenty-five-customers part.

[Build a New Oven: 0/25 Customers Served, 0/25 Clay, 0/25 Stone]

My brow furrowed. Zero of twenty-five? "Hey, Sweet Potato?"

Something thunked in the other room, and somebody started coughing like they were choking on their sandwich. I glanced into the cafe's dining area, but they were both sipping tea and smiling at me like nothing had happened. Strange, but okay. Actually, I could ask Dave about this, except he was here on a break. I should honor that and let him relax for once.

"Why does my quest say I didn't serve any customers?" I asked the system. "I've served at least a dozen people since I picked up that quest."

[People are not the same as customers. A customer is defined as one that purchases a commodity or service.]

"Seriously? I guess I'll have to start charging people, then . . ."

[Correct.]

Something else caught my eye in my menus: My level bar was almost empty. "Did I lose XP when I fell off the cliff?"

[Affirmative. An adventurer's XP resets back to 0 for the level they're on and must be regained.]

"Is that the price of teleporting me to the starting zone? Couldn't I just pay you in cookies or something?"

[No. XP must be lost. Cookies are not a proper form of currency.]

"I was kidding." I frowned, staring at that message. "Is everything okay? You seem a bit stiffer than usual."

[Running System Diagnostics]

[Trap Stability: 92%]

[Loot Stability: 96%]

[NPC Performance: Stable]

[Monster Count: 9,875]

[Adventurer Count: 7,589]

[All systems are running smoothly.]

My eyebrows rose. "There are that many people here? How have I only seen a few hundred?"

[The dungeon has many floors.]

I guess that made sense since all the adventurers were probably spread out throughout the dungeon. That was really good to know, but it felt a bit odd that the system had run a diagnostic right in front of me like that. Usually, it would have just said it was fine and moved on. Was the dungeon glitching out? That didn't sound good . . .

"Hazel?" Cole asked, pulling me out of my thoughts. "Any chance you have some tea left?"

"Just a minute." I put some more water in the kettle and decided to focus on what was right in front of me: this cafe and my customers. When I brought the tea out to them, I carefully poured it into their cups and joined them at the table. "So, what did you think?"

"It was amazing!" Cole grinned. "Best sandwich I've ever had."

Dave nodded. "It was pretty tasty, actually. I might need to come back for more."

"I'm happy to hear that." I smiled, sipping my own mug of tea. "Thanks for doing this dry run with me. I feel a lot better about opening the cafe now."

"Then we should get going." Dave started getting out of his chair, but Cole yanked him back down. "What?"

"Aren't you forgetting something?" He stared at the satyr pointedly. "About . . . you know what?"

Dave's mouth formed a silent O, and then he handed me a few coins. "Sorry about that. Your food is well worth the money. It was delicious."

Cole followed suit and handed me a few coins as well. I checked my quest, and it had updated to two customers served!

"Thank you." I smiled at them and put the coins away. "You just helped me figure out a new quest of mine. I really appreciate it."

"Anytime. Do you need help cleaning up?" Cole asked.

"Not a chance." Dave grabbed Cole by the collar. "You promised to catch up on all that work you left behind, remember?"

Cole's shoulders slumped. "Yeah, I remember."

"You two seem like good friends," I said with a laugh. "Come back soon, okay?"

Dave nodded, but Cole's eyes seemed to darken. Was he not intending to come back? Something about that didn't sit right with me. He was a little strange, but also sweet and caring too.

"We're going to befriend those goats once I level up more, right?" I prompted, hoping he'd take the bait. "And gather more ingredients sometime?"

His lips tugged into a smile. "Of course. I'll help you however I can."

"Until next time, then." I waved at the both of them as they left the cafe.

I leaned against the door as it closed behind them. The cafe hadn't been this empty in a while. I picked up Matcha. "Let's go bake something sweet, okay?"

Matcha nodded, nuzzling closer to me as we made our way into the kitchen. This cafe was about to become my training grounds, full of amazing food and hopefully great people too. There was nothing holding me back, not as long as I had all these slimes to help me and a garden full of ingredients. Time to get to work!

CHAPTER TWENTY-EIGHT

Fiona's Blacksmithing Adventure Part 2

No matter how many times Fiona tried, the metal just wouldn't keep its shape. Soot and sweat coated her skin, and her entire body felt the exhaustion of working at this for days on end. It was so different than fighting monsters. She enjoyed it but had also never felt so frustrated in her life. Every time she got close to making something wonderful, it fell apart like the metal was mocking her.

She tossed another hunk of twisted and burnt metal on the scrap pile. It had grown taller and taller each day, a constant reminder of her failures. She'd owe Brennic quite a bit for all the wasted metal. Maybe it was time to give up . . .

"Drink." Brennic shoved a glass of water in her hands and pinned her with a stare she'd come to know very well.

"I know, I know. Part of being a blacksmith is taking care of myself." She drank deeply, gulping the cool water down. "You're pretty good at taking care of people for a loner like you. Maybe you should get a pet. Hazel loves her slimes, but I think you're more of a cat guy."

He grunted something incomprehensible and started moving to his side of the shop to work on the day's projects.

"Wait." She grabbed his arm, and the heat of him sank into her skin like a warm campfire. "I know I'm wasting a lot of good metal, and I know I don't have a blacksmith class. But *you* do." She stared into those ever-watchful eyes of his, silently pleading with him. "Help me."

They stood like that for a while until he lifted his hand to her cheek with a sigh. "You know I can't. My class only lets me make weapons."

"I know you tried to make a pan while I was taking a break earlier." She held her hand up when he tried to interrupt. "Don't even try to deny it. It was a disaster just like mine. But what if we worked together? I've managed to get the shapes right, but the system knows I don't have the right class, so it fails. If I help shape it while you add the final touches, then maybe we can make it work."

A soft smile tugged at his lips. "Okay, let's do this. Together."

Brennic added another piece of metal to the forge, standing so close she could feel the heat of him. Or maybe that was something else welling up inside her. She was starting to care a little too much about that grumpy blacksmith after spending all this time here. She brushed her fingers over her cheek, feeling the lingering heat from his hand. He turned around, carrying the hot metal to the anvil for them to work on. She dropped her hand with an awkward shake of her head.

She needed to focus on this project.

They took turns hammering the metal into shape, working in beautiful harmony like they'd been doing it for years. When the metal started cooling, Brennic cupped his hands around it to add warmth without having to take it back to the forge. And when he struggled with the shape, she took over to mold that warm metal into exactly what they needed.

They were the perfect team, but the final touches were always when her projects failed, so Brennic would have to finish the pan himself. Hopefully his blacksmithing class would kick in and the metal would accept him. She held her breath while he did all the same steps as her, heating and cooling it slowly to take the stress out of the metal.

And the pan . . . held its shape!

"We did it!" Fiona held her fists up in joy, but Brennic was staring at something in his menus, his eyes wide. "What's wrong?"

"Nothing's wrong at all. I got a new skill that lets me craft more than weapons." He smiled wider than she'd ever seen and pulled her into a big bear hug, spinning her around the forge with newfound joy. When he set her back on the ground, his hands lingered on her waist. "This is all thanks to you for being so damn stubborn and convincing me this was possible. Thank you, Fiona. I couldn't have done this without you."

Him getting a new skill was amazing, but it was also more than a little frustrating. She was the one who'd been working herself to the bone, and yet the system had completely ignored her. They both should have gotten skills, not just Brennic.

"I'm so happy for you." She tried to smile, but hot tears rolled down her cheeks. She wiped them away as fast as she could, but he'd already seen them. "Sorry. I really am glad that you got a new skill, but how could the system just ignore me and my efforts? All that work and I've got nothing to show for it."

"You've got a pie pan." He motioned at the pan she'd fought so hard to make.

She choked out a laugh. "Any pie Hazel makes in that will taste like bitter defeat. I know you're the only reason it worked."

His eyes softened. "I'm sorry the system won't let you do what you were obviously born to do. You've got the heart of a blacksmith, and I can see that plain as day."

She swallowed hard and moved away from him. Hearing those words would have been wonderful yesterday, but now they stung a bit too much. Even if she had the heart of a smith, she didn't have the class, and apparently that was all that mattered here. She should stop fooling herself and get back to what she did well: fighting monsters.

"Thanks for letting me work with you the past few days." She took a deep breath and started gathering all the scrap metal she'd accumulated. "Let me just toss this out, and then I'll be out of your hair. I'd be grateful if you could make a few cookie sheets and other pans for Hazel though."

"You don't want anything for yourself?"

She scrubbed at the tears still falling down her cheeks and shook her head. "I don't need anything. Your help was more than enough."

His sigh was almost drowned out by the sound of his hammering, but she still heard it and felt horrible. All she had to do was be happy for him, but she'd started crying instead. Honestly, what was wrong with her? He'd been so kind, letting her use all this metal to work on a doomed project. One day she'd thank him properly, but it hurt too much right now. All she could do was clean up the shop, removing all trace of her presence there. It was for the best, no matter how much she'd enjoyed the past few days.

She wasn't a blacksmith, and she never could be.

Once she was done cleaning, she hid in the back room on the cot he'd let her use. The pillows and blankets had smelled like him that first night, smoky and warm. She'd slept so soundly, better than she ever had in the dungeon. Everything about this place felt right, like she was meant to be there. So why did the system refuse to let her be who she wanted to be?

She pulled her knees to her chest, curling up into a ball of anguish while Brennic worked hard on the pans she'd asked for. The *ting ting clang* of his hammer was soothing, and eventually her tears stopped. Everything would be all right. She was still a good fighter and would get out of here in no time if she kept focusing on leveling up. She had to believe that.

When the sound of his hammer eventually quieted, she held her head high and walked back into the forge.

"Thanks for everything, Brennic." She handed him enough coins to cover all the metal she'd wasted and the pans too, but he just shook his head.

"You helped me grow as a blacksmith, and that's worth every piece of scrap it took." He glanced away, staring into the forge for long enough that Fiona almost took it as a cue to leave until he shoved something at her. "Take this. You deserve something for all your hard work too."

She stared at the metal figurine in her hands. It was shaped like a cat and it looked like it was made from scrap metal. *Her* scrap metal, probably. A smile tugged at her lips as she glanced up at him. "You made a cat for me, huh?"

"You said I needed a pet," he mumbled. "Figured I'd make a metal one. That's my first try. I know it's not perfect, but . . ." His gaze finally met hers, warm and bright. "I didn't want you to forget about me once you leave."

Her heart pounded in her chest as she gripped the cat figurine tight. That man just kept surprising her in all the best ways. She stood on her tiptoes and kissed him on the cheek. "I don't need a scrappy little cat to remember you, and this isn't the last you'll be seeing of me."

"Then I'll keep making cats until you come back." His words felt like a promise deep in her bones.

No matter what happened next, she had somebody waiting for her. After she checked on Hazel, she'd have to come back and invite him to the cafe. Let him see those pans he'd made firsthand.

CHAPTER TWENTY-NINE

Time for a Haircut

The garden was growing so well under the care of the dirt slimes, especially the tea, which had taken over the new garden plot. We'd even managed to grow a patch of glowing blue mushrooms somehow. I'd never use them for food, not in a million years, so I replanted them in front of the cafe like a glowing path that would lead adventures here. It seemed like a fantastic way to use a gross ingredient, and it was pretty cool-looking too.

I brushed my hands off and went back to the tea grove, where Matcha was rolling around the plants and the dirt slimes were hopping in and out of the dirt. Every time they hopped out, Nugget would move into the hole they left behind and do a little chicken wiggle like she was a slime too. Being raised by slimes was giving her some odd tendencies, and I couldn't help but laugh.

I loved spending time outside with them like this and was actually getting a lot done too. The new drying trays were perfect. I'd already filled most of them with beautiful green tea leaves, splaying them out on the ground in front of me so I could examine them.

[Tea Leaves: Uncommon]

[Tea Leaves: Uncommon]

[Tea Leaves: Uncommon]

[Tea Leaves: Rare]

My eyes widened. That was only the second rare I'd seen since we started harvesting the tea. How were most of the leaves from a plant uncommon while a few were rare? I just didn't get it. The system seemed entirely random, but I had a feeling I just didn't understand it yet. If I was going to keep leveling up and eventually make legendary food for the final boss, then I needed a more consistent source of rare ingredients.

"Hey, Sweet Potato, remind me how I get rare ingredients again?"

[Some things you need to discover for yourself.]

I sighed. "Yeah, I thought you'd say that."

Maybe it had something to do with how the plants were grown. I hadn't used any fertilizer or special techniques. I honestly hadn't checked on them that often at all since I'd gotten so busy with all my other quests. If the dirt slimes hadn't been helping, the garden would probably be a disaster.

I carried the drying trays to the big rack the system had given me as a reward, slotting them into place so the tea could continue drying out for the next few days. From now on, I'd have to pay more attention to the plants here. Maybe with a little care and attention, I could grow rare ingredients more often.

At the very least, all this work had gotten me a few more cafe points. I desperately needed another table and chairs if I was going to actually serve guests at the cafe. Barely anyone had shown up so far, but that would change. I just had to get the word out somehow, draw people in to taste all the delicious food I'd been making.

While I snagged another table-and-chairs quest from my menu, Matcha peeked into the drying racks with far too much curiosity . . .

"Don't even think about it." I stared him down, daring him to eat a single one of those leaves I'd spent all day picking.

He tilted his body, gazing up at me with an innocent smile before nudging a tray that was a little crooked into place.

I doubted that was his original plan, but I just shook my head with a smile. "Why don't we take a break? I'll even make us some tea."

Matcha trilled, bouncing with far too much excitement. Being around all this tea without eating it must have been tough. I gathered enough leaves for a few pots and added them to my inventory. They weren't completely dry yet, but maybe the fire slimes could help me with that.

As we walked back inside, I bent down to pick a few weeds and stopped to water every dirt slime we came across with my bottomless watering can. I accidentally watered Nugget too, and the little chicken clucked up a storm, feathers flying.

"Sorry!" I leaned down to dry her off while the dirt slimes crowded around to do the same. "You're such good slimes. Thanks for the help."

They bounced happily as I poured more water on them, being careful not to get any on Nugget this time. The little chicken stared at the slimes dancing in the rain and seemed to make a decision. She squeezed in between them, standing proud as she got completely drenched.

"Oh, Nugget, you don't have to like everything they do." I pet her soft feathers, realizing something was different about her. "Have you gotten taller?"

Nugget puffed up her feathers and stood as straight as she could. Yup, she was definitely getting bigger. Our lil Nugget was growing up.

Matcha chirped, pulling my attention to the front yard, where he was bouncing up a storm.

"Yeah, yeah, I know I owe you tea." I gave the dirt slimes and Nugget one last pet before I stood up, muscles burning from all the gardening we'd done today. "Just give me a minute, Matcha."

He trilled louder, bouncing strangely like he was trying to get my attention. I frowned and picked up the pace. He gazed out at the jungle with rapt attention, but I didn't see anything unusual. Vines hung from the dungeon's ceiling, swaying in the breeze, while a few trees stood tall and unmoving. Other than that, I saw a whole lot of nothing.

Wait, no, there was something moving between the trees. A monster? No. They were definitely human shaped.

"Are we about to get our first customer?" I felt myself bouncing a bit with Matcha, his excitement flowing over to me as the figure got closer and closer. "I hope it's somebody nice. Who likes slimes."

Matcha tilted his head back, gazing up at me with those big eyes of his.

"Of course they'll like slimes." I picked him up, hugging him close. "If they don't, then they're not welcome here. We'll have Boss kick them out."

The big blue slime was pretty intimidating, but I didn't really love the idea of using him as a bouncer. Maybe he'd enjoy it though, getting a bit of harmless revenge on silly adventurers. I'd have to ask him later, but right now, our customer was almost here, and they had shockingly red hair . . .

"It's just Fiona." I sighed, shoulders slumping a bit as she walked closer. "Welcome back."

"Don't *welcome back* me, I heard that comment earlier. 'Just Fiona.'" She shook her head, looking utterly disappointed in me.

I winced. "Sorry, I didn't mean it like that. I meant it like, *Oh, it's just Fiona!*"

"Put whatever cheerful tone you want on it, the words don't change," she said with a laugh. "Were you expecting somebody else?"

"Customers?" My voice sounded far too hopeful. "It's hard running a cafe that nobody knows about."

"A lot of things are hard in this dungeon." Fiona headed inside, saying hello to every slime she came across before slumping into a chair. "And even more are entirely unfair."

"Does that mean things didn't go well with the blacksmith?" I asked softly, joining her at the table. "It's fine if the pans didn't work out, but you've been gone for a while. I was getting kind of worried."

"The pans went fine." She opened her inventory and pulled out two pie pans along with a few cookie sheets and even a muffin tin!

My eyes widened, taking in all the beautiful baking pans on the table. "They're amazing! I can't believe you really did it! Thank you."

She crossed her arms and averted her eyes. "Don't thank me yet. Brennic did all the work. I couldn't even manage a single pan on my own." She huffed and grumbled a bit before glaring at the pans. "I don't have a blacksmithing class, so it was pointless for me to even try."

Sadness clung to her like a weight pulling her down. The past few days obviously hadn't gone well for her. The system was just so rigid when it came to these classes and forcing people to fight. What was the point if they weren't happy?

"I'm sorry." I leaned forward and moved the pans off the table, adding them to my inventory so she didn't have to look at them anymore. "Thanks for trying. I'm sure you put a lot of work into these even if the blacksmith ended up making the final ones, right?"

"Well, yeah. I messed up so many pieces that his smithy turned into a scrapyard." Her lips twitched like she was resisting a smile. "I even helped him get a new skill too. Brennic can make all sorts of things now, so feel free to hit him up for more pans if you need them."

She'd gone from sad to proud way too fast. Something was up here.

"Sounds like you had a good time with Brennic, then, huh?"

"We got a lot done, yeah." A faint blush swept over her cheeks. She stretched her arms out, leaning back until the chair was only on two legs so she could peek inside the kitchen. "Are there fire slimes in your stove?"

"Yes?"

She burst out laughing. "Of course there are. I don't even know why I asked."

"Why don't I make us some tea so we can catch up." Hearing her laugh like that made this cafe feel so much more alive. As I walked past her, I leaned down to hug her quickly. "I missed you. Thanks for coming back."

"Did you think I forgot about you?" She stood up to hug me properly, gripping me tight in a bear hug before sitting back down. "Not a chance."

I smiled and went into the kitchen, placing the teapot on the stove and feeding Spark a piece of the fresh bread we'd made earlier today. The fire slime blazed bright as he gobbled it up, heating the water in no time. I started to remove the tea leaves from my inventory to see if Spark could dry them out a bit more, but Matcha kept nudging me and brushing his own tea leaves against my hand.

The tea plant growing from his head had been getting bigger and bigger, to the point where it felt like a small tree was sprouting from inside him. The leaves kept falling in front of his eyes too, and a few small white flowers were blooming.

My green thumb skill nagged at me, not in words, but in a feeling every time I looked at Matcha. I thought . . . his tea was ready to trim? Relief coursed through me as I felt the rightness of that. Yes, Matcha needed a haircut.

"Do you want me to trim those leaves back?" I asked. He bounced up and down but then went out into the dining area by Fiona. "And you want Fiona to do it?"

He swayed back and forth. No, that wasn't it.

"Ummm, you want Fiona to hold you while I do it?"

Again, he swayed in a clear no, but then he wiggled so his leaves shook.

Fiona leaned down, fingers brushing against the leaves. "Maybe he heard we were making tea and wants to help?" Matcha's eyes widened as he frantically bounced up and down, almost hitting Fiona, who just laughed and leaned back in her chair. "See? I'm basically a slime whisperer at this point."

"Riiight." I laughed along with her until we were both wiping our eyes and taking deep breaths. "Okay, come on into the kitchen, Matcha. We'll steep some tea with your leaves and make it extra special."

The slime cheered, bouncing into the kitchen like he was returning in triumph. Spark hopped out of the oven and joined him in a little slime dance, hopping in circles around the room. They were so adorable. I went out back for my garden shears, and a few dirt slimes popped out of the ground, staring at me with excitement in their eyes.

"Sorry, this is for Matcha." Guilt swept over me as they slunk back into the ground all dejected-like. "I'll come out to garden again later though. We'll harvest lots of food and maybe plant more seeds, okay?"

Dirt exploded everywhere as they shot out of the ground, doing their own slime dance. Everyone had gotten so cheerful lately, as if the work we'd been doing was helping more than just my level. The slimes were enjoying being useful and having fun with it. We all were.

Thankfully, Spark had cooled down, so the water wasn't boiling over, but Boss had squeezed himself inside the kitchen as if Matcha needed a friend for this. We barely all fit in here, but I was glad he had backup if he was worried. The little tea slime was perched on big blue's head.

"You ready for this?" I asked.

Match nodded and bounced down so I could reach his tea leaves, pruning them back to where the green thumb skill led me to. Boss loomed over us, as if any wrong cut would be trouble. He'd become such an overprotective slime, and seeing their close friendship made me so glad we'd been able to rescue him. Fiona leaned into the kitchen to join the fun even though she couldn't actually fit. I'd really need to expand the cafe again at some point. Between the slimes and potential customers, this place was just too small.

After a few more snips, Matcha shook himself with a happy sigh, as if a great weight had been lifted. Boss leaned back, settling into a more comfortable position now that the stressful part was over. My hands were full of Matcha's beautiful tea leaves, which shimmered with magic. These were special, grown by Matcha himself. I'd keep them set aside just for us.

[Tea Slime Leaves: Rare]

Interesting. Did all the slimes grow rare food? I thought back and shook my head. The dirt slimes usually gave me uncommon ingredients, not rare. Either this was another random rare, or there was something special about Matcha. Our bond, maybe?

"What will tea with those leaves taste like?" Fiona asked. "Is it green tea? Or matcha like you named him?"

I shrugged. "No idea. Guess we'll have to try it and find out."

Spark had already hopped back into the stove and was keeping the water at the perfect temperature. I added the leaves to the teapot, which now had a built-in strainer, and waited. Every kind of tea took a different amount of time to steep, but I wasn't even sure what this one was. Once steeped, tea usually became a shade of light green, golden brown, orange, red, or even more of a white, but this tea was completely different.

It was vivid green, as if the essence of the plant itself was in our cups.

"Do you want to try it first?" I asked Matcha, not sure if drinking tea he'd grown would be weird or not, but he bobbed his head excitedly. Of course he wanted tea! I filled his pot, waiting for him to hop in while I got some for Boss and Spark too. Matcha wiggled, settling into the pot with his eyes closed like it was a warm bath. "I'm guessing it's good, then?"

Fiona reached over to take her cup, handing me mine too. "Only one way to find out."

Steam curled around me as I lifted it to my lips, inhaling the refreshing scent of freshly cut grass. Green tea always smelled so bright and vegetal, but this one was even clearer, as if we were lying outside in the garden on a sunny day. I breathed it in, letting its scent invigorate me before I even drank any. When I took my first sip, the delicate flavor danced across my lips, sweeter than any green tea I'd had before, and it soothed my soul more and more with each sip.

So that was the power of a rare drink. It was magical and made me even more curious about epic and legendary food.

"Thanks for sharing this with us." I bent down to pet Matcha softly. "It means a lot."

The little slime cooed, spinning in his pot like he was on a lazy river. His body shimmered, as if the tea was filling him with a magical sparkle. I sat on the floor next to him, pushed up against Boss, drinking tea with my adorable slime friends. Fiona sat cross-legged in the doorway, and we just sipped tea, enjoying the vibes. So what if no customers had come today? This was too precious to share with them anyway.

This was the magic of slimes and good tea. I never wanted to forget this moment.

"I missed this," Fiona said. "Blacksmithing was interesting, but there's something homey about your cafe too."

"That's exactly the vibe I was going for." I smiled against my teacup. "Come back whenever you want."

She nodded. "No matter what floor I'm on, I'll find a way."

"No matter what floor . . ." I frowned, feeling an idea coming on but not sure how it would work. "Imagine if we could connect the cafe to other dungeon floors. Like how the key that Cole gave me works, but for other people."

Her eyes widened. "Then you could get customers from anywhere!"

"Exactly. The lower floors could probably use some good food and a break even more than the early ones." I finished my tea, feeling completely invigorated by this idea. "How would that even work though? Magical doors? Portals? Hey, Sweet Potato, what do you think?"

[You're amazing.]

"I meant about the idea," I stammered, suddenly feeling way too hot in this cramped kitchen. "Do you think we could connect other floors to my cafe?"

[You'd have to keep growing and expanding to do that.]

[But anything's possible if you work hard enough.]

Anything was possible, huh? Well, then, I'd have to work so hard that this cafe took over the entire dungeon. Then, once I'd progressed far enough, I could walk right out onto the final floor and finally go back home. Wherever that was.

"Okay, I'll keep working hard, then." I glanced at Fiona. "Got any good ideas to get adventurers here?"

"A few." She set her cup down, staring at me hard. "And none of them have to do with a glowing trail of mushrooms that screams *trap ahead*."

"No way," I scoffed. "That was a great idea. Nobody will think it's a trap."

She raised her eyebrows. "Have you seen anybody here since you did it?"

"Well, no, but that's beside the point." I leaned back against Boss, cradled by his squishy body. "Okay, maybe it's a little bit suspicious . . ."

She snorted, pouring herself another cup of tea and refilling Matcha's pot too.

"Okay, fine, what would you do, then?" I asked, crossing my arms. "What's your grand idea?"

"Post a quest in town." She sighed with contentment as she drank her tea, patting Matcha's head absently. "Ask adventurers to bring you something, and they'll rush here in droves if you've got a good enough reward."

My mouth dropped open. Was it really that simple? I just had to post a cool job for people to do and they'd come find me on their own? Wait, that could make so many things easier! I wouldn't need to hunt down ingredients or risk going outside! I could just stay in the cafe and bake.

"You're brilliant," I told Fiona. "Absolutely brilliant."

"Oh, I know." She gave me a smug smile, sitting a bit straighter. "So, what's the quest going to be?"

I tapped my finger against my teacup. "Ingredient gathering. If they bring me ingredients, especially rare ones, then I'll cook something special. The best thing they've ever tasted."

"That's not hard when all they've tasted is cardboard."

"Exactly." I laughed, suddenly feeling so much better about this cafe plan. "I'll get customers for sure this way."

A blue message box appeared in front of me.

[You are so full of creativity, Hazel.]

[Keep working hard and make your cafe into something this dungeon can't live without.]

"Is that an order? A new quest for me perhaps?" I raised an eyebrow at the messages. A quest like that better have one damn good reward. "Or maybe you're just hoping I succeed?"

Fiona gave me a strange look. "The system doesn't hope, Hazel. It just runs things."

That didn't feel quite right. From all the conversations we'd had, the system seemed to have feelings just like everyone else, even if it didn't know how to talk about them very well. Maybe how it talked to Fiona was different than how it talked to me? Why would that be though?

[Good luck.]

I smiled, holding my mug tight as Boss snored behind me. The system had wished me luck, and the slimes were happy. With those two things, I felt like I could do anything. Even lure adventurers to my cafe carrying armfuls of ingredients for me.

CHAPTER THIRTY

Mission Bake Sale

Cookie sheets and pie pans were great, but I couldn't use them until I finished the new-oven quest. Even after gathering all the clay and stone it required, I still had to serve twenty-two more customers. Which meant I had to find people fast because those pans were itching to be used. Fiona and Brennic had put far too much effort into them to let them go to waste.

"Almost ready to head out?" Fiona leaned into the kitchen, eying the dough I was making. "Ohhh, what's that?"

"Flatbread. I thought it might be fun to cook at the table to show off my skills and make people feel like they're part of the experience." I sectioned off the dough into smaller parts and added them to my inventory for later. "I'm going to add some cheese in the middle to make it nice and gooey too. I also made a few batches of cookies. Think it'll be enough to get twenty-two paying customers?"

She grinned. "I think it'll be enough to get fifty. Dream big."

I laughed and cleaned up the dishes quickly so we could leave. We were going to the safe zone to post that ingredient-gathering quest, but I thought doing a bit of a bake sale at the same time might entice other adventurers to visit my cafe. Or at the very least, I'd get closer to finally having an oven of my very own. Excitement rushed through me, so I picked up the pace, saying goodbye to all the slimes.

Leaving them was a lot easier this time since they'd taken care of themselves just fine the last two times I was gone.

"We'll be back soon." I hugged Matcha tight and waved to the others. "Wish me luck."

The slimes all cheered and bounced extra high, like they really were wishing me luck. That was so sweet. I put a hand to my chest, eyes tearing up as I watched all those colorful slimes cheer me on. Even Nugget joined in from her perch on top of the cafe, clucking and raising her wings high.

"They'll be fine, come on." Fiona tugged my arm, pulling me toward the door to the safe zone. "There's no official way for you to post a quest, but you can add it to the request board in town. Adventurers use it to find new party members, so I bet a lot of people will see it there."

"Sounds great. Lead the way."

We walked up the stairs to the safe zone, coming out in the middle of the marketplace close to what looked like the board Fiona had mentioned. There were all sorts of notes pinned to it looking for party members, requesting help with bosses, and even a few offering bodyguard missions. It looked like the perfect place to add my request.

Looking for rare ingredients in exchange for a delicious home-cooked meal made by a culinary mage. Taste guaranteed. Come to the Slime Serenitea Cafe on floor six for your reward.

There. That should do it. I nodded and turned back to Fiona. "Okay, let's go find somewhere to set up and sell some food!"

We wandered around for a bit, ending up back at the group of picnic tables we'd baked potatoes at last time. Hopefully Marvin was doing okay. If he showed up again today, maybe he'd be willing to visit the cafe and meet the slimes this time. Knowing there were adventurers who were just stuck here with no way to get out or find happiness really bothered me, but I could only do so much on my own. My food was the best way to connect with people and show them that life didn't have to be that way.

I set my portable stove on the table along with a skillet and all the dough I'd made earlier. I added cheese to the middle of each piece of dough, twisted the tops to seal them, and then rolled them out until they were flat. A few adventurers wandered over, silently watching while I added the dough to the pan with some butter. The soft sizzling was such a comforting noise as the scent of buttery toasted bread filled the air. I flipped the flatbreads, and the bottoms were a beautiful golden brown.

Some of the adventurers moved closer, sniffing the air with looks of surprise.

Fiona nudged me with a grin before calling out. "Come on over and get your slime sweets and dungeon treats! We've got cheesy flatbread guaranteed to warm you up and chocolate chip cookies that are so delicious you'll never be able to eat just one of them."

I grabbed the cookies from my inventory and laid them on the table for everyone to see. "Cookies are one gold apiece and the flatbread is two gold. I promise you haven't tasted anything like my food in this dungeon before, so get it while it's hot."

Once the flatbreads were ready, I pulled them off the pan and brushed garlic butter on top for that extra bit of flavor. A few curious people bought some, biting into the bread with trepidation. The cheese inside pulled in a perfect string, and their eyes went wide.

"It tastes amazing!" one woman said while another mumbled their agreement around a full mouth.

"I'm glad you like it." I smiled and motioned at the cookies. "Do you want to try some of these too?"

Her eyes sparkled. "Absolutely."

And then everyone started clamoring for food faster than I could make the bread. It was all going exactly how I'd hoped, and my quest would be done in no time if this kept up. But unfortunately, that's not how things ever seemed to go in the dungeon.

A stern-looking woman walked over, followed by a group of stocky adventurers pushing everyone else out of the way.

Fiona stood up, hand twitching as if she wanted to grab her hammer. "There's a line for a reason, you know. We've got enough food for everyone if you just wait your turn, Varka."

"You know them?" I whispered, but Fiona just motioned for me to stay put.

Varka laughed. "Like I'd want any of this nonsense." She held up the request I'd posted earlier. "I can't believe you're trying to send adventurers out for something as silly as rare ingredients. There's no such thing."

Hmmm . . . most people probably couldn't see the quality of ingredients without an ingredient insight skill, so that made sense, but I really didn't like her tone. This had to be about more than just my request, especially since all my customers disappeared the moment she and her goons came over. I was so close to finishing that quest too!

Fiona crossed her arms. "You've seen rare weapons and potions, so I'm sure you can guess what rare ingredients are. Now, are you going to buy some bread or keep moving?"

"You don't even need to buy it; it's on the house." I took a fresh piece of flatbread off the skillet and held it out to her. "Once you try my food, you'll understand why I posted the mission."

Varka slapped the bread out of my hands. "I don't care *why* you did it. I just want you to stop. Good food doesn't help you in a fight, so you're wasting everyone's time."

"Not everything's about fighting!" I stared at the bread I'd worked so hard on lying in the dirt, my fingernails digging into my palms. "You're allowed to do things just because you enjoy them too. That's what a good meal's all about. If you don't enjoy life, what's the point?"

"Hazel's a culinary mage," Fiona said. "Cooking's how she levels, and leveling up is all that matters, right?"

The two of them glared at each other like they were about to test the no-fighting aspect of the safe zone. I sighed and packed up the rest of the cookies and bread. If Varka wasn't willing to consider my point of view, then there was no reason to stay here any longer. I doubted any customers would come while she was looming over us like that.

"Come on, Fiona. Let's get going." I turned back to glance at Varka. "If you change your mind and want some good food, we'll be at the Slime Serenitea Cafe."

"The *Slime* Cafe?" She laughed and nudged her cronies. "Of course she'd like slimes. Maybe we should pay them a visit for some nice XP."

And that was where I drew the line at being nice.

"It's a safe zone, so don't even think about it." I leaned closer. "Plus, I can buff stats with my food. Imagine what I could do if I focused on debuffs and made it my mission to stock all the markets you go to with them."

Fiona smirked. "I wouldn't test her, Varka. She might look innocent and sweet, but I bet she'd do a lot to defend her slime friends."

The other woman rolled her eyes. "Whatever. Enjoy your food and slimes. Just don't get anyone else mixed up in your nonsense."

"That's not really up to you." I opened a door back to my cafe and stepped through, putting Varka and her bad vibes behind me.

There would always be people like her who didn't stop to enjoy the little pleasures in life, but hopefully she was the exception and not the norm. Otherwise, my cafe was doomed to fail before it even started.

CHAPTER THIRTY-ONE

The Dungeon's Post-Vacation Blues

Cole had only been gone for a day, two at most, so why had it taken him almost a week to recover from all the chaos his absence had caused? It was like the entire dungeon had rebelled. Traps weren't running properly, loot wasn't refilling, and the monsters were so unbalanced. They'd taken a cue from the living trees and decided to become overpowered and run rampant. Honestly, what had his automatic system programming even been doing?

His flames sputtered, weak and exhausted. This was not how he'd planned his little break to end. He was supposed to go off on an adventure, have fun, and come back refreshed. But instead, he'd abandoned his post, almost gotten Hazel killed, and completely screwed everything up. He was a failure of a dungeon core, playing at being human.

Hazel had trusted him, believed in him even, and he'd still taken her to a floor that was far beyond her capabilities. He was the one who'd set up the levels, so he knew how difficult facing a higher-leveled monster would be. His overconfidence had done nothing but hurt her. She might have forgiven him, but he had a ways to go before he forgave himself.

He was a dungeon core. His place was here, running the dungeon from behind the scenes.

But even so, he hadn't disposed of his human avatar yet. It was locked away in a magical box that would keep it sustained on the off chance that he needed it again.

"You look awful." Dave added some more coal to the fire. "I know I said you shouldn't shirk your responsibilities, but don't you think you've been pushing yourself a little too hard? Even a dungeon core needs to rest some-times. That's why the automatic system exists."

Using that was what had gotten him into this whole mess in the first place. It didn't have enough reasoning capabilities to tell the difference between jokes and reality. It had even started running a system diagnostic right in front of Hazel! If she'd seen the whole thing, she'd have learned way too much about how the dungeon worked. Too much about him . . .

Dave frowned. "The automated system does seem a bit rough around the edges, but that's why it's supposed to only be used in short spurts, not for days at a time. It'll be fine to use it again."

Cole considered it but devoured the new fuel instead and brightened his flames even more. He was a dungeon core, and the gods were trusting him to do his duty.

"I understand, but I don't like seeing you run-down like this. I hate to admit it, but you seemed happier with Hazel. If we planned your next out-ing better, I'm sure you could visit her again soon."

Hope surged through his flames, but he clamped down on it. Visiting her was too risky. If she ever found out who he really was, then her falling off a cliff would be the least of her problems. He relayed that to Dave, mak-ing sure he knew to never reveal the secret of who Cole really was. If the gods found out, they'd wipe her memory again. She'd forget about the slimes, her cafe, and about him too. Nothing was worth risking all her hard-earned progress like that.

She deserved to level up and progress through this dungeon just like everyone else. And then . . . she deserved the best reward he could give her.

Cole felt his mind wandering to the cafe as Hazel played with a few dirt slimes in the garden, harvesting vegetables. He remembered the taste of the soup she'd made, the warmth. She'd been doing nothing but baking and working in the garden since he left. She seemed more determined than ever, and that was how things should be. Her leveling while he watched from the sidelines, helping her however he could.

"My lord?" Dave asked softly. "There's something I wanted to talk to you about."

He pulled himself away from the ember shards outside Hazel's cafe, focusing on Dave instead. The satyr straightened his shoulders, which had been slumped with exhaustion and anxiety lately, then took a deep breath.

"I don't know why the gods chose you to run this dungeon, but their rules are too harsh. All these secrets are weighing on me, and I'm tired of getting yelled at by frustrated adventurers. I'd like a break."

A break? Cole's flames flickered, casting shadows on the stone walls. Did Dave want to quit?

"No, no, nothing like that," Dave assured him. "Just, maybe, you could make another Dave for a bit, and I could . . . explore or something. See what else is out there. Ever since Hazel got here, things feel different. She's done nothing but break the rules, and yet, it feels like she's winning at something bigger. And then there's you—you'd never have run off to play adventurer like that in the past. Things are changing, and I think that I—" He paused, wringing his hands. "That I might want to change too."

Ah, so it was already that time for him. It was happening much faster than with the others, but Dave was evolving. Every NPC created by the dungeon could gain a soul if they so wished and become more than just a pile of parts. They could become real, with feelings and desires just like anyone else. It was one of the things he loved about the dungeon, seeing how everyone evolved and grew. But he was oddly sad to see this Dave leaving so soon. He'd grown attached to him. Something about his nagging felt kind of nice, like Cole always had somebody checking in on him.

Without tutorial Dave, the dungeon core would need to take on a lot more responsibilities again. Getting a new Dave up to speed would take time, especially since the tutorial zone was the hardest to deal with. Adventurers were always so grumpy in that area, not wanting to listen even for a moment. They skipped past most of the Daves after a minute or two, leaving them feeling unhelpful and alone. But this Dave had been different. He'd forced his training on the adventurers, keeping them safe and sound as best he could. He didn't let himself be skipped over.

And maybe that's why he was evolving so quickly.

Cole's flames dimmed as he relayed that it was more than fine if Dave went out adventuring on his own. Cole would make another Dave to take his place, just like all the other Daves before him. It would be fine. Dave deserved his own life if he was ready to reach out and grab it. Funny how Hazel had sparked that in him so thoroughly. It was like her being here was changing the very concept of the dungeon. Changing its core.

His flames surged at the thought. Meeting somebody so amazing that they could change things just by existing was like a new kind of magic. One he craved more and more of.

"So you're okay with this?" Dave asked. "I promise I'll come back when you need me."

It was fine, the dungeon relayed to his most-trusted Dave. Go, explore, and find out what you truly want to do.

Dave let out a deep sigh. "Thank you. I was worried you'd say no."

Cole would never refuse a request from such a hardworking supporter. Dave had leveled up in his own way today, and the dungeon core was proud of him.

"That means a lot, thank you." Dave scratched at his horns, glancing back at the door. "Well, I guess I should get going, then?"

The dungeon core sent all his support and best wishes through their ember shard connection, but where would Dave go first?

Dave sat down on the stone ring around Cole's fire. "Honestly, I'm not sure. Maybe I'll see if Hazel needs a hand at the cafe. Or see how that new seamstress is doing. I could even hire myself out as a guide, I guess. For the first time, it feels like I have options."

Cole didn't want to lose one of his best workers, but he knew the feeling of wanting to be somewhere else all too well. His mind wandered back to Hazel as she replanted even more glowing mushrooms in front of her cafe, creating a bright blue road map hundreds of mushrooms long to her business. If he could laugh in this form, he would.

Dave leaned over to watch Hazel too. "She's just so weird. I'd never think to use glowing mushrooms like that, especially since they're poisonous, but look at her go. It's eye-catching, that's for sure."

It really was. Now if only he could create some kind of grand opening for the cafe. Maybe make a quest for adventurers to—

"Nope, no way." Dave shook his head, ears flapping. "No more big group quests like the attack on the living trees. Try sticking to cafe upgrades and rewards for her skills. Keep her busy, keep her leveling, and keep her happy." He stared into Cole's flames. "Think you can handle that?"

Cafe upgrades . . . now that gave him a good idea. The only reason she had to go after the goats was for milk, but if she had easy access to basic ingredients, she could focus on improving her skills and leveling up without worrying about disappointing customers. Maybe he should give her some kind of unlimited pantry upgrade path.

It would need to be balanced, of course, so she couldn't gain XP for using those ingredients, but at least it would let her cook freely. He should make it kind of tough to unlock too, maybe have her visit those living trees again and see just what her overenthusiastic fertilizer had done to them.

Dave chuckled, patting the stone around the core's flames. "Sounds like you're on the right track. I'm going to head out for real this time, then." He turned back at the door, eyebrows knit together. "Are you really going to be okay on your own?"

Cole's flames sparked. He was the core of this dungeon. Of course he'd be fine on his own. Besides, Dave wasn't quitting, remember? Cole expected him back eventually, even if it was just to update him on all his adventures.

"Deal." Dave smiled, waving goodbye. "I'll be back soon."

The room felt a bit chillier after he left. Cole would have to work even harder now and do what he did best: create a challenging but rewarding dungeon. His human avatar would just have to stay tucked away, safe in its box. That was the best for everyone involved.

CHAPTER THIRTY-TWO

Quest for Courage

I completed the second table-and-chairs quest, marveling at how the wood reshaped itself like magic. Fiona had told me to dream big, and two tables were a much bigger dream than one. This cafe was going to draw in customers. It had to.

Matcha rolled across the floor, playing with Spark. Their little chirps and giggles usually would have put me at ease, but today it worried me. What if there were a lot more adventurers like Varka who thought slimes were just fodder for XP? I'd joked about Boss being a bouncer, and about making debuff food, but I didn't want it to actually come to that. I wanted the slimes and adventurers to feel at home here.

Safe and happy.

Voices drifted through the open window, and I lunged over to see who it was. A man and a woman were walking toward the cafe! "Fiona! We've got customers!"

"Customers or troublemakers?"

I winced. That was a good point. The slimes were lively, and there were new people visiting. That could end so many ways, but I chose to think it would end in good food and new friends.

As the visitors drew closer, the woman's voice got clearer. "These glowing mushrooms scream trap . . ."

Fiona gave me a pointed look, and I rolled my eyes in return. Okay, so the trail of glowing mushrooms was probably a bad idea, but they were there now, and I wasn't about to dig them up again. I thought they looked nice.

"A trap?" The man moaned, sounding far too overwhelmed for some mushrooms. "No, no, no. They said this was a safe place! But we're going to end up as some giant mushroom's dinner, aren't we? Just bring me back to the safe zone. If the slimes don't eat me, something else will."

"What about your quest for courage?" The woman laughed. "Stay strong. I bet you'd at least make it to the door."

The man mumbled about rude bets, and his voice sounded so familiar. I peeked out the window again to see the adventurer I'd made potatoes for earlier.

I turned to Fiona. "It's Marvin!"

"I didn't think he'd really come." She glanced out the window herself and smiled. "Good for him."

Good for us too. Even though he was scared, he came all the way out here to visit. This was going to be okay. I rolled my shoulders, stretching out my arms to loosen up. I just had to cook my heart out and win them over. They'd see the charm of this place, just like Fiona and Cole had.

The door creaked open slowly, revealing the point of a dagger.

"Hello?" A short but stocky woman covered in leather armor walked inside carefully, gaze darting around every corner as if she was looking for trip wires. When her gaze settled on me, she frowned. "Are you the one who posted the ingredient-gathering quest?"

"Yes, welcome to the Slime Serenitea Cafe!" I smiled and motioned for her to come in. "Take a seat. I'll make some tea, if you want."

"The *Slime* Serenitea Cafe?" Her face fell. "Please don't tell me the rumors are true. This isn't a trap and we're not on the slimes' menu, right?"

"Wait, what?" I opened my mouth and closed it a few times, not even sure how to respond to that. Matcha bounced over, looking up at me with those big green eyes of his. "You really think I'm feeding people to slimes? I thought that was a joke."

She gripped her daggers tight. "Well, they are ravenous."

"True, but I can't imagine you taste very good," I snapped. She glanced over at Marvin, and I instantly regretted my tone. "Sorry. I know you've had bad experiences, but those slimes didn't have a choice. These do. And they prefer sweets."

"Hear that, Marvin? We're not sweet enough for them." She sheathed her weapons, chuckling as she sat down. "I actually prefer sweets too." Her eyes sparkled as she leaned forward. "I was lucky enough to try one of those cookies you were selling in the safe zone, and it was divine. It reminded me how much I love food. I haven't been able to think about anything else since."

"That's really nice to hear." Warmth filled my chest as I motioned for Marvin to join us. "Thank you both for coming. I was worried that whole thing with Varka would stop anyone from visiting the cafe."

Marvin hovered by the door, wringing his hands. "Well, it kind of did. I was the only one willing to go when Astrid asked."

His eyes widened as Spark bounced over to greet him. Spark was such a friendly slime, but Marvin was so nervous that all he could do was back away. He squeezed his eyes closed, mumbling something to himself that sounded like a protective chant.

Fiona sighed and grabbed Marvin by the collar. "Oh, just come inside and sit down. You got the courage to leave the safe zone; be proud of that. Anything you do now is just the cherry on top."

"Th-thank you," he stammered. "It's only because Astrid was so curious about your food. I thought it would be best if I introduced you all."

Astrid smirked. "Don't let him fool you. He wanted to visit ever since you made him that potato, but he needed a good reason to get moving. He told me to get him here no matter what and to ignore anything he said afterward."

"That sounds terrifying," I said softly. "Why did you want to come here so badly?"

He blinked. "You said you'd help me get over my fears." He turned to Fiona. "And you said you'd help me protect myself."

Astrid had called this his quest for courage, which made a lot more sense now. He was here to move past his fears so he could finally leave the safe zone and continue adventuring. This was a big moment, one that I respected and wanted to help with.

"Why don't I go make some tea while you get acquainted with the slimes?" I went into the kitchen and put the teapot on the stove.

Once the water was hot enough, I added the new leaves I harvested earlier, letting them steep for a few minutes. The water turned darker than the tea I'd made before, almost black. I inspected the leaves carefully.

[Black Tea: Uncommon]

Wasn't that green tea before? I wasn't really sure what the difference was, but my green thumb skill was nagging at me. Maybe I harvested it wrong. Or dried it wrong? Yeah, that felt right. I left it outside on those drying racks instead of . . . what? The answers eluded me, so I'd just have to make black tea for a while until I leveled up my skill enough to harvest green tea properly.

I took a sip of the tea, grimacing at how weak and watery it tasted. I'd have to steep it longer than the green tea apparently. I played around with times, wishing I had an actual clock to judge it by, until I finally caught on to the color changes that meant it was ready.

[New Skill: Perfect Timing]

[Through trial and error, you've learned how to tell when things are ready to serve. This skill will push that feeling even further, letting you sense when things are done even if you can't see them.]

"That's exactly what I needed! Thank you." My lips pulled into a grin as I filled four mugs, setting them on an old shield before walking back into the dining room. "Sorry that took so long."

"No worries." Astrid reached out for a mug, taking a sip without even waiting for it to cool down. "Ouch, that's hot! But it's so good too!"

"Careful." I shook my head as I tried to hand Marvin his, but he was too focused on Matcha to even realize I was there. "Everything okay?"

He dug his fingers into his arms, nodding. "Yup. Just fine."

I somehow doubted that. I handed Fiona her mug and set the rest down so I could pick up Matcha instead. Marvin's eyes widened with each step I took, and he kept scooting his chair back. He reminded me of a scared animal, easily startled and prone to fleeing.

"It's okay. We can take this slow." I held my hand up and stopped walking.

But Fiona got up and stood behind his chair. "No more backing away. If this is really your choice, then you've gotta own it. Matcha is the nicest slime here, so you should say hello."

"That's the spirit!" Astrid held her mug in the air like she was toasting him. "You can do this, Marvin. Don't make me take you back to the safe zone in defeat. You know they'll treat you even worse."

"I know, but that doesn't make this any easier!" His gaze locked on Matcha like he was a terrifying beast.

"If it helps," Fiona said, "Matcha's too small to eat somebody your size."

"Fiona!" I gasped as she clapped him on the shoulder with a grin.

Marvin actually seemed to straighten up at that though. "You're right. That slime is far too small to eat me. The other ones were way bigger."

Fiona raised her eyebrows at me and mouthed, "See?"

I rolled my eyes and walked up to Marvin. "Remember how I told you that I knew a blue slime who drank so much tea that he evolved into a tea slime? This is him." Matcha wiggled in my arms, like he was proud of his evolution. "He's been with me since the tutorial zone and he's my very best friend. He takes care of me, so there's nothing for you to fear."

We all seemed to hold our breaths as Marvin studied the tea slime, nobody moving except for the slight bounce of the slime.

"He-hello, I'm Marvin." He held his hand out, fingers shaking. "Nice t-to meet you."

Matcha chirped, bobbing forward to tap his fingers softly. Marvin squeaked and jerked his hand back, but Fiona held his chair firm so he couldn't fly out of the cafe. Matcha just kept bouncing with a big goofy slime smile on his face.

"Look at him." I held Matcha out to Marvin. "How can you be afraid of such a sweet smile? He likes to be pet, if you want to try that."

Astrid laughed. "You are one crazy lady, but I kind of like it. This place might grow on me."

Marvin took a deep breath and reached out to the slime. Even though his hands were trembling, he dared to pat Matcha's head. The slime cooed, happy as can be.

"He's warm," Marvin whispered. "Like holding a cup of tea."

Matcha leaned into his hand, leaning even farther when Marvin pulled away. I held on tight so he didn't fall right out of my arms while Marvin stared at his hand, moving it in the air like he was shocked it was still attached. Man, he must have really been terrified of slimes. I respected him even more for trying his best to befriend them. Or at least, not fear them as much.

"You're doing great," Astrid said.

"Thanks, I think I might—" His voice choked up as Matcha careened out of my grasp and landed in his lap! He flung his arms in the air, sweat beading on his face. "You said it wouldn't eat me! I'm not sweet, I promise. I'm stringy and dry and probably taste terrible."

"He's not trying to eat you," I said. "He's just very friendly and apparently has no boundaries." Matcha swayed back and forth, doing a little slime dance like he was so proud of himself. I shook my head, determined to teach him slime manners one day. "I'm sorry. I'll take him back if you want."

Matcha nuzzled up to Marvin like he absolutely wouldn't be letting that happen. I sighed. What had gotten into him?

"It's f-fine," Marvin forced out as he awkwardly lowered his arms. "I can handle this."

My eyebrows shot up, but Fiona eventually stepped out from behind his chair. If Marvin thought he could handle this, then I guess she didn't need to stop him from fleeing anymore. He had to stand on his own and prove that he could hold a slime without panicking. Maybe Matcha knew this was what he needed, a calm slime to chill with for a while. Matcha's green eyes slowly closed as he fell asleep in Marvin's arms. His little slime snores sounded like thunder in the silence that had suddenly filled my cafe.

"He's asleep?" Marvin whispered. "What now?"

Fiona patted him on the shoulder. "Now you sit there while Hazel cooks something delicious."

"I have to sit here?" He gulped. "With a slime?"

I nodded. "Yup, think of it like training. Once you're comfortable enough around him that you don't scream when he moves, I'll introduce you to the others."

He stared at Matcha, slowly relaxing when the slime didn't wake up and cause any chaos. This might actually work if he spent enough time around them.

"Good job, Marvin. I knew you had it in you." Astrid pulled a few things out of her inventory, glancing up at me with a grin. "So, now that we're all acquainted, it's about time we discussed that ingredient-gathering quest you posted. I went out adventuring just for you and brought back some things I'm hoping are rare enough."

[Golden Strawberries: Rare]

[Rock Sugar: Rare]

[Sugar Stinger Honey: Rare]

[Glowberries: Uncommon]

[Valerian Root: Rare]

My heart raced seeing all the ingredients she put on the table, especially the golden strawberries that I'd failed so badly to make jam with last time. I wanted strawberry redemption, and now I could finally get it.

"These are amazing!" I picked up the strawberries, sorting out the few normal ones that weren't rare. "Where'd you get all this?"

She shrugged. "Here and there. I've always been drawn to food, but I wasn't really sure why. It clicked when I tried your cooking though. I love food, so I went back to all the places I'd seen interesting ingredients. The strawberry trees on the early floors, the rock sugar caves on floor seventeen, and even the sugar stinger hives on floor nine. The glowberries were a random find on our way here, and I don't remember where the valerian root came from."

I hadn't realized how much I was missing staying cooped up here. An entire cave full of crystalized sugar sounded beautiful! Maybe I'd have to adventure out once my skills were a bit stronger, but for now, I had to figure out what to make to pay her back for all these beautiful ingredients. My fingers brushed over the strawberries and rock sugar while an image tugged at my mind.

Fruit encased in sugar that was as beautiful as gemstones.

"Mind if I use these?" I asked.

"Not at all!" Astrid leaned forward, already way more eager than my normal customer. "What are you making?"

I opened my mouth to answer but ended up staring at Fiona instead. I had no idea what it was called.

"Hey, don't look at me." Fiona sipped her tea with a shrug. "I just eat the food; I don't name it."

We all laughed at that, even Marvin, and the atmosphere became much more relaxed as I washed and dried the strawberries. I removed the stems and set them aside, wishing I had skewers of some kind. Wait. I had a few from those chicken skewers that I'd cleaned and saved. I pulled them out and slid the strawberries on them.

Once the fruit was ready, I took out my portable stove and a big pot to crumble the rock sugar in with some water. As that heated, I filled another bowl with water too, but something didn't feel right. I thought that was supposed to be cold . . .

I held my hand over the bowl. "Mana Mix-In! Use ice cubes!"

Shimmering cubes of ice rained down into the water, chilling the bowl quickly as Astrid's eyes practically bugged out of her head. "That's so cool! How can I get a skill like that?"

"You'd have to be a culinary mage, sorry." I winced as she deflated. "I'll make whatever you want if you keep bringing me ingredients like these though."

She nodded and we both watched as the sugar melted and mixed in with the water, darkening into a warm amber color. After a while, my new perfect timing skill nudged me, and I picked up the strawberry skewers. It was time to dip them in and hope this worked.

I swirled the strawberries in the sugar, coating every inch of them before pulling the skewer out and dunking it in the ice water. The sugar hardened beautifully, creating a candy shell around the fruit that shimmered in the light like diamonds.

[Sweet Tanghulu: Rare]

I stared at the fruit in awe. That was the first rare thing I'd made besides Matcha's tea, and it felt amazing. If only I could grow rare ingredients, then everything I made would be this awesome. Fiona nudged me and I blinked, pulling my gaze away from the treasure in my hands to find Astrid practically drooling over it.

"You should be the first one to try this." I laughed and handed her the skewer. "It's called tanghulu, and it's basically fruit with a hard-candy coating."

She bit into the first strawberry, her eyes widening as the sugar crunched. "It's delicious!"

That look of utter joy was one of the reasons I loved baking so much. Being able to share an experience like this made all the hard work worth it. I grabbed the next skewer and coated those strawberries in sugar too, doing it over and over until I had enough for everyone and I could finally try one myself.

The sweetness of the strawberries burst in my mouth, fresher than anything I'd tasted before, while the sugar created a wonderful textural difference. The whole thing felt decadent and playful at the same time. I bet I could use all sorts of fruit for this, like grapes or oranges. I closed my eyes, enjoying the moment with everyone until colorful lights burst around me.

[Level Up: Culinary Mage Level 6]

[Making rare desserts is a big step toward defeating the final boss. Keep working hard and leveling up. I know you can do this.]

I finished up my last strawberry with a smile. Things were really starting to come together for me. There would always be adventurers like Varka around, but hopefully there would be even more like Astrid and Fiona. This dungeon needed people who were excited about things, no matter what those things were.

But then there was Marvin. I bit my lip, watching as he dared to feed Matcha a strawberry.

Was him not being afraid really all that mattered? There should be more to life than that, like how much joy this one tiny dessert had brought all of us. That's what he should be striving for: finding the thing that would make him as happy as baking made me.

Everyone was so focused on the fight that they neglected the small pleasures in life, like good food and even better company. If my cafe could help people slow down and enjoy themselves for a bit, then maybe they could let themselves dream of a better life too. One that was full of happy moments like this one.

I might not be able to change how the system worked, but I could improve people's lives one delicious meal at a time.

"Hey, Marvin?" I asked. "What would you think about staying here for a while? I could use some help in the garden, and working around all these slimes could really help you get over your fears too."

He froze. "You want me to stay?"

"Only if you're comfortable with it."

Fiona devoured the last of her strawberries and patted her stomach with a happy sigh. "That was amazing. If you stay, you'll keep getting good food like this. The whole area around the cafe is a safe zone, so you'll be fine camping outside like I do."

The whites of his eyes got bigger and bigger with each word she said. Matcha must have sensed his discomfort since he finally woke up and stared up at him blearily.

"Think you can handle that?" Astrid asked. "Or should I take you back to the safe zone?"

He closed his eyes and took a deep breath, then glanced down at Matcha. The little slime bounced on his lap, smiling up at him. "I think . . . I'd like to try."

"Good." Astrid stood up, stretching her arms in the air. "Then I'm going to head out and look for more ingredients to bring back for Hazel. I can't wait to try what you cook up next." I started gathering up the rest of the ingredients she'd brought, but she just shook her head. "Keep them, it's fine. I'm sure you'll find a good use for them."

"Thanks! If I make anything really good, I'll let you know." I added the honey and glowberries to my inventory, already dreaming up new recipes as she waved goodbye and walked out the door.

Marvin's shoulders tensed, but he didn't chase after her, so that felt like a good start. I couldn't force him to change, so this would only work if it's what he really wanted for himself. Hopefully the slimes and I could make a real difference in his life and prove how necessary this cafe was.

Because it was more than just a way to level up now. It was a safe haven.

CHAPTER THIRTY-THREE

Slime Gardening

If Marvin was going to stay here, then he had to meet the other slimes and see if he could handle this or not. I didn't want to overwhelm him, but I also didn't want him hiding away like he did in the safe zone either.

I took a deep breath, decision made. It was time to introduce the dirt slimes and see how he reacted. I needed to be able to trust him around them even if he was afraid sometimes, and I couldn't do that if he reacted badly every time a new one appeared.

"Ready to meet some more slimes?" I opened the door and stepped outside. "I'd love to show you the garden and everything we're growing back there. There are so many things to harvest that I honestly can't even keep up."

He nodded and followed me to the back of the cafe. Lush greenery was everywhere, from the tea plants to the trailing strawberry vines slowly taking over the garden to the sweet potatoes growing happily in the corner. I'd probably need to replant a few things to keep them separated better, but right now, I was just happy to see the fruits of our labor.

Fiona's eyes widened. "It's grown so much since the last time I was here."

"We've been working hard. I even leveled up my green thumb skill."

Marvin gasped. "You've got a gardening skill?"

"I'm a culinary mage with a cafe-owner title, so I have a few . . . unique skills." I stepped into the garden, feeling the soft dirt beneath my feet and inhaling the fresh green scent of the plants. I loved it out here. It was so soothing, and I wanted to share that feeling. "Okay, the first rule about slime gardening is that this is their garden and we're just guests here."

"Sl-slime gardening?" The whites of his eyes shone starkly.

Fiona snorted, trying to cover up a laugh as I pressed on.

"The second rule about slime gardening is that you should never, and I mean never, cut or uproot anything without permission from the slimes." I gave him a stern look, remembering that poor dirt slime I'd hurt when I haphazardly clipped any plant I saw. When he nodded, I continued. "And the third rule is that if you see something flying through the air, catch it, because it's probably food."

Marvin wrung his hands. "So you're telling me that there are slimes out here?" His gaze flitted from plant to plant. "Where? I don't see any."

"Look closer." I knelt next to a little dirt slime poking out of the soil. Bright red strawberries curled around her head like a crown. When she saw me, she leapt up, bounding into my arms like a happy puppy. "Hello, little one."

I pet the dirt slime, trying not to bump any of the strawberries. She was one of the smallest I'd seen so far, barely filling my cupped hands. Mossy seemed to be able to make more slimes whenever he wanted, but I wasn't sure how. They just appeared from the ground more and more each day. Soon we'd be overrun with adorable dirt slimes growing all the food we could ever need.

I walked back to Marvin, cradling the strawberry-covered slime close. "See? They're part of the garden. It's their home, but they welcomed me into it."

"It's so tiny!" His eyes softened as he watched the little slime rock back and forth on my palms. "Does it have a name?"

"Not yet. Also, she's a girl." I moved the slime closer to him. "Want to help name her?"

"You want me to—to *name* her?" He shook his head, backing up a step and almost tripping over another dirt slime who'd scooted up behind him. He spun his arms, catching his balance. "They're everywhere, aren't they?"

Fiona finally let out the laugh she'd been holding in. "Yes, they really are. So watch your step."

He lifted one of his feet and stared at the ground below it, then lifted the other, letting out a breath when no slimes jumped up. As if I'd let him step on a slime!

But maybe it would be best to keep the smallest ones out of reach. I moved the little strawberry slime to my shoulder, letting her nuzzle against my braid like it was a blanket. I ran my index finger over her side and the slime giggled, leaning into me further. Adorable. I'd call her Strawberry for now and see if she continued to prefer berries or other types of plants later on.

"Okay, Marvin, let's start you off with something easy." I clapped my hands together. "How do you feel about watering the garden?"

He stared at me for a bit before nodding. "I can do that."

"Fair warning, the slimes love being rained on." I grabbed the bottomless watering can for him. "They'll probably bounce and cheer if you water one of them. Try not to be too startled."

"Startled? Me?" He laughed, reaching out with shaking hands to take the watering can. "You'll both be here, right?"

Fiona nodded. "Of course. You're safe. I promise."

He gripped the watering can tight, taking a few deep breaths, before tipping it over and watering the strawberries next to him. When nothing jumped out, he seemed to steady himself and started walking. When the first happy dirt slime jumped up, dancing in the rain, Marvin fell straight on his backside, dropping the watering can and everything. He didn't yell at them or try to hurt them though, so he passed my test just fine.

"You okay?" I held my hand out to help him up while the dirt slime who startled him bounced over, nudging his leg as if to ask the same thing. I patted the slime's head. "It's not your fault; Marvin's just new here. He's not used to being around dirt slimes yet."

Berry leaned forward, almost tipping off my shoulder trying to see what was going on. I steadied the slime with a smile. They were always so concerned about people, even when they were total strangers. How anyone got into fights with them was mind-boggling. Maybe they were fiercer when they were defending themselves?

The dungeon was set up for adventurers to fight monsters and monsters to fight back just as hard. That wouldn't change just because I wanted it to, but if even one more adventurer could see slimes as friends, then there was hope for more.

Marvin dusted his clothes off and picked up the watering can again. He gave me a determined nod and kept going without saying a word. His fingers gripped the can so tightly his knuckles were white. I glanced at Fiona, who seemed like she was staying close to him in case he got startled again.

Another dirt slime popped out of the ground, wiggling in joy as Marvin poured water on him. This time, Marvin smiled a little bit and the tension building in my chest disappeared. Working in the garden was more than just pulling weeds and pruning plants; it was about taking care of the slimes too. It seemed like he might be okay with that after all, but he wasn't the only one I had to worry about.

This was Mossy's garden, so he'd get the final vote on who worked in it.

The strawberry slime bounced on my shoulder, probably eager to get down and join in the fun. I laughed and set her in the damp soil with the others. Three slimes danced under the rain of the watering can, chirping and giggling like they were having the time of their lives. Marvin didn't back away. He just kept watering them with an odd look on his face.

"So, what do you think?" I asked. "Can you handle working out here for a bit each day?"

"Maybe . . ."

Fiona raised an eyebrow at him. "Maybe? Come on, I can already see a change in you, and we've barely been here. Imagine how far you'll come if you spend a few hours working with the slimes every day. Astrid won't even recognize you when we're done."

His face flushed, but he just mumbled something and kept moving. His hands weren't shaking nearly as much though, so it felt like she was right. This garden full of slimes was good for him.

A tomato shot through the air, arcing over my shoulder too high for me to grab. "Somebody catch that!"

Marvin scrambled after it, almost dropping the tomato as he fumbled it from hand to hand, but he managed to hold on tight. So tight that he squished it and juice shot all over his hands.

I winced at the look of horror on his face. "It's okay. It was your first attempt, and slime gardening isn't exactly normal. You'll get it next time."

He stared at the smashed red tomato in his hands, a laugh spilling from his lips. "The food really does just fly through the air! I thought you were kidding."

"I never kid about slime gardens." I laughed with him while Fiona handed him a cloth to clean his hands with. "The dirt slimes know when the food's ready better than I do, but they usually wait until one of us is here to toss them up in the air. There was food all over the ground the first few times I came out, so I make it a point to garden a little each day to give them a chance to harvest their food."

Marvin nodded and looked like he was about to say something, but a keening noise pulled my attention to a dirt slime caught in a tangle of weeds.

I rushed over, pulling at them carefully to free the poor little thing. "Sorry about that. Are you okay?"

The dirt slime harrumphed, glaring at the weeds like they were monsters. I stomped on them, making the slime giggle, before I picked them up to make sure they didn't reseed in the soil. I glanced up at Marvin, who was watching closely.

"Weeds are vicious invaders." I showed him the ones I'd just pulled. "Eventually you'll need to tell the difference between plant and weed, ripping the bad ones out by the root so they can't multiply. Dirt slimes seem to attract weeds even faster than normal gardens, so you'll have to be mindful of them. Slay the weeds and keep my slimes safe, that's your mission here."

He nodded solemnly, taking the weed from me for a closer look. The ground shook a bit as a massive slime rose from the middle of the garden, dirt falling off him in waves.

Marvin's eyes bulged as he scrambled backward. "That slime is definitely big enough to eat me!"

"Calm down," I said, but he was already halfway out of the garden. Fiona hurried after him while I patted Mossy on the side. "Sorry about that. He's skittish." The big slime leaned into me, almost knocking me over, but I stood firm as his moss tickled my cheek. "You're such a good slime, taking care of all these youngins. I was hoping Marvin could help you out with that."

But maybe that was too much to hope for so soon.

Nugget strutted over, attacking the weeds with her beak. Tiny puffs of smoke curled around her too, like she was trying to burn them out but didn't know how yet. I grinned and sat down to help the brave chicken. She was really growing fond of the dirt slimes. Together, we pulled up handfuls of weeds and cleaned up quite a bit of the garden while Mossy swayed slowly, moving side to side in a comfortable rhythm.

"Are you thirsty?" I reached up on my tiptoes to pour water on Mossy's head. His eyes closed, a soft hum emanating from his body. He was a gentle giant, but a giant all the same, so I could see why Marvin ran away. Still, there was no getting over his fear if we couldn't have him work with the slimes. He'd run into Boss or Mossy eventually no matter where he was.

"Maybe this wasn't a good idea after all," I said softly, gaze following drops of water running down Mossy's sides. "I pushed him pretty hard today. Meeting Matcha was probably enough."

Mossy turned his big slime body toward me, blinking slowly.

"I know, I know. The dirt slimes are amazing too, and he was doing well." I sighed. "He's just afraid of big slimes like you after some bad experiences."

Mossy burrowed into the ground, wiggling deeper and deeper until he was only around knee height. I bit my lip, trying not to laugh.

"I don't think looking smaller will help, but you're so sweet for trying." I hugged him tight. "It'll be okay. He'll see how great you are soon enough."

After a while, Marvin and Fiona returned, but he was shaking like a leaf.

I held my hand up to stop him. "You don't have to do everything on the first day. Maybe we can meet Mossy tomorrow?"

"No. I refuse to keep running away." Marvin shook his head, standing tall as he gripped that weed so hard that he almost ripped it apart. "Hello, my name is Marvin and I'm ha-happy to meet you."

He held his hand out to the slime, but when Mossy didn't move, he dropped it to his side, staring at me mournfully. Mossy probably didn't want to scare him again, plus, he was a pretty slow mover. But the carrot on his head was wiggling . . .

"Hold out your hands again," I whispered to Marvin. "Hurry!"

Marvin jerked his hands out, eyes wide as one of Mossy's carrots popped up out of the slime's body and elegantly arced into the adventurer's outstretched hands. Marvin stared at it, cradling it like a prized possession.

"I did it," he whispered. "It just fell right into my hands. Almost like . . ." He glanced over at Mossy, who was sinking farther and farther into the dirt. "Almost like the slime made sure I'd catch it."

Mossy stared at Marvin while the little slimes we'd been watering earlier circled around us, bouncing like they didn't have a care in the world. Marvin was still staring at the carrot, mouth hanging open like he couldn't fathom the idea that Mossy had gifted it to him.

"Does that mean you approve of him?" I asked the big slime. "I was hoping he could continue working out here for a while, tending the garden and playing with the slimes. But only if you're okay with that."

Mossy nodded slowly before disappearing back into the ground entirely. He'd only have done that if he believed Marvin was worthy of being here and that he'd treat the dirt slimes right.

"Enjoy that carrot," I said with a grin. "It's a sign of your new friendship with the dirt slimes."

"My new . . . friendship?" Marvin gulped. "With slimes?"

Fiona clapped him on the back, setting a dirt slime on his shoulder. "Look at how far you've come in such a short time. Soon you'll be sleeping with the slimes, just like our dear Hazel here."

I rolled my eyes. "Don't knock it till you've tried it." I turned to Marvin, smiling at the little slime on his shoulder, who cooed and wiggled in joy. "You really did do well today, but maybe we shouldn't push our luck?"

"Oh, thank you." He let out a giant breath, shoulders drooping so much the little slime tumbled right off. He gasped, catching it in his hands along with the carrot. "Sorry!"

The slime gave him an upside-down smile and we all laughed. It felt magical, like this garden had given us more than just dirt slimes and food. It had given us a bit of joy too, and we probably weren't the only ones who needed that.

CHAPTER THIRTY-FOUR

Slimes and Marshmallows

Turns out that three people and tons of slimes didn't all fit in one tiny cafe very well. The fire slimes were especially tricky with their tendency to light things ablaze when they were playing. They really deserved their own place where they could hang out and escape to if things got busy.

I searched the cafe menu for something suitable, but nothing stood out as far as slime habitats went. So, I'd have to make one myself as a surprise gift for helping me cook so often. A firepit seemed like a good idea, and the dirt slimes were more than eager to help. Okay, they were more than eager to play, leaping in and out of the dirt like it was water, but it helped break the ground up really well so I could shovel it.

The firepit was going to be way bigger than I'd originally planned, but the slimes deserved it. I wanted them to feel comfortable no matter what was going on in the cafe, even if it meant me spending hours digging a hole.

A *glomp* noise drew my attention to the pile of dirt next to me. It was half the size it was before with just a tiny dirt slime wiggling next to it. She was the one with strawberries on her head, and her smile was full of joy as she opened her mouth wide, devouring even more of the dirt. She cooed, bouncing like it was the best meal ever.

"That can't taste good," I said. "Is that how you all evolved? You ate a lot of dirt?"

She bobbed, nodding. Well, to each their own, but it made me want to feed them so many delicious things. Except, dirt probably was delicious to them. Hmmm . . . maybe I could make them a dirt cake? The slimes squealed cheerfully as we removed the last of the dirt from the firepit, leaving a nice big empty space for the fire slimes to get cozy in. Now we just had to line it with rocks in case their fiery playtime got out of hand.

The garden would be my best shot at finding rocks suitable for the job, but Fiona and Marvin were training over there, and it was honestly a bit too painful to watch. Marvin flinched every time Fiona raised her sword, even when she downgraded to a long stick. When it was his turn to attack, he often stumbled and injured himself instead of her.

Overall, not the best student. Which would be fine if he was enjoying himself or actually wanted to fight, but sheer misery was etched on his face every time I looked over at them.

"Come on," Fiona said, "you hit like a wet noodle!"

"Maybe I should be a chef, then, like Hazel," Marvin joked. "Because I'm obviously terrible at this."

Fiona sighed. "You know that can't happen. Hazel is special. She's the only one who can get away with baking her way through the dungeon."

The slimes and I quietly gathered our rocks. Was I really that special? Sure, it seemed like I was the only person who could get XP from something besides fighting, but there had to be other people out there enjoying themselves, right?

"Hey, Sweet Potato?" I whispered. "Why did you give me this class? Was it really just because I chose Dave's grilled cheese as a weapon?"

[Of course. It was on the weapons' table, so it was only fair to grant you a class worthy of it.]

I stared at my hands, which were covered in dirt. "And what if we put something else on that table? Would it unlock new classes?"

[. . .]

[That is not possible.]

"But why not? Some people just aren't meant to be fighters." I glanced over at Marvin, who was careening toward the ground with his hands flung out trying to steady himself. "If they could be something else, like a gardener or a tailor, then maybe they'd level up faster. Everyone works harder when they enjoy their work."

[Hmmm . . . so you're saying that enjoyment is the key to progress?]

"Well, of course it is." I shook my head, chuckling as I handed a dirt slime a smooth, flat rock to carry back to the firepit. He balanced it perfectly on his head, bouncing along like it was a new hat. "See that slime? He's happy, so he's working hard. They all are, growing food every day to help my cafe. It's why I bake so much too. Sure, it helps me level, but I love it too. I can't imagine going a day without baking something."

[You do seem to glow when you bake. Like a fire's burning in you, warming everyone around.]

I stared at the message box. "You think I look like that?"

[Yes. It's beautiful.]

The system . . . thought I was beautiful?

The blue box eventually faded away, along with its kind words, but they wouldn't fade from my mind anytime soon. Just what was the system, really? Sometimes it felt like a real person, but then other times, it felt like a machine. Like when it was running diagnostics a while ago. I couldn't seem to get a handle on it, so every time it said something like that, it threw me off guard. If the system was being run by a person, I hoped I could meet them one day.

And ask why they'd created such a frustrating dungeon.

Matcha cannonballed into a puddle, splashing all of us within distance. The cold water pulled me from my thoughts as Matcha gave a big, goofy slime grin, spinning in the water. He always found enjoyment in the little things, and I loved that about him.

It made me want to be bold.

"Sweet Potato . . ." I paused, not sure how to even ask this. "Are you a person?"

[I am a dungeon.]

I sighed. Of course it was a dungeon. What else would it be?

A slime nudged me, waiting for another rock. I smiled, piling them up high like a tower. Every dirt slime was doing their part making this surprise for the fire slimes, so I shouldn't get distracted either. Not even if the system thought I glowed when I baked.

Together, the slimes and I lined the inside of the firepit with the smaller rocks, saving the biggest ones for the ring around the top. I cleared the grass away, wishing we had flat paving stones to make a seating area too. This would have to do for now though. Once I added the last rock, we all stood back and admired our handiwork. Well, I did. The dirt slimes just kept bouncing into the firepit and back out, sighing like they already missed playing in the freshly dug soil.

"Sorry." I patted their heads. "Why don't we go find the fire slimes and show them our little surprise? I even made a special treat for the occasion."

They cheered, leaping out of the firepit and following me into the cafe. I'd managed to make fresh marshmallows with the honey Astrid had brought and a few other ingredients I had. I couldn't wait for the fire slimes to try them. They crowded around me the moment I stepped inside, pushing against my legs like I'd been gone for years.

I laughed. "Calm down. I was only gone for a little while."

Spark jumped on top of another fire slime, and then a third slime jumped on top of him, piling themselves up like scoops of fiery ice cream. The fire slimes wobbled, swaying back and forth as if they were trying to see what was on the table before I got there. I had a feeling they'd tried that a few times while they were waiting, but thankfully, the marshmallows were all still in one piece.

"It's time," I told the slimes. "Want to try out your new firepit?"

The tower of slimes collapsed, rolling toward the door with excitement. I grabbed the trays of marshmallows, carrying them outside carefully. The slimes had gathered a bunch of roasting sticks for us too, so everything was just about ready. I added a bunch of logs to the firepit, laying them flat so the slimes could sit on them more easily, and then placed Spark right in the middle. The fire slime looked around, eyes widening as his flames licked the wood that we'd found just for them.

I would have helped the other fire slimes inside, but they'd all jumped in already too. They snuggled up against one another, nestling into the burning logs. The dirt slimes cheered, bouncing in their own little dance.

"You all did a great job." I smiled at the adorable slimes surrounding me. "Thanks for the help."

Spark moved to the edge of the firepit, trying to snag a marshmallow off the pan all sneaky-like. I laughed and grabbed a tiny stick for him, spearing the sticky treat.

"Here you go. You'll want to heat the marshmallow, but not burn the stick, okay?"

The slime nodded, wrapping a little trail of fire around the stick. Spark held the marshmallow above his head, following it with his eyes. The white outside slowly started toasting, turning a beautiful golden brown.

"Okay, now you get to eat it." I motioned for the slime to hurry up and devour it. Spark opened his mouth wide, gobbling the marshmallow up. His eyes sparkled as he wiggled happily. I put a hand to my chest, my heart feeling very full right now. "I'm glad you like it."

The other fire slimes hopped forward, reaching for their own little sticks and marshmallows. Soon the air was full of the scent of caramelized sugar and my stomach was rumbling. Spark let his next marshmallow go past golden into charcoal land, giggling as he held it out for another slime. The other fire slime devoured it, cheering. Apparently that one liked charcoaled food.

"Hey, Fiona, Marvin, get over here," I called out, getting a few larger sticks ready for us. "I don't think these marshmallows will last long. They look too tasty!"

I held my own over the fire as Spark moved closer, toasting it even more perfectly than his first one. He smiled as I bit into the warm marshmallow. It was sweet and gooey, exactly what I was hoping for. If only I had graham crackers and chocolate too, this would be the perfect snack.

[New Quest: Serve 25 S'mores to Upgrade the Firepit]

Fiona grinned as she watched the fire slimes play. "This looks like quite the party. Mind if I join?"

"It wouldn't be the same without you." I handed her a stick and a marshmallow. There was something about sitting beside a campfire with friends that just felt so cozy. "Hey, everyone, get over here for some tasty treats!"

I'd probably need to make more marshmallows, but it would be worth it. Matcha bounced over, followed by Boss. Halfway to us, the big slime froze, his eyes panicked.

"What's wrong?" I started to get up, but Marvin grabbed my arm in a tight grip. "It's okay, he's friendly."

But Marvin wasn't listening. He and Boss were locked in a death stare.

"He's the one who ate me." Mavin's voice was hushed. "Twice."

Boss puffed himself up, looking larger and more imposing than usual, except his body was trembling even more than Marvin's hands. Hands that were wrapped around the hilt of his training sword. He pointed it at Boss and took one stumbling step forward.

Before I could react, Boss fell apart. Literally. Dozens of little blue slimes cascaded onto the ground like a waterfall, all bouncing in different directions. It was chaos, blue, bouncing chaos! I tried to pick one up, but they kept squirming away, fleeing.

I spun around, staring Marvin down. "What. Did. You. Do?"

"I didn't—I wouldn't—no," he sputtered, dropping his sword like it had stung him. "That slime was the one who ate me."

"And now you're going to be the one to save him." I shoved Marvin after the fleeing blue slimes. "And you better catch 'em all, because neither of you can get past this if you don't."

Marvin gulped as he, Fiona, and I ran after the slimes, trying our best to corral them safely. There was no way I'd let Boss fall to pieces like this, not without a fight. There had to be a way to put him back together again, right?

CHAPTER THIRTY-FIVE

Gotta Catch 'Em All

'd learned something important today: Little slimes could run much faster than big slimes. Boss usually moved at a languid pace, easy to catch up with, but tiny Bosses? It was like trying to herd cats, and I was apparently terrible at that.

I collapsed on the ground, breathing heavily. "This isn't working."

"I'm sorry," Marvin muttered as he tried and failed to catch another slime. "I'm useless."

"We'll figure this out, don't worry."

He'd been working hard, even if nothing he did was helping, so it was difficult to stay mad at him. He hadn't actually attacked Boss or meant him harm. He was just afraid, and that wasn't his fault. Marvin was an adventurer who Boss had eaten multiple times, which meant they'd fought each other multiple times. I felt bad for both of them, but that's how the dungeon worked. It pitted human against monster until they either had to fight or be miserable.

It was the dungeon's fault for being set up this way.

The light-blue slime bracelet Boss had given me shimmered on my wrist, mocking me. We supposedly had a bond, but I couldn't even keep him safe at my own cafe.

"This dungeon sucks." I shook my head, leaning back on my hands to stare up at the embers in the ceiling. "We got thrown in here with no memories, forced to fight for no apparent reason, and then we're supposed to deal with it no questions asked. It could take us years to get to floor one hundred, and we're just supposed to keep mindlessly fighting that whole time?" I stood up, brushing off my hands. "We deserve more than that."

Fiona was the only one of us still dashing around, but even she'd only caught two slimes, and it didn't really feel right putting them in the cafe like we were locking them up. Boss should come back because he wanted to, not because we were forcing him to.

"New plan." I opened my inventory and pulled out sugar, vanilla, slime jelly, and two empty pots. "If we can't catch the little Bosses, then we should lure them to us. And what do slimes love most? Tasty snacks. Can one of you get me some water from the kitchen?"

Marvin rushed forward to grab the pot before a slime could. "I'll do it."

"Thanks."

He was trying so hard to fix his tiny moment of fear. I guess I was completely done being mad at him now. It was time to forgive and move forward. With marshmallows.

"Will you help me with this, Spark?"

The fire slime nodded so fast that he tumbled off the logs he was sitting on. I grinned, handing him the pot to hold with his flames. It wasn't ideal, but I didn't want to leave Boss outside all by himself. So we were going to cook over the open flames instead of in the kitchen. Spark bounced back onto the log, situating himself firmly before holding the pot over his head. Guess it was time to start baking.

I added sugar and water to the pot, but I was out of honey, so I'd need something else . . .

"Mana Mix-In! Add corn syrup!"

The entire pot glowed as the new ingredient poured into the mixture. Spark curled his flames around the pot, cradling it carefully as he added just the right amount of heat while I got a pan full of powdered sugar ready to coat the marshmallows with.

Once the sugar mixture was bubbling, I removed the pot from the fire and added slime jelly, whisking it with as much gusto as I could manage. After a few minutes, I switched arms, hating how much my muscles were burning from doing this multiple times in the same day. Baking was quite the workout. After another minute or two, Fiona walked over with a grin on her face.

"Need help?" she asked sweetly.

I stirred the marshmallows harder, willing them into their nice fluffy form, but it was no use. I sighed, pushing the pot at Fiona. "Have at it."

She mixed the marshmallows firmly, whipping them into a beautiful white fluff that only a strong baker could achieve by hand. Dave apparently had a good point about upgrading my other stats even if I wasn't using them to fight.

I opened my menu and found one stat point still waiting to be used. "Hey, Sweet Potato? Could you please upgrade my strength?"

No message boxes appeared.

"My darling dungeon?"

Still no response. It was like the system was ignoring me, but why would it . . .

"Is this because I said the dungeon sucks? Because I meant the setup of it, not the actual system."

[The system sets up the dungeon; they are one and the same. Not that your comment bothers me. I am just a system.]

I winced. That message was darker blue than usual, as if it was full of sorrow. How could I insult the system after it had been so kind to me? Who cared if I didn't agree with everything it did, it had been treating me well since the moment I woke up in that meadow. At the very least, I could be polite about the issues here and find a way to discuss them without flat out saying the dungeon sucked. Even though it kind of did.

"I'm sorry," I whispered. "You're not just a system. Not to me anyway. You're my friend, and you didn't deserve me being rude."

[. . . So you don't think this dungeon sucks?]

"Well, no, I do, but there had to be a nicer way to say it." I sighed. I was just digging myself a deeper hole here. "You really don't see the issue with making people fight monsters nonstop as their only option in life? Where's the freedom to do what you love? Where's the joy?"

[Joy doesn't make you stronger.]

I rolled my eyes. "That depends on what kind of strength you're after. Because happiness definitely strengthens the soul, and that's the only kind of strength I care about. Once you find the thing that brings you joy, the rest of your life just gets better. Like adding sugar to a pie. It doesn't change what the pie is, but it makes every bite sweeter."

[People are not pies.]

Maybe I actually was talking to a system and not a person running a system. For them to not understand why happiness mattered was baffling. Or very, very sad.

Spark chirped, bringing my attention back to the now-bubbling sugar mixture. I had to focus on getting Boss back right now. I'd finish this conversation with the system later. A small blue slime darted across the lawn, pulling my attention away from the message boxes. I wanted to have this conversation, but now wasn't the right time.

"I'm sorry for hurting your feelings, Sweet Potato. I hope that one day I can show you what I mean by happiness being a strength, but right now, I really need to help Boss."

[My feelings are not hurt. Enjoy your newfound strength.]

The soreness in my muscles faded away. I flexed my hands, feeling strength coursing through them. Too bad Fiona was already done with the marshmallows, because it felt like I could whip them into shape in no time now.

[Perfect Timing: Level 2]

[Your grasp of food has grown, letting you not only *know* when things are ready but be able to jump to that time as well. This skill takes a lot of mana, so use it sparingly.]

My eyebrows shot up. That was a pretty advanced skill upgrade, and I'd just gotten the original a few days ago. Was that the system's way of proving they didn't suck? I'd have to be so much more careful with what I said from now on. Sweet Potato was more sensitive than I realized, and I felt like a jerk.

"Thank you, Sweet Potato. You're always so kind and I really do appreciate it."

[You're welcome. I want to see more of this happiness you speak of. Show me its strength and I'll try to understand.]

The back of my neck grew warm. The system was so strange sometimes, but seeing it want to understand what being happy meant to me was beyond sweet. Even humans often didn't care that much. What was this system, really?

Fiona cleared her throat. "Everything okay?"

I jumped, almost knocking over the pot of marshmallows. "Yeah, I'm fine."

"You forgot I was here, didn't you?" She shook her head with a smirk. "You and that system sure enjoy talking to each other. My messages don't make me blush like yours do."

My face burned hotter than ever. "I just got a cool new skill, that's all."

She was grinning like a fool, so I ignored her and started scooping the marshmallow mixture into a pan. I spread it out evenly but then stared at it. This was usually when I'd let it sit for a few hours, but we really didn't have time for that. Sweet Potato had said my upgraded perfect timing skill would let me jump to when food was ready. Did that mean that I could skip all the time it took for these to set properly?

If so, maybe we could lure Boss over here a lot faster than I thought.

I held my hand over the pan and shouted, "Perfect Timing!"

Marvin jerked upright, looking around in a panic while the marshmallow fluff instantly set into a solid mass. That was so handy! I glanced at my mana bar, which was almost empty between that and the mana mix-in skill. I'd have to use perfect timing sparingly, but it would definitely be helpful in a pinch.

I poured powdered sugar on top of the marshmallows before cutting them into squares and dusting the edges too.

"It's time." I speared a marshmallow with a stick and handed it to Marvin. "Are you ready to help me bring Boss back?"

He stared at the marshmallow for a while before taking a deep breath and grabbing hold of the stick. "I'm ready. Let's bring your friend home."

Together, we all held our marshmallows over the fire, toasting them to golden perfection as the scent of caramelizing sugar drifted over the entire area. A little blue slime bounced in the corner of my vision again, but when I turned to look, he hid behind a bush.

My chest ached seeing him this out of sorts still. I went back to toasting marshmallows instead of staring at him to hopefully lessen the pressure while Marvin and Fiona slowly went back into the cafe to give us some privacy.

"You know that you're a boss in name only, right? You never have to go back to that other floor again." My voice was so quiet that I wasn't sure he'd heard me until a few more blue slimes crept forward, inching closer and closer to the firepit. "You're safe here, and your only job is to eat good food and spend time with friends." I held a stick out to one of the small slimes without looking at him. "These marshmallows are delicious, you know."

I felt the stick pull down as the slime ate one. He cooed, bouncing closer with stars in his eyes.

"You liked that, huh?" My lips tugged into a smile as the tension in my shoulders eased. "We've got plenty more. Do you think that, maybe, it's time to pull yourself together again?"

Little Boss tilted this way and that, swaying in place. I offered him another marshmallow, which he gobbled up in record time with a big grin on his face. Another Little Boss joined us, bouncing onto the first one's head. I fed him a marshmallow too. Slowly, the top slime seemed to merge with the bottom slime, their bodies vibrating just like Boss had when he first fell apart.

One by one, other Little Boss slimes joined us by the fire, gobbling up marshmallows and merging with one another. Eventually, Boss was eye level with me while I was sitting. That felt like his normal size, but how could I be sure none of the slimes were missing?

I leaned my shoulder against the big slime. "It's good to have you back. I was worried."

Boss snuggled closer until he was practically in my lap, like a big dog who didn't realize they weren't a lapdog anymore. I wrapped my arms around him, hugging him tight. My bracelet glowed softly, shimmering against Boss's body as the slime turned to look at me. His big eyes were full of an emotion I couldn't quite identify.

[New Skill: Slime Sense]

[Your bond with slimes is growing, and they don't want you to worry about them anymore. Whenever you focus on a slime you've bonded with, you will be able to sense where it is and bring its location up on your map. In the same way, the slimes who've bonded with you will always be able to find their way back to your cafe.]

"Now I'll never lose you again." I swallowed the lump in my throat, tears pricking the corners of my eyes as I focused on Boss, trying to sense if there were any others of him out there all alone. The only thing tugging at my mind was the big slime right next to me though. He'd put himself back together after all.

I buried my face against his smooth slime, hugging him even closer. "Thank you for bonding with me. I'll do my best to protect you and make sure you have a wonderful life. You never need to fight again."

Boss shuddered, a big exhale leaving his body. We sat like that for a while, watching Spark and the other fire slimes play in their new firepit, until the scent of roasting marshmallows seemed to be too much for Boss. He moved forward, leaning into the firepit for Spark to feed him a marshmallow. He munched on it before opening his mouth wide for another. Soon the fire slimes made a game out of it, toasting marshmallows and launching them into Boss's mouth like it was a goal.

All the slimes gathered together, giggling and playing like Boss had never fallen apart and they were just enjoying a chill day out by the fire. Fiona joined us again, smiling and feeding the slimes marshmallows without a word while Marvin bowed low to Boss.

"I—I'm sorry." His voice was shaky, but he stood in front of Boss anyway. "I never wanted to hurt you in the first place, but I thought I had to. To get to the safe zone. I had to fight."

Tears fell onto the ground, but Marvin didn't look up. Not until Boss bounced closer, nudging him. The big slime held a stick with a perfectly roasted marshmallow on it, offering the treat to Marvin. My chest warmed. A slime offering somebody their food was a big deal, but Marvin just kept glancing between me and Boss.

"What do I do?" he whispered.

"Eat the marshmallow!" I shooed him forward. "Honestly, do I need to explain everything around here? He's trying to be your friend. Toast a few marshmallows with him and see how it goes. Maybe you'll realize you have a lot more in common than you think."

Marvin's eyes widened as he pulled the marshmallow off the stick, getting sticky sugar all over his fingers. He winced, eating it the best he could. Then he smiled at Boss. "Thank you."

The big slime nodded slowly, then went back to playing with the fire slimes, who were charcoaling marshmallows before devouring them. Marvin shook like he was shaking water off after it rained, then took a deep breath and held a marshmallow over the fire too. I smiled. They'd gone through a lot, but it felt like this was a big step toward healing.

Fiona sat down next to me. "You did a good thing here."

"Me? I just made some marshmallows." I nodded at Marvin and Boss. "They did all the real work."

"But they wouldn't have thought to try without you." She glanced at the cafe before grabbing another marshmallow to toast. "This place feels important. It's changing things, making them better. You're giving people a place to relax and understand one another. That's not nothing."

Maybe she was right. Good food had a magical way of bringing people together and taking some of the stress away. It was hard to be frightened when you were covered in sticky marshmallow eating a delicious treat. If I could do that for Marvin and Boss, then maybe I could do that for other adventurers and monsters too.

"Does that make me a monster therapist?" I laughed. "Imagine the business I could make. A dragon sitting at one table, a slime at another, while adventurers sat between and tried not to be terrified."

Fiona grinned. "Hey, you mock it, but it sounds pretty awesome to me."

She was right; that did sound wonderful. My cafe was a safe zone that actually let monsters inside of it. I'd never really considered how unique that was, but now it felt like a big opportunity. One I had no intention of letting slide through my fingers.

This cafe was going to become the best spot in the whole dungeon. A place every adventurer yearned to visit.

CHAPTER THIRTY-SIX

New Customers

Fiona had left for a quest and Marvin was deep in thought in the garden, so that left me and Matcha to spend some time together inside the cafe. I'd been experimenting with drying times for the tea leaves but still hadn't managed to get any more green tea out of it. Tea making was an art, one I apparently knew nothing about.

I set a big pot of black tea down for Matcha and he hopped in. His eyes closed in bliss as he soaked, slowly spinning around in the pot. The leaves on his head were starting to change color too, like he was absorbing the darker tea into his slime.

As long as he was happy, I wasn't too worried, especially since tea counted as a bonus no matter what kind it was. I'd love to have a little more variety though and let people choose from a whole basket of tea flavors. Maybe even grow coffee one day.

Matcha slurped up the last of his tea and jumped out of the pot, chirping at me.

[Quest Completed: Serve 25 Cups of Tea]

[Reward: Tea Guide and Assorted Teas]

A book dropped into my hands with a beautiful cup of tea on the cover surrounded by lush greenery. I flipped through the pages, eyes wide at all the information. Green tea and black tea came from the same plant, but you had to heat the leaves after harvesting them to stop the oxidation process if you wanted green tea. You could pan-fry the leaves or steam them, both of which made the tea taste slightly different.

"This is perfect! Thank you!" I kept flipping the pages, staring at all the other kinds of tea I could make, from rooibos to herbal teas to chamomile. "Where can I get seeds for all these?"

[New Quest: Harvest 50 Ingredients]

I bounced on the balls of my feet, barely containing my excitement. Hopefully this gardening quest would start a whole questline like the tea had so I could get lots of seeds out of it. Before I could dig into the book too much more, the sound of a woman singing drifted through the open window. I peeked outside to see four people heading our way with the one in front skipping while she sang about an adorable little cafe in the woods full of monsters.

Wait, was she singing about *my* cafe?

I picked up Matcha, setting him on my shoulder before opening the door. Fiona was with the new group of people, but her armor was covered in dirt and scratches.

"Are you okay?" I asked, hurrying outside.

She nodded. "Yeah, these adventurers bailed me out. I thought I'd bring them by for a meal as a thank-you."

Fiona was usually the one who bailed other people out, so what kind of trouble had she gotten into on that quest of hers? Was she on another floor? I'd have to ask her later, because the group was eying my cafe like it was going to eat them for dinner. The big burly man in front had a sword almost as tall as me, and the mage behind him was tiny, but her staff was giant. Then there was the singing blond woman, who was leaning over the slime's firepit so far that she almost fell in with them. She and the slimes laughed together, and my tension eased a bit until the mage moved closer, frowning at the cafe.

"So, this floor not only has abnormally strong tree monsters but a bizarre slime cafe too, huh?" She clicked her tongue against her teeth in disapproval.

"I wouldn't call it bizarre," I started, but froze when I noticed their levels. They were all level thirty and above. If anything was bizarre, it was them. "What are you doing on such a low-level floor, if you don't mind me asking?"

Fiona winced, but the big guy in front was the one who spoke up. "Dungeon-extermination quest. They happen from time to time when monsters get out of control."

"Buttttt," the woman with long blond hair said, "I thought we should get some food first. Adventuring on an empty stomach is terrible for morale. When little Fiona here mentioned your cafe, I just had to see it!"

"Little Fiona?" I raised an eyebrow at her, but she just shrugged her very broad shoulders. Yup, this group was definitely bizarre. "Well, come on in, then. I'm more than happy to cook anything you want. If I've got the ingredients, of course."

The big guy in front grunted. "It's not like food tastes good, so I'll have whatever. Name's Garrik, by the way."

"And I'm Dahlia," the blond woman said, pushing Garrik inside. "Don't mind him. He's always grumpy."

"It's fine." I smiled, waiting for all of them to file into the cafe before joining them. "Welcome to the Slime Serenitea Cafe. What can I get you to drink?"

Dahlia smiled at Matcha, who was still sitting on my shoulder. "Is he the slime on your sign? How adorable! I'd love some tea, then, to really get into the right vibe here."

The others nodded, saying they'd take the same as they sat down. Matcha hopped off my shoulder, slowly bouncing over by Dahlia. They stared at each other for a moment before Matcha leapt right into her lap, wiggling into a cozy position like he'd known her all his life. Her eyes widened, but she started giggling instead of screaming, so it seemed fine. She wiggled along with Matcha while the other people in her party just sighed, as if she was always doing weird things like that.

"Mind taking care of him while I make the tea?" I asked Dahlia, who shook her head adamantly. "I'll be right back, then."

Matcha was so good at putting people at ease with his carefree attitude. I'd have to make him an extra treat later. Maybe add something to his tea? Or make baked goods with tea as the main ingredient? That could be tasty.

Now that we were finally getting customers, I'd have to stop by the safe zone for more mugs. I grabbed four, pouring hot tea into them before heading back out to get their orders. Dahlia was balancing Matcha on her head, holding her hands out on each side to catch him if he fell. Matcha had the biggest grin on his face, giggling up a storm.

"I see you two are getting along well," I said with a smile. "I'm glad."

Garrik sighed. "Don't encourage her. She's the reason we had to go back to the first floor to begin with. Her and her weird antics keep getting us killed."

"Oh, hush." She waved a hand at him. "You know it's more entertaining traveling with me than without. And you'd never have gotten that good quest if we hadn't reset."

"Good quest?" I raised an eyebrow, turning to Fiona. "It sounded like you got a good quest too, recently. Were they related?"

She rested her arms on her knees, staring at the ground. "It was to exterminate the living trees you befriended. The system is offering an even bigger reward than last time, pulling in adventurers from higher floors to deal with them."

No, no, no. I gripped the edge of my apron tight. Had I really caused all this? Forced the dungeon to make a quest to exterminate those trees just because I interfered? Those poor trees. They hadn't done anything to deserve that! It was my fault . . .

"Did she just say," Garrik paused, squinting at me, "that you befriended the trees? Slimes I can see, okay, they're weak and kind of adorable—"

Dahlia patted Matcha. "See, even Grumpy Garrik thinks you're adorable."

"Let him finish, Dahlia," the mage said, grabbing her staff from where it was leaning against the wall. "We might be in danger here. Those trees are not normal. If this woman's a mage, she could have messed with them, and we have no idea what evil plan she has for those tree monsters."

They all turned to me, even Matcha, who was currently upside down in Dahlia's lap like he'd tumbled off her head. Fiona stood up, hand reaching back for her hammer, but she didn't draw it. The tension in this room had suddenly skyrocketed, and I didn't like it one bit.

"Let's just calm down and order some food, okay?" I held my hands out in a calming motion. "I am a mage, but I'm a *culinary* mage. As in, I make food, not evil monster plans."

Dahlia nodded. "You're overthinking it, Camellya. Let's eat." She turned to me, setting Matcha right side up. "I'll have some fried rice." She rummaged around in her item box, pulling out a massive bag of rice. "Will this be enough?"

My eyes widened as I took the rice from her, almost dropping it. It had to be at least fifty pounds! "More than enough. I could make you all heaping plates of it if you wanted."

"And poison us?" Camellya asked. "No thank you."

I plastered a smile on my face. I just needed to hurry up and cook their meals, because delicious-smelling food was a powerful magic all its own. Hopefully it would be enough to sway her.

"Ignore my sister," Dahlia whispered. "She loves fried rice and *will* eat it."

The two glared at each other like only sisters who fought often but still loved each other could. This was the first time I'd seen relatives in the dungeon, and now that I thought about it, that was really strange. Unless I just hadn't asked anyone about it maybe? I mean, they were both blond and had flower-inspired names, so it probably should have been obvious.

Camellya leaned forward. "Are you going to cook the food or keep staring at us?"

I smiled one last time and escaped to the kitchen, where there weren't any judgmental adventurers. I enjoyed getting to know new people, but it was always weird in the beginning. I was looking forward to having repeat customers who already knew the cozy vibes here and didn't question it. Or me.

"Okay, Spark, time to get cooking." I dropped the bag of rice with a thunk and filled a pot with water.

Fried rice usually needed leftover rice, not freshly cooked, so hopefully my perfect timing skill could work here. I opened the bag, scooping out enough rice to make a meal for everyone with some leftovers, and then started washing it. My body seemed to remember doing this as I went through the motions with ease, washing and straining, putting the water on to boil, waiting for the rice to cook, and then letting it steam. It all felt natural.

Once it was done, I held my hand over the pot of rice. "Perfect Timing!"

The steam disappeared and the rice clumped together a bit, as if it had been sitting out for a while. Perfect. I gathered a few eggs, vegetables, and everything else I needed and got to work. Fiona was keeping the adventurers chatting in the other room, diverting the conversation every time they got too focused on slimes being monsters or talking about how to kill the trees.

My chest ached as I stirred the fried rice, and not even the nutty scent of it could lighten my mood. What was I going to do about those trees? I couldn't let them get slaughtered because of me, but I also couldn't just leave them there. They were way too strong for this floor and obviously causing some chaos. If my food could make them grow, then maybe it could make them shrink back to normal too? I had no idea how that would work or if the system would even cancel the extermination quest if it did.

What were my other options here?

I plated up enough fried rice for everyone and carried the dishes out to the dining area two by two. Dahlia beamed, leaning over the plate to smell the food with an overexaggerated inhale, but before she could take a bite, Garrik pulled her plate away.

"Let Camellya try it first," he said. "You know she's got better poison resistance than you."

Dahlia pouted. "But it's going to get cold! And it looks perfectly edible."

"It really is," I promised, being bold and taking a bite off Garrik's plate. I chewed it slowly and swallowed it with a smile. "See? All good."

He grunted, waited a moment to see if I'd collapse or something, then nudged Dahlia's plate back at her. She dug into it with gusto, making happy noises as she ate. She even fed some to Matcha, who was circling her plate like he was ravenous. The slime cooed happily, so she fed him even more. Dahlia really did seem like a nice person, and her cheerful spirit was rubbing off on the others as they dug in too. Camellya's eyes widened at her first bite. She quickly forced a frown on her face, as if she was trying to keep up the suspicious pretense, but the way she was wolfing down that food told the real story. She loved it.

Maybe it was a good time to bring up the living trees again, now that everyone was in a good mood with food in their bellies.

"So, about that extermination quest," I said. Fiona stopped eating, raising an eyebrow at me. I took a deep breath. "Do you mind if I come with you?"

Dahlia shrugged. "Sure, why no—"

"No." Camellya shook her head firmly. "Why would we bring a rookie like you along?"

Fiona leaned closer to me. "It was pretty dangerous, and I was only there to gather information. The trees are drawing in other monsters, so you'd have to get through them before even making it there."

"That makes me want to go even more," I whispered. "This is my fault. I should be the one to fix it."

Garrik finished the last of his rice and leaned back in his chair, staring at me. He glanced at Matcha and then at Spark, who was peeking out of the kitchen to see who was here, and grunted. He stood up and the others followed. I glanced at Fiona. Was that a grunt of approval or disdain? I couldn't tell. The man was a mystery.

Dahlia hugged Matcha tight before setting him on the table and paying me for their meals. "I'll be back later. I promise. We'll eat so much good food you won't know how to get rid of me."

The little slime chirped with a smile, but I still wasn't sure what to do. I had to fix this, and the only way I could do that was by talking to the trees again. I stormed outside, Fiona following with a sigh.

"I'm coming with you." I stared up at Garrik, crossing my arms. "I'll just follow behind you anyway, so you might as well let me join."

He stared at me for a while before nodding. "I was hoping you'd say that. A good adventurer always takes responsibility for their actions. If you really caused all this, then it's your job to fix it, and I'm more than happy to help you get there."

Wait. Had that been a test to see if I was a good adventurer or not? I glanced at Dahlia, who just smiled and linked her arm through mine.

"We'll take care of you, don't worry." She patted my arm. "Let's go see these trees of yours."

I waved to Matcha and the other slimes in front of the cafe. "I'll be back soon. Keep the place running for me, okay? And keep an eye on Marvin too!"

Camellya rolled her eyes, pushing past us to lead the way herself with Dahlia, Fiona, and me following behind. Garrik took up the rear, his heavy footsteps grounding me. I had a feeling he was the cornerstone of this group, keeping everyone safe and sound. I'd never adventured in a party like this before, but it felt kind of nice being surrounded by people as we headed out. Like a real team.

CHAPTER THIRTY-SEVEN

Taming the Raging Trees

The jungle floor was full of activity today with all sorts of monsters I hadn't seen before, from giant vine snakes to terrifying gorillas, Venus flytraps, and massive walking mushrooms. I kept close to Dahlia as Fiona and Garrik rushed out to defeat them each time. They were like a well-oiled machine even though they'd just met. One would go high while the other went low, or one would lure a monster while the other set up a trap. They also had the support of Dahlia's and Camellya's magic. It was all so well thought out, as if Fiona belonged with their party.

I didn't like it one bit, but fighting monsters was how they leveled and that's what the dungeon was made for. I needed them to get me to the living trees, so there wasn't much room for me to make demands no matter how much I wanted to. We all knew I'd never make it alone, not with the dungeon this out of control.

Plus, it was a system quest, so even if I convinced this group of adventurers to leave the trees alone, there would be more to take their place. Apparently, that's what happened whenever the dungeon was out of balance: A cleanup team showed up to fix it.

Was that going to happen to my cafe one day too? Or was I exempt because it was a mini safe zone?

I reached into my inventory, holding the key Cole had given me tight. It was still warm, as if it had been sitting by a fire, and it made me think of Cole all piled up with fire slimes sitting outside the cafe. What had he been up to lately? I assumed he'd be back for another meal, but it felt like a long time had passed. Maybe he'd found something else to pique his curiosity . . .

Fiona slung her hammer across her back, rejoining our group with a grim look. "This doesn't even feel like floor six anymore. It's like we've jumped ahead past floor ten."

Dahlia shuddered. "That boss is tricky. It's a creepy mushroom that has way too many spore attacks."

"What's after that boss?" I asked.

"Water, lots and lots of water," Camellya said. "Hope you like swimming. It's a bioluminescent underwater adventure."

"Really?" Fiona whistled. "That sounds pretty awesome, actually, but I think my hammer might weigh me down."

Garrik shook his head. "Everything's weightless in the water. You also can't drown. It's a bit unsettling at first, never breathing but still swimming."

Dahlia smirked. "You should have seen him panicking the first time."

"As if you were so put together," he snapped back. "Why don't you join us, Fiona? We can help you get past the boss and onto those floors. Honestly, with your skills, you could catch up to us pretty quickly."

My chest tightened. I hadn't really thought about her leaving, but she'd need to eventually . . .

Fiona shook her head. "Thanks, but I'm good."

"Strength stagnates if you stay in one place too long." Garrik rested a hand on her shoulder. "You've gotten too comfortable here. I bet you haven't leveled in a long time. You get better XP from monsters who are stronger than you, but these are all so much weaker."

"Is that true?" I asked. "Have you been stagnating like Marvin?"

Fiona caught a vine snake in her bare hands, tossing it aside before it could get to me. My heart thudded in my chest. I hadn't even seen it coming! She really was far too skilled for this low-level floor, wasn't she? Garrik gave me a knowing look, as if he expected me to do something about it. Wait. Was I the one who was holding her back?

"Fiona," I started, but the words stuck in my throat. A buzzing that had sounded like background noise at first was getting louder and louder the closer we got to the forest. Giant, fluffy, black-and-yellow creatures flew around us on glassy wings that glittered in the light. "Are those . . . bees?"

"Sugar stingers." Garrik cursed. "Keep your guard up! We're getting closer to our real targets."

Fiona gripped her hammer tight while Garrick drew his sword, Dahlia pulled out her spellbook, and Camellya held her staff at the ready. I was the only one who didn't really have a guard to keep up. Unless he wanted me to pull out [Dave's Lunch]. I had a feeling the others would leave me to fend for myself if I did that. It didn't seem like the bees were after us though. It was more like they were flying formations around the forest, keeping guard in case we tried to get too close to the trees.

I hadn't needed weapons against the tree monsters last time, and I wouldn't need them now either. We would come to an understanding over good food and kindness, just like before. The trees weren't evil, just stressed out and tired, probably terrified too with adventurers coming from all over the dungeon to attack them.

"Remember not to kill any of the trees." I locked gazes with all of them, making sure they'd heard me. "This is my fault, so I'm going to be the one to fix it."

Camellya rolled her eyes. "Do you even have the quest to defeat them?"

"Doesn't every adventurer have it?" I frantically pulled up my quest menu. I hadn't actually seen it, not once, even though Fiona obviously got it a while back. I scrolled through the cafe upgrades, but there was nothing there. "Umm . . . Sweet Potato? Any idea why I don't have a dungeon-wide system quest?"

[You are a culinary mage.]

"Yeah, but I'm still an adventurer," I whispered. "Shouldn't everyone have it?"

[. . . but you don't enjoy fighting.]

My frown deepened. "When has that ever stopped the system from trying to make people fight? Did I do something wrong?"

[No, of course not. You just kind of break things sometimes and this really needs to get fixed.]

I stared at that blue message box until the color faded. The system hadn't given me the quest because I broke too many things? Seriously? I shook my head, laughing to myself. If it thought I'd been breaking things so far, it better buckle up, because I was about to break even more.

"I'll fix it, I promise." I crossed my arms, drawing stares from the rest of my party. "Just give me the quest already."

[. . .]

[Adventurers don't usually order the system around like that, you know.]

[But since it's you, I guess I don't mind. You can have your quest . . .]

[New Quest: Exterminate the Raging Living Tree Monsters on Floor 6. Reward: One Full Level-Up]

The new quest appeared in my list, bright and shiny and ready to be broken. I grinned, reading those words very carefully. If the system wanted to get rid of the *raging* living tree monsters, then all I had to do was calm them down, right? Once they weren't raging, the quest would no longer make sense.

"Thank you." My grin stretched from ear to ear now, and Fiona was giving me a concerned look. I picked up the pace as if nothing had happened. "I won't disappoint you, Sweet Potato."

[Are you sure? Because your tone is kind of saying otherwise.]

[It's fine. Just deal with the trees, please.]

And deal with the trees I would. In my own way. I searched through my inventory while we walked, relying on Fiona to guide me a bit. I had some chamomile tea from my last quest reward, which might help, but didn't feel like enough to calm a raging tree down if it really was raging. Hmmm . . . I had rose hips as well and just enough valerian root from Astrid to really make this drink sing. Or sleep, I guess.

If only I had some nectar for the bees, then we'd be set. I glanced around the area, spotting big, purple, bell-shaped flowers growing on vines nearby. I hurried over, reaching high to pick a few.

They smelled sweet and were hopefully fragrant enough to appease the bees.

"If you're done smelling the roses," Camellya said, "then maybe we should get going?"

This time it was my turn to roll my eyes. Her lips quirked up in a smile as she raised her staff at a bee.

"Wait!" I held the flower up instead, offering it to the bee and trying not to cringe as the massive insect flew closer to me. This would work. It had to work. My arm trembled as the bee seemed to sniff the flower. "We aren't here to hurt anyone. I just want to talk to the trees."

"Do lines like that really get you anywhere?" Camellya asked. "Or have you just never been stung by one of those beasts? I promise you, it's not sweet and sugary like the name makes it sound."

Fiona stepped closer, but I shook my head, holding the flower up higher. "I'm fine, but I'm glad to know you care, Camellya."

The two sisters exchanged worried glances as the bee grabbed the flower, tugging it away from me as it took off toward the trees. I let out a breath as my knees gave out and I collapsed on the ground.

"I can't believe that worked." I laughed, shaking my head as the adrenaline swept over me. "Let's pick some more flowers."

Garrik snorted. "Here I was thinking you knew what you were doing, but you were just flying by the seat of your pants. You've got courage, that's for sure."

"Maybe a bit too much courage." Fiona held her hand out to help me up. "Be more careful. Not every monster is as nice as your slimes."

I had learned that the hard way after meeting the Solhorn goats, but I had to at least try. If a monster didn't attack me, then I wasn't going to be the one to start the fight. Every time I befriended a monster, it let other adventurers know it was possible too. And if enough of us kept doing it, then maybe the dungeon would start changing for the better.

After we each gathered a handful of flowers, we continued on toward the forest ahead. Adventurers dangled upside down from tree limbs with their weapons littering the ground while others were climbing the trees and getting swatted by painful-looking branches. A group of sugar stingers gave chase to about a dozen adventurers while a higher-leveled party watched on from the outskirts, as if making their plan of attack based on everyone else's failures.

My stomach turned. This was wrong. I had to put a stop to it before things got even more out of hand.

Garrik nudged me. "If you're going to do something, now's the time."

"Right, of course." I took a few steps closer to the trees. "Hello, you remember me, right?" One of the biggest trees lurched forward, slamming its roots on the ground so hard I almost fell over. "Okay, maybe not. I made you some tasty fertilizer and you gave me wood in return. Ring any bells?"

The trees groaned as they moved closer to me, their wood creaking with the effort. Roots cracked like whips, making me dodge more than once to avoid getting clobbered by them. Maybe they remembered me, but they just didn't *like* me. I was the one who put them through all this pain after all. They probably hated me and wanted to send me back to Dave in the tutorial zone.

My pulse raced as my head started to spin. What was I doing out here? I was a baker! I should be at home, in the kitchen making pies, not having a standoff with some angry trees.

Fiona stepped up next to me and rested her hand on my shoulder. "It'll be all right. Just talk to them. If it doesn't work out, we'll jump in to back you up."

I glanced over my shoulder to see them all nodding, even Camellya. I took a deep breath to steady my nerves and pulled the biggest pot out of my inventory along with my portable stove.

"Would you like some tea?" I forced myself to take another step toward the angry tree who had tried to knock me over. "It'll calm your nerves and reduce your stress. You don't have to keep fighting if you don't want to. I'll help you."

The trees swayed, noises traveling over the wind like they could somehow communicate through their leaves. While I waited, the other adventurers in the area started whispering too: about me. They thought I was an idiot about to get herself killed. Maybe they were right, but I still had to try, so I sat down right in the middle of all the chaos and got to work preparing the tea.

I added water to the pot. "This is my fault. I only wanted to help you, but I accidentally overpowered you so much that the system took action to fix it. I didn't really know how my skills worked at the time and I used them without thinking." A tree took a big step forward, branches swaying dangerously close to me. I held my hands up. "Let me make it up to you!"

The trees stopped moving, as if waiting.

I pulled out the chamomile tea leaves. "See these? They're very tasty when steeped in water. I'm sure you'll like them."

"You're really making tea right now?" Garrik asked.

"What else do you suggest?" I whispered back at him. "The problem isn't that the trees are overpowered, it's that they're raging. If tea can calm them down, then I might as well try, right?"

[That's your grand plan? Sleepy-time tea?]

"Pretty much, yeah." I couldn't help but smile at that message, grateful that the system was interested enough to keep watching. The whole thing hinged on me being able to convince it to cancel the quest once the trees were calm again. "Keep your eyes on me, Sweet Potato. I'm about to do something pretty impressive."

[You have my full attention, as always.]

My hands froze, dropping the tea leaves in the water. "As always?"

But the system didn't answer, and the adventurers weren't waiting. A group of them charged the trees.

"Stop!" I shouted, but Fiona was already darting out ahead of me to intercept them, just like when I had decided to rescue Boss. She was always so reliable, backing up every crazy plan I had. I'd have to find a way to thank her.

"The lady said she'd handle this," Fiona said as she gripped her hammer, "so I'd suggest you stay back and let her try to calm them down."

The adventurers eyed her warily as one of the guys spoke up. "Those trees are using half our party as playthings. I don't care if she can calm them down or not. I'm going to kill them."

I winced, adding the rose hips and valerian root to the pot as well. They had a point, even if I didn't like their plan. The sweet floral aroma of the tea wafted through the air as it steeped. I took a deep breath as one of the trees moved a bit closer, leaves reaching for the pot.

"Careful, it's hot." I took it off the portable stove to cool. "Why don't you let the adventurers down first, then once the tea cools, I'll make sure you all get as much as you want."

Garrik sighed, joining Fiona as a defensive line between the two groups. He seemed pretty reliable too, and I was glad they'd shown up at the cafe today.

"Please. We had a deal, remember?" I stared at the trees, searching for one in particular. The old gnarled tree who'd needed my fertilizer the most. "Honor our deal and I'll find a way to keep you safe."

The tree in question rocked forward, standing far taller than I remembered. It snapped its leaves against the other trees' bark as it shambled by, as if chastising them. The other trees groaned, but eventually dropped the adventurers, who thudded to the ground painfully. They stood up, rubbing their shoulders and backs before picking up their weapons. Thankfully, they seemed too dizzy to attack right away, so they just stumbled back to their groups.

"Is that good enough for you?" I asked the man who said he wanted to kill the trees. "They gave you back your party members, now why don't you let me do the rest?"

Fiona and Garrik got into fighting stances, as if to say they'd make them agree by force if they had to. This quest had a really good reward of gaining an extra level, so I knew those adventurers wouldn't back down easily. Maybe if I gave them something else to think about? I reached into my inventory again, pulling out some cookies I'd made earlier for Boss.

"Here, take these as an apology." I walked over to the group, handing out cookies one by one. "They'll change your life, I swear."

Dahlia rushed over, dropping her spellbook like she didn't care about this fight at all. "Ohhhh, you've got cookies? I want to try one!"

I laughed, handing her the rest of them. When she bit into it, she moaned, rushing over to shove one into Camellya's mouth too. "You've gotta try this!"

Camellya mumbled something I couldn't understand around the cookie, but it sounded like she was irritated. One by one, the other adventurers tried them too, even the dangerous one in front who wanted to kill my tree friends. Their eyes widened as the delicious taste of chocolate started to win them over. I smiled, going back to the pot of tea, which was still warm but not hot enough to burn the trees. I'd normally strain it, but they might like the leaves and herbs too. So, I'd leave it as is for them.

"Okay, it's ready." I picked up the pot, lurching from the weight of it, and carried it over to the elder tree. Its branches swayed, curling around me like it wanted to drag me in. "Ummm, should I just pour it on your roots?"

That's what I had done with the fertilizer, so it made sense to do the same thing now. I gently ladled the tea onto its roots, which shivered. The elder tree's branches shook, then settled as it seemed to sigh. I poured some on the angry tree nearby too and its roots instantly calmed down, no longer thrashing the ground in anger. It looked like it was working!

I made my way around the forest of monsters, giving each tree a generous drink of the sleepy-time tea. When the pot was empty, I made another. And a third. Eventually every tree had had their fill and the forest was quiet, unmoving. Their rage had dissolved just like this tea seeping into the ground.

[Living Tree Defeated]

[Living Tree Defeated]

[Living Tree Defeated]

The messages went on and on until eventually a new one showed up.

[Quest Completed: Defeat 10 Monsters]

[Reward: Wood, Seeds, Syrup, Gold]

[New Quest: Defeat 25 Monsters]

Wood and my other rewards rained down from the sky, falling into my inventory before they even got close to hitting me. I'd almost forgotten about that quest since I didn't mess with monsters very often. The slimes and I had a bond, so I never seemed to get any rewards for feeding them. Besides their friendship, of course.

"She actually did it," Garrik said. "I knew her food was good, but not good enough to calm a rabid monster. That's crazy."

Dahlia rushed over to hug me, practically knocking me over as she did. "I knew you could do it! You're the best baker ever."

Fiona nodded but kept her eyes on the other adventurers. She must have expected them to attack still, so I needed to finish this quest for real.

"Okay, Sweet Potato," I called out, "I finished the quest. There isn't a single raging living tree here."

[. . .]

[You just had to find a loophole, didn't you?]

I grinned. "Isn't that what you like about me? I keep things interesting."

[You definitely do that. Congratulations, Hazel.]

[Quest Completed: Exterminate the Raging Living Trees]

[Reward: Level-Up]

Music chimed through the air as my level went from six to seven, my mana and health bars increased, and my entire body refreshed like I was a whole new person. I used the stat point on my charisma, feeling like I could use all of that I could get if I was going to keep conning bee monsters with flowers and terrifying trees with tea.

Fiona pulled me into a side hug. "Hey, I leveled up too and we didn't even need to fight! You did a great job."

Garrik grunted. "I guess she did. We all leveled, so we're good."

"More than good, we're hungry," Dahlia said with a laugh. "Got any more cookies?"

I shook my head. "Sorry. I can bake more though, if you want to stop back later and pick them up."

"Sounds like a plan to me!" She turned to Garrik. "Please tell me we can come back."

He frowned. "I would, but it's just not that simple. It took a long time to come all the way back to this floor. Maybe if she had a teleport or something, but without that, I just don't see it happening."

Dahlia's face fell. "You're right. Sorry I got so excited."

"Well." Camellya scuffed her boots in the dirt. "I do have something that might help."

She pulled two sets of lanterns from her inventory, shrouded in smoke with a flame flickering inside each one. One set was bathed in a warm golden light while the other had deep purple flames, creating a magical aura like I'd never seen before.

Garrik sucked in a breath. "You're really giving those up?"

"What are they?" I leaned closer for a better look. There didn't seem to be a wick or anything keeping the flames lit; they just hovered in the center of each lantern. "And why are you giving them to me?"

"For Dahlia." Camellya shoved the golden set of lanterns at me. "So she can eat cookies whenever she wants."

Dahlia leapt into Camellya's arms. "Aww, you're the best! I knew you liked that cafe too."

"Oh, shut it," she said, but hugged Dahlia back. "Now are you going to take them or not, Miss Baker?"

"Definitely taking them!" I grabbed the lanterns before she changed her mind. "But what do they do?"

Garrik sighed. "We'll explain on the way since we need to link them to your cafe now. Great job, Camellya."

Dahlia grinned. "Yes, great job, sister!"

Fiona and I exchanged glances. "Great job?"

The others marched forward like we were on a new mission. I hung back, staring at the trees. Leaving them here would just cause more issues and they'd probably get enraged again, especially if people kept attacking them. I walked up to the angry tree who'd ended up loving my tea the most.

"Would you like to come back to my cafe with me?" I touched its bark softly, glancing at the elder tree too. It seemed to be waiting for the others to decide this time though. "Nobody will hurt you, and I promise you'll get lots of tasty treats."

The tree's branches swayed as it turned back to the others, who didn't budge an inch.

I smiled at them. "It's a monster-friendly place as long as you promise not to attack anyone. There are dozens of slimes there already, so why not at least come check it out?"

The giant trees groaned as they inched closer, swaying back and forth until they surrounded me. I leaned my head back, marveling at how tall they all were compared to the scraggly trees I'd first encountered.

I patted the tree's bark. "Let's go home."

It wrapped a branch around my shoulders as its leaves patted me on the head. I bit my lip, trying not to laugh at how absurd this must look. A tree patting a woman on the head. I knew these trees were kind, I just knew it. I turned to head home, the trees following in my wake one by one like a line of very slow-moving ducklings.

At least the slow speed would give me time to think on what to do with them once we got back.

CHAPTER THIRTY-EIGHT

Settling In

We didn't run into any trouble on our way back to the cafe, not with an entire forest of living trees trailing slowly behind us, but there was a soft buzzing in the background that made me think at least a few of the sugar stingers had tagged along too. A giant hive dangled from one of the trees, which made me hopeful for honey if the bees liked their new home enough. Mmmm, tea with honey. I bet Matcha would love it.

"You really are strange," Camellya said. "You're looking at that beehive like it's delicious instead of dangerous."

"Well, honey's good for a lot of things!" I tapped my chin. "I could make honey cake, baklava, toffee, all sorts of pies, you name it."

Dahlia moaned. "All of them. Make all of them and invite me over."

I laughed as we walked up to the cafe. The fire slimes were all cuddled together sleeping in their new firepit, but the rest of the slimes were nowhere to be seen. Which was probably for the best until I figured out what to do with the trees. They towered over the cafe by at least ten feet, casting huge shadows that would probably concern any adventurer who came by. And Marvin.

Suddenly this whole plan felt a little haphazard.

I turned around and put on my most professional smile. "Welcome to the Slime Serenitea Cafe. Feel free to look around and see where you might want to settle in." A soft breeze rustled through their leaves as if they were debating before one walked straight up to the cafe's front door. "Wait! I don't think you'll fit inside, I'm sorry. Maybe we could go out back?"

The tree creaked as it leaned over, touching the ground with one of its branches. Leaves and twigs sprouted from it, twisting and curling into a cozy little bench beside the door.

"That's amazing!" Dahlia exclaimed as she stared up at the tree, patting its bark affectionately. "You're such a good tree monster."

"Agreed. That bench looks wonderful!" I hurried over to try it out, sitting down with a sigh of contentment. It was perfectly shaped and much smoother than I'd imagined. "Thank you for the gift."

The tree patted my head with its soft leaves before rumbling off to rejoin the others, who were wandering around the yard. The fire slimes had woken up and were currently trying to use one of the other trees as fuel. I raced over, snatching them away from the poor tree.

"I'm so sorry!" I held the fire slime tight, patting the spot where her flames had touched the tree. It was warm but not charred at all. "The fire slimes love to play, that's all."

The tree swayed, lifting its branches over the firepit. Chunks of wood rained down, filling the firepit to the brim. The fire slimes cheered as they climbed the giant pile of wood, bouncing and wiggling like they were the happiest little slimes ever. I let out a breath, grateful that the trees didn't seem to mind sharing wood with us.

"Hey, Hazel?" Fiona called out. "Is it okay if we hang those lanterns up for you?"

"Unless you're busy hugging trees," Camellya said. "I thought you'd be more excited about my gift, but no, you're just trying out furniture and building bonfires."

I winced. "Sorry, but I don't actually know what they do. I'm guessing it's something travel related?"

Dahlia grinned. "See? I told you she probably didn't know. You can't just expect every mage to be an expert in magical relics."

"They should be." Camellya marched over, holding her hand out for the lanterns. "Give them here. We'll attach them to each side of the cafe's front door, anchoring them to it. As long as the flames are lit, we can create a portal to your door from any other door we link our lanterns to."

"That's amazing! But are you sure you want to just give them to me? They sound pretty useful."

Camellya nodded. "Keep feeding us good food and we'll call it even."

"And," Dahlia joined in, "if you could make us a huge batch of cookies, I'd really appreciate it."

"Deal. Do you want any buffs on them?" I asked.

Garrik raised an eyebrow. "You can buff food?"

"Yeah, I've got a buff baking skill that lets me buff any one stat when I make food." I bit my lip, glancing at the giant trees. "That's actually part of the reason these trees got so out of hand, so I haven't used it much since then. It works normally for humans, so you'll be safe to try it."

Probably.

He stared at me for so long that I started to get uncomfortable. Maybe I shouldn't bring that skill up so casually until I did more testing with it to see how long the buffs lasted and if they could be stacked or not. I didn't want people to start relying on them too much either.

The silence was getting a little awkward though, so I pulled the lanterns out of my inventory and held them up by the front door. "Is this how you wanted them, Camellya?"

"Yeah, we've just gotta find something to hold it up with." She started going through her inventory, but before she could grab anything, a large tree branch leaned in over her shoulder. It tapped the wall of my cafe, letting the wood grow and curl around the handle of the lantern, securing it in place. "Oh, well, that works too, I guess."

Camellya shuffled over to the other side, motioning for me to hold a lantern there too. I did as she asked, waiting to see if the tree would help us out here as well. A branch slowly moved over my hand, bringing the cafe's exterior to life as the wood grew around the lantern as if it was designed that way.

"That is so cool," I whispered, smiling at the tree. "Thank you for your help."

Its leaves fluttered and I could have sworn I heard a happy little chirp. Wait, no, that was one of the slimes. Matcha rolled out of the cafe, bouncing against the tree's trunk as a stopping point. The tree reached out one of its leaves to touch the tea leaves on Matcha's head. The slime froze, then giggled as if the tree had tickled him. He bounced happily as the tree picked him up, setting the slime in its branches.

"Glad you approve of our new guests." But something was still bothering me. Garrik's stare was burning a hole in my back. I took a deep breath and turned toward the burly adventurer. "Is something wrong?"

He tilted his head, frowning. "I just don't get it. You can cook food that not only tastes good but gives people buffs too. Is that how you get XP?"

"Yes?" Based on how hard he was staring at me, it felt like I should be keeping that information secret in the future. I didn't want to attract unnecessary attention. I just wanted to bake, level up, and play with as many slimes as possible. "That's how the culinary mage class works. I level up through baking and defeat monsters by feeding them."

Camellya's eyes widened. "So that's why all that wood and honey dropped even though you hadn't killed anything? That's insane."

"How'd you do it?" Dahlia whispered, moving closer. "How'd you get a new class?"

All eyes were on me, like I had the secrets of the dungeon locked away somewhere. I searched for Fiona, but she must have wandered off somewhere. So it was up to me to answer them.

"Ummm . . . I'm not really sure." I shrugged. "I just got to the dungeon and picked up a sandwich instead of a weapon."

It sounded kind of ridiculous saying it out loud, but that's what happened. Honestly, me getting this class probably had more to do with the system than anything I did. It had never really explained why it gave me the class, but it felt like it was bored. Like it wanted to try new things. Maybe it would be open to other new classes if somebody opened its mind to the idea.

Matcha bounced in the tree, making a few leaves rain down on me. The tree moved, walking over to the others with Matcha chirping out noises like he was directing them somewhere.

"Matcha?" I called out, but they were on the move already. I turned to the adventurers. "Sorry, but I should probably see what they're up to."

Dahlia nodded. "We'll wait inside with Fiona and discuss a few things."

That sounded a little ominous, but I didn't have time to think about it while the trees were heading toward the backyard. Was Matcha bringing them to the garden? They'd probably enjoy all the plants back there, so it was a good idea. Maybe they'd want to settle in around it, like living guardians.

The dirt slimes would probably love having new friends to play with too. As long as the trees didn't mess up the garden with their root attacks or something . . .

I picked up the pace, catching up to the trees in no time. "This is our garden. Mossy, the big dirt slime in the middle, takes care of everything with his dirt slimes." A few slimes bounced over, eying the trees like they weren't sure what to do. I patted their heads, smiling. "Slimes, these are our new friends, the living trees. They're going to stay with us for a while."

Matcha rolled down a branch, dropping out of the tree like a rock. I rushed to catch him as he giggled up a storm, wiggling like this was a new game. I shook my head, laughing. He was adorable but such a handful. When I set him on the ground, he hopped on an empty patch of dirt and nodded at the trees. They dug their roots into the ground, ripping up the soil and flinging dirt everywhere. I took a few steps back, but the dirt slimes literally dove in.

They leapt under and over the tree roots like they were running an obstacle course, and the trees obliged by moving into different positions to keep it interesting. All wariness left the slimes as they sank into the freshly turned soil the trees had opened up for them. I picked up the watering can, drizzling not only the dirt slimes but the trees too. Their leaves perked up and one of them patted me on the head again.

"You're kind of adorable." It was the same tree who'd knocked me down and the first one to drink the sleepy-time tea too. "Hmmm . . . do you mind if I name you? It would be easier to tell everyone apart with names."

The tree tapped a branch against its bark before bending forward slightly like it was nodding. Which meant I now had to think of a bunch of tree names that they'd be happy with.

"Ummm, what about Barkley?" I shook my head, already disliking it. "Or Leafie? Maybe Rootbert?"

None of them really fit this tree's vibes. Sure, it attacked me, but it had also been willing to try my tea right away. After that, the tree had been nothing but sweet, giving me head pats and hugs with its twiggy branches ever since. It even gifted me that new bench and helped with the lanterns. It deserved a good name, something sweet and kind so nobody thought of it as a monster anymore.

"What do you think of Sappy? Because you're sweet as syrup?" I frowned. "Syrup is actually kind of nice too, but you're not a maple tree, so maybe it wouldn't make sense."

The tree held up a branch and it reminded me so much of a person holding up their finger to say wait that I couldn't help but smile. The tree started shaking, all its leaves falling to the ground in a torrent of greenery.

"Are you okay?" My eyes widened, but it continued holding out its branch to keep me away. "If something's wrong, maybe I can help."

The tree trembled, shaking until every single branch was bare. My chest ached as the other trees watched on in silence. Weren't they going to help their friend? Unless trees didn't think of one another like that, or maybe this tree wasn't actually in pain? It looked like new buds were forming on its branches. New leaves sprouted, even bigger and healthier than the old ones, and they were shaped almost like a star.

Or a maple leaf . . .

My mouth dropped open as the entire coloring of the tree changed. "Are you a maple tree now?" The tree bobbed in a nod. "You didn't need to do that for me or anyone else. You were perfect the way you were." The tree patted me on the head so softly that tears pricked my eyes. I rubbed them away, smiling. "Well, if this is what you want, then okay. I'll call you Syrup from now on."

It threw its branches in the air and swayed in a happy dance. The other trees turned to one another, wind rustling through their leaves as they discussed something. Then they all started trembling, shaking off their old leaves and growing new ones too. Some became maple trees like Syrup, but others grew glowing leaves like I'd never seen before, illuminating the garden in cool blue light. Others turned white like birch trees and still others morphed into fruit-bearing trees full of apples, pears, and cherries.

"Sweet Potato," I whispered, marveling at the beautiful myriad of trees in front of me, "what's happening to them?"

[They're evolving beyond the jungle limitations of this floor . . .]

"Evolving? Like the slimes?"

[Not quite. More like they're choosing who they want to be for now. Living Trees can change with the seasons, but it takes a lot of energy, so they only do it when they feel safe. They'll need to rest and recharge if you want them to stay healthy.]

The trees were a dazzling array of colors now, some I recognized and some that felt completely fictional, like the ones growing glowing berries like lanterns. It was all so overwhelming, but I was happy that they felt safe enough to become who they really wanted to be here. It was beautiful and magical. They started moving around the perimeter of the garden, creating a beautiful barrier between the dirt slimes and the rest of the dungeon.

They slowed down, rooting into the soil at a snail's pace, as if it would be their last time moving for a while.

I walked over to Syrup, patting its bark softly as the tree settled into its new home. "You're safe here. I'll make sure you get all the rest you need."

The tree patted my head one last time before going dormant. No matter how long I was here, this dungeon kept surprising me. I put my hand to my chest, appreciating my cafe more and more. It not only let me level up, but it gave others a safe place to call home too.

I wanted to keep providing that sense of safety in the middle of this crazy dungeon, so I'd work hard to make this cafe the best it could be. This was my own little sanctuary in the dungeon, the one place that I could help anyone I wanted and meet all sorts of new friends. I loved it with all my heart.

CHAPTER THIRTY-NINE

Cookies for Everyone!

Dahlia's party was getting ready to set off, but before they left, she handed me a small bag of coins. "For the cookies. I'll be back later to pick them up, okay?"

"Sounds great, thank you!"

The coins clinked softly in my hands, and I couldn't help but grin. The gold wasn't what I was most excited about though, it was what the gold meant. Dahlia had been my twenty-fifth customer. I opened my quest menu to make sure.

[Build a New Oven: 25/25 Customers Served, 25/25 Clay, 25/25 Stone]

It was finally ready to complete! I rushed into the cafe, zooming past Marvin and Fiona in a blur on my way to the kitchen. This oven was what I'd been wanting since my very first day in the dungeon and I was finally about to get it.

I laid out all the clay and stone the quest needed, my hands shaking with excitement. "Okay, Sweet Potato, time to do your thing. Let's complete that quest."

[Quest Completed: Build a New Oven]

[Reward: Oven]

The clay and stone lifted into the air, spinning and swirling around each other as they morphed into different shapes, becoming tall and rounded like a brick-style pizza oven. The oven slid against the far side of the kitchen with a chimney that went through the cafe wall for venting. A wide-open circle in front, big enough for a large cookie tray, revealed an open dome inside where I could place the food.

Spark poked his head out of the old stove to see what was going on, and his eyes grew as big as saucers. He bounced closer, hopping up a set of tiny stairs built into the side of the stove, before going inside to explore for himself. There were circular indentations perfectly shaped for him to rest on, like little slime chairs inside the oven itself.

Had the system intended for slimes to run the oven? I leaned down, verifying that there was a place for me to add wood as well in case I wanted to bake the normal way, but with how Spark was wiggling, I had a feeling I'd never need to.

His big smile lit up the entire oven, casting a warm glow on the new appliance.

"It's beautiful." My voice was full of awe for this amazing dungeon. "Thank you, Sweet Potato."

[You did all the hard work yourself. You should feel proud of what you've accomplished.]

I stepped back to admire the new oven, but it filled so much of the small room that I'd have to work on an expansion quest next. I wanted full counters lining the kitchen instead of the makeshift ones I'd made out of crates, and an even bigger dining area. A cold storage area would be nice too. Every time I upgraded one thing, it felt like there were ten others that could benefit from an upgrade too.

This cafe was a never-ending source of upgrades. I scrolled through the list of quests, taking as many as my cafe points would allow.

[New Quest: Gather 25 Stone, 25 Wood, and 5 Ice Crystals to Build a Cooling Cellar]

"What do you mean by ice crystals? Is that just snow?"

[No. These ice crystals will never melt, but you'll need to explore quite a bit farther to obtain them.]

I bit my lip, staring at the message. Dahlia's party had said water floors were after the next safe zone, so it would be at least another ten floors before I had the potential of seeing any ice floors. Unless there was ice in the water areas somewhere. I sighed, wishing I'd asked more questions.

"Okay, I'll just grab a few other quests to work on in the meantime, then."

[New Quest: Gather 50 Wood, 50 Stone, and Serve 50 Customers to Expand Every Cafe Room by 50%]

I raised an eyebrow. "That's a lot of fifties. You might need to work on your creativity."

[Do you want the quest or not?]

"Yes, I definitely want it!" I laughed and accepted the quest. That took all my cafe points, but it would be worth it for the extra space to move around in here.

Speaking of moving, Spark was peeking out from the new oven, chirping and bouncing like he wanted something. With how much he enjoyed me cooking, I had a feeling I knew exactly what was on his mind.

"Think we should try it out?" I asked the fire slime, who nodded before going back to his oven chair. "Okay, then, let's make some cookies."

I pulled out flour, butter, eggs, chocolate chips, and everything else I'd need for the cookies and started working on the dough, using mana mix-in for the baking soda. Boss tried to squeeze through the kitchen door while I was mixing everything together, but there wasn't really anywhere for him to sit now that the oven took up half the kitchen.

"Sorry, Boss, but I don't think you'll fit." The big blue slime sighed, deflating a bit. I scooped out a bit of cookie dough for him and held it out. "Want a little snack? We're about to try the new oven."

His eyes widened as he leaned forward to gobble up the cookie dough. I laughed as his slime tickled my skin. He settled down right outside the room, watching my every move as I shaped the cookies into balls. Fiona had made me a beautiful set of baking pans that I hadn't been able to use yet, so I pulled those out and filled them with balls of cookie dough. Then I slid the pan into the oven where Spark nudged them into place. The slime's flames danced, bright and happy as he kept the oven at the perfect temperature.

"You're amazing, Spark." I smiled at him and started on the next tray of cookies.

Boss closed his eyes, apparently falling asleep while I rolled cookie after cookie. I started humming that song Dahlia had made up about my little monster cafe in the woods. It was actually pretty catchy. I'd have to have her sing it properly next time she was here.

When the first batch of cookies was done, I pulled them out and set them on the makeshift counter to cool while I put the second tray in for Spark. It looked like the oven was big enough for multiple trays at once, but I had a feeling I'd need multiple fire slimes then. Especially since there were three little slime chairs inside, like the system had already thought of that.

I reached back to snag a cookie for Spark since he was doing all the hard work, but the counter was empty.

"What the . . ." I frowned, staring at the tray that used to be full of cookies. I held my hand over it, feeling the warmth emanating from it still. I glanced up at Boss, but he was still snoozing outside the kitchen, too big to fit inside anymore. "What happened to the cookies?"

Boss opened his eyes blearily, blinking at me like he had no idea. My frown deepened, but since the slimes couldn't talk, I probably wouldn't be getting an answer anytime soon. I rolled a few more cookies into balls and filled the next tray up. I kept glancing back though, trying to spot anything unusual happening.

When the second tray was done baking, I set it on the counter next to the first, determined to keep an eye on it this time. Whatever cookie shenanigans were happening, I was going to find out.

Except, nothing happened.

The cookies cooled on their tray like normal and Spark started chattering for more. I added the next tray to the oven, glancing sideways at the cooled cookies. Tiny blue slimes hopped up on the counter and grabbed a few cookies each before scuttling off to Boss.

That tricky slime! I had no idea he could separate at will now and send his little cookie bandits into my kitchen on their own!

I focused on Spark, giving the Little Bosses enough time to scamper away with all the cookies. He deserved a good treat after everything he'd been through lately, even if it was a little devious to take them when I wasn't looking. Maybe he was just trying his new abilities out. Or maybe he was sad that he was too big to fit in the kitchen with me now.

Either way, I'd let him steal as many cookies as he wanted.

I baked another three trays of cookies, feeding some to Spark and eating a few myself before Boss snatched them up. He seemed to be ravenous today, unable to fill his slime stomach no matter how many I made. It was kind of worrisome, but each time I looked back at him, he seemed to be a little more . . . golden? Like he was so full of cookies that his slime was becoming cookie-colored itself. It reminded me of the time Jellybean evolved into Matcha, actually.

If Boss was trying to evolve too, then I should keep feeding him as much as I could. Cookies had always been his favorite.

Dozens of cookies and many, many Little Boss cookie bandits later, it seemed like Boss was finally full. At least, the last batch of cookies I made was still on the counter cooling without being snatched up. This was the first time I'd managed to get two trays cooling at once, so it felt like a good sign.

"How are you feeling, Boss?" I asked as the slime continued to pretend to sleep. "Want a cookie?"

The big slime shook his body slowly, golden-brown slime jiggling back and forth. Chocolate chunks dotted his body and there was no trace of his original blue slime left. He'd completely transformed into a chocolate chip cookie slime, just like Matcha had turned into a tea slime! A delicious buttery scent wafted off him, as if he was the embodiment of a cozy cookie now. I walked out of the kitchen to give him a big hug, burying my face in his golden body.

"Aww, Boss, you evolved! Congratulations!"

He wiggled, nuzzling closer to me until I was almost buried in his slime body. I laughed and pulled away before I couldn't breathe, patting his new cookie-slime form. Matcha and a few other slimes seemed to hear our celebration, because they bounced over to join in the fun. We all danced, cheering for Boss's evolution into a cookie slime.

"Do you still like the name Boss?" I glanced at the big cookie slime. "I can think of something more fitting if you want?"

He scrunched his face up, but didn't make any noises, and eventually shook his body back and forth.

"Okay, we can always think of something later if you want." I gave him one more hug, squeezing him tight. "Congratulations. Now I'm going to go finish the cookies for Dahlia's party while I'm at it. Might as well keep going since I'm on a roll."

And since Boss was too full to eat any of them anymore. I chuckled to myself as I went back into the kitchen, gathering even more ingredients for cookies. I wanted to branch out and make other kinds of baked goods soon, but for now, the warm comfort of a classic chocolate chip cookie felt like what people needed. Something comforting and warm, that could soothe their souls and make them smile.

I got into a groove of mixing ingredients, rolling dough, and putting them in the oven for Spark to bake, zoning out a bit as the process became more and more familiar. The counters were filling with cooled cookies, and the scent of chocolate filled the air.

Boss's soft snoring was making my eyes feel heavier. I should probably sleep after the next batch of cookies, but using this oven was just so satisfying and it was hard to stop. This was how baking was supposed to be!

I reached for the next pan to remove it from the oven but yelped as the heat of it burned my skin. I grabbed the pan without a pot holder! So stupid. I ran my hand under water, cooling it off. Thankfully, it didn't seem too burnt, just a bit tender. Boss was fully awake now and trying to squeeze into the kitchen, almost knocking over the makeshift counters and spilling all the cookies.

"I'm fine." I held my hand up. "See? Just a little accident. Nothing to worry about."

Spark squeaked from inside the oven, peering out at Boss as they chattered away at each other. Boss nodded, backing out of the kitchen like they'd come to some sort of conclusion. Once again, I really wished I could speak slime. An acrid scent wafted over to me.

Dammit, the cookies were burning!

I snatched them out of the oven, hating how dark they'd turned out. I'd have to toss them, except, the slimes had been eating every scrap of leftovers we had. So maybe they'd want them even if they were a little charred? I set them aside to check later, but for now I had most of a bowl of dough left and couldn't just let it go to waste. That cold storage quest was a long way off, so once something was started, it had to be finished.

After two dozen more cookies, the bowl was finally empty. I let Spark hop inside it to gobble up all the crumbs, but he wasn't as enthusiastic about it as usual. He kept staring at me, like if he took his eyes off me, I'd burn myself again. Or like he thought it was his fault?

"I'm sorry I scared you." I patted the fire slime's head softly. "I'll be more careful from now on. I just grabbed it without even thinking."

Spark cooed, leaning into my hand, carefully avoiding the spot where I'd burned myself. I never meant to worry them, so I should probably heal it even though I wasn't really that hurt. I grabbed one of the cookies I'd put a healing buff on and munched on it, watching the slight redness on my skin fade entirely.

I held my hand out to Spark. "See? All healed up."

The slime chirped and Boss leaned back into the kitchen. I shook my head, smiling as I held my hand out to him too. He nuzzled against it, as if he could tell if I was injured or not by touch, until he leaned back and nodded in approval. Sheesh. These slimes were like mother hens.

"Burns happen sometimes when you're baking, but they're not usually that serious."

The slimes stared at me like they weren't convinced, so I just moved on to the next step: storing the cookies. I wasn't sure what to give Dahlia's party the cookies in since I didn't have to-go boxes, so hopefully an empty treasure chest would do the trick.

I lined the chest with delicious chocolate chip cookies, piling them high. Cookies were the true treasure in this dungeon now, better than gold and weapons, that's for sure.

"Hey, Sweet Potato, you can steal my idea if you want. Your treasure chests can be full of tasty food from now on, and people would love you for it."

[Honestly, that's not a terrible idea.]

I grinned. "Maybe I'd even want to explore more if you had treasures like these."

[Deal.]

I blinked. "Really? It's that simple to change the dungeon?"

[. . .]

[No, of course not. I was just already thinking about doing that myself . . .]

Sure it was. I smiled to myself, closing the lid on the treasure chest full of cookies. This system was kind of adorable, and I really wished I could meet them in person. If they were a person and not just lines of code. Even if they were lines of code, they must have some kind of main form. Like a computer or a control room. Now *that* would be worth exploring.

I leaned down to grab the bowl Spark had been cleaning crumbs out of so I could wash it, but the room started spinning. Black spots swept over my vision. I reached out to steady myself on a counter, accidentally pulling the crate over. I stumbled, and this time Boss did push himself inside to steady me.

"It's okay," I mumbled, leaning against him. "I'm okay."

But my entire body was saying the opposite. It felt heavy, so I slid onto the floor, leaning against Boss as a backrest while my empty mana bar blinked. All those mana mix-ins had finally caught up to me.

"I'm just going to rest my eyes . . ."

Darkness overtook me as I fell into a deep sleep.

CHAPTER FORTY

Is the Dungeon Smitten?

Hazel collapsed!

Cole threw his mind into his human avatar and raced to the cafe as fast as he could. She'd been fine one moment, joking about cookie-filled treasure chests, and then she was on the floor the next. It all happened so fast that he didn't even have time to think. He just had to see her.

His heartbeat thundered in his ears as he jerked the cafe's door open.

The tables had been shoved to the side to fit a mound of blankets and slimes in the middle of the room, piled up so high that he could barely see Hazel through it all. He rushed inside, pushing past Fiona to get to Hazel's side. Her breathing was deep and even, and she was wrapped in a cozy blanket surrounded by slimes.

Relief washed over him. She was okay. She was just sleeping.

"Excuse me." Fiona shoved herself between him and Hazel. "Who the hell are you and what gives you the right to barge in here like that?"

Her hammer was drawn, ready to knock him right out of this cafe if he didn't answer her correctly. He forgot that they'd never met in this form. That put a dent in his plans, but it was nice knowing Hazel had such a good bodyguard around her.

"Sorry, my name's Cole. I'm a friend of Hazel's." He held his hand out in the way he'd seen many adventurers greet each other before. "I was worried about her and didn't think. Sorry for startling you."

Her eyes narrowed. "You're Cole, huh? I've heard *a lot* about you."

"Oh? Good things, I hope?"

Hazel had been talking about him? His heart soared as he peeked over at her sleeping on the floor. He wanted to get closer to check how she was doing, but he couldn't move until Fiona trusted him. This being-a-human thing was so complicated.

"Mixed bag. Can't believe you took her to floor twenty-eight." Fiona gripped her hammer tighter. "If you're going to do things like that, you need to be strong enough to protect her."

His stomach tightened, remembering her falling off that cliff. "You're right and I'm sorry. It won't happen again. But it was floor thirty-eight, not twenty-eight. That probably makes it worse though, so I'm going to shut up now."

Fiona relaxed. "Guess you really are Cole, then. Come on over and check on her. She's fine. She just got so excited about the new oven that she ran out of mana baking cookies."

"Wait, that's it? She just ran out of mana?" Cole sank to the floor, forcing Spark to jump out of the way. The little fire slime stared up at him with concern before hopping in his lap. Cole felt more than a little ridiculous for running over here so fast, and he couldn't seem to pull his focus from the way Hazel's chest was rising and falling, breath going in and out. She was sleeping, not injured. Sleeping. "She'll be fine after she gets some rest."

"Exactly." Fiona pinned him with an uncomfortable stare. "But one thing still doesn't make sense. You ran in here like a bat outta hell, but how did you know she fainted?"

His gaze jerked to Fiona as she tilted her head, studying his every move. His heartbeat raced again. What could he respond with that would make sense? Any form of *he was watching her* would be beyond creepy without explaining that he was the dungeon core, which would cause way more issues than it solved.

But what else was there to say? Maybe he could make up a skill, something that would give him a special bond with Hazel so he'd know when she was in danger.

Hazel shifted in her sleep, her hand falling out of the blankets. He felt the urge to reach out and touch her, to take her hand in his to reassure him that she was okay. But that would imply a bond he didn't actually have with her yet. Sure, he watched over her, but that was his job. To her, he was practically a stranger. Just the unreliable adventurer who'd taken her to a dangerous floor.

"I'm still waiting, you know," Fiona snapped. "There's something not quite right about you, but I can't put my finger on it. First, you can bring people to different floors, and now you know things when you're not even here. It's definitely weird."

Alarm bells rang in his head. This conversation was dangerous and had to be handled carefully.

He cleared his throat. "I, uh, I brought her to that floor with a one-time item. It was a rare drop."

"And you used it on her?" Fiona raised an eyebrow. "Either you're covering something up or you're completely smitten. I can't tell which yet . . ."

"Smitten? With Hazel?" His face warmed as he shifted awkwardly, moving Spark off his lap. "Man, these fire slimes are really warm, huh?"

Fiona sighed. "Smitten it is, then. Okay, I get it. I'll leave you be for now, but I'm watching you."

She pointed two fingers at her eyes and then at Cole's, before sitting in a chair on the other side of the room. Which left him basically alone with Hazel and the slimes, and honestly a bit puzzled. Was he smitten?

He didn't have access to his knowledge stores in this form, but he was sure that word meant he was attracted to her. Intensely attracted. But wasn't he just watching out for her like he would do for any other adventurer?

Hazel burrowed deeper underneath the covers, and her hair fell across her face. Cole reached out, brushing it back behind her ear. His fingers grazed her skin, soft and warm, and he felt himself lingering. He cupped her cheek. She looked so peaceful sleeping like this, but he also missed the excitement in her eyes when she was baking. He enjoyed every version of her, appreciating all the new things she'd shown him. He hadn't been able to take his eyes off her since the moment she chose that sandwich as a weapon.

Was that what being smitten felt like?

If so, then he might be doomed. A dungeon in love? That was ridiculous. Unheard of.

He slowly pulled his hand away from her cheek, but she mumbled something that sounded a lot like *Sweet Potato* and reached for him, holding his hand tight between hers like she refused to let him go. His heart pounded in his chest so loudly he was surprised it didn't wake her up. Hazel was holding his hand!

He sat perfectly still, not wanting to disrupt this moment for anything, not even the slimes who kept shifting from Hazel to him. They bounced and chirped, making far too many little slime noises as they circled the two of them.

"Shoo," Cole whispered. "She needs her rest."

Matcha poked out from underneath the blankets, and Hazel shifted in her sleep again. All this activity was definitely going to wake her up. Maybe he should go and let her rest in peace. He tried to stand, but her grip tightened on his hand. He swallowed hard, staring at that beautifully calm expression on her face as she held onto him like he was hers, only able to come or go as she pleased. It made him oddly happy.

Hazel made an adorably sleepy noise, her eyelids fluttering as she started waking up. "Cole?" She started to pull away, then froze, staring at their intertwined hands. A faint rosy color tinged her cheeks. "What are you, um, what brings you here?"

Cole glanced over at Matcha, who was snuggling up to a fire slime. "Me? I was just passing by . . ."

"And decided to come watch me sleep?" She laughed, gripping his hand one last time before letting it go so she could sit up. "I'm guessing somebody told you I depleted my mana, huh? I really need to pay more attention to that bar."

"You definitely should, yeah." He nodded, happy to have an easy excuse for being here, but already missing the warmth of his hand in hers. "Maybe you should take it easy for a bit?"

Boss bounced closer, moving behind Hazel so she had something to rest against. The poor slime must have really taken it hard when she collapsed on his watch. Cole understood that feeling completely and would have to reward the slime for taking care of her. He'd already evolved into a cookie slime though, so what else could he want? More food? A skill maybe?

Hazel patted Boss's side as the other slimes bounced closer, as if checking on her. She pet them too, smiling. "I'm okay, really. I just needed some sleep."

She yawned widely, pointing out how little sleep she'd actually gotten. All the talking must have woken her up when she really needed her rest. She leaned back, settling into Boss and closing her eyes as she hugged Matcha tight. She looked so cozy and at peace. Did he really need to keep her so busy with all these quests?

He leaned back on his hands, watching her slowly drift off to sleep again. He'd been running this dungeon for so many years he couldn't keep track anymore, and everyone followed the script eventually. He'd give them a class, they'd fight hard to level up, and then they'd leave with an intense feeling of accomplishment, knowing they'd earned every bit of their freedom.

So why was Hazel so determined to do things her own way?

He'd created a bit of a mess trying to make her new class work, but she still pushed against the system for more. She was working just as hard as the top-ranked adventurers though, striving to make her cafe the best it could be. That's what this dungeon was for, right? To give people a sense of purpose and drive, to make them feel like they accomplished things.

That's what growth was all about.

So maybe, just maybe, Hazel wasn't breaking the dungeon as much as he feared . . .

Cole sighed, watching as Hazel slipped farther down Boss's side until she was back on her blankets. He reached over to tuck her in, pulling the blankets high over her shoulders. She snuggled into them, smiling and hugging Matcha close.

His chest felt warm and fuzzy as he watched them, and it was impossible to ignore the feelings he had for her—feelings that had gotten him into this mess in the first place. He couldn't help it though. She was like a treasure he'd accidentally stumbled over and wanted to guard with his life.

If that's what being smitten meant, then Cole was absolutely, unimaginably smitten.

And that was a dangerous feeling.

CHAPTER FORTY-ONE

Food Catastrophe

My blankets were soft and cozy, practically willing me to stay in bed and sleep, but sizzling sounds drifted from the kitchen like somebody was cooking. If Fiona was hungry, I should probably get up and make breakfast since she didn't have any culinary skills to make the food taste good.

I started to sit up, but Matcha chirped from under the blankets. I lifted them up so he could bounce outside, joining all the other slimes surrounding me. Dirt slimes, fire slimes, plain blue slimes I'd never seen before—it was like every slime in the area had gathered around me. And then there was Boss, the big cookie slime watching over me. He nudged closer, pressing against my back.

Tears pricked my eyes as all their love surrounded me. "Thank you for taking care of me, but I'm all right now." Matcha tilted this way and that, as if unconvinced, so I patted his head and smiled. "Really. I feel great. You guys helped me sleep so well. I appreciate it."

I stretched my arms up high as the sound of metal clattering on the floor pulled my attention to the kitchen again.

"Dammit," a very male voice said, "how does she make it look so easy?"

That sounded a lot like Cole. In my kitchen. Cooking breakfast?

Now I had to get up and see what was going on. Flames shot up from the stove as something charcoaled in a pan. Spark and another fire slime danced in the chaos, making the flames even bigger like they were having the time of their lives. Cole's sleeves were rolled up and he had a big smear of flour on his face while a bowl of dry ingredients lay scattered all over the floor. He looked utterly out of his element.

"What's going on in here?" I asked softly, not wanting him to drop anything else.

"Hazel, you're awake already?" Cole winced as I took in the absolute disaster of a kitchen. "Umm, I wanted to make you breakfast, but it's my first time cooking. I'm sure you could tell that though."

Flour dusted his long black hair, which was pulled back in a ponytail that looked far too good on him. Honestly, the whole vibe of him cooking in my kitchen would have given me butterflies, if only it wasn't on fire.

I picked up Spark and set him on the stove. He sighed, then devoured the flames like a good little fire slime. Cole obviously didn't know how to control the chaos a fire slime could bring when they were having fun, but it was an acquired skill. He'd learn if he was here more often.

Wait, did I *want* him here more often?

I shook my head, rolling up my sleeves with a smile. "Why don't you let me make breakfast? I promise it'll taste delicious."

"You're supposed to be resting." Cole frowned at the burnt lump of something on the stove. "Let me try again. It'll be better next time. Unless you don't want me to?"

His sad tone tugged at my heart. If he wanted to help that badly, I couldn't really refuse. He had been nice enough to stop by and check on me, even staying to make breakfast too.

"No, no, please keep cooking. I can rest while I teach you how to make . . ." I paused, trying to figure out what he'd been trying to cook. There were blueberries and lots of flour, cornstarch, potatoes, an entire cup of salt, and no sugar. "Sorry, what are you trying to make?"

"Muffins," he mumbled, glancing awkwardly at the ingredients he'd laid out. "Is this not right?"

I pressed my lips together, trying not to laugh. "Well, you need more sugar than salt for one, and you definitely don't need potatoes. Unless you're making potato pancakes or something savory."

"I thought potatoes made things sweet though?"

"Only if you're using sweet potatoes. But that's a whole different thing." I chuckled to myself a bit over that, thinking of the system. "Let's clean up and give these muffins another try."

He gave me a sweet little half smile as he grabbed a chair and a blanket from the dining area so I could get cozy while he cleaned up the entire kitchen by himself without me lifting a finger. It felt kind of nice sitting back while somebody else did the work, even if he was the one who'd made the mess. Vague, half-asleep memories tugged at my mind of him holding my hand and brushing my hair out of my eyes. The butterflies from earlier came back with a vengeance.

"What next?" Cole's expression was so eager and full of excitement, like cooking for me was the thrill of his day.

I swallowed hard, my mouth suddenly dry. "Um, take the stems off the blueberries and wash them. Once they're dry, you can coat them in flour. It'll prevent them from sinking to the bottom of the muffins."

He nodded, picking each stem off the blueberries with care and precision before washing them. Then he turned to me again, awaiting instructions. Muffins were actually kind of difficult for a first-time baker who didn't have a recipe, so I wished he'd started with something easier. Like eggs.

"Why don't I measure everything out for you?" I got up to help him, but he shook his head.

"You just focus on relaxing." His voice fell to a whisper. "And let me take care of you for a while, okay? You have no idea how terrifying it was seeing you collapse."

His gaze held mine, dark eyes full of an intense emotion I'd never seen before, but it had my entire body feeling strange. Like I was waiting for something, but I wasn't sure what.

Honestly, what had gotten into Cole all of a sudden? It was like he was an entirely different person from the silly guy who was headbutted by a goat. He felt so sure of himself now and in control, like he knew what he wanted and nothing was going to get in his way. I hated to admit it, but it was kind of . . . attractive.

I sat back down, feeling a bit uncertain. I was here to level up, not find romance, but he was being so kind that I couldn't help but let him stay. I *had* been working hard lately. I'd earned a break.

"Okay, I'll just sit here and watch you work, then." I pulled out my cookbook, opening to a new blank page. "Do you have something to write with though? This might be easier if you had a recipe to follow."

Mine usually just filled in with magic as I baked, but I hadn't made muffins in the dungeon before. I felt like I knew how though, so if I could just write it down, I knew he could figure it out. Cole flipped through his menus, pulling a black pen out of his inventory. It had smoky tendrils swirling around it and an amber stone at the top.

"Try this." His fingers brushed against my skin as he handed me the pen. He smiled and dipped his head shyly. "Some pens can fly and take notes for you on their own, but this one is just a normal pen unfortunately."

"Just a normal pen?" I laughed. "That's like saying a soufflé is just a cake. This pen is beautiful!"

Cole smiled as he started flouring the blueberries. I set the pen's tip against my cookbook and started writing a muffin recipe down. The ink swept across the page so smoothly that I almost believed it was a magical pen after all, with dark ink that shimmered in the light. Cole finished the blueberries far sooner than I finished the recipe, but he just waited and quietly played with the slimes. It was a comfortable kind of quiet, like we'd known each other for a long time.

When I was done adding notes for everything I thought he might need, I handed the cookbook over to him. "Let me know if you have any questions."

His gaze moved back and forth, reading everything I'd written, flipping the page to the notes section. "I think I'm good to give this a try. Thanks."

"You're welcome." I leaned over to the pan of burnt potatoes he'd set to the side to cool. There were a few bits that weren't charcoaled, so I snagged a bite. It was absolutely tasteless, just like I'd expected. "It's not as terrible as I thought it would be."

He grinned. "Gee, thanks."

"I meant that you can't expect anything to taste good without a culinary skill." I shook my head, laughing. "It was supposed to be a compliment."

"You should work on those." He tilted his head, measuring out the flour. "And how do you know I don't have a culinary skill?"

I toyed with my braid, which had gotten pretty messy from sleeping with it in, trying to give myself time to think of a polite answer besides that his food was awful. Based on everyone's reactions so far, it felt like I was the only one in the dungeon with a culinary mage class, so he couldn't possibly have any skills like that. Right? But once I finished rebraiding my hair, I had nothing left to be distracted by.

"Well, I mean, your food tastes like all the other food in the dungeon," I said softly. "Without a flavor boost skill, it's just kind of . . . bland? Sorry, I don't mean to be rude. The dungeon just doesn't have good food."

"Hmmmm, that is a good point." He scooped flour into a bowl before adding in the other ingredients, then stirred everything together, mixing and mixing and mixing until I held out my hand.

"You're overmixing it!"

He froze. "Sorry. I got lost in thought."

Cole pulled the cookbook over, checking the next steps before adding the blueberries, mixing them in carefully so they didn't get mushy like my note said. He really was trying hard, so no matter how it tasted, I'd love it. Nobody had ever spent this much time baking for me before. Maybe we could bake together next time and make something extra tasty.

He buttered a muffin pan I didn't recognize, flouring it so the batter wouldn't stick.

"Where'd you get that pan from?" I asked.

He froze, batter dripping from the spoon in big glops. "Um, I stopped by the blacksmith earlier to get an apology gift for the whole goat fiasco. Do you like it?"

"I love it. Thank you."

I couldn't believe he'd gotten me a gift like that; it was perfect. I wrapped the blanket around my shoulders, curling into its warmth as Spark climbed the stairs into the oven with another fire slime. Their grins lit up the oven, shining brighter than ever before.

"Careful not to overheat it, Spark," I called out as the slimes started doing that fire dance they'd been doing when I first walked in. Spark sighed, lowering the flames a bit. "Thank you."

They giggled as Cole carried the muffin pan to the oven. He paused, turning back to me. "Why don't you put them in? Maybe your skills will take effect then."

"I don't think that's how it works . . ."

Flavor boost said my cooking would have flavor as long as I had mana, but how much of the cooking did I actually have to do for that to trigger? Just putting something in the oven really didn't feel like enough, but I'd give it a try for Cole. I got up and slid the pan in, letting Spark pull it into position. The slime nodded, smiling like he would bake them to perfection for me.

"Now what?" Cole asked. "We just . . . wait?"

"Pretty much." I went back to my chair, sighing as I sat down. "I kind of like this taking-a-break thing, by the way. I should make it a daily quest. The quest for relaxation."

He laughed. "Careful, the system might add that for you if it overhears you."

"Ohhh, that would be cool." I leaned forward. "What do you think, Sweet Potato? Want to reward me for being a little lazy every day?"

"I think it's more taking care of yourself than being lazy, but sure." Cole's eyes widened. "I mean, sure, *I* think that's a good idea, but I doubt the system really tracks your well-being." His smile faltered and he lowered his voice to a whisper. "Maybe it should though."

That sad look of his tugged at my heart. "You're right. The system seems nice, but at the same time, it doesn't seem to care if we're happy or not. So many people are struggling, stuck in classes they hate and feeling more and more miserable each day. It's not fair to keep us trapped in this horrible grind without any real choices." I pulled my knees to my chest, resting my chin on them. "I'm the only one who got exactly what I wanted, and it makes me feel so guilty whenever I run across people like Marvin. I wish I could give him a better class too. I got unbelievably lucky, but everyone else deserves to be happy too. The very least the system could do is require them to take breaks once in a while."

Cole didn't answer me, but his shoulders were tense and his hands clenched at his side. Something I said must have bothered him, because the warm and teasing atmosphere from earlier had vanished. Before I could ask, system messages started appearing.

[Calculating . . .]

[Breaks do not increase your level, so they serve no purpose.]

[Quest denied.]

I frowned. "Well, that was harsh. Why are you so sweet sometimes and so sour the rest of the time?"

[Because I am an automat—]

Cole walked right through the system message, obscuring it entirely. "Did it say no? Maybe I can reward you instead?"

His smile didn't quite reach his eyes and his words felt overly cheerful, like he was trying to lighten the mood again. What had upset him so much in the first place? I leaned to the side, trying to see what the system message said, but it was already fading.

I glanced up at Cole. "Is everything okay? Did I say something wrong?"

"No, nothing at all." His tone was casual, but there was enough hesitation that things still felt awkward.

Maybe he was one of the people who actually loved his class and enjoyed fighting his way through the dungeon. We sat there for a bit, not really saying anything, until Fiona peeked into the kitchen like a breath of fresh air.

"Something smells good in here," she said. "What are you making this time?"

She was looking at me as if I'd made it, but I just shook my head. "The muffins are all Cole, he did the work while I just sat here resting. He insisted."

Fiona's lips curled into a grin. "Maybe he's not so bad after all, then."

"He's pretty okay, yeah." I glanced up at him with a sly smile, trying to get back to the easy conversations we'd been having earlier. "Maybe even great."

A soft smile touched his lips. "You two aren't the best at compliments, are you?"

We laughed and he joined in too, banishing any leftover awkwardness entirely. Having all three of us here, all cozy and warm in the kitchen while the scent of blueberry muffins filled the air, was really nice. This was how every day should start. We continued chatting while the muffins puffed up, creating beautiful muffin tops, until they were finally ready to take out of the oven.

Cole grabbed a towel and removed the pan, placing it on the makeshift counter to cool. Then we dug in. The streusel on top was buttery and crumbly, a perfect texture against the soft muffin and bright pops of fresh blueberries. The flavors practically exploded in my mouth, so delicious I couldn't ask for anything better.

Fiona stared at the muffin in her hands. "These are amazing, but didn't you say that Cole made them?"

"She put them in the oven though," Cole said quickly. "So her skills activated."

I nodded, grabbing a second muffin. "I honestly didn't think it would work that easily, but man, are these delicious. Thank you for making them, Cole."

He smiled, bringing the tray into the dining area so we could all sit down properly and invite Marvin to join us too. Cole even filled four glasses of water and made sure my blanket was fully covering my shoulders. He was a lot more thoughtful than I'd realized before, taking care of everything before I could even ask for it.

A girl could get used to this . . .

CHAPTER FORTY-TWO

The Dungeon's Dilemma

Hazel's words kept replaying in Cole's mind: It doesn't seem to care if we're happy or not.

That wasn't true. It couldn't be. The system had been helping people for centuries, giving them a new purpose with goals that they could achieve if they worked hard enough. He believed in that system and in the quests he gave out.

Everything he did was to ensure people's happiness. Maybe not in the moment, but in the long run. They deserved to move through this dungeon with confidence, their abilities growing every day.

He walked outside, wandering into the garden surrounded by living tree monsters that had no business being there. That wasn't how he had set up this floor. Every time he let Hazel get away with something, she changed the design.

And people seemed happy about it.

So why was he so uneasy? She kept turning his world upside down. He usually enjoyed it, but at the same time, every little change was like she was saying that his way wasn't good enough.

That *his way* was the broken one.

He dragged a hand over his face. None of this was her fault, but he couldn't let it keep happening. He was supposed to be helping the entire dungeon, not playing favorites and experimenting on a whim.

"Everything okay?" a man asked softly.

Cole jerked, almost stumbling into Marvin. "Yeah, everything's fine, but can I ask you something? Are you happy here?"

"Yeah. Happier than I can ever remember." He cradled an armful of vegetables with a big grin on his face.

"Even though you're not leveling up anymore?"

Marvin shrugged. "I guess. I wasn't leveling before either and I was miserable. At least here I'm having fun and doing something I actually enjoy. Getting to floor one hundred seems impossible for somebody like me, so I'd rather keep working here. I got pretty lucky finding Miss Hazel and Fiona, so I'm not about to give that up."

Lucky. Hazel thought she was lucky too, getting a class that nobody else had, but it wasn't luck. Cole had made that happen because she chose a sandwich as a weapon. Maybe the system wasn't the problem here. Maybe putting too much stock into a decision people made right after waking up was.

"What if you had a different class?" Cole asked slowly. "Maybe you'd be better as a mage or an archer."

"Maybe? I still don't think I'd like fighting, but not having to be up front would be nice. I hate being the first one to get hit. Or eaten." He cringed, gripping the vegetables to his chest. "It's not like I can try the other classes, but I think I'm good at gardening. Which feels kind of awesome, so I'd rather stay here where it's safe."

Where it's *safe*. That was another thing Cole probably shouldn't have done.

Making this cafe a safe zone allowed people to shirk their duties and hide away here. Sure, it helped Hazel, but it wasn't what Marvin needed. He should be out adventuring so he could grow stronger instead of stagnating here even worse than he was in the safe zone. At least back there, he had dreams of going out again, but now he was so happy gardening that he didn't even care.

Maybe he just needed a class that fit him better. He'd probably make a wonderful mage if Cole tweaked the rules a bit to let him have a do-over of that first decision. It might even help other people too.

He should talk to Dave first though. Dave was really good at seeing all the ways things could blow up in his face, and Cole desperately needed somebody like that right now. Plus, he'd already been gone for over a week. Surely he was ready to come back soon.

Dave had tried everything from being an adventurer to a musician to losing a drinking contest at a tavern, but the last time Cole had checked in on him, he was sitting on top of a deserted mountain all by himself.

"Tell Hazel I'll be back soon." He waved to Marvin before grabbing his dungeon keys and opening a door to floor seventy-two.

The slide didn't give him the same thrill as it had the first time. His thoughts were too jumbled to enjoy it, and all too soon, he was shooting out the other end. He landed softly on the rocky ground next to a pool of water. Steam curled through the air and lanterns rested on the surrounding rocks, lighting a hot spring in a warm glow.

Dave sat in the water, head tilted back and arms resting on the outer edge, not even noticing Cole had shown up. Usually, he was a lot more attentive than that, but today he seemed to be completely relaxed. He even had a drink floating on a wooden tray beside him.

Cole dipped his hand in the water with a small smirk. "You really took this whole vacation thing seriously. You're so relaxed a Solhorn could head-butt you and you wouldn't even see it coming."

"My lord?" Dave lurched forward, splashing water everywhere and sending the floating tray rocking toward Cole. "What are you doing here?"

He nudged the tray back. "Maybe I just wanted to say hi."

"If that was true, you'd have joined me in the hot spring instead of standing there awkwardly." He leaned back against the smooth rocks again. "Just tell me what's on your mind and maybe I can help."

"You probably can, but . . ." Cole frowned, staring at the water. "When did we build a hot spring here? What purpose would it serve?"

Dave took a long drink before replying. "I added it for background scenery when you were building the boulder run. Figured it couldn't hurt to have random things for people to find. Plus, hot springs are nice." He slipped deeper into the warm water with a sigh. "Very nice. You should really add more of them. An entire floor maybe."

"So even more people can sit and be lazy instead of trying to get out of here?" Cole shook his head but removed his layers of clothing anyway. If Dave liked a place like this, then there had to be something interesting about it.

Steam rose from the water like fog, reaching out for him in wispy tendrils. The water was verging on hot as he stepped in, sinking beneath the water until it lapped against his shoulders. A sigh of contentment escaped his lips. Maybe Dave's idea of an entire hot springs floor wasn't so crazy after all. Warriors needed a place to relax and ease their aching muscles, right?

Maybe small changes like that would improve the conditions here and help people find the happiness Hazel spoke of.

"See? I knew you'd like it." Dave took a drink, frowning at the glass. "Honestly, you really should upgrade how things taste around here too. This alcohol might give a buzz, but it tastes terrible."

Cole nodded absently, still lost in the warmth of the hot springs. Hazel would probably love this, but it would take a while for her to make it to this floor. Especially if she never left the cafe . . .

Dave sighed. "Okay, spill it already. What did Hazel break this time? You keep giving these intense looks, and she's the only one who brings out that kind of response in you."

So even Dave knew he had feelings for her. He was a terrible dungeon core. How could he have let this all get so out of hand?

He sank even deeper into the water until the steam obscured his face. "I . . . think I'm smitten with her. And I don't know what to do about it."

Dave choked on his drink, sputtering. "You just realized that?"

"Oh, shut up and help me fix this." His face burned even hotter than usual. "I just keep giving her whatever she wants. Every time I try to stand firm, she gives me a smile that melts me to the core, and I agree with anything she says."

"That sounds like a you problem, but it feels like there's something bigger going on?"

"She hates the dungeon and everything it stands for." His voice was barely above a whisper. "And now other people are doing weird things too. Fiona almost tried to become a blacksmith, and Marvin is becoming a gardener. He's completely stopped leveling, but he's happy about it. Like really happy. How am I supposed to force him to fight when all he wants to do is hang out at Hazel's cafe?"

Dave was silent for a while, like he was gathering his thoughts. "I've been wondering the same thing. The more time I spend out here, the more I see little glimpses of happiness that have nothing to do with leveling. Taking this vacation is just the start. I think there's a lot more we could do to change things."

Cole's mouth dropped open. "You want to change things? *You?*"

Dave had always been the one to hold the rules above all else, especially when anyone tried to bend them. If even he was starting to doubt things, then maybe the system really wasn't as perfect as Cole thought.

"Yeah, me." Dave laughed and gazed out at the valley below. "I know why we're doing all this, but I don't think it would hurt to add some more amenities and make this place . . . I don't know. Wholesome?"

A wholesome dungeon. Now there was an idea that really turned everything upside down. Maybe Dave had spent a little too much time in vacation mode. Cole would have to figure this one out himself.

He couldn't fix what he'd broken with Hazel's culinary mage class until she was safely out of the dungeon, but if he could nudge a few things here and there, then maybe he could help people and make her happy without breaking so many rules.

If he could get Marvin leveling, then things might settle down and she might believe in the system again.

Believe in him.

Even if he was starting to wonder if *her way* might be better . . .

CHAPTER FORTY-THREE

Baking Lessons

After a full day of mandatory rest, I was finally back in my kitchen with my hands in a bowl of dough. Watching other people work was nice, but I really did enjoy baking, and I was happy to be back at it myself. Especially since Cole had decided to stick around for some lessons.

Right now, we were working on shaping bread dough into buns, but Cole's were all different sizes and a mix of round to square to flat. I laughed under my breath, covering my mouth so he wouldn't hear.

"Something wrong with my buns?" He glanced sideways at me with a smile. "You've got flour on your face." I tried to wipe it off, but he just laughed, warm and bright, as he reached over and brushed his fingers over my cheek. "There. All better."

My eyes widened. When had he gotten so casual with his touches?

I focused on my bread, rolling it to a perfect shape and trying to ignore the fuzzy feelings sweeping through me. Having Cole here was kind of nice, fun even. I grabbed the bowl of egg wash, brushing it over every roll before putting them in the oven.

Cole and I washed the extra flour off our hands, his fingers grazing over mine every so often. His shoulder brushed against me, and everything in me wanted to lean into him.

What had gotten into me? This was ridiculous.

I dried my hands quickly and hurried into the dining area, where Fiona was playing with the slimes while she waited for our next creation. She'd been our ever-dutiful taste tester for this baking adventure, and she'd thoroughly enjoyed it.

"What's up next?" she asked, smacking her lips together. "Something tasty, I hope?"

"Fresh rolls with herb butter." I leaned closer. "If Marvin manages to pick some herbs, that is."

"I heard that!" he called out from the backyard before coming in with an armful of fresh veggies and herbs. "And I'll have you know, the garden is doing great. The slimes are literally throwing food at me they're so happy."

Fiona frowned. "Don't they throw food at anyone once it's ripe?"

"Well, yeah, but I like to think we've got a special bond. Don't we, Strawberry?"

The little dirt slime on his shoulder cooed, leaning into him with a giggle. They really had been growing close lately, like he'd fully gotten over his fear of slimes. Or at least, his fear of the slimes here. Out in the dungeon was another story, since he was still too afraid to leave our cozy little safe zone.

Fiona pushed a muffin his way. "Here, their muffins have gotten way better. Try one."

His eyes widened and he dropped all the ingredients in his arms, vegetables thunking to the ground one by one as he stared at the air in front of him. He was probably seeing a system message, but he looked like he'd seen a ghost instead.

"What's it say?" I asked.

He opened his mouth and closed it a few times, apparently unable to get the words out. Slimes started crowding him to eat all the food he'd dropped, but he didn't seem to notice that either.

He moved his hands stiffly to open his menus. "I've got . . . a class-change quest."

"A what?" Fiona and I said at the same time.

"It says I'm supposed to go to the ancient training grounds and prove myself to its guardian to receive a new class." Marvin's voice trembled. "My level will apparently be reset to one and all my skills will be lost." Marvin gulped as he removed a key from his inventory. "And I'm supposed to use this to activate it."

Cole stepped out of the kitchen with an appreciative whistle. "Sounds like you got really lucky, especially since you were just talking about trying out a mage class or an archer one. How great is it that the system wants to help you out?"

"Help me out?" Marvin shook his head. "No way. Did you hear the part about proving myself to some guardian? And what about this key? Special quests that need those are always extra difficult and terrifying. I'm just going to stay here and garden. I'm getting pretty good at that. Right, Strawberry?"

The little dirt slime nodded, bouncing softly on his shoulder as he pet her with his index finger.

"Just because something's difficult," I said softly, "doesn't mean you shouldn't try. This sounds perfect for you. The system gave you a gift, don't waste it."

He didn't answer, but he dropped his hand and looked away.

"Cheer up, Marvin!" Fiona slapped him on the back, almost knocking poor Strawberry right off his shoulder. "We'll go with you and make sure you get out of there in one piece. If you hate all the classes, then I'll drag you back here myself and throw you into the garden again. Sound good?"

"Sounds a little violent—" Marvin paused, as if debating his options. "But okay. If you're both with me, then I'm sure it'll be fine."

"Fiona and I will definitely go with you." I glanced over at Cole. "What about you?"

"Fine, I'll go too. But only to keep you three out of trouble." He sighed, giving me an odd look as if he thought *I* was the biggest troublemaker. All I ever did was bake and play with slimes! Before I could ask him about it, he offered me his hand. "Ready to go?"

I glanced back at Marvin. "I don't know, are we?"

"Not really, but why not?" He carefully set Strawberry on the floor. "You should stay here where it's safe." Marvin leaned down to whisper, "I wish I was staying here too, so go grow lots of food for when I come back."

The little slime nuzzled against his leg. Marvin was really good with them and seemed to honestly enjoy gardening, far more than anything else the dungeon had tried to get him to do. If he had the option to change his class, would it be possible for him to get a unique class like mine? If he could become some kind of plant mage, I bet he'd be a lot happier.

But how could we make that happen?

I'd gotten my class by choosing a sandwich from the weapons' table, so maybe I should bring something gardening related just in case . . .

I led Strawberry back into the garden, casually picking up a hand trowel and adding it to my inventory. If Marvin really did hate the other classes, I'd use it as a last resort.

As I walked back inside, Spark chirped, reminding me about the rolls we left in the oven! I hurried to take them out so they could cool on the counters. We probably wouldn't have time to eat them, so I took them out of the pans and laid them out for Spark.

"Make sure to share these with everyone else while we're gone, okay?"

The fire slime nodded, eying the buns like he had no intention of sharing. I grinned and snagged a few, not wanting to leave without at least trying Cole's rolls. I split one in half and steam rose out along with the delicious scent of warm bread. The butter melted as I spread it across, tossing the roll from hand to hand so I didn't burn myself.

"We'll be back soon," I promised. "Don't go crazy while we're gone."

Spark giggled, nodding so hard he almost rolled over. That was not reassuring at all, but I knew Boss and Matcha would keep things under control. They always did.

Cole was waiting by the door, feeding a slime some leftover muffins. "Let's head out. I think it would be better if we didn't drag this out . . ."

Probably good advice since the longer I took getting ready, the more anxious Marvin had gotten. He was sitting on the floor with his knees pulled up to his chest while Fiona murmured reassuring things, staring at me with a *do something* kind of look.

"Okay, Marvin, let's get you a new class." I offered him my hand to help him up. "I promise we'll make sure you like it. No matter what."

The trowel had to work, it just had to. Marvin was counting on us to help him through this, and I didn't want to let him down. Not that I minded his help at the cafe, but I'd rather he be here because he wanted to be, not because he was too afraid to go anywhere else.

"The system is giving you a chance to be happy," Cole said. "You've got to at least try."

Marvin stared at Cole. "You really think so?"

"Yeah, why else would you get a quest nobody else has ever gotten before?" He opened the door leading outside, motioning for Marvin to hurry up. "It's time to take charge of your life."

Fiona nodded. "He's right. This is a great opportunity for you, exactly what you'd been hoping for. Don't waste it."

"Okay, okay, I get it." Marvin managed a weak smile and walked outside. "Let's go change my class."

When I passed by Cole, I paused, handing him a roll. "That was kind of you."

"Everyone needs a helping hand once in a while." He bit into the bread. "Okay, this is really good. It must be one of yours, right?"

I smiled, shaking my head. "Nope, it's one of yours. You're a quick learner."

"Only because you're a good teacher," he said softly, closing the door as we walked outside together. "After this quest is done, think you could show me how to make something else?"

"Sure, anything you want."

Baking with him had been more fun than I'd expected, and I wasn't ready to call it quits so soon. Teaching him let me get to know him better too, which was something I found myself wanting more and more of. He was strange, but somehow so very familiar at the same time. I couldn't put my finger on it, but it felt like we'd known each other for a long time. Or maybe we just got along really well.

Once this quest was over, I'd ask him if he wanted to go somewhere. Just the two of us. Maybe I could really get to know him then and see what kind of things he did for fun. He'd mentioned working with Dave once, and that might be interesting to see too. I just wanted to know more about him, get a glimpse into his life like he'd experienced mine through baking.

There wasn't any harm in getting to know somebody better, right?

CHAPTER FORTY-FOUR

Class-Change Quest

The special key for this quest unlocked a training ground full of stone statues covered in faintly glowing moss. There was a table in the middle loaded with different kinds of weapons that looked eerily similar to the one in the meadow I'd woken up in. Add in the campfire and I half expected to find Dave lurking around somewhere ready to teach me how to be a better adventurer.

Fiona walked out ahead, scouting the area, but she just turned back and shook her head. "Nobody's here."

"What now?" Marvin asked from inside the dungeon corridor. He hadn't stepped out to let the door close yet, as if he was planning on dashing back to my cafe at any moment.

Cole crossed his arms. "Now you come over here so the quest activates."

"Sorry, but I think he's right," I said. "This is your quest, so you probably need to actually step outside to start it."

"Unless you want to give up," Fiona said. "That's definitely an option. It's not a good option, but it's an option."

Marvin seemed to take a minute to seriously consider that before shaking his head. "No. I want to do this. I want to be stronger."

Good. It was nice seeing him take charge and step out of that corridor all on his own. Even if this wasn't exactly what he wanted, it was still a step toward something better. Marvin deserved to have a life that fit him, and if I could help him get even a little closer to that, then maybe the system would realize that people were happier when they had real choices.

And if it couldn't see that yet, then maybe I'd just have to give it a nudge.

When Marvin walked over to the table, the moss on the stone statues glowed brighter. The one in front depicted a chubby little dragon with a big smile on its face and a paw on its belly like it was laughing. Marvin stepped onto a round stone in front of the table, and the dragon came to life, flapping wings of creaking stone and shaking itself like a dog that had just gotten out of a bath.

Marvin fell back, landing hard on the ground.

Fiona rushed toward the statue, hammer at the ready. "Who are you? Are you friend or foe?"

"Friend. Probably." The dragon statue opened its mouth wide in a yawn. "Slept too long. Need food."

The statue turned to me, leaping through the air on tiny stone wings that should not have been able to actually fly. It sniffed me, searching my pockets just like that little goat monster had last time.

I calmed my racing heart and handed it one of the rolls Cole and I had made. "Here you go. My name's Hazel. What's yours?"

The dragon ripped into the roll, devouring it in two gulps. It rubbed its stomach, making an *mmmmmm* noise. "Bread good. Name's Smudge."

"Hello." I held my hand out, then paused. It was a dragon, not to mention a statue, so it probably wouldn't shake hands. I dropped my hand back to my side, fiddling with my apron as I glanced over at Cole, who nodded like I should continue. "We're here for a class-change quest."

"All of you?" Smudge asked. "Or just the scaredy-cat over there?"

"Hey, I'm not—"

"Rawr!" Smudge growled and pounced at Marvin, who scurried away. The little dragon laughed boldly, straight from its belly. "Sorry, sorry. Had to test your fighting skills. They're bad."

Fiona took a step back, guarding Marvin, but it didn't seem like she really needed to. It felt like the dragon statue was part of the quest, and it didn't seem violent. Honestly, that little rawr was adorable and I kind of wanted to see it again. Maybe the dragon was like Dave, a helper meant to guide adventurers through their choices.

I walked over to Marvin. "I think the dragon's here to help change your class. Why don't you ask it for help?"

"Okay . . ." Marvin stood on shaking legs, glancing between the weapons' table and the dragon statue. "Mr. Smudge, I'd like a new class."

The dragon flew over the weapons' table upside down, smiling at him. "Would you? Then return your weapon and take a new one. Believe in yourself."

Marvin nodded, stepping closer as the rest of us watched on. He pulled out his battered sword and dropped it on the table with an unceremonious clatter.

Smudge sighed, landing on the table. "Respect the weapons or they won't respect you."

"Sorry."

Marvin held his hand out to take a different weapon, but he couldn't seem to decide which. He hovered over swords, daggers, bows, spellbooks, staffs, but he didn't touch a single one. The dragon eventually started thwapping its tail against the table and rubbing its belly.

"Hungry. This is taking too long." Smudge leapt up, pounced on Marvin's hand, and forced it down onto a spellbook. The dragon gave a goofy grin. "There. Decision made."

"Wait, no, you can't just do that," Marvin stammered, backing away from the table. "What if I don't want to be a mage?"

I crossed my arms, staring the dragon down. "Isn't this supposed to be his choice? Why would you do that?"

"Just training." Smudge rolled its eyes. "No choices yet. Grab a weapon. Train. See what you think. Then decide."

"Oh." I glanced around the area, realizing the other statues were set up like training dummies with targets on them and everything. "Is this a new way of making sure people choose a class they like?"

"Yes, yes." Smudge flew little figure eights in the air. "Hurry and train. Hurry and choose. Smudge is ravenous."

I laughed, going through my inventory to see what I had for the hungry dragon statue. If this was a new quest, how long had Smudge been waiting here for us? Maybe the area had always been here, but served some other purpose? I didn't know much about how the dungeon worked, but hopefully I could satisfy it. I handed the statue a few cookies and its eyes widened.

"For me?" The dragon's mouth fell open, eyes shining even brighter. "For me!"

Then it gobbled up the cookies and rolled around in the air, grinning. Everyone liked cookies, even stone dragons.

While the statue was distracted, Marvin finally gathered up the nerve to pick up the spellbook. The symbols on it glowed as it hovered in the air in front of him, exactly like my cookbook did. Was my cookbook a spellbook too? Huh, that was kind of cool. Good food was magical after all.

"What now?" Marvin whispered, gaze begging Fiona for help. "Do I just say the spell?"

She shrugged. "How would I know? I'm not a mage."

Cole stepped in. "Yes, say the spell loud and clear, with intention. Feel what you want it to do and say it proudly. You can even shout it if you want."

I frowned as his words tugged at my mind. I'd heard that somewhere before. It was similar to when the system had told me to shout my skills, but maybe it told everyone that. Wait, what class did Cole even have? I'd never seen him use magic before, so why would he know how a mage class worked? The more I got to know him, the less sense he made.

Marvin stepped up to a statue, held his hand out, and shouted, "Fire Blast!"

Flames licked his fingers, rolling over his spellbook and exploding in a big puff of smoke. He coughed, waving his hand to clear the smoke as Smudge laughed hysterically.

"Ohhhh, adventurer," the statue said between laughs, "that weapon is not for you. Try again. You'll find one that fits."

The soot marks on Marvin's face kind of said otherwise, but I hoped the dragon was right. I still had that trowel in my inventory, but I honestly wasn't sure what it would do if I added it to the table. So I watched while Marvin tried to throw daggers, ducking as he somehow threw them behind himself instead of ahead, before fumbling with a bowstring that snapped him in the face, leaving a big red welt. Weapon after weapon wasn't the right fit, and Marvin was getting pretty frustrated.

"I suck." His voice was thick with emotion, verging on tears. "I really am just terrible at everything. I should just go back to the safe zone and never leave. I'm a complete failure."

The dragon statue flew lower, patting him on the shoulder. "Nobody is a failure here. Just experimenting. You'll find one that fits you."

Except, the statue had said that at least a dozen times now like it was on repeat, and Marvin definitely wasn't finding anything that fit him. There were only a few weapons left for him to try, and they were pretty much the same as the others. More blades, more bows, and more magical items. He didn't mesh with any of them because they were all focused on fighting and that's just not who Marvin was. How could the system not have realized that by now?

Fiona leaned closer to me, whispering. "This is getting hard to watch. We need to do something."

"Trust the system," Cole said. "It'll find something that works for him."

"Will it really?" I asked. "The system doesn't seem to have a clue how people think. There's more to life than fighting, and until the system realizes that, people like Marvin are going to keep being miserable."

Marvin yelped, dropping whatever weapon he'd been trying this time and sucking his finger like he'd cut himself. This wasn't just painful to watch, but he was literally in pain. He couldn't keep going like this. I took a few steps back, blending in with some training dummies behind us, and opened my inventory to pull out the gardening trowel.

While Smudge was distracted teaching Marvin how to throw axes, I casually placed the trowel on the table. I half expected the system to yell at me or throw it back, but nothing happened at all. I let out a breath, stepping away as Marvin dropped the axes on the table with a sigh.

"I'm hopeless," he said. "I don't even want a new class anymore. I should just go back to the cafe and pretend like this never happened."

"No. I'm supposed to help you." Glowing tears dripped from Smudge's eyes. "*I* failed. Not you."

Those tears tugged at my heart. "Neither of you failed. The system is the one who's the failure." I patted Marvin on the shoulder. "Maybe you should try one more weapon. I'm sure there's something here that you'd enjoy."

"I really don't think—" He froze, staring at the gardening trowel. "Was that here before? I didn't even notice it. It looks just like the one I use at the cafe."

I bit my lip. It wasn't just like it, it *was* it.

Cole turned to me, eyes wide with horror. "What did you do?"

Before I could answer, Marvin picked up the trowel. The table flickered, almost like it was an illusion that had grown unstable, and Smudge fell to the ground with a thud.

"Are you okay?" I set the dragon upright, heaving the heavy stone into place. It didn't move, didn't blink, didn't act anything like before. "What's wrong?"

The moss glowed so bright I could barely look at it. I squinted, turning away as the rest of the training ground flickered, bright lights shooting through the sky like lightning. Fiona pulled me away from the statue as cracks of light burst through it.

My body felt strange. Lighter than usual. I ate a healing cookie hoping that would help, but it was tasteless.

"What's going on?"

[Plant mage class does not exist]

[Failure]

[Failure]

[Failure]

The system messages scrolled through the air over and over for all of us to see while Cole seemed to pull at the campfire's flames, tugging them this way and that like they were strings of light.

"What are you doing?" I frowned at how odd the flames looked in his hands, almost like he was controlling them.

His gaze met mine, eyes wide in panic. "Sleep."

And then everything went dark.

CHAPTER FORTY-FIVE

All the Secrets Are Revealed

My eyelids felt as heavy as stones as I pried them open, blinking in the flickering light of a campfire. Fiona was on the ground next to me, breathing deeply like she was asleep. I turned to find Marvin farther back, his chest rising and falling as he slept too. I let out a breath, happy they were both okay. There was something off about them though, like they were fuzzy and out of focus.

I rubbed the sleep out of my eyes but froze when I saw my hand. It was translucent, the light of the fire shining right through my arm. No. That wasn't possible! I flipped my hand back and forth, seeing through it no matter how I looked. My breath caught in my chest.

"Am I a ghost?" The words felt like ash in my mouth as I searched the area for any other explanation. My gaze landed on Cole, who was still playing with the fire like he was some kind of god. "Did you do this?"

He jerked his hands out of the flames. "You're not supposed to be awake."

"So sorry to ruin your plans." I forced myself to sit up even though the ground felt like it was swaying beneath me. "What did you do to us?"

"Calm down." He held his hands out. "I can explain everything if you'll just hear me out."

My tongue felt thick in my mouth, like I hadn't drunk anything in a while, so I just nodded.

"The system glitched when you added that trowel to the table and that's why everything started flickering . . ."

Everything he said after that blurred into background noise as my stomach sank. All I'd wanted to do was help Marvin be happy, but instead I might have ruined his quest and gotten him stuck in a class he might not even want. If the trowel had even worked . . .

My fingernails bit into my palms. I should have talked to him first instead of assuming I knew what was best. The way I lived my life wasn't necessarily how everyone else wanted to live theirs. Sure, being happy felt universal, but everyone's version of happy was different.

And now, Marvin might be stuck with mine.

I glanced over at his sleeping form, making a silent promise to fix this.

"Hazel!" Cole's hands gripped my shoulders, shaking me hard enough to pull me from my thoughts. "Everything's going to be okay. I just put them to sleep so they wouldn't see anything they shouldn't."

"Like you *playing with fire*?"

He groaned. "Yeah, like that. I'm sorry. I never meant to hide things from you, but it's dangerous if you know too much. You should really go back to sleep and forget this ever happened."

"No way." I shook my head, clearing the last of the fuzziness. "I know this is my fault, but I need to know what's going on. Are you a god?"

A laugh burst out of his chest, and he sank to the ground, sitting cross-legged across from me. "No, I am definitely not a god. Think of this dungeon like an in-between. A place where you can rest and recover."

"In between what?" The answer felt like it was at the tip of my tongue, but I couldn't bring myself to say it.

His eyes softened as he took my hand in his. "In between lives, Hazel. Your old life is over, but your new life is waiting for you at the end of this dungeon. Reincarnation is the reward you've been working so hard for."

Reincarnation . . .

No matter how many times I tried to figure out this dungeon, I never would have guessed that. Never would have guessed that I was . . .

Dead.

I swallowed hard, gripping his hand like it was my only lifeline. Everything else felt so far away, so fuzzy, except for him.

My eyes started watering and I brushed the tears away before they fell. "So that means I'm dead, then, huh?"

He pulled me into a hug, wrapping his arms around me firmly. Feeling his hands pressing into my back made me feel whole again. I wasn't just a ghost. I had a body, even if it was translucent.

I was real.

"Hazel, you're more full of life than anyone I know." He pulled back, his eyes misty. "Nobody ever really dies. Our souls are like embers, and this is where they get the fuel they need to shine bright again."

Everything I thought I knew was crumbling around me and I could barely wrap my head around it. I was dead, but I wasn't really dead, and I was in some kind of limbo dungeon . . .

"That's . . . a lot to take in all at once." I wrapped my arms around myself, trying to make sense of it all, but one thing kept nagging at me. I glanced at Cole's kind expression. He was obviously concerned about me, but he knew far more than he should if he was just another adventurer. "Who are you really? If you're not a god, then why do you know all of this?"

"I knew you'd ask that eventually, and it's past time I told you." He took a deep breath, straightening his back and catching my gaze with a serious look. "I'm the dungeon's core, the one who keeps the system running smoothly. You can think of me like its heart."

I don't know what I expected him to say, but it definitely wasn't that. If he was the one who controlled the system, then . . . I froze, eyes wide. "Are you Sweet Potato?"

All the pieces started falling into place. The reason he could take me between floors on a whim, how he seemed to know things he had no business knowing, and how he once in a while answered me when I was talking to the system.

"Hazel . . ."

"No way." I shook my head, moving back to put some space between us. "You can't be Sweet Potato. That would mean you've been lying to me this whole time. Which, I guess everyone's being lied to about the whole limbo thing, but this feels different. It's personal."

Cole started to reach out but dropped his hand mid-thought. "I'm sorry. I didn't realize how much you'd mean to me until after I'd already lied. Adventurers aren't supposed to know anything about their reincarnation. The gods wouldn't be pleased if I suddenly started telling everyone about it. They've got a plan and I've trusted that plan for centuries." His voice softened and he fiddled with a blade of grass. "I was a soul once too, but I chose to be the next dungeon core instead of reincarnating. I wanted to help people like you move on to a better life. I never thought I'd feel this way about anyone. I never thought . . ."

His voice trailed off and I couldn't help but feel for him. If he really was Sweet Potato, then he'd done so much for me. He'd made this dungeon not only livable but fun in a way that nobody else could have. He'd given me the tools I needed to live the way I wanted to live, and I couldn't thank him enough for that. I should be grateful, not upset over a little thing like his name.

Cole was Sweet Potato, and I owed him everything.

I held my hand out to him. "Hello, I'm Hazel."

"What are you doing?"

"Just go with it." I took his hand in mine to shake. "It's nice to finally meet you properly, Sweet Potato. Thank you for giving me a culinary mage class and watching over me this whole time. You made me feel safe, like somebody had my back."

"Does this mean you're not mad?" His lips pulled into a grateful smile as he gripped my hand, shaking it so fast that I felt like my arm might fall off. "I'm glad. I don't know what I would have done if you hated me. And you can keep calling me Cole, if you want. That way nobody will get suspicious."

"True, but it's just the two of us right now, so I'll keep calling you Sweet Potato."

"You are a beautiful soul, Hazel." Cole pulled me against his chest, hugging me tight.

The scent of campfire smoke surrounded me as I leaned into the hug, daring to wrap my arms around the heart of the dungeon. He was the man who'd given me my class and kept me company whenever I was lonely. He'd joked with me, cared for me, and even baked with me.

He leaned back, kissing my forehead softly. "Since you already know way more than you should, there's a few more things I want to show you."

I glanced over at Fiona and Marvin, still sleeping soundly. "What about them?"

"They'll be fine, but they won't wake up for at least a few hours, and we'll be back before then. I promise." Cole summoned a door in front of us. "Do you want to see where everyone goes when they first get here?"

"Isn't that Dave's meadow area?"

Cole shook his head with a grin. "No, that's where you wake up. You were somewhere else for a while before that though. Somewhere that might help this all make more sense."

"Okay, let's go." I took a deep breath and stepped through the door.

Warm light filled a vast room with hundreds of glowing cocoons hanging from the ceiling like lanterns. Their golden lights sparkled brilliantly, pulsing like heartbeats. Some were faint while others were so bright I could barely look at them.

Cole led me down a path to the middle of the room where the warmest light was. "This is the Hall of Embers. It's where souls come when they first arrive in the dungeon. Think of it like a resting period between their old lives and the tutorial zone. It's a time for them to transition and let go of the pain they felt before."

I spun in a circle, staring at all the souls filling this room. There were hundreds, no, thousands, just waiting to become adventurers like me.

"So I was here too?" I asked, transfixed by the beautifully pulsing lights. "I was a big ball of light like them?"

He nodded. "And you'll be here again. It's the cycle of life, and this is your time to rest."

"Wait, have I been here before? How many times have I reincarnated?"

"This is your first time, and believe me, I'd have remembered you. Nobody else breaks my systems quite like you do." He laughed, smiling just as warm as the lights around us while the back of my neck burned.

"Am I really that much of a menace?"

He grinned. "You have no idea. Dave was so overwhelmed trying to fix it all that he had to take a vacation." His tone felt teasing as he laced his fingers through mine. "And I wouldn't have it any other way. I was bored beyond belief before you came here, but now my days are full of excitement and wonder. You brought my flames back to life."

He lifted my hand, his gaze never leaving mine as his lips brushed my knuckles in a fleeting kiss. My breath caught in my chest as the lights danced in his eyes. He had an otherworldly beauty to him that should have been my first clue that he was something . . . more. He led me around the cocoons, showing me all the souls who were resting and recovering here.

"This is where I first met you," he whispered. "Your soul burned bright even then. Watching you change the dungeon by sheer force of will has been a pleasure."

Knowing he'd cared about me even then, when I was just a bright light in a cocoon, was a little overwhelming. He really was part of this dungeon, the one running things, but also the one willing to bend the rules when I needed him to the most.

And if he was willing to do that for me, then maybe he'd be willing to do that for other people too.

That train of thought was what had gotten us into this mess in the first place though. I still wasn't sure if adding that trowel to the weapons' table had been a good idea or not. Maybe it had changed things for the better, or maybe it had just . . . made a mess. But if I didn't at least ask Cole about it, then the system would keep trapping people in lives that didn't suit them.

"There has to be some way forward that lets people be happy without me breaking things," I mumbled. "Some system change that would let people choose the life *they* want to live. That's what this limbo dungeon is all about, right?"

"It is, so I think I'd like to see where this happy worldview of yours leads."

His thumb brushed across the back of my hand in a slow, steady motion that left me a little weak in the knees. I leaned against him, gazing out at the brilliant souls in front of us. This room felt like it held so many possibilities, and maybe, just maybe, we could turn them into something wonderful together.

CHAPTER FORTY-SIX

The Dungeon's Spark

If they were really going to change the system, then they had to do it from the Core Chamber. Which meant that Hazel was finally going to see Cole's true form. Hopefully she'd accept that as wholeheartedly as she'd accepted the truth about the dungeon's true purpose. Otherwise things were about to get awkward.

"So, there's something else I should probably tell you." Cole gripped the handle of an intricately carved black door, unable to bring himself to open it.

He glanced back at Hazel, studying her kind green eyes. What would she do when she saw his true flames? Would she think they were beautiful? Or really, really weird?

"Everything okay?" she asked.

"Yeah, just . . . try to keep an open mind, okay? What I'm about to show you might be a little weird."

"Weirder than me being a soul who was wrapped in a cocoon of light before being sent out to level up in a dungeon so I can reincarnate?" She raised an eyebrow, a smile tugging at her lips. "I think I can handle whatever you need to show me."

She really was an amazing woman, and he hadn't been giving her enough credit. She'd already accepted so many things with a genuine smile, and he knew his flames would be the same.

"Welcome to the dungeon's Core Chamber, then." Cole pulled the door open and warm light spilled into the hallway. "This is where all the magic happens, so to speak, and it's my home." He turned to walk inside but stopped short. Somebody was already there. "Dave?"

The satyr stood by the hearth with his arms crossed, hoof tapping the ground. "About time you got here. I knew something was up when you came to visit me at the hot spring, but then I felt a weird tug and knew I had to come back. The core is changing."

Dave stepped out of the way and the full impact of his words hit home. Cole's flames weren't just orange anymore; they had tendrils of gold running through them, burning brighter and taller than ever before. Something had changed in him so profoundly that the core itself had evolved.

Only Hazel could have done that.

Nothing else in his hundreds of years as the core had left an impact quite like she did. He rushed inside, staring at the flames he once knew inside and out. They were stronger now and more brilliant than ever.

"What's been—?" Dave froze, gaze locked on the doorway. "Hazel? What's she doing here?"

Hazel waved awkwardly. "Oh, hey, nice to see you again, Dave."

Cole winced. "About that . . ."

"You brought a *date* here?" Dave dragged a hand over his face with a groan. "I know you like her, but this is ridiculous. The gods will definitely pay us a visit if you keep doing foolish things like this. I bet you even told her what's really going on, didn't you?"

"Well, yeah, but it's fine." Cole motioned for Hazel to join them. "We can trust her, and, well, I didn't really have a choice. She sort of added a gardening trowel to the weapons' table during Marvin's class change and the system kind of . . . exploded."

Dave sighed. "I knew I should have just gone with you right away. I was selfish, dragging out my vacation like that. But I'm here now, so let's fix this." He turned and stared at Hazel. "We could make her forget again."

"No!" Hazel and Cole shouted at the same time, before Cole continued. "She's got a better plan to fix things if you'd just hear her out."

Hazel nodded. "I think the dungeon would run a lot smoother if everyone got classes that suited them. My culinary mage class has made me want to level because I love it and I'm having fun, not just because I have to. Imagine if everyone was that driven. People like Marvin wouldn't have to struggle so much, and they'd learn who they really wanted to be so much easier. That's got to matter when they reincarnate, right?"

Dave glared at Cole. "You really told her everything, huh?"

"Yeah, I did, and I won't even apologize for it." Cole stood beside Hazel. They were in this together now and he wouldn't let anyone, not even Dave, stop that. "She cares about the souls here and I want to give her ideas a try. We've both seen how fast she's grown and how much of an effect she's had on other adventurers. I truly believe this will make the dungeon better."

Dave was silent for a while, staring into the flames like they had all the answers for him, before he met Cole's gaze again. "I think you're right. I'm tired of seeing people stagnating. So what can I do to help?"

"Seriously?" Hazel grinned and nudged Cole's shoulder. "Look, even Dave's on board!"

Cole laughed. "I didn't expect that at all, but I'm grateful. That vacation must have really changed you."

"It opened my eyes to a few things, yeah." Dave pulled out his trusty clipboard. "So, where should we start first?"

Hazel leaned against the hearth. "First, I want to know why me adding that trowel messed everything up so much. Nothing broke nearly that bad when I chose Dave's lunch as my weapon, so what was different this time?"

Cole hesitated but knew he had to tell her the truth. He squared his shoulders and turned to face her.

"Last time, I was here in my true form." Cole nodded at the flames. "And I could handle any glitches that came up. But this time I was with you, in a body that wasn't connected to the system, and it didn't know what to do when you changed the game like that."

Hazel blinked, her eyes darting from the fire to Cole and back. "So you're saying . . . that that's *you*? You're a *fire*?"

"Pretty much, yeah . . ." Cole's shoulders tensed. "I'm the dungeon's core. My flames fuel the system."

Hazel's shoulders shook with silent laughter as she tried to keep a straight face but failed entirely as a grin took over. "Sorry. I just realized why the fire slimes keep piling on you like you're their leader. You're literally made of fire!" Her laughter finally spilled out, filling the room with the wonderful sound. "Remember when they followed you to my cafe like ducklings? Then slime piled you and wouldn't leave your side? Fire knows fire!"

She doubled over like that was the funniest thing she'd ever said, wiping tears from her eyes, and even Dave cracked a smile.

Cole wrapped an arm around Hazel's waist, pulling her close enough to kiss her temple. "Thank you for being so completely you all the time."

"You're welcome . . ." A faint pink blush bloomed across her face, but she leaned into him casually, as if this was something they'd done many times. "You too. Thank you for always being here for me."

He had worried that his feelings for her would become a problem, but now, he felt like they were the solution to everything. Opening himself up to her had opened his mind to other things as well. Things that would change this dungeon at its core.

Dave cleared his throat. "Sorry to interrupt . . . but we should probably fix all this before the other two adventurers wake up."

"You're right, sorry." Hazel pulled away from Cole. "I really want Marvin to get a class he'll enjoy. Like a gardener or something. Honestly, a lot of people would probably like noncombat classes like mine."

"Agreed," Cole said, "but what do you think, Dave? I don't want to make such a big decision on my own again. I need you on my team if we're going to do this right."

Dave scratched the base of his horns. "Well, I like the *idea* of giving people new classes, but we need to be more careful than you were with Hazel's. They need to be balanced and well thought-out before anyone starts using them. Deal?"

"Deal."

Hazel let out a breath. "Man, I really didn't think you'd be that easy to win over, Dave. I thought I'd have to bribe you with good food or something."

"Good food? Now there's an idea." Dave tilted his head, studying them. "If we're already going to be changing things, why not make the food here taste better too?"

Cole glanced at Hazel and whispered, "Is that okay? Will people still go to your cafe if—?"

"Please don't tell me you think my food is only popular because it's the only food that has flavor." She crossed her arms, tossing her braid over her shoulder. "My food can handle a little friendly competition, thank you very much."

Dave laughed in a way Cole had never heard him laugh before, light and carefree. His vacation really had been good for him, like a weight had lifted from his shoulders. Changing the dungeon was the right decision, for all of them, and Cole would do whatever it took to make it happen. If the gods showed up, he'd handle it. As long as they saw the benefits of their plan, they'd go along with it. They weren't vengeful gods, just ones who wanted order and to make sure the dungeons weren't overflowing with souls.

This would work. It had to.

"So what now?" Dave casually leaned against the hearth, as if that was a totally normal thing to do. This new, chill Dave was going to take some getting used to. "How many new classes are you thinking about? And do we release them all at once or one at a time as new adventurers get classes?"

"All at once," Cole said. "Let's give everyone the option to change their class and make it a big event."

"Like a game expansion." Hazel grinned. "That sounds perfect. And if people don't like their new class either, they can always change it again until they find something that fits."

"Whoa now." Dave held up his hands. "There's got to be a limit. We can't have adventurers changing their classes every day, otherwise they'd never make it out of the dungeon. Keep in mind that that's still our main priority here."

"True, we need to find a good balance." Cole glanced around the room, wishing it had chairs. It wasn't really well suited for human bodies wanting to discuss big ideas. "Resetting to level one should prevent too many changes in the higher levels, but it won't prevent it in the beginning, which is where most adventurers get stuck in the first place. Maybe we add other quest requirements that take time to do?"

"That might just add to the procrastination," Dave said. "What do you think, Hazel?"

Her eyebrows pinched together. "What do *I* think? Are you sure you're the same Dave?"

"Of course I am. The other Daves wouldn't even entertain this idea. They're a bit tight-laced, if you ask me."

Hazel's eyes widened as she turned from Dave to Cole and back again. "Other Daves?"

Huh, apparently he hadn't told her all the secrets yet after all. This dungeon had been around for generations, so telling her everything would take time. Time he'd gladly spend with her, talking and baking and just enjoying their lives together.

"There are many Daves," Dave said proudly. "There's one of us for every safe zone and the tutorial zone, of course. We Daves keep everyone safe and sound, giving them a feeling of familiarity and solid ground."

"Do you share the same memories?" Hazel asked, leaning closer as if to study him. "You know, I remember thinking you looked fluffier a while back when I first found the cafe. Was that a different Dave?"

He sighed. "Oh yes, that's fifth-floor Dave. He likes his fluff."

"I have so many questions," Hazel said, "but I don't want to leave Marvin and Fiona waiting for too long. So we should probably figure out a class for Marvin first since he's the one who prompted all this."

"Agreed, he deserves to be happy." Cole scooted closer to her until their shoulders brushed up against each other. "So, what do you have in mind?"

She glanced at him sideways, a soft smile on her lips, before lacing her fingers through his. "Something wonderful."

Cole's flames burned brighter than ever before, dancing in the hearth like they couldn't be contained. His heart felt full in a way he'd never realized he craved before, but now, he couldn't imagine life any other way.

CHAPTER FORTY-SEVEN

Designing New Classes

N o, no, no." Dave shook his head, sitting on the floor across from me. "You can't let him grow his own little plant pets, because little pets become big pets and it'll be the living trees all over again." He gave me a pointed look. "Don't think I didn't hear about how you found a loophole in that quest. Exterminating their *rage*, really?"

"I don't know what you're talking about." I gave him my best innocent look as I leaned back against the warm hearth behind me. "If you don't like plant pets, then maybe we could have plant golems with buffs who can run around spreading their awesomeness to the rest of the plant life."

Cole laughed. "I feel like you'd enjoy that more than Marvin would. Honestly though, plant pets aren't a terrible idea as long as they only level as the adventurer levels."

"Ohhh, now there's a good idea." I leaned my head back, smiling up at him as he twisted the flames in the hearth into intricate designs. "Maybe it could be a secondary path like my slime friend title gave me."

Dave sighed. "If we're going to do that, we might as well let people pick two classes. One that's more focused on fighting and one that's not. That way if people change their minds about how they should make their way through the dungeon, they don't need to start over entirely."

We'd been going back and forth like this for what felt like hours, not really coming to any solid decisions. There were just too many ways to go, and each had an upside and a downside to it. I turned the ember shard in my hands over, watching Fiona and Marvin sleeping in the meadow. Cole had promised they were fine, but seeing them for myself made it much easier to take the time to sort this out properly.

"Okay, let's start at the beginning," I said. "Plants need sunlight to grow and recharge. Why don't we make some kind of sun-based recharge skill?"

Dave raised an eyebrow. "Like how a cat naps in the sun and wakes up all refreshed?"

"Wait, are there cats in the dungeon?" I reeled around to stare at Cole. "Please tell me there are cats. We could make a whole pet-based class for people."

"Do cat *monsters* count?" Cole asked. "Because I think monster tamer would be a very cool class. Kind of like what you've been doing, but on purpose."

I grinned. "Yeah, let's do that for sure."

"And what about the plant mage?" Dave tapped his hooves against the smooth stone floor. "We can't keep them sleeping forever."

"Right." I slumped back down, focusing on the ember in my hands. Marvin and Fiona were both counting on me to do this, whether they knew it or not. "Okay, how did you pick things for my culinary mage class? Maybe we can start there."

Dave leaned forward, elbows on his knees. "Yeah, Cole, tell her how we picked things for her class."

He focused on the flames, pointedly ignoring the satyr so much that it made me curious. I stood up and wandered over by Cole until I was so close that he couldn't ignore me. He glanced at me, then away, then back, until he finally sighed.

"Fine. I'll tell you." He took his hands out of the fire and crossed his arms. "I just went with whatever sounded interesting."

Dave snorted. "You mean whatever *Hazel* thought sounded interesting. He basically made the entire class based on what you were excited about. Honestly, I knew he was in love with you way before he did. It was so obvious."

"Dave!" Cole shouted before waving a hand at me. "Ignore him, he's just being ridiculous."

"Right, yeah, of course." I held my hand against my chest as butterflies danced in my stomach. "Let's go with the rule of cool, then."

"The rule of cool?" Dave asked. "I'm not familiar with that one."

My palms were sweaty, and my face felt like I'd been standing over a bonfire. Which I kind of was. I backed away, leaning against the cooler outer wall of the chamber. I knew Cole liked me, but love? It was way too soon for that. I'd only just realized I liked him back. I couldn't go around using words like that so casually. Not even if he made my heart beat faster whenever he was nearby. Nope. Not even then.

Cole flipped through invisible menus. "The rule of cool isn't in here, but I'm guessing you just go with whatever sounds fun?"

I swallowed hard, determined not to let them see how much that love talk was throwing me off. "Basically, yeah. We should start with whatever sounds the coolest, and then we can decide what needs to be set up to get there."

Dave nodded. "That's an okay plan. You're more sensible than I gave you credit for."

"Gee, thanks." I rolled my eyes at him. "So, what are some cool plant abilities? Sun healing? Vine attacks? Faster growth?"

Cole tapped his fingers against his thigh. "What if we gave him multiple skill options to choose from with some that focus on combat and others that focus on noncombat options? Like carnivorous plants on one side and calming flowers on the other. Then he could get a mix of both kinds of skills, but he could focus on the area he wants to go after most without needing two entirely different classes."

Dave grinned. "Now you're talking. That would give people more options without having to reset their class. I've learned that making choices is important for life."

"And what choices have *you* been making?" I asked, tilting my head. "Cole said you've been off on vacation?"

"Yeah, doing totally normal things." Dave scratched his horns, staring at a corner of the room with nothing in it. "Soooo, anyway, I like the plan. Let's start with something simple like a growth skill and an emotional skill like the calming flowers. Both of those can evolve into combat or noncombat things, depending on how he uses them."

As we dove into the specifics, we realized that this would probably work for every class. A blacksmith could be a craftsman and a warrior, depending on how they used their skills. Same with a baker like me or a seamstress even.

As long as it gave people more options, I was all for it. I was tired of the tiny box that only a few people fit into.

"Why did you make the dungeon like this in the first place anyway?" I asked Cole. "It's so rigid, only focused on fighting. What does fighting have to do with souls resting?"

He hesitated but eventually answered. "It's how the dungeon was when I reincarnated as the new core, so I just kind of kept doing it that way. The god who introduced me to the system told me that fighting and getting stronger made souls feel like they accomplished something. When an enemy was difficult to defeat, it made it all the more exciting when the soul eventually won. By the time they got to the one hundredth floor, they were so full of pride that they were ready to move on to their next life feeling like they earned every bit of it."

"That makes some sense," I said softly, "but how often do people actually get to floor one hundred?"

"More often than you'd think." Cole took a deep breath. "I know you don't like the system, but it's worked pretty well for the most part. No, it doesn't fit everyone, but it works great for the majority. I never realized how unfair that was until you came along though. What works for one person shouldn't have to be what everyone else does. Every soul deserves a chance to feel accomplished in their own way, whether that's through fighting or baking or even gardening."

"Or drinking," Dave added with a sly smile. "Don't forget about making the alcohol taste good around here."

I grinned. "Wait, don't tell me you went off on some drunken adventure? No, you're Dave the rule-following tutorial guy. My entire worldview is shattered."

He shrugged. "What can I say? I'm a satyr of many mysteries. We should make a distiller class."

Cole ran a hand over his face. "Really, Dave?"

"Hey, they work hard too," I said with a grin. "Why not make a class out of it?"

And from there we devolved into making up dozens of classes, laughing and joking all the while. It was nice spending time with the two of them like this. We still had a long way to go, but at the very least, we'd come up with a class for Marvin, which meant it was time to head back to the meadow where we'd left him and Fiona.

Cole and I walked through the doorway leading to the training grounds. The stone statue was slumped over in the grass beside Marvin and Fiona, who were sleeping soundly, soft smiles on their faces like they were having the best dreams ever. Cole was right. They were perfectly fine. I felt bad that I'd have to keep this all a secret from them, but both Cole and Dave had thought it was for the best.

They'd said something about drawing the attention of the gods, and that didn't sound fun, no matter what kind of gods they were. So I lay down on the grass, settling into position so Fiona wouldn't notice anything was amiss.

"Thanks for bringing me back just in time, Sweet Potato."

He blinked faster, opening his mouth and closing it like he didn't know what to say as a rosy hue swept across his face. It reminded me of when those system messages had turned pink instead of blue. How had it taken me so long to put all of that together?

Everything about Cole reminded me of Sweet Potato. They were both easily flustered, adorable, and fun to talk to. Knowing the truth made everything make so much more sense, and I was happy he'd felt comfortable sharing it with me.

I glanced up at him as he toyed with the flames, curling them into beautiful forms. I wasn't sure what a new life would hold for me, but for now, I was really enjoying this one. I couldn't wait to help adventurers find their true passions, bake wonderful food, and learn even more about my Sweet Potato.

Yup, this in-between life was pretty damn nice.

Fiona mumbled something incoherent next to me. She rubbed her eyes, staring blearily at me for a moment before surging to her feet. "What's going on? Is everyone okay?"

"I think so?" I got up to join her, moving slowly as if I had been asleep this whole time too. "That was so weird, but it looks like everything's fine now. Maybe I didn't break anything this time."

"Right, and those failure messages were just for show." Fiona rolled her eyes as she hauled Marvin up. "What about you? You good?"

He patted himself down, as if he expected to be injured or something, then nodded. "I think so?"

"Good!" The dragon statue stretched its tiny arms wide with a yawn. "Sleep is fun. Time to work now though." Smudge turned to Marvin, eyes glowing bright. "Time to test your weapon."

"My weapon?" He lifted his arm, staring at the gardening trowel gripped tightly in his fist. "Oh, right. I picked this up a little bit ago, but how do I use it?"

The dragon statue paused, scratching its belly and staring up at the sky. "Dig?"

I tried not to laugh at the little statue trying to wrap its mind around how to train with a gardening trowel. Cole walked over, moving closer enough to whisper. "He'll figure it out."

"I hope so." I glanced sideways at Cole, who was smiling. "What's got you so happy?"

He shrugged. "Just enjoying being here with you when a new thing's about to happen. We did this. Together."

Warmth spread through my chest as we watched Marvin dig a small hole in the ground and plant a seed the statue gave him. His hands glowed green, and the seed sprouted violently from the ground, shooting vines up that wrapped around Marvin like a cocoon.

"He-help!" he shouted, struggling against the vines. When Fiona ran over to cut him down, he shook his head. "Wait, I don't think they're trying to hurt me. It actually kind of tickles. Wait, they're hugging me?"

Marvin laughed and patted the vines. They released him, moving as if they had a mind of their own and he could somehow understand them.

"Did we do that?" I whispered to Cole. "I don't remember us doing that."

Cole shrugged. "You never know what's going to happen with new skills. That's half the fun. Trial and error."

I stood there watching Marvin go from confused to terrified to absolutely thrilled each time he planted something and tested out the skills of this new class. We'd decided that the training grounds should let people experience a few skills they hadn't earned yet to give them a real taste of the class, and this was exactly what I'd been hoping for. Everyone deserved a class that made them as happy as Marvin looked right now.

This was really going to work. We were going to change the dungeon and make it better. I'd always thought that was impossible, but it was happening right here in front of my eyes. Marvin was finally enjoying himself!

Eventually Marvin turned to Smudge with the trowel cradled against his chest. "I'd like to take this class. I think I'm going to like it a lot."

The little dragon cheered, fluttering through the air in circles and dropping confetti. "Yes! He likes the class!"

"Congratulations." Fiona clapped Marvin on the back. "Now we can start training all over again."

Marvin groaned. "Not that. Anything but that." He glanced at the various plants he'd grown. "Well, maybe that. As long as the training involves gardening. I am a botanical mage now, after all."

"A botanical mage, huh?" I grinned. "That sounds pretty amazing. Maybe you can grow some flowers around the cafe for me and make things even more beautiful."

"I can absolutely do that!" Marvin nodded quickly. "I bet the dirt slimes would love it too. We should go tell them the good news."

"Really?" I smiled, patting him on the back. "You've come a long way from the terrified adventurer we met on floor five. I'm proud of you."

He dipped his head, smiling. "Thank you."

Fiona ruffled his hair. "Come on, let's go celebrate. You earned it."

"Ohhh, we should throw a party at the cafe!" I grabbed Cole's arm, grinning. "We could invite everyone we've gotten to know so far and celebrate all the new things about to happen."

Cole smiled softly. "And what new things are those?"

Shoot. I was supposed to be keeping the class changes a secret for now until he alerted the entire dungeon.

"Marvin's new class," I said, "and my cafe upgrade! I've been working on a quest to expand it, and what better way to celebrate than a party?"

Fiona nodded. "Sounds good to me. Let me know what I can help with."

"Are you sure?" Marvin asked, wringing his hands. "You don't need to go through all that trouble just for me."

"Trouble? Pretty sure that's my job." I grinned, opening a dungeon door back to the cafe. "A party will be fun for everyone and a good way to show off my cafe, so all you need to do is have fun and show us all the cool new skills you unlock by then."

Fiona pulled him into the dungeon corridor. "Think you can handle that?"

"I think so," he said softly. "I'm really glad I met all of you."

Me too. I didn't know what I would have done if Fiona hadn't found me in that tree surrounded by crispy cluckers or if Cole hadn't taken an interest in my strange class. I linked my arm through his, strolling side by side through the corridor.

We'd done something wonderful together, but Marvin's class was just the start. Soon there would be an entire dungeon full of people chasing what made them happiest. Now *that* was a life worth fighting for.

CHAPTER FORTY-EIGHT

Party Time!

Marvin had spent the past week trying to unlock new skills, which included planting beautiful flowers outside my cafe. From deep reds to calming blues, they added so much color to the area, and the slimes loved them too. I'd often catch them stopping to stare at the flowers, swaying in the wind with them like they were transfixed. It was honestly pretty adorable.

I leaned down to smell one, inhaling the beautiful, sweet scent as the sound of Dahlia singing drifted over. Camellya and Garrik walked beside her, humming the tune as well.

In the middle of a dungeon
An unexpected light
And a sweet smell on the air
So warm and oh so bright.
A little sign declares the place
For adventurers to stop on their way.
I've stumbled upon
The Slime Serenitea Cafe.

Fire slimes in the oven
Baking tasty treats.
Dirt slimes help the garden grow
Fruit for us to eat.
If you're lonely, then the tea slimes

*Give you friendly company
And there's more slimes coming all the time.
Come stop by the Slime Serenitea Cafe!*

The slimes were bouncing like the song was all about them, and I couldn't help but laugh. I should hire her to sing the tales of the Slime Serenitea Cafe all over the dungeon to draw customers in.

I waved them over with a grin. "Sounds like you finished that song you were working on last time. I love it. Thank you!"

"You liked it?" Dahlia raced over and gave me a giant bear hug. "I'm so glad! It's good to see you again."

"It's good to see you too! I'm glad you could all make it."

"Of course we'd make it," she said, leaning closer to whisper. "Even though we got a bit lost . . ."

"Hey, we were just taking the long way around to get more XP," Garrik grumbled. "Leveling is important and now we get a nice reward for it."

I raised an eyebrow. "A reward?"

"Your food, dummy." Camellya rolled her eyes, resting on the edge of the firepit where I had s'more ingredients laid out. "What's all this?"

Dahlia's eyes widened as she picked a marshmallow up, squeezing it between her fingers to puff the sides out. "It's so fluffy! Is it really food?"

Strange. Even though nobody remembered their old lives, they usually didn't question the food I made. Could she have never had marshmallows in her old life? But marshmallows felt so common . . .

Spark handed Dahlia a small stick to roast the marshmallow with, but she just frowned. "What do I do with this?"

"Spear the marshmallow." I picked up my own stick, showing her how it worked. "Then hold it out over the slimes so they can toast it for you. The marshmallow will turn golden brown and delicious."

"That sounds exciting." Dahlia carefully added her marshmallow to the stick while Camellya stabbed hers soundly, holding it over the fire slimes like that had been pretty enjoyable for her.

Garrik joined in too, smiling at the fire slimes, who were eager to toast the marshmallows for them. A little too eager, actually, as their flames burned brightly.

"Careful," I said, right before Dahlia's marshmallow lit on fire. I winced. "Sorry, that happens sometimes. You can feed it to the fire slimes though, they love the charred taste."

"But this one was mine," she said softly. "I was supposed to make it golden."

Camellya leaned over, eating Dahlia's marshmallow right off the stick with a big bite. She wiped sticky mallow off her face. "Mmmm . . . nice and burnt, just like I wanted." Then she held out her perfectly golden-brown marshmallow. "Here, you can have this one. It's not quite done enough for me."

"You're the best, sis." Dahlia smiled as she delicately removed the marshmallow from the stick. She bit into it carefully, probably trying to avoid the sticky mess Camellya had gotten herself into. Her eyes widened. "It's so sweet and warm, toasty too. It's amazing!"

I grinned, passing them graham crackers and chocolate. "Now try it with these next time. The graham crackers go on the outside with the marshmallow and chocolate between them like a sandwich."

Garrik raised his eyebrows. "A dessert sandwich? What will you come up with next?"

"Tasty things, I assure you." I smiled at them before turning to see Dave walking up with the seamstress from floor five. "Welcome to the Slime Serenitea Cafe! I'm so glad you could make it."

"Who could say no to a party?" Dave's hair and fur were brushed to perfection, taming all the wild curls that usually fluffed up in random places. He was even wearing a nice new outfit too. He glanced at the seamstress. "She really wanted to come too, so thank you."

"Yes, thank you." The seamstress held out a beautiful golden ribbon, her button eyes shining. "For you. Nobody has ever invited me out before."

"Well, it's long past time, then, and thank you for the gift." I untied the last ribbon she'd given me so I could try the new one on. "What do you think?"

Her smile widened. "It's beautiful, just like you."

Dave glanced at the seamstress like he had something to say but turned to me instead. "So, uh, is Cole here yet?"

"Smooth," I whispered, shaking my head. "He's working on the last parts of that job we were talking about. He'll be here soon, I'm sure."

"Oh, right, the job . . ." Dave winked at me before leading the seamstress over to the firepit. "Have you ever had s'mores before?"

The woman shook her head. "No, but I'm excited to try new things."

"And I'm excited to show them to you." Dave speared a marshmallow like a pro even though I had a feeling he'd never done it before. He frowned at the fire slimes, holding his marshmallow out unsteadily. "Like this, right Hazel?"

I nodded. "Exactly like that."

The seamstress oohed and ahhed as they toasted the marshmallows, sheer joy shining out of her as she tried one. I really should have visited her again, but life had gotten so busy since that shopping spree. I could use more clothes though, so I'd make it a point to visit her and the other shopkeepers again soon.

Speaking of, Fiona was heading over with the blacksmith she'd made my baking pans with. I was pretty sure his name was Brennic? Bright orange glowed underneath his skin, like lava beneath a rocky volcano. He nodded at everyone as he approached but didn't say anything.

"Looks like the party's already started," Fiona said. "Sorry we're late. This one didn't want to leave the forge."

The smith grunted, brushing soot off his clothes. "And I wouldn't have if you weren't so damn stubborn."

Fiona shrugged and stuffed a marshmallow in his mouth. The smith's eyes widened and he made an *mmm* noise as if he liked it. He wandered over to the seamstress and took his own stick from Spark, who shone even brighter like they were kindred spirits.

Excellent. This was all going so well already! If only Cole would hurry up, and Marvin too. What had he gotten sidetracked by?

"Hey, Strawberry? Could you go get Marvin for us?"

The little dirt slime who'd taken such a liking to Marvin bobbed in a nod, the strawberries on her head tipping over and scattering over the ground. She flipped them back up with a well-practiced bounce and headed for the garden to grab our new botanical mage. We couldn't have a party without the guest of honor, after all!

"Did he really get a new class?" Dahlia whispered. "I know that's what you said when I picked up our cookies, but it doesn't seem real. Nobody's ever gotten a new class."

Not yet at least. I could barely keep my excitement to myself. I had a feeling that Fiona and Dahlia might both want new classes too. Dahlia felt more like a singer to me than a fighter, so we made a bard class just in case. We'd also planned a blacksmithing class, if Fiona wanted to go that way too. It felt a little selfish focusing on classes for my friends, but Cole and Dave had created a bunch of other ones too. There would be so many options that people wouldn't even know what to choose now.

Movement pulled my attention to the back of the cafe as Mossy, the big giant dirt slime that he was, bounced out of the garden for the first time since I'd come here, leading all the other dirt slimes with Marvin at his side. The man couldn't stop smiling as he held an armful of fresh flowers that he'd grown just for this occasion.

The slimes surrounded him, pushing him forward like they were prouder of him than anyone else. Mossy was slow-moving, so it took a while for the group to make their way over to the firepit, but when they did, I couldn't help but stand and clap. Everyone cheered, the slimes bounced higher than I'd ever seen, and Marvin just kept grinning and hugging those flowers tight.

"Thank you," he whispered, eyes getting a bit misty. "I grew these for all of you."

Marvin passed out the flowers, which had special buffs on them so they'd calm your senses, invigorate you, or even put you right to sleep. We'd found that one out when I caught Marvin passed out, surrounded by a dozen dirt slimes snoring up a storm. His new class took a bit of trial and error, but that's where the fun was. He got to choose his own skills and really make it his own.

It reminded me of the first time I was experimenting with mine, shouting out my skills like nobody could hear me. I still hadn't talked to Sweet Potato about that little joke of his yet. Where was he?

As everyone congratulated Marvin on his new class, smelling the different flowers and smiling, I craned around searching for Cole. He had to get here soon. I'd promised I wouldn't upgrade my cafe without him here and we couldn't really go eat until I did that, so he better hurry up. People could only eat so many s'mores.

[Quest Completed: Serve 50 S'mores]

[Reward: Upgraded Firepit]

I whipped back around, staring at the group of people gobbling up all the s'mores I'd left out. They were laughing and chatting, playing with the fire slimes, and just having a good time while also finishing up my quest. I hadn't even considered that me laying out all the ingredients and showing them how to make the s'mores would count as serving them, but I guess making them yourself was part of the experience.

"Everyone, stand back for a moment," I called out, lifting the slimes out of the firepit. "I just finished a quest and I have no idea what it's going to do."

The stones from the firepit rose into the air, spinning and reforming themselves. Other stones got added in, dark ones like lava rocks and reddish-orange ones too, until eventually there were so many stones that we could make four firepits. The red ones flattened, pushing themselves into the ground around the old firepit to make a giant patio.

"What the hell?" Dahlia's eyes widened. "Is that how all your quests work?"

"Kind of?" I nodded, remembering the first cafe expansion and the stove. "Things just reshape themselves, I guess. It's pretty awesome, actually."

Once the patio was done, the rest of the stones formed an even bigger firepit with perfectly designed patterns of shapes and colors instead of my haphazard garden rocks from earlier. It was beautiful. Absolutely beautiful.

"Thank you, Sweet Potato," I said as the fire slimes leapt into their new home with squeals of joy. "Thank you so much."

"Anytime," Cole whispered so softly that I almost didn't hear him. His warm breath sent a pleasant shiver down my spine.

"When did you get here?" I asked with a smile.

"Right about the time your quest finished." He grinned, leaning over the new firepit to say hello to the fire slimes. He turned back, still smiling wide. "I'm glad you like it."

"Like it? We love it!" Dahlia raced forward to play with the fire slimes. "Hazel's cafe is the best."

I laughed. "Wait till you see the cafe upgrade itself. That quest is ready to finish too, but I was saving it for just the right moment."

They all turned to look at me with excitement in their eyes. Even Dave had taken a small step forward like he wanted to get a closer look. Guess it was time, then. I opened my menus and pulled out all the wood and stone I'd need to finish that quest.

[Quest Completed: Cafe Expansion]

[Reward: 50% Larger Cafe]

The wood formed itself into planks as the cafe's walls literally came apart at the seams to make room for the new additions while the stones lined up along the bottom, creating a solid foundation.

When everything settled down, my cafe felt like it was twice the size. The quest had said it would only get 50 percent bigger, but I couldn't help but stand there and stare at it. I could fit so many more slimes in here than before. Even giant slimes!

Matcha bounced over, staring up at me with wide eyes until I picked him up. He crooned in my arms, bouncing slightly like he wanted to get moving.

I laughed and took a few steps forward, opening the door to my newly upgraded cafe.

Light shimmered through the windows, casting a warm glow on the wooden floors. The lanterns were more spread out now, adding to the warm ambiance nicely. Three tables and sets of chairs stood in the dining area, way better than the makeshift ones I'd made out of old crates.

I hurried to the kitchen, followed closely by Spark. We both gasped as we saw how spacious it was now. Shelves lined one wall, ready to be filled with containers and cookware, while counters spread out across the other, perfect for cooling pies or cookies on. The oven no longer looked massive and out of place either, and Boss finally fit inside the room with us again!

Tears pricked my eyes, and I blinked faster to stop them from falling.

"We really did it, Matcha." I held the little slime closer, hugging him tight. "We found a safe place, met so many wonderful people, and built a home for ourselves." He nuzzled against me, vibrating softly like he was purring. "Thank you for taking this journey with me."

We stood there like that for a while before I heard the others finally entering the cafe to see the new upgrades as well. I wiped my eyes, ready to join them, but Cole pulled me aside before I could.

"I've got a surprise for you, if you don't mind coming with me for a moment." His amber eyes sparked with excitement. "I promise you're going to like it."

"Okay?" I followed him out of the kitchen, turning into an area of the cafe that didn't used to be there before. It was a new room. "What's this?"

He held the door open for me. "It's your bedroom. I thought you deserved a place all to yourself after all the hard work you've been doing. Plus, rearranging the dining room every time you want to sleep must be annoying."

Now the tears really did fall no matter how fast I blinked. He added a bedroom to the cafe upgrade just so I didn't need to sleep on the floor anymore? In the middle of the room was a giant fluffy bed with the blanket I'd gotten from the seamstress on top. A few slimes had already jumped onto it, snuggling under the blankets while Matcha hopped down to join them.

A dresser sat in the corner of the room with a small table next to the bed. It was all so cozy and wonderful, exactly what I needed.

I turned to wrap my arms around Cole's neck, pulling him to me. "Thank you. For everything. From giving me this amazing class, to helping me through the dungeon, to being willing to give my ideas a chance. This room and everything else mean so much to me."

"You are more than worth it." He pulled back, leaning his forehead against mine and cradling my face in his hands. "You've brought life into this old dungeon and made me happier than I ever knew I could be."

His eyes were warm and bright, like his true flames. How he found the time to dote on me like this while running an entire dungeon was beyond me, but I was so grateful for every moment I got to spend with him. He'd literally changed my life.

I leaned up, pressing my lips against his. He gasped and pressed a hand against his chest.

"Are you okay?" I asked, putting my hand over his. "Is something wrong?"

"No, far from it. My heart is beating so forcefully it just took me by surprise."

The smile that spread across his face told me everything I needed to know as he pulled me close, kissing me with such tenderness that I felt cocooned by his warmth. My sweet Sweet Potato.

Matcha squeaked from across the room, and I would have ignored him, but the sounds of other people talking outside snapped me back to reality.

I pulled away with a small smile, keeping his hand in mine. "Think it's about time?"

"Yeah, let's do it together." He opened his menus, manipulating things so I could see them as well. A large blue button hovered in the air.

[Upgrade Class System?]

[Yes]

[No]

Our intertwined fingers hovered over the menus. He glanced at me, as if double-checking that this was the right thing to do, before we pressed the [Yes] button. Chimes rang out through the area as everyone's system messages alerted them of a new optional quest to change their class. Excitement broke out in the dining area mixed with shock and amazement.

I gripped Sweet Potato's hand tighter. "This is the start of a whole new adventure for us, isn't it?"

"One I'm happy to go on with you." His soft lips brushed against my cheek in the whisper of a kiss. "This is our system now."

My heartbeat pounded in my chest as the reality of that finally hit me. I was dating the dungeon and had somehow convinced him to break everything for my crazy idea of a better world. I'd gone from struggling against the system to helping create a new one that would benefit everyone. Being able to help people like that filled me with such joy.

I wrapped my arms around Cole, tucking myself against his side. There was so much more to life than fighting, and we were about to see that for ourselves. People might hate the new classes or love them, but either way, I was exactly where I wanted to be.

By Cole's side as the entire world changed around us.

I couldn't wait to see what happened next.

Acknowledgments

To my wonderful Royal Road readers and Patreon subscribers: thank you for loving these adorable slimes as much as I do and for making my first LitRPG so much fun to write. Your encouragement helped me push past my doubts.

Many thanks to my book coaches, Cathy Yardley of Rock Your Writing and Rachel May of Golden May Editing, my developmental editor, Isaiah Belli, my song writer, Emily McNally, and my cover designer, Nicole Gustafsson.

About the Author

Pandora Pierce is the author of the Slime Sweets series, originally released on Royal Road. She loves penning cozy fantasy stories in which monsters are charming, whimsical magic is prevalent, and the adventures are delightfully low stakes. She has a weakness for slimes, red pandas, and other adorable creatures, and they inevitably sneak into her tales. When she's not writing, Pierce connects with readers, writers, and gamers via her Twitch stream.